Acclaim for
Blown Awa

C000045394

"*Blown Away* by Perry Wynn is an intelligent and exciting political thriller, fascinating in its exploration of the alarming lengths to which the Christian right could go to destroy the left, particularly gay men and lesbians.

At the same time, *Blown Away* gives us a honeyed glimpse of gay utopia, an independent state carved out of a sultry piece of Florida, governed by beautiful, athletic lesbian activist attorney Elizabeth Nix, who has survived her share of tragedy, betrayal, and romantic passion.

The characters are deeply human, the plot fast-paced and engaging, and the issues could not be more timely. A wonderful novel populated by smart, powerful lesbians who are doing their best to create a safe and abundant world for all of us."

Carla Tomaso
Novelist, author of *Maryfield Academy*

"Perry Wynn offers a chilling near-future speculative fiction examination of an America so divided over homosexuality that the only solution is the creation of a reservation for homosexuals to separate them from everyone else. Domestic terrorists and neoconservative fundamentalists set the course, leaving the rest of the country floundering in their wake. The "bad guys" come across as one-dimensional, but Wynn is able to develop some of the "good guys" into multidimensional characters. In the end, the story is less about homosexuality and political intrigue, and more about the ripple of decisions based on love and hate."

Anna Creech, MSLS
Serials & Electronic Resources Librarian,
Central Washington University

More Acclaim . . .

"*Blown Away* is a thoroughly impressive debut novel. This is the story of a right-wing America unleashed. When the right-wing administration decides that a "territory" where gays and lesbians can either freely relocate or be sent if they are facing criminal charges for illegal sexual conduct is the solution to the "gay problem" facing the country, the already tenuous solidarity of the gay community is threatened.

A romance, a political statement, a not entirely unrealistic vision of our nation's future, *Blown Away* is a real page-turner—best left to be read when you don't have to put it down, because putting it down before the final page is turned won't be easy."

Andrea L.T. Peterson, MDiv,
Freelance writer/editor

NOTES FOR PROFESSIONAL LIBRARIANS AND LIBRARY USERS

This is an original book title published by Alice Street Editions™, Harrington Park Press®, the trade division of The Haworth Press, Inc. Unless otherwise noted in specific chapters with attribution, materials in this book have not been previously published elsewhere in any format or language.

CONSERVATION AND PRESERVATION NOTES

All books published by The Haworth Press, Inc., and its imprints are printed on certified pH neutral, acid-free book grade paper. This paper meets the minimum requirements of American National Standard for Information Sciences-Permanence of Paper for Printed Material, ANSI Z39.48-1984.

DIGITAL OBJECT IDENTIFIER (DOI) LINKING

The Haworth Press is participating in reference linking for elements of our original books. (For more information on reference linking initiatives, please consult the CrossRef Web site at www.crossref.org.) When citing an element of this book such as a chapter, include the element's Digital Object Identifier (DOI) as the last item of the reference. A Digital Object Identifier is a persistent, authoritative, and unique identifier that a publisher assigns to each element of a book. Because of its persistence, DOIs will enable The Haworth Press and other publishers to link to the element referenced, and the link will not break over time. This will be a great resource in scholarly research.

Blown Away

Blown Away

Perry Wynn

Alice Street Editions™
Harrington Park Press®
The Trade Division of The Haworth Press, Inc.
New York • London • Oxford

For more information on this book or to order, visit
http://www.haworthpress.com/store/product.asp?sku=5706

or call 1-800-HAWORTH (800-429-6784) in the United States and Canada
or (607) 722-5857 outside the United States and Canada

or contact orders@HaworthPress.com

Published by

Alice Street Editions™, Harrington Park Press®, the trade division of The Haworth Press, Inc.,
10 Alice Street, Binghamton, NY 13904-1580.

PUBLISHER'S NOTE
The development, preparation, and publication of this work has been undertaken with great care.
However, the Publisher, employees, editors, and agents of The Haworth Press are not responsible
for any errors contained herein or for consequences that may ensue from use of materials or information contained in this work. The Haworth Press is committed to the dissemination of ideas and
information according to the highest standards of intellectual freedom and the free exchange of
ideas. Statements made and opinions expressed in this publication do not necessarily reflect the
views of the Publisher, Directors, management, or staff of The Haworth Press, Inc., or an endorsement by them.

This is a work of fiction. Names, characters, places, and incidents either are the products of the
author's imagination or are used fictitiously, and any resemblance to actual persons, living or
dead, business establishments, events, or locales is entirely coincidental.

Cover design by Jennifer M. Gaska.

Library of Congress Cataloging-in-Publication Data

Wynn, Perry.
    Blown away / Perry Wynn.
        p. cm.
    ISBN-13: 978-1-56023-607-8 (pbk. : alk. paper)
    ISBN-10: 1-56023-607-8 (pbk. : alk. paper)
    1. Gays—Fiction. 2. Same-sex marriage—Fiction. 3. Religious right—Fiction. 4. Exile (Pun-
ishment)—Fiction. 5. Epidemics—Fiction. 6. United States—Politics and government—21st
century—Fiction. 7. Political fiction. I. Title.

PS3623.Y65B55 2006
813'.6—dc22
                                                                                    2006005561

To Leigh
with love and gratitude

Editor's Foreword

Alice Street Editions provides a voice for established as well as upcoming lesbian writers, reflecting the diversity of lesbian interests, ethnicities, ages, and class. The cutting-edge series of novels, memoirs, and nonfiction writing welcomes the opportunity to present controversial views, explore multicultural ideas, encourage debate, and inspire creativity from a variety of lesbian perspectives. Through enlightening, illuminating, and provocative writing, Alice Street Editions can make a significant contribution to the visibility and accessibility of lesbian writing and bring lesbian-focused writing to a wider audience. Recognizing our own desires and ideas in print is life sustaining, acknowledging the reality of who we are, as well as our place in the world, individually and collectively.

Judith P. Stelboum
Editor in Chief
Alice Street Editions

Chapter 1

Meagan Sullivan walked up Eleventh Avenue South, turned north on Seventeenth Street, and walked a half block to Chris Landry's law office. This time of spring the Five Points South area of Birmingham, Alabama, was especially welcoming, bursting with flower beds full of color and an occasional ivory magnolia bloom stretched out for the sun. Meagan made the walk every day, weather allowing, to spend her lunch break with the woman she loved.

A simple bronze plaque, CHRIS LANDRY, ATTORNEY AT LAW, attached to the corner of a century-old brick building, marked the stairway up to the office. Meagan turned by the plaque and bounded up an aging wooden stairwell to the second-floor landing. She pushed open the door to the left and strolled in.

"Hi, Linda. Is she busy?" Meagan asked, breezing by the secretary's desk.

"Is she breathing?" Linda replied in her no-nonsense voice. As usual, she kept typing. "She's not with a client, so go on back."

Meagan strolled down the hall to the opaque glass door at the end of the small suite. Two lines were stenciled on the glass, the top line in large capital letters read CHRIS LANDRY, and the bottom, in smaller type, CIVIL RIGHTS ATTORNEY. Meagan tapped the door and went in.

Across the office Chris Landry sat at an oak table, surrounded by thick law volumes and yellow legal pads, dwarfed in her large but unfortunately cramped office. Chris was a small woman—just three inches over five feet tall—but her quiet, confident manner projected a formidable presence. Chris had fine, angular bones that delicately framed her face, and light brown eyes that encouraged trust. But her best physical feature was a smooth, silky voice that calmed like a lullaby.

"Hi, baby. Is it that time already?" Chris asked without looking up.

Blown Away
© 2006 by The Haworth Press, Inc. All rights reserved.
doi:10.1300/5706_01

"Yes, it's that time already." Meagan walked across the office and draped her arms over her mate. She kissed her and said, "You need to eat, you know. I really don't think you would if I didn't make you. You'd probably try to live off those damn cigarettes."

Meagan was right. Chris Landry spent most of her time thinking about the law, politics, and Meagan. If left alone, she often forgot to eat, but Meagan usually managed to get at least two meals a day into her.

"Are you ready to go?" Meagan asked. "I've got to be back at the ER on time today."

"I'm pretty swamped, but give me a minute." Chris begged Meagan's patience with a kiss on the back of her hand.

"Principle case or grocery case?" Meagan asked looking over Chris's shoulder and watching her write a line of notes in the margin.

"This one is a grocery case."

"Good. I don't feel bad about the interruption," Meagan said.

Just after finishing law school, Chris turned down lucrative offers from two well-respected law firms and a nonprofit in DC to pursue her own dreams, and over the next eight years she built a reputation as one of the top consulting civil rights attorneys in the country. Now she was in a position to choose her cases, but there were still bills to be paid. More often than she wanted, she worked cases for the money, usually class-action suits with lots of billable hours and a nice fee after judgment. Those were the grocery cases, the ones that paid the bills. As often as she could, she worked the principle cases—the cases she lived for, the cases that shaped America on their way to the Supreme Court.

It was Chris's passion for civil rights too, that brought her into Meagan's life just three years ago. Meagan first saw Chris standing on a small stage at a women's festival in north Georgia, delivering a speech on civil rights. Compared to the musicians and comediennes the Bill of Rights drew little interest, but like a skilled preacher Chris used humor and passion to draw in a crowd. After the speech Meagan waited two hours for Chris's admiring politicos to drift away, but when she finally walked up to Chris, Meagan found herself awkwardly lost for words. Chris saved her with an invitation to dinner.

Chris wrote another few lines in the margins before she closed the brief. She leaned back into Meagan's chest and flashed an apologetic smile. "Sorry for cutting into your lunch, but I'm trying to finish this case so I can focus on the Supreme Court preparations for the Thompson case." Chris stood up and arched her back in a long stretch, "I should get some relief soon, though. The ACLU decided to pony up for a legal clerk to help me out. As a matter of fact, she's supposed to be here this afternoon. Got a taste for anything in particular today?"

Meagan didn't answer. Her mind was stuck on the Thompson case. Distractedly she ran her hand across Chris's back and walked to the office couch.

Chris admired the view as Meagan moved across the room, knowing that she was still one of the most desired women in Birmingham. Meagan's sleek body moved with internal buoyancy, and her kind spirit radiated from her infectious smile. Gold and red strands of full, wavy hair fell past her shoulders, surrounding a round face and warm, welcoming, bright green eyes that sparkled when she laughed. Meagan instinctively knew how to make even casual acquaintances feel at ease, and her list of friends was endless.

Meagan settled into the couch and lightly ran her fingers through her hair. "Chris, I meant to ask you about a TV report I saw on the Thompson case. The reporter said something I hadn't heard and I wondered if he had his story right. Tell me again about the facts of that case."

Chris watched the long fingers of Meagan's hand glide through her hair and pushed back a burning desire to join Meagan on the couch for more than just the facts of the case. She satisfied herself with the promise of tonight and reached across her desk for a Marlboro Light. "I don't think I've ever told you the whole story, but if you want to take the time, I'll tell you what I can," Chris began, lighting the cigarette and blowing a column of smoke toward the lofty ceiling. "The facts of the case—*Roe versus State of Idaho*—how could a love story end up sounding so hard and cold?" She paused, looking down at the floor as she gathered her thoughts. "I think this is one of the toughest cases I have ever been involved with," she said after taking a long drag from the Marlboro. "Roe in this case is a young woman named Jessica

Thompson, who made the tragic mistake of falling in love with a young woman named Amanda Harkins. Amanda grew up near Pocatello, Idaho, the daughter of none other than Senator John Harkins. Jessica Thompson moved with her parents to the Pocatello area the summer before her senior year in high school, and soon after, Amanda and Jessica met and fell in love. They spent the school year and the next summer together, but then Jessica got a scholarship to the University of Oregon and moved to Eugene. Jessica and Amanda saw each other every chance they got, and when Amanda graduated she persuaded her father to let her go to the University of Oregon also, since her best friend Jessica was there. Of course, John Harkins objected to his daughter going to college out of state, but he finally agreed, after much begging from Amanda and some gentle persuasion from Amanda's mother." Chris paused for another drag and again exhaled a wispy stream toward the ceiling. "I think I told you that part of the story, right?"

Meagan nodded. "Yeah, I'm with you so far."

Chris continued, "Soon after Amanda moved to Oregon, the state of Idaho passed the legislation prohibiting civil unions and defining marriage to be exclusively the union of one man and one woman. As you know, Senator Harkins was the major player behind the scenes orchestrating all of the legislation. Meanwhile in Eugene, Amanda and Jessica were still very much in love, but they were also very deep in the closet. They knew if anyone, straight or gay, found out about them, it would mean big trouble. After a couple of years of that nonsense they decided to publicly come out, but they wanted to protect their relationship first. As soon as Amanda turned twenty, which is Oregon's age of consent for civil unions, they slipped off to the small town of Sisters and secretly entered a civil union. Unfortunately, the word had leaked back to Senator Harkins by the next day."

"Oh wow," Meagan said. "I can image his reaction, but since Amanda and Jessica were legally together by then, there was nothing Harkins could do, right?"

"You would think, but their trouble was just starting," Chris replied gravely. "Of course Harkins was outraged. He vowed the 'homosexual scourge' would never be allowed in his family, so he deceived Amanda into coming home and the rumor was he sent her to Colorado Springs for 'deprogramming.' But he wasn't finished. Harkins had major political damage to repair, so he went after Jessica Thompson."

"But she's just a kid," Meagan protested.

"She is, but unfortunately, her age is part of the problem. John Harkins applied pressure to the Idaho attorney general's office to have Jessica prosecuted for criminal conspiracy on the grounds that she enticed a minor into an illegal contract."

"Wait a minute. How could they do that? The civil union took place in Oregon, not Idaho," Meagan said.

"Exactly right," Chris replied. "This is where it gets interesting and the whole reason that the Supreme Court decided to hear the case. Remember when the question of civil unions came before the Ninth Circuit Court?"

"How could I forget? It's all you talked about for weeks."

"Well, as you know, the Ninth Circuit found that since some states have legalized civil unions, there is no compelling reason why other states should interfere with or prohibit other states' contractual statutes, but residency laws could be applied due to the wide division of community standards regarding the issue. In other words, same-sex couples can enter civil unions as long as they remain citizens of their state or a state with similar laws. The Circuit further found that the equal protection clause only requires prohibitive states to allow married gays to freely work, recreate, and do business in within the prohibited state, but equal protection did not require the prohibitive states to allow any state recognized marriage privileges, such as tax breaks and insurance privileges, to legal same-sex couples." Chris said as she ground out her cigarette.

"Yeah, but how does that apply to this case?"

"John Harkins and his puppets in the AG office assert that the equal protection clause does not protect Jessica because Amanda was still a legal citizen of Idaho when the contractual union was entered, even though she and Jessica lived in Oregon at the time. The state of Idaho is saying that Jessica unduly influenced a minor Idaho citizen into a contractual obligation that Jessica knew was illegal."

"Didn't Amanda have some culpability here?" Meagan questioned.

"You would think so," Chris answered. "However, the Idaho law that prohibits civil unions also included a section that requires its citizens to be twenty-one to enter a same-sex marital contract in another state or country, unless they have the consent of a parent or legal guardian. Idaho is asserting that Amanda Harkins did not have the legal capacity to enter the contractual obligations of a civil union until she turned twenty-one, and that due to Jessica's influence Amanda entered the contract under duress. The prosecution claims that Jessica was aware John Harkins still financially supported his daughter and considered her a dependent, therefore she knew Amanda was a citizen of Idaho and a parent's consent would be necessary for her to enter a same-sex marital contract."

Meagan raised her dark eyebrows, "Wow. What are they proposing to do to Jessica?"

"As it stands right now, she'll likely serve a year in jail."

"A year in freakin' jail!" Meagan protested. "Yeah, send her to an iron-barred love nest—that will fix her. Is such a severe sentence normal for Idaho?"

"No, usually a suspended sentence would be recommended for this type of offense, but you can be sure John Harkins is set on jail time, and Jessica will serve every day of that year."

"He must really hate her."

"Looks like." Chris walked to the window and watched the lunch-time crowd mill about on the street below. When she spoke again, her voice was distant, "You know I told you the story gets ugly?"

"Yeah. That's not the ugly part?"

"It gets worse," Chris said softly. "Jessica knew she was in trouble in Idaho, but she also knew the state of Oregon would not push to have her sent back to Idaho to face prosecution. So she stayed in Eugene. In the meantime, Amanda was coerced into staying at home, and following her extended vacation in Colorado Springs she found herself in an unbearable situation. Her father had her followed everywhere she went. She couldn't see any of her old friends from school; they were all suspect, and Harkins was insisting she would have to testify against Jessica."

"What do you mean she would have to testify against Jessica?"

"Harkins knew they needed evidence to persuade the judge that Jessica had used duress to influence Amanda into the civil union. So, he convinced Amanda that Jessica was already involved with someone else and she no longer cared about her. Harkins told Amanda that the only way she could gain his forgiveness and stay in the family was to testify against Jessica. He even told her that was also the only way to repent her sins and gain God's forgiveness."

"Is there no end to this man's vindictiveness?"

"There is more," Chris replied. "Lots more. For a while Amanda tried to conform to her family's expectations, but she became increasingly depressed. She wanted desperately to see Jessica, and the thought of having to testify against her was eating away at her. Several weeks after Amanda returned from Colorado Springs, her mother, Emily, walked into Amanda's bedroom to wake her up, but she couldn't. Then Mrs. Harkins saw an empty bottle of antidepressants lying on the floor. Amanda was rushed to the hospital and was revived, but later lapsed into a coma."

Meagan stared at Chris in disbelief, "Wait now, that's not how they said she died on the news report I saw."

"That's not surprising. Harkins's office covered up the suicide attempt and the mainstream press reported untreated diabetes as the cause of the coma," Chris said as she walked to her desk and took a single sheet out of a file folder. She handed it to Meagan, "We know differently because of this message Amanda posted on one of their favorite Web sites the night she OD'd. Fortunately, Jessica had a premonition to go back to the site and she found the message there. Amanda used the title of a song to catch Jessica's attention, and when Jessica saw the profile icon posted with the message she knew the note was for her."

Meagan read the note silently:

The ironic cruelties of this world are so great for those of us who must dare to love. My only sin was to love you so wholly, so completely, and with all that was in my soul. I know that God will not forgive me for this but I pray that you will. I never stopped loving you.
~A.

"Jesus! Amanda must have been totally committed to Jessica," Meagan said, still staring at the note.

"Yes, she was, and Jessica was committed to her. When Jessica saw the message on the board she returned to Idaho immediately. She was determined to find a way to see Amanda right away, even if it meant being arrested. When Jessica got to Pocatello she found out about the coma and went straight to the hospital. She waited until Mrs. Harkins left for dinner to sneak into Amanda's ICU room. Jessica says that when she took Amanda's hand and spoke to her, she saw the temperature on her monitor rise a couple of degrees. Amanda knew she was there. While Jessica was in the room, John Harkins came by and saw her holding his daughter's hand. He lost his shit, went nuts, and had Jessica arrested on the spot. Amanda died the next morning."

"That narrow-minded bastard," Meagan said. "If there is any justice in this world, John Harkins will come back in his next life as a black lesbian. Then he'll learn a thing or two about injustice."

"Amen," Chris said with a quick smile. "Anyway, I learned the real story when Jessica's attorney, Colton Rice, called and asked if I would help with the case. When he and Jessica told me the story, of course I agreed, but I never dreamed it would go all the way to the Supreme Court. I thought the case would surely be overturned in the Ninth Circuit. I see how wrong I was. Fortunately, this is the case that finally convinced my friends at the ACLU I could use some help."

"And here it is," Linda's voice boomed from across the room.

Abruptly Meagan and Chris turned to the door where Linda stood with a striking young woman.

"By the way, Meagan, I heard what you said about John Harkins. He couldn't handle it, baby," Linda said flatly. "I'm gone to lunch."

Chris smiled and motioned to the young woman at the door, "Hi. Come on in. I wasn't expecting you until later. Meagan, this is my new legal clerk, Elizabeth Nix."

Chapter 2

Elizabeth Nix was impressive on paper. Chris first read her résumé four weeks ago when the ACLU sent over a stack of applications. Chris sent back a list of three names, with Elizabeth Nix at the top.

At the University of Georgia Elizabeth Nix was an academic all-American hitter for the varsity volleyball team. A year after finishing her undergraduate work, she entered law school, again at the University of Georgia, and finished number four in her class. For two summers she worked for the ACLU, researching both local and nationwide civil rights cases. Her political experience came from working on the campaign of a newly elected congresswoman from Atlanta, and from her work with GAYLA, an organization dedicated to the protection and civil rights of underage gay youth. On her résumé Elizabeth listed five references. Chris called all five and found that although each of them spoke of different strengths, they all mentioned one common trait—that Elizabeth Nix was a natural-born leader, but willing to do the grunt work necessary to learn the system. She knew her niche, where she fit in the larger scheme of things, and knew when it was time to step into leadership.

At the interview Elizabeth was equally impressive and Chris connected with her immediately. Outwardly Elizabeth reflected the confidence of a woman who, at the age of twenty, had looked into the mirror and knew she liked the person looking back. Elizabeth was tall, five-eleven to be exact, with broad, square shoulders and the smooth, easy gait of an athlete. And, in spite of her accomplishments, Elizabeth was gracious, thoughtful, and usually soft-spoken, unless asked about a political passion. Then a passionate fire emerged.

Like Chris, constitutional law was Elizabeth's academic preference, and during her interview Elizabeth accurately summarized every Supreme Court case Chris asked, including the justice's opinions and the dissenting arguments. Chris asked her opinions on current national is-

Blown Away
© 2006 by The Haworth Press, Inc. All rights reserved.
doi:10.1300/5706_02

9

sues, and Elizabeth infused a keen historical perspective into her arguments that Chris knew would be invaluable. Chris interviewed two
other candidates for protocol, but she knew her choice was Elizabeth
Nix.

It was no surprise when Elizabeth arrived early for office orientation. Chris told her to come by sometime in the afternoon, and it was
officially after noon.

"Hi, I hope I'm not too early," Elizabeth said as she walked across
the office toward Meagan. "I moved into my apartment on Friday and
I was getting a little stir crazy. Nice to meet you, Meagan," she said
with a solid handshake.

"I understand," Chris said as she held out her hand to Elizabeth.
"It's no problem, but we were on the way out the door for lunch. Will
you join us?"

"Sure, as long as I'm not imposing on anything," Elizabeth said politely.

"Not at all." Chris smiled. "Meagan and I see each other almost every day at lunch, and about twelve hours every night. We'd enjoy
your company."

"So you are her partner, then?" Elizabeth asked, turning back to
Meagan. Elizabeth had noticed Meagan the minute she walked in the
door. Chris was a lucky woman.

"So it seems, but her real wife is the law," Meagan said with a quick
wink to Chris.

"Unfortunately, there's a little too much truth in that," Chris
shrugged.

"How do you feel about hamburgers?" Meagan asked Elizabeth.
"There is a place across the street that makes the best homemade bur-
gers in Alabama."

"Sounds good to me," Elizabeth replied.

THE FLAMING PIG had been in the same family since the 1950s,
and worked only to hold onto the loyal local customers. The Pig's ad-
vertised specialty was barbecue, but the only pig served was to folks
from out of town. The locals preferred the custom hamburgers.

"Hello, Charlie," Meagan said with a wink to the Pig's owner as she breezed past the front counter.

Charlie kept his eyes on his newspaper and lifted three fingers, "Meagan, Chris, good to see ya. Thanks for bringing your friend."

Meagan found a shiny red leather booth in the back of the narrow restaurant and slid across the far bench. Chris slid in beside her and Elizabeth took the opposite bench as Meagan dealt three greasy, worn menus from the stack pinned between the sugar and salt and pepper shaker at the end of the table.

"Now I'm telling you, Elizabeth," Chris said, halfheartedly browsing her menu, "you need to try one of these custom hamburgers. They're good, but not good for you."

"That's the best kind," Elizabeth began, suddenly interrupted by a loud commotion erupting from the kitchen. A young woman in baggy overalls hustled through two swinging silver doors carrying a tray of water glasses and a pitcher of sweet tea.

"Here comes Samantha," Meagan said without taking her eyes from the menu.

Three glasses of water slid across the table, stopping just in front of each of them. "Hi, Chris. Hi, Meagan," Samantha said, pulling out her order pad. Her eyes stopped dead on Elizabeth. "Who is your friend here?" she flirted.

"Samantha, this is Elizabeth Nix, my new legal clerk," Chris replied, watching Samantha with a mischievous smile, knowing what would be coming next.

"Hi, Elizabeth," Samantha stretched out her hand.

Elizabeth reached over and took it, smiling slightly when Samantha held on for an extra moment.

Samantha shot a final teasing glance before turning back to Chris. "Is she taken?"

"Why don't you ask her?"

"Not currently," Elizabeth offered through self-conscious smile.

"That's nice," Samantha said, looking again at Elizabeth. "You can call me Sam if you want. These guys say they like Samantha better, but most of my friends call me Sam," she said and turned back to

Chris and Meagan. "What are you guys going to have today? Your usual?"

Samantha finished the order, flashed one last flirtatious glance at Elizabeth and strutted to the kitchen.

Chris slowly shook her head, "Samantha is something else, but she's a good kid. She sure seemed to like you," she offered.

Elizabeth picked up her utensils and slowly unfurled the white paper napkin wrapped around them. "To tell the truth, I'm taking it slow right now. I just broke up from a five-year relationship and I'm still stinging a bit. We broke up a couple of months ago. It was tough for both of us, and I'm a long way from being over it. The last thing I want right now is another relationship." Elizabeth spread the napkin across her lap and looked up at Chris. "Besides, I expect you'll keep me busy enough to stay out of trouble."

"Yes, it may be good you're not planning to have a life," Chris replied, half smiling. "I know your main interest is the Thompson case, but I'd like you working on other cases as well. When we get back to the office, we'll go through my current caseload and your priorities."

"Does this mean I will see more of you?" Meagan interrupted.

"Why of course not," Chris teased.

Meagan mocked a grimace. "I don't know why I think I want to marry you."

"For my money, obviously," Chris smiled lightly.

Elizabeth watched them banter, remembering the many times her ex had asked for more of her time. In the end, Elizabeth wondered if all the long hours she put in for her causes, or her bosses, or her teams, had been worth it. She lost a woman she loved, and the world was still as screwed up as it ever was, in spite of her best efforts. But Elizabeth's deep-seated drive for justice kept her pushing, believing that someday she would find someone who was willing to sacrifice for ideals. For now, though, she just wanted to focus on the law. "Chris, I don't see how the justices can ignore the equal protection clause on the Thompson case."

Chris looked over at Elizabeth, startled, but slightly amused. "I agree with you, Elizabeth," she said. "I'll be interested in all your thoughts on the case, but I'd rather get to know you a bit first, and maybe we can fill you in on life in Birmingham. We'll hit the Thompson case this afternoon at our apartment. It's quiet there in the afternoon so I sometimes go there to work. You can stay for dinner, if you like."

"Sure. I'd like that," Elizabeth replied. "If it's okay with Meagan."

Meagan didn't reply. Her attention was fixed on the man sitting at the next table. He ordered barbecue, and hadn't turned the page of the paper in front of him for fifteen minutes. Meagan watched him for a moment, and then turned back to Elizabeth. "I'm sorry, what did you say, Elizabeth?"

"Chris invited me to stay for dinner," Elizabeth began.

"Oh yeah, that's fine."

"Meagan, what is it about that guy?" Chris nodded discretely toward him.

"He's listening to us," Meagan said quietly. "Poor guy is so bored he doesn't have anything to do but listen to other people's conversations," she said louder, fully intending him to hear.

Chris nodded and looked across at Elizabeth. "Another reason not to discuss a case at lunch," she said, raising her tea glass.

CHRIS AND MEAGAN lived five blocks from the law office in a stand-alone post–World War II era building subdivided into four apartments, two upstairs and two downstairs. Their apartment was downstairs to the right.

Elizabeth looked over the pots of annuals surrounding the front door as she waited for Chris to sort through an overgrown set of keys. Chris finally pulled out the right one and pushed the door open. On the other side a massive cat waited.

"Hello, Clarence," Chris said as the big tom wrapped himself around the hem of her pants. "This is Elizabeth. Elizabeth, meet Clarence Darrow."

Elizabeth kneeled and stroked Clarence the length of his body. His round, amber eyes coolly gazed up at her from a proud midnight face, sizing Elizabeth up as he rubbed against her outstretched hand.

"I've always wanted to meet you, Mr. Darrow," Elizabeth said.

"Mr. Darrow critiques all of my arguments," Chris said before she disappeared into the kitchen. "I'm afraid I've yet to impress him. Make yourself at home in there. Do you want something to drink?"

"Just water for now," Elizabeth answered as she looked around the den. There was no television—she noticed that first—but on the bookcase under the front window was a Bose stereo. In the far corners two chairs faced out into the room. The recliner with burgundy and tan upholstery sat by an end table filled with books, notepads, an ashtray, and a half-empty pack of Marlboros. In the other corner a matching oversized chair and ottoman was surrounded on each side by stacks of magazines, a few paperbacks, and a forgotten tea glass.

Elizabeth knew the two chairs were personal, so she settled into the long couch lining the back wall. She looked around the room again. There was a mirror by the door, and a painting above the couch of three women linked together in a circle of dance. Above Chris's chair was a modern artist's rendering of Lady Justice, and framed photographs of people Elizabeth assumed to be family members or friends were scattered on the bookshelves.

In a moment Chris appeared again, carrying two tall glasses of ice water, a wedge of lemon in each. She handed one to Elizabeth and set the other on her end table. "Colton Rice will be here in a few weeks to meet with us on the Thompson case. I'd like for you to be thoroughly familiar with the case by the time he gets here," Chris said, walking across the room to her briefcase. She took a brown expandable file folder out and handed it to Elizabeth. "This is the research I have on the case. You need to read all of the documents in the file, and then I want you to read these cases," Chris said. She handed Elizabeth a list scratched on the last page of a legal pad. "After you finish the reading, we'll go from there. And don't forget to refer to Thompson as *Roe versus Idaho* if you're talking about it publicly."

Elizabeth took the pad and scanned through the list. It must have contained at least twenty-five cases. "How soon do you want me to finish this?" she asked.

"Take your time, but be thorough," Chris replied. "I'll let you know if you're moving too slowly. Start with a complete review of the Thompson file. Make notes where you need. You'll see some of

Colton's and my notes on the margins. Don't write on any of the clean pages. Ask questions."

Elizabeth opened the file and pulled out the stack of documents. Six months ago she would have never dreamed of having the chance to read this file, much less make notes in it.

The next two hours passed in silence as Elizabeth pored over the file. At the final page, she slowly rubbed her eyes.

"Un-freakin'-believable," Elizabeth said. "The first thing I want to know is how Harkins kept the suicide note away from the press?"

"He doesn't know about it," Chris replied.

Elizabeth's eyes flew open. "*What?* Come on. How can he not know about it?"

"Well, I'm guessing he doesn't check Internet boards for one thing, and, fortunately, anyone who may have seen the message hasn't made the connection. Jessica says Amanda used a picture icon so Jessica would know the message was for her. Apparently the place pictured on the icon was significant to them, and Amanda was smart enough to keep her last words private."

"Then why haven't you gone public with this?" Elizabeth asked. "This could do serious political damage."

Chris pulled a Marlboro Light from the half empty pack and lit it before she answered. "First and foremost, Jessica asked us not to make the note public without her permission, and so far she hasn't given it. Second, Harkins would dismiss it, deny the note had anything to do with his daughter, and again Jessica would be caught in the middle of a public fight with John Harkins. Third, we don't know yet how much political damage we need to inflict on John Harkins. He may be just a bothersome senator, or he may be the next vice president of the United States."

Elizabeth looked at Chris through the rising smoke. "Do you think William Bucks wants him for the ticket?"

"I think Bucks needs him for the ticket," Chris replied. "I'm not sure what Bucks wants, but I think Harkins is the front runner. The lobby folks in DC tell me I'm probably right."

"So if Harkins is on the ticket you may go public with the note?" Elizabeth asked.

"I don't think Jessica will be up to fighting Harkins until after her case is decided, which of course is after the election. If the court decides in our favor, Jessica will probably let this whole thing lie. After all, she doesn't want Amanda's name dragged across the national spotlight. But if the decision goes against us, she may be willing to take one last swing at Harkins."

"Maybe it would be enough of a scandal to keep him from ever being elected president," Elizabeth offered.

"Maybe. Who knows anymore," Chris replied dryly.

The jingle of keys turned their attention to the front door. Clarence jumped from his post by Chris and trotted across the room. Chris followed, making it to the door just in time to take over two bags of groceries.

"Hi, babe," Meagan said as she kissed Chris and then swept Clarence into her arms. The big tom's purr filled the room as Meagan carried him to the kitchen.

After a rustle of plastic and the clink of a wineglass Meagan walked back into the den. She settled back in her chair and looked over at Elizabeth, then Chris, "Well, you two certainly look happy," she quipped. "Let me guess. John Harkins."

Chapter 3

John Harkins's mountain cabin sat nestled in a small, flat valley, flanked by a jagged mountain range to the north and south. A single-lane dirt road passed a few hundred yards in front of the property, and a hammered iron sign, ROCKING JH RANCH, hung from the middle of the timber pole arch that marked the long drive to the cabin. Harkins kept the vegetation around his property sparse to prevent fire, but on the west side he left a few tall fir trees to shade the corrals and barn.

It was still two days until the first official day of summer, but the weather was already hot and dry in the mountains of southeast Idaho. Harkins leaned back in a cane-bottomed chair and hoisted his dusty boots onto the log railing of his cabin porch.

Sitting next to Harkins was William Bucks, the man likely to become the next president of the United States. The two men relaxed as they alternated puffs on Cuban cigars with sips of Johnnie Walker Blue Label scotch and silently scanned the horizon for signs of forest fires. Inside the cabin Emily Harkins busied herself with the catch of the men's afternoon fly-fishing trip. Today the Harkins's place looked like hundreds of other weekend getaways scattered throughout the mountains of Idaho, except for the eight Secret Service agents milling about the property keeping their eyes busy on fleeting shadows.

In a moment Harkins squinted toward a faint column of smoke rising from a distant ridge to the south. "That one is right next to my property," he said evenly, keeping his eyes on the smoke, "They'll have a water drop on it soon. There aren't many fires this early in the season, so they get to 'em pretty quick." Harkins paused and glanced over at Bucks with a slow smile. "They know it's next to my place, too. That makes 'em nervous." Harkins paused and took another puff from the cigar. "I figure their extra attention is just part of my executive privileges."

Bucks pulled on his cigar and nodded silently, though Harkins's comment amused him. The senator from Idaho boasted constantly about being a self-made man, but along the way there had been more than a few turns of fortune.

Harkins had served two tours of duty in Vietnam as a helicopter pilot and returned to Pocatello for a job with a local helicopter contractor. Eighteen months later, he married Emily Anderson, the beautiful—and tough—daughter of a wealthy mining magnate. Emily's father agreed to finance a couple of helicopters for Harkins, and soon Harkins Sky Ships was in business and making money. All of Harkins's investments, including a dude ranch, made money, and fifteen years after returning from Vietnam, John Harkins was one of the true power players in the state of Idaho.

Most of Idaho liked their Senator Harkins. He stood tall and straight, his body still muscled and his eyes still clear. He looked like a model cowboy, an image he guarded and groomed. Politically, Harkins fought for a century-old way of life. Ranchers, loggers, miners, fundamentalists, independents, and an odd bunch of recreational developers backed Harkins, and he backed them. But John Harkins main political ally was an ultraconservative organization known as the Christians for Moral Accountability, or simply, the CMA.

Just as Harkins predicted, a helicopter appeared on the horizon, swinging a huge bucket from a long line attached to the ship's belly. It headed straight for the smoke and within a minute, the helicopter flew to the ridge, dumped the water over the smoke, and with the bucket still swinging, disappeared over the horizon. As the steady thump of the copter faded Bucks turned to Harkins, "John," he said slowly and softly, requiring Harkins's full attention, "you know I'm about to make the most important decision of my life. I'm going to the convention in August with the nomination in hand. You know you are on the short list to be my running mate." Harkins nodded slightly as Bucks continued, "My problem is my people are telling me I have to go with someone from a larger state, like California or Texas, to get the college votes I need. They're telling me that a ticket with candidates from a small Southern state and a small Western state won't work."

Behind Bucks the cabin's screen door opened and Emily Harkins walked out. She sat in a rocking chair next to her husband and pushed it into a gentle rock. Bucks nodded to her and continued. "Those spin boys are telling me I need to get either Holter or Leeman. But, what it boils down to, John, is that if I'm gonna convince the stuffed shirts that you're my man, I've got to show them you can deliver something to the ticket."

"What do you have in mind?" Harkins asked.

"John, you know these new campaign finance laws have got us up against the wall. With what we're taking in now, we figure we'll probably run out of money about mid-October, and as you know, the three weeks prior to the election are the most crucial. We've got to get more direct contributions, and to do that we've got to fire up our base. We need more money from individuals. We need folks like the NRA and CMA to get involved and get their constituents to make smaller contributions, but in a big way. You know that I'm not solid with those two groups and some of the other ideological conservatives, but I think putting you on the ticket could change that."

"I'm sure I could help there, Will," Harkins replied. "But so could both Holter and Leeman. Leeman has stronger ties with the NRA than I do."

"True enough," Bucks said, "and my folks know that too. But there is something else I think you can do for us that they can't."

"What's that?" Harkins asked as he squared his eyes on Bucks.

"Tap into Jason Johnson and the CMA."

Harkins kept his eyes steady on Bucks but offered no reply.

Bucks took a deep breath and looked over to Emily, then back to Harkins. "The bottom line is that the campaign has to have more money, John, more money that we have some control over. What I'd like for you to do is to work with Jason Johnson to tap into CMA money. We need to get the CMA to run issue ads . . . to . . . to push the country's attention to issues like gays, abortion, public participation in prayer—we need to get those hot-button issues into the fabric of this race, but we've got to be the ones weaving the fabric. We've got to make sure we push the right issues in the right places so we hold onto our base in the South and rural West, and pick up as many

Midwest states as we can get. If the CMA just goes out and starts pushing traditional issues everywhere, it could backfire and we could lose votes, especially in the Midwest. We've got to be sure the ads are run at the right times and in the right places, even down to the county level, and that's where we need the CMA's help."

"How's that?" Harkins asked.

"What we have in mind," Bucks began, "is for the CMA to funnel their money into other smaller, grassroots organizations which will in turn promote local activism. We figure if the CMA puts money into local coffers, the party leaders will know what issues to push at those levels. They'll sponsor local issue ads and campaigns and we'll be able to mask who's paying the bill for advocacy. The CMA can quadruple the amount they are currently able to spend on the campaign."

Harkins studied Bucks for a moment and stood and walked to the edge of the porch. Funneling money was illegal as hell and so was forming issue ad partnerships between presidential campaigns and nonprofits.

After a thick silence Harkins turned back to Bucks. "I've got no problem pushing for direct contributions," he began, "but this issue ad idea is different. I figure you're asking me to do this because of my relationship with Jason Johnson."

"Yes," Bucks answered. "You and Jason frequently work together, so we think the two of you can do this above any hint of impropriety."

"I don't like it," Harkins said.

"Neither do I," Bucks responded quickly. "But the party is pushing for alternatives, and I think this one deserves exploration. I believe it's low risk."

"Maybe," Harkins replied. "But it's our necks, isn't it?" He looked down and scuffed a raised nail with his boot, "Give me twenty-four hours, Will. I need to talk this over with Emily."

Emily suddenly stopped her slow rock and snapped her gaze squarely to her husband. "Dinner is ready," she said firmly as she stood and walked back into the cabin.

"She is on board with us, isn't she, John?" Bucks asked as soon as the screen door shut.

"She will be," Harkins said confidently. "She's a little concerned about all the extra attention the family will get during the campaign, but she knows we're a strong family. If I'm your man, she'll be right there with me."

WILLIAM BUCKS SLOWLY rolled his coffee mug in his hands and set it down. "I'd better get back to town," Bucks said as he stood and pushed his chair under the table. "Emily, thanks for a wonderful dinner." Bucks stretched out his hand to Harkins, "John, I need an answer soon," he said with a firm shake.

Outside the agents escorted Bucks to his black Suburban, their eyes busily scanning in all directions. Another couple of agents waited at the front doors of a matching Suburban stationed just behind Bucks's SUV. They slid into the front seat the instant Bucks's door closed.

Emily stood at the cabin door watching the whole ridiculous ritual with an incredulous smile. *The world would not stop turning if you all died today,* she thought. *Life would go on, just the way it went on after Amanda died.* The smile left her face. She closed the door and walked back to the kitchen, quickly moving past her husband without a word or a look.

"What is it now, Em?" Harkins demanded, following behind her.

"I'll tell you what it is," Emily said, spinning around to face her husband with an expression as drawn and angry as her voice. "I'm sick to death of our family's tragedy being used to win a few votes. You and Jason Johnson parade around and act as if you know all the answers. Well, let me tell you something, John; Amanda was our daughter and she was in love with Jessica. I know you can't stand to hear me say that but it's the truth. It wasn't about morals, and it wasn't about politics, and it sure as hell wasn't about winning. It was about love. You may vaguely remember love, John," Emily said as her eyes narrowed on her husband. "Damn it, John, it does seem like you could put away your political ambition long enough to realize how much this could hurt us all!"

Harkins's face flushed red. "I know she was our daughter, and I loved her, too," he growled. "I don't want what happened to her to happen to other people's daughters and sons. I do what I do for the good of this country!"

"That's bullshit, John, and you know it." Emily kept her glare on her husband's eyes. "Everything you do you say is for the good of the country. Well to hell with the good of the country. What about the good of this family for a change? What about that, John? What about the fact that a hired hand saw Ben take his first elk and taught him how to dress it? What about Katie's prom night, or even the night she had David? Where were you then, John? Or maybe you shouldn't answer that!" Emily leveled one last glare on her husband and turned for the door.

Harkins grabbed her arm. She looked down disgustedly at his hand and then slowly turned her cold stare back to his eyes. Harkins tightened his grip. "What's that supposed to mean?"

"I think you know what I mean," Emily said, pulling away from his grasp. The night their fourth grandchild was born, six weeks early, Harkins couldn't be found anywhere. Too many questions led Emily to a rumor of a mistress in Washington.

"Emily, you know that was just a rumor. I thought you knew me better than that." Harkins's angry brown eyes narrowed on his wife. "As I see it my political career has been damn good to us. Do you think we would have all of this if it weren't for my political career?"

"No," Emily replied as the edges of her mouth hardened. "We might not have your dream of the White House, but we would have plenty. And we would still have our daughter."

Harkins's reply exploded into the night air. "So you're still blaming me for that, are you!"

"I'll always blame you for that," Emily replied, keeping her voice low and even. She left him there and walked to her bedroom. In a moment she heard the screen door slam, and she knew her husband was storming across the yard, heading for the barn. In a few minutes he would have his favorite mare saddled and his gear gathered. Then he would be gone for the night.

EMILY HARKINS STOOD in front of her kitchen sink, looking past the open field in front of the cabin to the mountain peaks on the horizon. In the distance she made out the image of her husband riding in on the dirt road to the east. She watched him for a moment, remembering how she once loved him. She shook away the memories with a weary smile and walked to the refrigerator for eggs. She cracked the last one as her husband's boot steps fell soundly across the porch.

The door squeaked open and Harkins tossed his gear into the storage closet. He walked past Emily with hardly a look. "I'm going to wash up," he mumbled.

There was no hint of campfire smoke on Harkins's clothes when he came back and sat down at the table, even though last night's temperature had fallen below forty degrees. Emily set a plate of fresh biscuits in front of him, wondering where he had really spent last night.

"Emily, I'm going to call Jason Johnson soon. I've decided to do what Bucks wants, but I need to know you'll support me on the ticket," Harkins said as he buttered one of the biscuits.

Emily looked at him for a moment, and then sat down across the table. She poured cream in her coffee, stirred it lightly, and tapped the spoon on the mug. She kept her eyes on the coffee as she spoke to him soberly. "I'll do as I have done for the past five years, John. I'll stand by you in public and do whatever it takes to convince the public that our lives are perfect and that you have all the answers. I talked you into this political life and I suppose I owe you that much," she said, caressing her coffee mug in weathered hands. "But I will tell you this," she said, turning her focus to his eyes, "if I think for one minute you are using Amanda's death for your own political gain—it's over. I will bring you down. You know I've watched you and your bunch long enough and I've met the right people. I can do it, John."

"I have no doubt about that," Harkins replied.

"GOOD MORNING, NELL," Jason Johnson said with the same over-eager smile and voice he greeted his secretary with every day. He picked up his morning stack of letters and flipped through them as he spoke, "How are you this fine morning?"

"Fine, Jason," Nell replied. "Senator Harkins called about twenty minutes ago. I told him you were on the other line and you'd call him back."

"Harkins called?" Jason questioned. "Did he say what he wanted?"

"No. He didn't leave a message other than to call him."

"Okay. Buzz me when you have him on the line," Johnson said. He tapped the letters on her desk, gave Nell a wink, and retreated into his office.

Johnson's executive office was as plain as the rest of the headquarters building of the Christians for Moral Accountability. The building, like everything else associated with the CMA, was just another carefully calculated piece of a public façade designed to present an image that would neither alarm nor draw criticism from the secular voting public. The organization's name was kept below the radar, too. To see the title *Christians for Moral Accountability* fully written out was rare; the preferred name was simply "CMA." The image spin worked well, allowing the CMA to become one of the largest and fastest growing forces in American politics. Jason Johnson loved the power of his CEO position, and the ability to influence history.

Nowadays Johnson's power reached to the highest levels in Washington, so it took Nell only five minutes to get Harkins on the line.

"John Harkins is on line one, Jason."

"Thanks, Nell," Johnson said and pushed the line-one button. "Good morning, John. Sorry to keep you waiting, but you know how it is—everyone wants you to tackle their problems first. How can I help you this morning?"

"I know you're busy, Jason, so I'll get right to the point," Harkins began. "William Bucks was here last night. He's considering me for the ticket."

"That's what we've been praying for," Johnson gloated.

"Yes," Harkins replied. "But Bucks is getting heat from the party to name someone from one of the larger states, like Holter or Leeman. He thinks he can change the party thinking on that, but he's got to show that by going with me the party can hold the marginal states in the South and rural West and pull in most of the Midwest states."

"I see," Johnson replied. "I think it's obvious the party needs you on the ticket to do that. Bucks is way too soft. Our folks are really concerned about his potential appointments to the Court, and I've got to tell ya, I'm already hearing rumbling about staying home on election day. A ticket with you on it will go a long way toward easing those folks concerns and reenergizing our base."

"Well, I agree, Jason," Harkins replied. "But the problem is the party. Bucks has to convince them I can deliver more than just the conservatives." Harkins lifted the lid on his desktop humidifier and pulled out a cigar. He rolled it in his fingers as he considered his next words.

"How do you see us being able to help you out?" Johnson interjected.

"We need to show the party how I can help win the fence sitters," Harkins replied. "As you know, this election will come down to taking the undecided voter and getting our folks to the polls. Most people vote on emotional rather than real political issues, so part of our strategy will be to get our hot-button issues into the political conversation and then use our stand on those issues to get the independent and swing votes and to get our base to the polls. We've got to show those voters how important this election is for the future of their children and grandchildren."

"Your record is very clear on family issues."

Harkins took a reserved breath. "What we really need, Jason, is a way to stretch the money. We've got to leverage our dollars to push our message in the right places, places where our dollars will end up in votes."

"You mean by running issue ads," Johnson interrupted. "You know our issue ads will back your positions."

Harkins put the cigar in his mouth and impatiently bit down. "Yes, I know that, Jason. But the truth is we're going to need cash. What I'd like for you to consider is diversifying the CMA campaign contributions. We think you can do that by pushing dollars down to local groups and organizations. If you diversify your cash contributions through local organizations, you can maximize your contribution to the party."

A long silence followed before Johnson replied. "Basically you want us to launder contributions through our supporting organizations. We use our national clout to pull in money and then funnel it back to the local organizations where the party wants the money to go. The bottom line is we would be working directly with the Bucks campaign to illegally solicit campaign contributions."

"You got it," Harkins replied.

"What are the risks?" Johnson asked evenly.

"They're manageable. If we're ever investigated, and I don't think we will be, sifting through the financial resources of these small organizations would take weeks, and then it would be almost impossible to prove intentional fraud. I don't think anyone would ever bother to try it. If they did, a little black eye would be the worst we'd get."

"Yeah," Johnson said, taping his pen in a steady beat while he thought, "I think you're right."

"So, you'll do it?"

The beat of Johnson's pen quickened. "Yes. We've got to do all we can to win this election. But the CMA will be looking to protect our interests as well."

Harkins winced and eased back in his chair. "I'm listening."

"We'd want final approval on all Supreme Court nominations before they go to Congress. We figure there will be at least two openings in the first term," Johnson began without hesitation. "Also, we need assurance that Bucks will do whatever is necessary to protect the financial breaks for religious organizations, including tax exemptions and government grants for all churches and religious charities. Can you imagine the devastating effect taxes would have on the CMA's missions?" Johnson paused to measure Harkins's reaction. Hearing nothing, he said confidently, "If you can give us those two assurances, we'll give you the election."

Harkins pulled the cigar from his mouth and cradled his head in his hand, rubbing his forehead thoughtfully. "Okay, I think we have an understanding, Jason," he said. "I'll be in touch soon."

Harkins hung up the phone and looked down to the sparse notes he had just written. On the top line was the date, and then Jason Johnson's name underneath. Beside Johnson's name were the words *the Court* and *tax exemption*. It was scarce little to record the most important conversation of his political career, but it was enough. He picked up the phone and dialed, reaching Bucks's campaign bus as it barreled down I-84 on the way to another stump speech, this time in Portland.

"Mornin' Carl," Harkins grumbled to Bucks's assistant campaign manager. "Is your boss busy?"

Bucks picked up immediately. "Hi, John. You got good news for me?"

"I do," Harkins replied. "Johnson said they'll do it. But he wants a couple of things."

"I figured," Bucks said.

"He says they'll want you to ensure the CMA keeps their tax exemption and continue to allow government grants for faith-based organizations."

"That's no problem. What else does he want?" Bucks asked.

"He wants final approval on Court nominations."

Bucks said nothing.

"Are you still there?" Harkins asked after a long silence.

"Hell yes, I'm still here," Bucks replied. "That bastard went for the throat, didn't he? I haven't even got my feet in the Oval Office and I already have my hands tied. I don't like this, John. I'm going to have to talk to Carl and the staff. I'm not sure we can agree to the Court. I'll get back to you soon. Johnson will keep quiet, right?"

"Yes, he will. If there is one thing Jason understands it's discretion," Harkins replied.

"Good. I'll be in touch. It will probably be a few weeks before I can tell you anything certain. Thanks for your good work, John," Bucks said and hung up.

ELIZABETH FINISHED THE *last* of a generous portion of peach cobbler and set the bowl on the table beside her. She sat back, listening to the soft murmur of a Georgia summer rain falling on the tin roof above as she pushed her porch glider into a slow rock. Beside her, Chris Landry kept the same rhythm in an oversized white rocker. For now they sat quietly, just listening to the soothing rain.

The murmur of the rain slowly faded, soon replaced by the hypnotic drum of distant bullfrogs. In a moment, Nettie, the aunt Chris had idolized since childhood, bustled onto the porch to gather their dessert dishes.

Chris loved Nettie for many reasons, but mostly because Nettie was a woman who always said exactly what was on her mind, not caring one whit what anyone might think, and her tall, robust stature made her impossible to ignore.

"Are you girls okay?" Nettie asked, stacking their plates on top of each other. "You two are so quiet out here we were beginning to wonder if a banshee came and got you." Nettie laughed heartily at her own words. She nodded toward the window next to the front door and said, "Chris, your niece and nephew are sure giving Meagan the business in there. She's holdin' her own for now, but you know they won't go to sleep without one of your bedtime stories."

Chris lazily turned to the window and smiled. Inside, Meagan knelt on the floor in a Statue of Liberty pose, holding perfectly still as two children wrapped her in the red, white, and blue streamers they had gathered from the Fourth of July picnic. "Ah, Lady Liberty," Chris said, still smiling. "I never knew she had red hair."

"Or liked watermelon so much," Elizabeth offered.

"She's not going to fit her wedding dress if she keeps eating like that," Nettie laughed.

Chris shook her head and looked up to Nettie. "Don't dare say that to her. She's getting crazy about this whole wedding thing."

"Oh, your wedding's gonna be fine, baby," Nettie assured. "Your Aunt Nettie will see to that." Nettie nodded confidently and sauntered back into the house with the dishes.

The drumming of the bullfrogs again filled the air as Elizabeth rocked slowly, reflecting on the last three days. She had spent almost every waking hour in the North Georgia mountains with Chris Landry, and she couldn't think of a more gratifying time she had spent anywhere with anyone else. The days had been filled with long walks spent talking about the law, or fishing with the twin seven-year-olds, or spitting watermelon seeds for penny bets. Elizabeth watched Chris move heartily through the days, realizing that it was passion that drove Chris in every phase of her life. Elizabeth wondered why, then, Chris would settle for a marriage that was less than legal.

"Chris, do you mind if I ask something personal?" Elizabeth asked over the baritone of the bullfrogs.

"It depends on what it is," Chris replied lightly. "Go ahead, but I reserve my right not to answer."

"Why do you and Meagan want to have this commitment ceremony?" Elizabeth asked.

"I'm not going to insult your intelligence by saying because we love each other, but maybe I can better answer your question if I know why you ask."

"Well, for one reason, because a commitment ceremony doesn't have the benefits of a legal foundation, and because I still question the wisdom of following the dubious social experiment of freewill marriage."

Chris chuckled and said, "So I'm taking it you view modern marriage as a dubious social experiment."

"Not always," Elizabeth replied. "But about half do end in divorce."

"And about half do not," Chris countered. "But based on what you've just said, I'm guessing you question whether a lifetime commitment is a realistic blueprint for relationships."

"Yeah, I suppose that is what I'm really getting at," Elizabeth replied.

"To tell the truth, I would have been inclined to agree with you before I met Meagan, but it's different with her. In every other relationship I was ever in there were definitely two individuals involved, me and the other person. With Meagan it's not that way. I see her as a part of myself, so a ceremony to acknowledge that bond, to her and to others, seems perfectly natural."

"In that case, why don't you move to a state where you can be legally married?"

"We probably will eventually, but as long as I'm doing what I do we need to stay where we are. The deeper the South the better," Chris said.

"Why? What difference does it make?"

"It makes a lot of difference. You can't win a war if you're fighting it from distant shores. I need to be here, in the middle of the emotion, the prejudice, even the hate. I need to know what motivates the enemy, what they are thinking, where their beliefs and fears are. I have to be able to understand them if I hope to have a chance to beat them. I can't do that if we're living comfortably in Massachusetts, or California, or wherever."

Elizabeth studied Chris for a moment, wondering what it was, deep in her psyche, that pushed Chris, that made her sacrifice the freedom of her youth to fight this seemingly endless war. She realized that Chris Landry truly believed she could change the world, or at least change her own world. Elizabeth did not know yet how they were going to do it, but she decided she would follow Chris every step of the way. "Well, I guess that means I'll be staying in the South for a while, too."

Chris smiled widely. "Good."

Meagan's laughter turned their attention back inside the house. "I see Meagan escaped," Chris said as she watched Meagan walk toward the door, her body still half covered by paper streamers.

Meagan walked onto the porch and over to rub Chris's shoulders.

"So I see you survived," Chris said.

"Yes, and I appreciate all the help from you guys," Meagan said sarcastically, teasing Chris with a squeeze to her shoulders, a little too hard. "Those two are wild tonight. They were so charged about doing the fireworks. Then it rained and they had all that energy to get rid of."

"It's too bad about the fireworks," Elizabeth offered. "The Fourth of July isn't the same without them."

"It's just as well with me," Meagan said. "I've seen so many firework accidents come into the ER. The firecrackers are the worst— I just don't understand why people buy them. I never liked explosions."

Chapter 4

Elizabeth cursed under her breath, weaving her Subaru Outback through six lanes of rush hour traffic, pushing to make the Birmingham International Airport in time to meet Flight 1917 from Atlanta. Veering right onto the exit ramp she caught the green and accelerated the last mile to the terminal. At the first Delta sign she pulled in to let Chris and Meagan jump out. They were already ten minutes late.

Elizabeth lucked into a front-row space and quickly made her way to the terminal. Fortunately, the flight was late too. Elizabeth found Chris and Meagan waiting by the baggage carousel and sat down with them. Right now the terminal was mostly quiet, except for the man across the corridor who had just scurried up to one of the phones, his face bright red as he pulled out his wallet to fumble for a phone number. Elizabeth watched him punch the numbers and turn to the wall. In a few minutes he slammed the phone down and stormed away, more red faced than before. Elizabeth watched him disappear around the corner, knowing exactly how he felt, but doubtful his anger had actually helped. One day, she reminded herself, she had to learn to control her own temper.

"There they are," Chris said after a moment, pointing to the family of five at the top of the stairs.

Gracie, the youngest, held her mother's hand and swung a rag doll as she hopped down the stairs. The two boys, Lucas and Trent, were just behind, a couple of steps in front of their father.

The oldest boy, Lucas, had the same dark hair and eyes as his mother. Trent, the middle one, was a carbon copy of his father. His fine, sandy blond hair naturally parted on the right with the exact same crook toward the front, and his light blue eyes actively studied everything around him.

"Welcome to Birmingham," Chris said with her hand out to Nancy, then to Colton. She turned to Meagan and lightly touched her shoulder. "This is Meagan Sullivan, my partner, and your Orlando tour guide," she said with a welcoming smile to Nancy.

Meagan had volunteered to go with Nancy and the Rice children on a trip to central Florida, leaving Colton free to work the sixteen-hour days needed to prepare for the Thompson case.

"And this is Elizabeth Nix," Chris continued.

Colton took Elizabeth's hand and shook it firmly. "Nice to finally meet you, Elizabeth. Chris has told me a lot about you. I'm glad to have you on board," he said sincerely. He turned to Meagan. "But you have the toughest job, keeping up with these three and showing them the ins and outs of Disney World. Give me the Supreme Court over the Magic Kingdom any day," Colton mused.

Chris looked at him with a teasing smile. "I've done both. Better be careful what you wish for."

ELIZABETH FOLDED HER HANDS behind her head and leaned back, studying the slowly turning fan blades above her. It was nearing five o'clock, but the hot, humid air of late July still crept into Chris Landry's office with stifling oppressiveness. Elizabeth hadn't noticed, though. For the past four hours her attention had been glued to the pages of the three thick constitutional law volumes in front of her.

Rubbing the stiffness from her neck Elizabeth turned to study Colton as he pecked intently on his laptop, making notes from an article in *American Law Review* and seeming to be oblivious of the hours he had just spent without leaving his chair, or to the fact that Elizabeth was watching him.

"What do you think about arguing the First Amendment?" Elizabeth asked reflectively. She turned back to the ceiling fan as she waited for an answer, she didn't care from whom.

Halfway across the room Chris was stretched out in her massive desk chair, reading a brief from an appeals court case in Florida, "I think we are going to argue equal protection," she said decisively before looking up from the brief. "But let's hear your argument anyway."

"The way I see it, religious-based moral issues are the whole basis for the civil union law in Idaho as well as in the other states denying us partnership privileges," Elizabeth said as she stood and began to pace. "It seems if we can attack the basis of the law—religious beliefs—we have in essence shown there was no reason for Jessica Thompson to be arrested, and in the meantime we will destroy the argument for discrimination in marriage laws. Now, supposing you take out acts of sexual intimacy, there is no compelling reason for our government to deny the formation of the stable, committed types of relationships found in marriage or civil unions. We know the whole 'marriage for the sake of rearing children' is a wash because as a culture we encourage marriage for straight people who cannot bear children, such as older or infirm couples, or couples who just don't want children. So that leads us back to discrimination based on sexual practices, but without sodomy, what basis does the state have for declaring homosexuality, or 'the homosexual lifestyle,' whatever that means, immoral? What could possibly be immoral about a bond of lifetime commitment between two consenting adults if the sexual conduct is removed? Now, the Court ruled on sodomy in the *Lawrence versus Texas* decision, basically saying the government has no business or need to make laws dictating the sexual habits of its citizens in their own homes so long as it is consensual and out of the public eye. So, with the new defense of marriage laws, homosexuals are the only group of people the government continues to discriminate against based on sexual conduct," Elizabeth said.

"The government also regulates people who pay for sex, both parties consenting," Chris said dryly for the sake of argument. "But go on, why shouldn't the states be allowed to enact marriage-type laws that discriminate based on sexual orientation?"

Elizabeth paced again, letting the resounding rap of her feet beat a natural rhythm for her words. "The right to privacy in our homes was established in *Griswold versus Connecticut,* which was also the case that gave us the least restrictive means test. Using *Griswold,* the Court found for the first time that the government has no compelling interest in dictating the sexual lives of its citizens," she said forcefully.

Colton pushed back from the laptop and listened closely.

"But isn't it in the government's, or should I say the people's, interest to discourage relationships and sexual conduct the collective citizens consider in some way immoral based on whatever standard they wish to apply?" Chris asked rhetorically.

"Again, for same-sex partnerships I would ask immorality based on what?" Elizabeth countered. "As I said, *Lawrence* struck down sodomy laws, therefore establishing that the government has no say in the private sexual acts of its citizens. So let's get down to bare bones individual civil liberties. We know the First Amendment prohibits the government from establishing a religion. Now, based on that principle, is it a stretch to say that the government also cannot establish a 'moral code' if you will based solely on religious beliefs? I would argue that religion, unlike sexuality, is strictly a behavior of choice, not something innate, such as race and gender. Therefore we can look at it this way: we know the founding fathers made religion the first part of the First Amendment because they wanted to ensure the government would not in the future dictate a particular religion or religious belief to its citizens, as had happened in Europe for centuries. Now, my point is that in the same way, laws that discriminate against citizens based solely on 'traditional values' stemming from religious beliefs are using the powers of government to force religious views and interpretations on the civil liberties of all of the citizens. I believe that since the First Amendment prohibits establishment of a religion, then all laws based solely on strict, conservative interpretations of religious scriptures violate the spirit of the First Amendment. And, what I find most ironic about the same-sex marriage dilemma is that the government is currently denying full participation in the benefits of marriage to thousands of same-sex couples already married in a religious ceremony. For these people the religious and spiritual bond is not being allowed full recognition in civil statutes. In other words, their *religious* marriage bonds are viewed as less than are their heterosexual counterparts. Is the government saying that the religious bonds of one group of people are somehow superior to the religious bonds of another? In many cases, the same minister has performed both same-sex and opposite sex marriages. Now tell me, how do you reconcile that without calling the First Amendment into question?"

Chris looked at Elizabeth for a moment, making sure she was finished, and turned to Colton with a pleased smile. "How did she do, counselor? I believe she hit everything but the Fourteenth Amendment, which I'm sure she would have hit next. She got *Griswold* and *Lawrence,* she got least restrictive means and compelling governmental interest, or lack thereof, and she made a good argument based on the First Amendment. I'd say I picked a winner, Mr. Rice," she said. Chris turned back to Elizabeth. "In a few years you're going to be hell, Elizabeth. I'm looking forward to watching you put the old boys through the mill one day."

Colton agreed. "It's a good argument, Elizabeth. Polish it up and you may get a chance to use it when the time is right." Colton stood and stretched his long arms over his head. "But, as Chris may have told you, we considered arguing the First Amendment, but we don't want to risk losing this thing for Jessica, so our strategy has been to go with our cleanest argument for this case, which is equal protection. We all want a good marriage discrimination case to come through the courts in the worst way but this doesn't seem to be the right one."

"Yeah, I know," Elizabeth said. "I just had to throw it out there and see how far it would go," she said with a confident smile. She walked to the window and looked out. After a moment, she turned back to Colton. "How is Jessica doing, Colton?"

"Fairly well considering everything she has been through. She's thinking of law school if she can find a way to afford it. Her parents don't have much money," Colton answered.

"How is she affording you?" Elizabeth teased.

"Pro bono, until we got the ACLU's attention."

"Pro bono, huh," Elizabeth said. "I guess the least I can do is buy you dinner tonight. Are you guys ready?"

"Yeah, let's go," Chris said as she pushed her chair back.

The three walked out together, but Chris left the lights on. In an hour they would be back.

THE DAYS THAT FOLLOWED were Elizabeth's dream—being smack in the middle of Supreme Court preparations. The sixteen-hour days stretched to eighteen hours and still flew by, seeming too short, despite the physical and mental demands. Elizabeth reported to the office at six, rushed home twice a day to take Rico, her two-year-old yellow lab, out for a quick run, then back to the office for nights of endless coffee, and finally home after midnight to grab four or five hours sleep. Elizabeth thrived on pressure, and her mind clicked with increasing efficiency until, on the eighth day, her heart sank the second she heard the tiny footsteps of Gracie Rice running through the door to get her dad for the trip to the airport.

"Hi, baby girl," Colton said as his daughter ran and jumped into his arms.

"Hi, Daddy," Gracie said, leaning into Colton's cheek for a sloppy, wet kiss.

The rest of Colton's family followed closely behind. Meagan was with them, too, relaxed from her days in the sun. Elizabeth allowed herself a long look at Meagan. *God, I wish this woman didn't get to me.*

Elizabeth turned away and looked over to Lucas. "So what did you think of Florida?"

"It was okay," he shrugged, staying cool.

"I thought the politicians were going to drive us nuts, though," Nancy said in exasperation. "Every time we turned on the television it was nothing but a bunch of politicians, smiling and slinging mud at their opponent." She turned to Colton and said, "Bucks is really spending the money down there. Have you heard anything else on his running mate?"

"I'm sure it will be Harkins," Colton replied as Gracie hung upside down from his waist. "And the minute he announces there will be about five hundred more reporters interested in this case. Harkins will have his spin worked out, though. He'll play it to his advantage."

Chris moved around to the front of her desk and leaned against it, "It may be difficult to stay focused on the case with reporters constantly calling for a story. I think we can handle them, though. They'll have to get through Linda first, which I believe they'll find damn near impossible. How about on your end?" she asked Colton.

"I'll start by getting an unlisted number. Other than that, I won't know for sure until it happens," Colton answered. "But we'll get through it." He pulled Gracie up and turned to Elizabeth. "How about you, Elizabeth? This will be a new experience for you. Do you think you're up to it?"

"Yeah, I think so," Elizabeth replied. "I know it won't be a picnic, but I'll be fine. I've had experience with reporters from back in my volleyball days and again when I worked on the congressional campaign. I've watched some damn good PR folks at work, and I picked up a few things from them."

"Good," Colton nodded, and then turned to his wife. "Well, let's go then," he said as he took her hand and led his family out of the office.

ACROSS THE STREET in a small rented office above the Flaming Pig a stocky red-haired man stood behind the lone, shaded window, watching the Rice family file down the stairs and into their rental. He called his boss as he watched them drive away.

"Senator Harkins, please," the man said to Harkins's secretary. "Tell him it's Rusty Dalton."

"Hello, Senator," Dalton said as soon as Harkins answered. "I have the information you need on their Supreme Court argument. I'll get the highlights of their conversations to you tomorrow. But there's something else you need to know, sir. They know Amanda's death was suicide."

Dalton waited silently until Harkins finally spoke. "Find a way to discredit them," Harkins commanded. "And make it good enough that no one will believe a word they say."

Chapter 5

Crisp October air blew softly into the loft bedroom where Meagan slept. The coolness of the morning breeze brushed her face, and she idly opened her eyes to a strong beam of sunlight streaming through the window. For a moment she watched the lazy dance of the sheer curtains gently swaying in and out as she basked in the morning glow of her wedding day. Meagan smiled and flung her legs over the bedside, pulled on her slippers, and bounced down the stairs of Aunt Nettie's house.

Downstairs Elizabeth slept soundly on the couch, until Meagan's playful pop to the back of her head. "Wake up, girl," Meagan said happily as she walked to the kitchen. "Go for a run with me."

Elizabeth grunted to life and looked sorely at Meagan, one eye yet refusing to open. "A run—are you crazy? What time is it anyway?"

"It's six-thirty. Time to get up," Meagan answered.

Elizabeth watched Meagan through half closed eyes, debating whether to get up. Last night they talked until 3 a.m. about everything, especially marriage, children, and Chris. Elizabeth decided for more sleep and flopped back down on the pillow, wrestling it to shape beneath her head.

Meagan's banks and clanks in the kitchen made it useless.

Elizabeth reluctantly rolled off the couch and staggered to join her. "Are you really going for a run? I would think you would want to save your energy for tonight," she said with a tired but sly smile.

"That's the problem, I've got too much energy," Meagan said as she busily dished four scoops of coffee from a Mason jar. "If I'm gonna make it 'til tonight I've gotta get rid of some of it."

Elizabeth watched her drop the final scoop into the filter and flip on the machine. "I don't think that will help," she said pointing to the coffee streaming into the glass pot below.

"It's decaf, dear," Meagan said. She walked to the refrigerator and pulled out the cream pitcher shaped like a cow.

"What's the use then?" Elizabeth said dryly.

"Taste, and all the other good things that come with coffee," Meagan replied, much too cheery for morning.

Elizabeth picked out a clean mug from the cluster on the counter. She poured the coffee and leaned against the kitchen counter, watching Meagan survey the contents of the refrigerator. "So how many of Chris's family are coming to the wedding?" Elizabeth asked.

"I think just her sister Audrey's family and Aunt Nettie," Meagan replied. "I know her other sister Janet won't be coming. She got run over by the Southern Baptist train a few years ago and doesn't speak to Chris anymore. I suppose marrying a woman will only add to Chris's long list of grievous sins in Janet's book." Meagan picked out an orange from the fruit drawer and began peeling it. "Chris's brother is still on submarine duty or else he would probably be here. Her parents may show up at the last minute—who knows. Would yours?"

"Would my what?" Elizabeth groggily asked.

"Would your parents come to your wedding?"

"Absolutely," Elizabeth assured. "My parents are a rare breed of Southern liberals who don't give a damn what anybody thinks. Everyone at home thinks they're aliens." Elizabeth smiled at Meagan's intrigued look. "My sister and I were taught first and foremost that women have no boundaries; we can do with our lives whatever we choose. My older sister is expecting her first child and her MD license this fall. So, my parents' philosophy seems to have worked pretty well so far. It was a great way to grow up."

"So how did they handle your being gay?" Meagan asked curiously.

"Believe it or not, my mother suspected it when I was going through puberty, so she took me to this child psychologist in Atlanta who explained the prejudices I may have to deal with and how Mom and Dad could help me get through the teen years, being different from most other kids."

Meagan stared at Elizabeth for a moment, wondering if she was really serious. "You're kidding me," she said finally. "Your mother said something first? There are no straight parents in the world like that."

"Mine were," Elizabeth said plainly, and then she smiled playfully. "I told you they're aliens," she said. "Don't get me wrong, my parents didn't let me go wild. They expected me to be sexually responsible and they explained the whole sex and intimacy thing. They just understood that I would most likely be sexually attracted to women."

"Wow," Meagan said. "I hope Chris and I can be that kind of parents."

Elizabeth eyed Meagan mischievously. "Marriage and babies, I swear I don't know what this queer world is coming to."

"I know," Meagan said in mock exasperation. What would the old dykes think, huh?" She looked down at the orange and said thoughtfully. "Chris and I both want children, and I think they need to know their parents are committed to each other to give them assurance that their parents will be committed to them as well."

"I agree with that," Elizabeth reflected. "I just wonder sometimes if all this domestication will eventually lead to a sedate and boring gay culture."

"Speaking of sedate," Meagan said. "Are you going running with me or not? I'm only going a mile or two."

Elizabeth pushed her hands through her thick, morning hair, thinking of her seemingly endless list of duties for the day. But, she hadn't expected to be awake this early. "Yeah, I guess I'll go," she finally said. "It'll give me one last chance to talk you out of this marriage thing." She smiled.

"Not a chance, baby." Meagan smiled back. "Not a chance."

THEY RAN TWO FULL miles and turned back on the dirt road leading up to Nettie's. "Race!" Meagan challenged and broke into a sprint.

Elizabeth slipped a half step and fell three feet behind. For a second her competitive spirit pushed to close the gap. Then her eyes glimpsed Meagan—the easy swing of her sleek, muscular legs, her tight, slender hips moving in perfect unison with squared shoulders that framed the golden red ponytail swaying back and forth with ev-

ery step. Elizabeth dropped her pace and fell back for the guilty pleasure of watching a beautiful woman run, even if she was already
taken.

At the house Meagan skipped across the stepping stones of the
walkway and bounded up the porch steps two at a time. She taunted
Elizabeth with a quick laugh and disappeared into the cabin.

Elizabeth watched her until the door closed and then sat down on
the steps. She watched the drops of her sweat fall to the ground below, catching her breath and thinking of Meagan in a way she wished
she didn't. Elizabeth took marriage seriously, and knew that after tonight her commitment to the success of Chris and Meagan's relationship must be unyielding. Meagan would never know that in moments
of weakness Elizabeth silently watched her, longing to follow the
beautiful groove of her back with a single fingertip, to allow her lips to
linger on the soft skin of the delicate hollow at the base of Meagan's
neck. And move down slowly.

Elizabeth swept the sweat from her eyebrows and climbed the steps
to the house. She met Nettie in the kitchen, heading for the coffeepot.

"Did you sleep well?" Nettie asked as she shuffled over to sit at the
counter next to Elizabeth.

"Yes, ma'am, I did," Elizabeth answered. "Except Meagan kept me
up half the night talking."

"You're a good friend," Nettie said as she patted Elizabeth's hand.
Nettie took a sip of coffee, and then her face suddenly twisted into a
scowl. "Damn decaf," she swore.

NETTIE'S FIELD SAT high on a grassy ridge where the sky fell away
in all directions, seeming to leave it on top of the world. The final crop
of hay had been harvested, leaving a smooth blanket of golden brown
covering the rust soil beneath.

The moon hung at a quarter, giving way to a clear black sky and
the brilliance of a thousand stars hanging above the field like a dome.
At the end of the field, a line of white candles ran the length of the ten
rows of guests, and then converged behind an altar made of twisted
river wood, tangled into a strong, solid form. Looking down the aisle
Meagan saw the exact vision of her weeks of planning.

"Are you ready?" Chris asked, standing beside her.

"Yes, I am," Meagan said with a joyous smile.

Chris took her hand and together they walked forward, their silver clothes bold against the night sky.

From her front row chair Elizabeth caught a glimpse of a falling star. *Nature's fireworks,* she thought. *Somebody up there must approve.* Elizabeth turned back to her friends, standing close, totally focused on each other. Chris and Meagan, as it should be, Elizabeth told herself. That was it. No room for discussion.

Chapter 6

"How soon can you get here?" Chris yelled the instant Elizabeth answered the phone.

"In a couple of minutes," Elizabeth replied, struggling to keep her voice calm as her mind began racing through dreadful scenarios of what could have happened. It couldn't be Meagan; she would have been at work at least two hours, and Chris had just talked to her a half hour ago before leaving to go home and pick up a forgotten file. A break-in wouldn't be enough to send Chris into this kind of panic. Chris was never one to lose her cool. "Chris, what is it?"

"Just get over here," Chris urged and hung up.

Elizabeth grabbed her keys and bolted past Linda and down the stairs. In less than two minutes she made the five-block drive to the apartment.

Chris stood waiting, holding Clarence in a blood-soaked towel. She pulled him close and sprinted for the car.

"What the hell happened? Did a car hit him?" Elizabeth asked, opening the passenger door.

"No. I'll tell you on the way. Just go."

"You know where the vet is, right?" Chris asked, gently rocking Clarence in her arms as his weak cries rose from the bundle.

"Yeah, sure," Elizabeth said. She slammed the Outback into second gear and floored it. From inside the bundle Clarence cried weakly.

They hit the first traffic signal on red and Elizabeth slammed to a stop, pounding the steering wheel and desperately searching for a way through the traffic. "Damn it, shit, shit, shit, I can't believe these fuckin' lights."

Chris shot a glance out the corner of her eye, telling Elizabeth to cool it. Clarence could sense the tension, and he didn't need any more trouble. Chris held him lightly in her arms as they drove, gently

Blown Away
© 2006 by The Haworth Press, Inc. All rights reserved.
doi:10.1300/5706_06

stroking a small tuft of black hair and softly whispering, trying to comfort the big tom in what she already knew would be his last minutes.

Elizabeth pulled into the veterinarian's office parking lot and drove to the back door where a technician waited. She watched quietly as Chris gathered Clarence close to her chest and walked inside. The door closed slowly and Elizabeth fell back against the seat and closed her eyes, for now just wanting to shut the world away.

The drive back from the vet's office was silent. Chris sat still as granite, staring directly ahead until they pulled up to the apartment and parked. Without a word Chris slowly walked inside and went straight for the liquor cabinet. She poured a healthy glass of bourbon and took a huge swallow, then lit a Marlboro.

Elizabeth stood silently in the hallway, watching Chris down another swallow and then two more drags. "Chris, do you know what happened?" Elizabeth finally asked.

Chris looked up from the whiskey with a vicious expression Elizabeth had never seen, and would never see again. "Somebody decided to torture Clarence, that's what happened," Chris seethed. "Acid— how's that for you? Fucking acid. By the time he crawled to the front door his skin was already bleeding. The shit had already dissolved his hair and was eating away his skin. Is that enough for you or should I tell you more?"

Elizabeth dropped her shoulders against the wall and turned her eyes to the floor. "No, Chris, I know." She waited as Chris took another swallow of the bourbon. "Do you have any idea who might have done it?"

"Take your pick, Elizabeth," Chris replied, throwing her arm out in an angry sweep. "Maybe it was the same ones who wrote 'burn in hell dyke' on the windshield of my car, or maybe it was those guys who waited for me to go to the grocery store and tailgated me all the way there and back. What do ya think, huh?" she asked cynically, and fell into her chair.

Elizabeth walked over and kneeled beside Chris. She silently studied her for a moment, looking into Chris's eyes for some clue of what she needed, of what could be said. What Elizabeth saw worried her.

Chris Landry almost looked defeated; her eyes hollow and distant as she sat quietly holding her head in her hand, alternating between the whiskey and the smoke.

"It's all such bullshit," Chris said as sudden, hot tears filled her eyes. "'Love thy neighbor,' they say. 'We're all God's children,' they say. It's all just bullshit," she said, rocking her head in her hand.

Elizabeth reached over to put her hand on Chris's arm. "Whoa, wait a minute Chris, you're losing me here," she said gently. "What does that have to do with Clarence?"

"*Why* do you think someone did that to Clarence?" Chris replied coarsely. "We've been living here over two years. Everyone loved Clarence. Why do you think someone decided all of a sudden to torture our cat?" Fierce anger shot from her eyes as she turned to Elizabeth. "It's because of that chicken shit propaganda that's all over the airwaves and newspapers around here lately. They're scaring people to death with that crap about pedophiles and gay affirmative action and teaching kids to be gay and God knows what other lies they can make up about us *queers*! How do those ads go, 'Working for a better America'?" she asked in an enraged, mocking voice. "Paid for by the Christians for Moral fucking Accountability. No political endorsement implied, of course," she said and bolted up from her chair. "Don't you see? Clarence was tortured for the same reason that gang of cowards beat up that guy downtown last week. It's for the same reason the Rice children have lost playmates. Lies and phobias, I think that's the main reason Clarence died, Elizabeth." Chris stormed back to the liquor cabinet.

"Well, I'm not going to let those bastards win, Elizabeth," Chris said after she poured more whiskey. "You can stay with me or you can get out right now. But I'll tell you, if it's the last thing I do, I'm gonna beat those bastards."

Chapter 7

Elizabeth had been to Washington, DC, five times, but never as a player. She wasn't sure if it was that or the fact that two weeks ago the country inaugurated the first Republican president in eight years that made the town feel so foreign. Whatever the reason, she felt strangely unsettled by the sight of the Capitol dome, the White House, and the massive columns of the Supreme Court Building.

This morning she woke from a light sleep before the alarm, threw on some sweats, grabbed a small box from the nightstand, and headed to the breakfast lobby, expecting to find it deserted. She smiled as she turned the corner and saw Chris sitting at a table sipping coffee and reading a paperback of morning meditations.

"Sleep much?" Elizabeth asked, pulling out a chair opposite Chris.

"A little," Chris replied. "Meagan worked on me until she got me in bed, then she made sure I relaxed," she said with a quick smile.

Elizabeth returned the smile, but her mind was elsewhere. She fingered the small box she held under the table, turning it over as she considered what she wanted to say. Her tone was soft but urgent tone when she finally said, "Chris, I know that handling the press for you and Colton today is important and I'm glad to do it. But I was wondering if you will wear something into the courtroom for me; well really for both of us." Elizabeth looked down at the box, opened it and took out a silver ring. She held it out to Chris, "I'd like this ring to be a token of moral support for you, and it would mean a lot to me to know it's in the courtroom today."

Chris studied the ring. The delicate hand-carved flowers and sunbursts encircling the band had become blurred through the years, but the ring still held the character of the generations who had worn it. "It's beautiful, Elizabeth. Should I wear it?" Chris asked.

"Yes, I'd like for you to." Elizabeth replied. "My grandmother gave me that ring, and her mother, who was a suffragette, gave it to her. I

doi:10.1300/5706_07

wanted you to have it with you today, to remind you of the people who'll be with you, and that some fights for justice can be won."

Chris slipped the ring over her index finger. "Thank you. What a great honor. I'll be proud to wear it."

"I just wish I could be in the courtroom," Elizabeth said.

"I know, but we need you with the press."

The opening elevator door took their attention. Colton Rice stepped off and walked toward them with an uncharacteristic frown. "So much for a quiet morning," Colton said as he tossed the newspaper on the table. He took the chair between Chris and Elizabeth and laid *The Washington Post* flat. JUSTICES TO HEAR *ROE VS. IDAHO,* stretched across the top headline in bold one inch letters. "I had hoped they'd still be preoccupied with the Bucks administration and leave us for page two, but it looks like we have the spotlight for today."

Colton looked over to Chris. "How are you with the argument? Are you ready?"

"Yes, the argument's ready; it's the questioning that has me worried," Chris replied. "I'm expecting hell from Thaggard."

"Yeah, Thaggard will grandstand all right, but don't let that rattle you. We can forget him, Hill, and Ortez. No way we'll get them. It's five of the other six we have to get, but, *my God* we've got to get those five."

"We'll get them, Colton," Chris said decisively. "John Harkins's arms don't reach that far."

MEAGAN RECLINED IN the hotel room's corner love seat, cuddled under a blanket and reading the latest *Newsweek*. She heard the key slide into the door and smiled, then went back to the editorial.

"Is that any way to start a morning?" Chris asked as she crossed the room to kiss her mate.

"No, and neither is waking up without you," Meagan replied, stretching from her blanket to meet soft, warm lips. She wrapped her hand around the back of Chris's neck and pulled her closer, savoring the kiss for an extra moment. As their lips parted she teased Chris with a sly, seductive smile. "Maybe I'll go with you," she said. "Or

maybe I'll just keep you here." Teasingly she trailed her fingers down
the hollow of Chris's neck.

Chris closed her eyes, "You don't know how good that sounds,
baby. But I'm afraid if you go with me, Nancy will kill you, and if I
stay here with you, Colton will kill me." She opened her eyes again
and planted her arms to stretch over Meagan. "Just wait till I get back
this afternoon," she whispered as she nuzzled the soft skin of Meagan's
cheek. "I promise it will be worth the wait." The tips of her fingers
drifted down to Meagan's breast and she lightly caressed it, then
locked her eyes on Meagan as she pushed from the love seat and
slowly walked backward to the bathroom.

"Tease," Meagan smiled as she watched Chris disappear behind the
wall.

"Bait," Chris replied just before the burst of the shower.

Meagan smiled and slipped back into their bed and reached for the
remote. The early morning news anchors told of two car crashes and
an overnight shooting, just everyday news for a city the size of DC,
but today it unsettled Meagan. She hit the power button and wrapped herself around Chris's pillow and breathed in the lingering fragrance of her, drifting off to sleep.

Forty-five minutes later Meagan woke to Chris's familiar nuzzle.
With a low moan Meagan rolled onto her back and propped on her el-
bows. The sight of Chris blew her away.

"Oh, wow," Meagan said. She flopped down against the bed and
pulled the sheets over her head, then peeped back over the sheets to
check out Chris again. "Damn woman," she said. Her eyes wandered
up and down, to the shoes, the skirt, the square shoulders of the suit
coat, and up to the strength of her face. "You're ready, baby. Go give
'em hell."

"I'm not sure hell is the right thing to give the Supreme Court,"
Chris replied cautiously, turning a pensive smile as she reached down
for Meagan's hand. "But for thirty minutes this morning I'll have
their attention. And then I'm certain they will give me hell. There's
nothing quite as intimidating as being grilled by the Supreme Court
of the United States." Chris took a deep breath. "Pray for me, baby.

I'm going to need it." She leaned down and gave Meagan a final lingering kiss.

"I'll see you this afternoon," Chris said as she walked to the door. With one last look she picked up her black leather case and turned the doorknob. "I love you," Chris said, and she was gone.

BY EIGHT-THIRTY Meagan had had enough of morning television. She flipped off the TV and rolled out of bed and sent up a quick but earnest prayer for Chris. On the bedside table she found the notepad with the Rice's room number. She picked up the phone and dialed 7-321.

Nancy Rice answered on the first ring. In the background a fight between Trent and Grace hit high-pitched frenzy.

Meagan smiled, remembering the fights she refereed in an Orlando hotel room six months ago. "Hey, it's me. Sounds like you have your hands full already."

"You could say that," Nancy replied in a tired voice. "We've got to get these kids out of here. They're going nuts in this room," Nancy said as she shot a warning glance to Trent. "Can you be ready by nine-thirty? We've still got two showers to go, but we should be ready by then."

"Sure, nine-thirty's fine. I'll see you then," Meagan said and hung up. She walked to the closet and decided on a beige cotton sweater and black jeans. In the shower she lingered a bit longer than usual, daydreaming of tonight. Spending the day touring the city with the Rice clan would be exciting, but tonight, holding a relaxed Chris in her arms, would be spectacular.

The clock on the bedside table read 9:17 when Meagan walked out of the bathroom. She reached for her sweater and pulled it on. Then she heard the scream—a loud, excruciating woman's scream, and it sounded like Nancy Rice.

Meagan jumped into her jeans and ran out into the hall. The scream came again, this time followed by a moaning wail—and it definitely came from room 321. Meagan sprinted to the door and slammed her palms against it. "Nancy, it's Meagan!" There was no answer. Meagan pounded the door again, this time with her fist.

"Nancy, please!" She pressed her face against the solid wood and shouted, "It's Meagan. Please open the door!"

The door slowly opened and Meagan stepped inside. Her eyes darted around the room. Lucas was behind her, leaning against the wall with his eyes fixed on the floor. Nancy sat on the bed with her arms around Trent, holding his head tightly against her shoulder as they stared blankly at the television. Grace stood next to them, pulling on Nancy's arm. "Mommy, what's wrong? What's wrong, Mommy," Grace pleaded as she jerked Nancy's sleeve.

Meagan walked across the room, growing sick with fear as the TV screen came into view. "To repeat," the reporter said, "at nine-oh-five a.m. a [bomb exploded] in the United States Supreme Court Building. No report on injuries or casualties is available at this time. We do know the court had just convened to hear the controversial *Roe versus Idaho* case. . . ."

Meagan's blank eyes stared as the scenes flashed on the screen: an aerial view of a building consumed by flames and destruction, a ground view of smoke and dust billowing out from tangles of steel, crumbled marble, and shards of glass. On the streets ambulances, fire trucks, police officers, paramedics, and news reporters madly rushed to their jobs. A lone camera followed a bloodied and terrified survivor, wandering aimlessly until one of the merciful led him to safety.

Terror hit Meagan full force. She doubled over as she ran into the bathroom, her stomach convulsing in dry heaves. The television images flashed through her mind. Where was Chris? Was she even alive? Nausea shot to Meagan's core. She convulsed savagely, spit, convulsed again and sank to the floor. She lay still against the cool tile, barely able to breath—until she heard the phone ring.

"Elizabeth!" Nancy's voice rang through the suite. "Thank God! Are you okay? Is Colton there?"

Meagan pulled herself up and listened. After a moment Nancy spoke again. "Yes, she's here. Let me get her," Nancy said, struggling to speak through her shaking voice.

"Meagan," Nancy knocked lightly on the door. "Can you talk to Elizabeth?"

"Yes." Meagan said, "Just a minute." She pushed herself from the floor and stood in front of the mirror, wiping her mouth with a wet bath cloth. She dabbed her eyes and set her nerves with a deep breath.

"Hello, Elizabeth," Meagan said calmly, working through the fear to keep her voice steady. "Are you all right? Are Chris and Colton with you?"

Elizabeth's response came slow and deliberate. "No. I don't know where they are, Meagan. I haven't seen them since they went into the courtroom this morning. You wouldn't believe what it's like down here. But I've heard there are survivors inside the courtroom," she said, and paused.

Meagan said nothing.

"Listen, there is a police officer here who says he'll help me check the hospitals," Elizabeth began again. "If you want, we can come over to get you. I think Nancy should stay there and wait with the children, but I thought you would want to go with me. Do you think you're up to it?

"Yes. Of course." Meagan's voice caught and she bit her lip. "I'll meet you in the lobby," she said and hung up quickly.

The four Rices stared, waiting. Meagan looked first at Grace, then the boys, and finally to Nancy. "Nancy," she said, finding the calm voice of her ER training, "Elizabeth is coming by to pick me up. She and I will check all the hospitals and as soon as we find Colton we'll call you."

Nancy nodded and reached her arms around Trent and Lucas to pull them to her. "You will call as soon as you know?"

"I will," Meagan replied. She walked over and wrapped her arms around Nancy, holding her for a moment. "I'll call you soon," Meagan whispered. Unable to find any words for them, she rubbed Trent and Lucas's hair and hugged Grace, and left the room without looking back.

MEAGAN WAITED NEARLY thirty minutes before the police officer walked into the lobby. "Are you Meagan Sullivan?" he asked. Meagan nodded. "I'm Officer Carson. Ms. Nix is waiting in the cruiser."

Meagan gasped when she first saw Elizabeth. A layer of gray dust covered her face, and sweat and dried blood soaked through her dirt-covered blue blouse.

"It's not mine," Elizabeth said as Meagan slid into the backseat with her eyes fixed on the blood. "We were doing what we could," Elizabeth said softly. She took Meagan's hand and answered the question she knew Meagan feared to ask. "Meagan, I don't know where Chris is," she began. "I tried to find her and Colton, but it was chaos down there." With the most confident look she could muster Elizabeth continued. "We'll find them soon. They'll be all right, Meagan. A lot of survivors are coming from inside the courtroom."

Meagan nodded and returned a vague, sad smile, then fell against Elizabeth's shoulder.

Elizabeth pulled Meagan close, stoking her hair as the cruiser made its way to Westside General Hospital, rallying all of her own emotional strength to keep from breaking down.

Their first glimpse of the madness swirling around the emergency entrance of Westside General came from the freeway. On the street just below them a line of white and yellow ambulance vans, bright red paramedic trucks, and police cruisers queued up in a gruesome line, stopping at the curb just long enough to drop off the injured and dead before making another breakneck drive back to the blast site. Officer Carson made the next two rights and headed for emergency.

The wail of the sirens became deafening as they drove nearer to the ambulance line. Meagan stared out at the line and set her mind with purpose. Chris could be somewhere in that line, laying on a gurney, waiting for her.

"Let us out here," Meagan said to Officer Carson. Her eyes impatiently searched up and down the line of gurneys as Carson put the cruiser in park and opened the back door.

"Let's go," Meagan said. She grabbed Elizabeth's hand and pulled her along, weaving through the gurneys holding bodies covered by blood and white sheets.

Meagan had trained for this at the South Highlands ER. Her specialty was triage, and she knew that somewhere, someone was making ten-second decisions—treat immediately, treat later, don't bother.

One of the bodies, one of the ten-second decisions, could be Chris, and Meagan knew those ten-second decisions were partly based on the staff available.

"I'm going to see how I can help. I'm sure they can use me," Meagan said as they stepped inside the emergency entrance.

Elizabeth scanned the maddening confusion near the admittance desk, the rush of doctors and nurses hustling in and out the doors to treatment rooms, and the anxious and panicked faces in the waiting rooms. "Of course, go ahead," she said. "I'll try to find out if they admitted Chris or Colton. If not, I'll start on the other hospitals."

"Let me know," Meagan began.

"As soon as I know," Elizabeth assured her. "You just go. I'll find you."

Elizabeth watched Meagan disappear through the swinging doors to the treatment rooms and turned back to the bedlam surrounding her. The admittance desk was stacked ten deep with minor traumas and frantic family members. It could take hours to get through the lines, and even then she wasn't sure they would give out information to nonfamily.

"You need some help, don't you?"

Elizabeth spun around to Officer Carson.

"Yes," Elizabeth replied. "But shouldn't you be going back to the bomb site?"

"No," Carson said. "I've got hospital security duty right here. Come with me." Carson led Elizabeth past the admittance desk, through a door marked NO ADMITTANCE, and into a strangely quiet hall. At the end of it was a tight, dimly lit room.

"This is the security room for the first floor," Carson said as he opened the door and waited for Elizabeth to walk through. Inside, two security officers sat intently watching the four banks of security monitors, three lining the back and one on the side wall. "Guys, I have a friend here who needs a place to rest. Mind if she waits here while I look for her friends?" Carson asked.

One of the officers briefly turned around. "She can stay as long as she can stand it," he said.

Elizabeth scanned the furious activity filling each black-and-white monitor, one for every trauma room, one for the hallways, two for the waiting room, two for the admittance desk, and four for the entrance and parking lot.

"You can wait in here as long as you like," Officer Carson said to Elizabeth. "There's coffee and magazines over there if you want them," he said, pointing to the counter on the opposite wall. "I'll go find out what I can about your friends. What are their names again?"

"Chris Baines Landry and Colton D. Rice," Elizabeth replied softly.

Carson wrote the names on his notepad. "If they're here, I'll find them," he said as he put the pad back in his shirt pocket. "I'll be back as soon as I can." He stopped at the door and turned back to Elizabeth. "Would you like some clean clothes?"

Elizabeth nodded and returned his slight, understanding smile. "I'll steal some scrubs," he said and left the room.

Elizabeth sat down across the room from the monitors, her mind enveloped by the sounds of the crammed ER, the wails of ambulances and fire trucks, shouts of doctors and nurses, cries of pain and curses from the critically injured. There was nothing she could do now, no one to protect and no one to help. She turned to the wall and lowered her head into her hands to finally let go her silent tears.

AN HOUR PASSED before Carson came back. "I hope these will do," he said as he held out a set of worn, green scrubs to Elizabeth. He sat down next to her, fidgeting a bit. This wasn't the first time he'd had to do this, but still he never knew what to say, or how to say it.

Elizabeth gave him an out. "It's not good, is it?"

"No, ma'am, it's not."

Elizabeth dropped her head in her hands and took a deep breath. "All right, tell me."

"Ms. Nix, it looks like Colton Rice is dead," he said slowly. "The coroner will need a final positive ID, but Mr. Rice's driver's license was found in a victim's wallet. They took the body from the blast site directly to the morgue."

Elizabeth stood up on weak legs and walked to the back wall. She wanted to put her fist through it, to embark on a rage of vengeance and settle the score, to leave her own body count. But who should die? No one knew who had done this. No one knew where to find revenge.

"And what about Chris?" Elizabeth asked, keeping her voice calm.

"The news is better there," Carson replied. "Ms. Landry is in surgery right now. She's in the OR so I couldn't find out much, but one of the ER nurses told me she was conscious when she came in. She said she was asking for your friend Meagan."

Elizabeth nodded slowly. "I need to be the one to tell her. Can you find her for me?"

"Yeah, I think I know where she is."

Carson found Meagan at the ambulance entrance and led her back to the security office. "Elizabeth is waiting for you in here," he said outside the door, and quietly left her.

Meagan pushed the door open and froze, unable to move or speak.

"Chris is alive," Elizabeth said right away. She grabbed Meagan just as her body went limp. "She's in surgery, but she's alive," Elizabeth said, tightly rocking Meagan in her arms.

"And Colton?" Meagan asked while Elizabeth still held her.

Elizabeth pulled her closer without an answer.

"He's dead, isn't he," Meagan said.

"Yes. It appears as if Colton is dead."

"Does Nancy know yet?"

"I don't think so," Elizabeth said. "I would go to tell them, but I don't want to leave you here alone." Elizabeth thought for a moment and said, "There are grief counselors on standby here at the hospital. I'll ask them to send a team to the hotel. The counselors will know best how to handle this situation with a family. They'll know how to tell the children."

Meagan nodded. "Thank you for staying with me. I don't think I could do this alone."

"You won't have to," Elizabeth replied. "I won't leave you alone, believe me. I'll stay as long as you want." She looked down at Meagan and gave her a reassuring smile, "Now, let's go find the OR."

THE OR WING was two floors up and across the hospital from the emergency wing, but the thick atmosphere in the waiting room was the same as emergency. Worried and pacing family members filled the large room, anxiously waiting for word of an operation that was likely the last-ditch attempt to save a loved one. Fortunately, one of the ER staff spared Meagan and Elizabeth and led them to a deserted staff break room to wait. An excruciating four hours slowly passed before a surgeon walked through the door.

"Meagan Sullivan?" the doctor asked as she pulled a worn chair next to the small couch where Meagan sat by Elizabeth.

Meagan nodded.

"Meagan, I'm Dr. Fallon. I understand you're here with Chris Landry."

"Yes," Meagan replied anxiously.

"Ms. Landry is in recovery," Dr. Fallon said. "She made it through surgery, but she still has a long way to go. We had to remove her right leg just above the knee, and she lost a lot of blood before she got to the hospital. Chris has some internal injuries, but none that look life threatening right now. I wish I could tell you something more encouraging, but at this point there is nothing we can do but wait. I'll have a nurse keep you informed of any changes in her condition." Dr. Fallon gave a quick reassuring pat to Meagan's hand and stood up. "I understand you're a nurse, and if this were a normal night I'd be happy to go into more specifics, but I have four more surgeries waiting."

"Of course. I understand. When can I see her?" Meagan asked.

"It may be a while. After recovery she'll be going into ICU, and as you know, hospital regulations prohibit everyone but family," Dr. Fallon began without thinking. "Are you her legal partner?"

Meagan's expression fell, "No, we're not legal partners."

"But you are her partner?" Dr. Fallon asked.

Meagan nodded.

"Well, I believe that legal stuff is bunk. You're close enough for me. As soon as Ms. Landry is in a room, I'll have someone find you. You'll be able to see her as soon as she's out of recovery."

"Thank you, Doctor," Meagan said.

"Can I get you anything, Meagan?" Elizabeth asked as Dr. Fallon walked out the door.

"A pillow, maybe, and a blanket," Meagan said. She pointed to a counter on the opposite wall. "There may be some things in those cabinets."

Elizabeth opened the bottom doors and found a stack of pillows and a few blankets. She grabbed a couple of pillows and a blanket and brought them back to the couch.

Without a word Meagan fluffed her pillow and laid it across Elizabeth's legs. She pulled the blanket across her body as she leaned down into Elizabeth's lap.

Elizabeth gently pulled the hair away from Meagan's eyes and lightly rested her hand on her back. There were times, in the past, when Elizabeth would admit to wanting a moment like this with Meagan. But since the wedding those desires had passed. Tonight, Chris was supposed to be celebrating the case of her life with Meagan. And the Rices were supposed to be out at the family-style Italian restaurant just around the corner from the hotel. And Elizabeth was supposed to be meeting with a group of gay law students in town from Harvard, one of whom, based on a few exchanged e-mails, she was definitely looking forward to meeting. Instead she was here with Meagan, and Chris was in a fight for her life.

But it was quiet here for now. The last ten hours had been madness, but at least they knew Chris was alive. Elizabeth laid her head back against the wall and closed her eyes, waiting.

After two and a half hours passed Meagan knew something was wrong. Chris should have been in ICU by now.

Elizabeth tried to assure Meagan that the hospital was just too busy, Chris had gotten lost in the shuffle, but she was all right. They would have her in a room soon. But after another half hour Meagan couldn't wait. She threw back the blanket and sat up, just as a resident walked into the room.

"Are either of you Meagan Sullivan?" he asked softly.

Meagan nodded slowly. "I am," she whispered uneasily.

The resident walked over and sat on the couch beside Meagan. He folded his hands together as he spoke, "Ms. Sullivan, there was a blood clot. . . ."

"No!" Meagan screamed.

Elizabeth grabbed Meagan and closed her eyes.

"I'm very sorry, ma'am. There was nothing we could do. Ms. Landry is dead."

Chapter 8

President William Bucks leaned back in his desk chair and stared out the window, watching rain fall on the world outside the Oval Office. It was 9:30 a.m., and already his tie was pulled loose and his black suit coat hung by the window. Douglas Whitman, Bucks's chief of staff, knocked lightly on the Oval Office door and walked in. Andrew Simpson, the FBI director; Attorney General Salvador Perez; Perez's Special Investigator, Robert Stark; and John Harkins followed. Thunder from a nearby storm roared against the window.

"Sit down, gentlemen," Bucks said, pointing to a pair of Colonial sofas as he walked to the chair between and sat down. Bucks slowly rubbed his palms together as he glanced from one man to the next, making the circle before finally letting his gaze settle on the blue carpet in front of him. "Boys, I'm gonna be honest with you," he began, still rubbing his palms. "I just don't believe that bullshit you fed me earlier this morning." Bucks looked over to Director Simpson, "I'm hoping you have something new to tell me."

"Mr. President," Simpson answered hastily, feeling the jitters of bottomless coffee. "It still looks like we have a lone bomber. We haven't been able to find any connection between Taylor and any other individuals or organized groups."

Bucks listened with a disapproving nod and then turned to Attorney General Perez. "Mr. Perez, do you have anything to add to what Mr. Simpson is telling me? Maybe your other guys at Justice can do a little better than the Bureau. Am I still to believe this Phillip Norton Taylor, a court recorder who had never caused an ounce of trouble, just casually walked into the courthouse of the Supreme Court of the United States and blew himself, half the Court, and fifty-one other people away? Is that what you want me to believe, Mr. Perez?" Bucks asked, his intense steel blue eyes drilling through Perez.

Blown Away
© 2006 by The Haworth Press, Inc. All rights reserved.
doi:10.1300/5706_08

Special Investigator Stark watched Bucks interrogate his boss, careful to avoid the president's eye. The last thing Stark wanted was to have Bucks on his ass, but he was fighting instincts to jump in and tell Bucks to go to hell. Ten minutes after the bomb exploded Perez assigned the case to Simpson and Stark. Practically every agent in the justice department was working for them, checking every lead, every bit of information, and every friend and relative Phillip Norton Taylor ever thought about having. They knew every magazine subscription Taylor had ever bought, every Web site he had ever visited, his credit card purchases, phone calls, and all the airline reservations Taylor had made in the past twenty years. In just twenty-four hours the agents had searched more than 100 data banks, interviewed more than 200 people, reviewed miles of security tape, and convened their five best psychological agents to build a profile. The progress they had made so far was commendable, if not exceptional. The president's imprudent sarcasm was pushing the little respect Stark had left for the office to the edge. Robert Stark never liked William Bucks as a man, either.

"Yes, Mr. President," Stark heard Perez answer. "From what we have so far, we believe that Taylor acted alone, though we still haven't established a motive. As you know, we've assigned the nonbureau investigation to Special Investigator Stark," Perez said and turned to Stark, "Mr. Stark, will you fill in the president on your end of the investigation?"

Stark sat straight and took a breath. "Yes, thank you, Salvador," Stark said. He looked squarely at Bucks. "Mr. President, in the past twenty-four hours we have gathered a great deal of information about Phillip Norton Taylor. We even know what he had for the last three meals of his life. If there is any connection to conspirators we will have them by the end of the week. They'll be in jail by this weekend," Stark said confidently.

"Is that right, Mr. Stark?" Bucks said. The president sat back calmly, but his eyes still shot impatient fire. "You will have them by this weekend, you say. Well, you know what Mr. Stark, I don't think that will be soon enough," Bucks said. He aimed a dissatisfied glare from man to man. "You see, gentlemen, at eight p.m. eastern standard time tonight I have to go on television, worldwide television, you understand, and tell everyone watching that at nine-oh-three a.m. yesterday a perfectly normal man without any apparent motivation strolled into the courtroom of the United States Supreme Court with a load of plastic explosives strapped to his body and blew himself into oblivion," Bucks said, still composed. "Well, I'm not buying that, gentlemen," Bucks continued as his voice began to grow indignant. "*And neither will the American people!*" Bucks locked his glare on Stark, then moved to Director Simpson. "Now you get back out there and find some answers, and find them quick!" the President commanded. "I want another full report at four p.m."

Bucks stood and walked away. "That's it," he said, keeping his back to them.

The five men silently stood and filed to the door.

"John, and Douglas, I want to see you two back in here this afternoon at three o'clock," Buck said. "The speech is on your shoulders, Douglas. I know you won't let me down."

AT EXACTLY 3:00 P.M. John Harkins and Douglas Whitman reported to the Oval Office and found the president with the phone to his ear and his feet propped on a desk drawer. Bucks motioned Harkins and Whitman in.

"Thank you, Jason," Bucks said over the phone. "I'll get back with you after the speech." Bucks swung his chair around and hung up. With an impatient sigh he looked up at his top two men. "As you may have guessed, that was Jason Johnson," Bucks grumbled. "That makes the second time today he's called me. Jason tells me his organization—and indeed all good Christian people—are very concerned about the state of our nation. I appreciate that, but I think that concern goes for all Americans, Christian or not." Bucks turned to Harkins. "I'll tell you what concerns me most about Jason—his main concern seems to be how I plan to fill the Court."

Bucks stood and walked to the window to watch pouring rain beat down on the White House lawn. "At least the son of a bitch had the decency to wait until today to call in his favors," he said to no one in particular. After a silent moment Bucks turned to Harkins. "But Jason does bring out an important point. We will, in fact, have at least six justice positions to fill, maybe all nine, if Thaggard, Hill, and Ferguson decide to resign."

Bucks went to his desk and picked up a file. "This is what I have on the candidate pool for potential justices. I never expected to have more than one, at the most two justice positions to fill at one time. So this pool is not nearly deep enough to fill a whole court," Bucks said. He tossed the file on the desk toward Whitman. "Douglas, I want you to get me a top-notch pool of candidates, and I mean quick. We've got to get the Court working as soon as possible. The American people will lose confidence if we let this thing drag out too long."

Whitman nodded and picked up the file.

Bucks walked around to the front of his desk, just in front of Harkins. "John," Bucks began earnestly, "I never anticipated we would be filling justice positions before *Roe versus Idaho* was decided. I know you are not officially linked to the case but politically there will be serious cries of conflict of interest if you are in any way involved in making the court appointments. We must do everything possible to avoid your involvement in the justice selection process. So, I want you to oversee the bombing investigation."

Harkins looked interested as Bucks continued, "I'll tell you I just don't have confidence in those clowns in justice. The whole law enforcement side of the department is downright soft or else incompetent. Most of the agents are just a bunch of overeducated yuppies that wouldn't know a terrorist from a priest."

Harkins nodded in agreement.

"Now, John, you're a man who's seen combat and you've been in the business world long enough to know a snake-eyed son of a bitch when you see one. And you've got resources and contacts around the world. I believe you're the man to find every scumbag that even remotely had anything to do with that bomb."

"I'll be honored to do it for you and the country, Sir," Harkins said.

"Good," Bucks continued. "I'll talk to the committee chairs on the Hill to get you a NSA task force. You'll have whatever you need to do the job. Just name it and you've got it. And remember, John, I don't want you even remotely involved in justice placements."

"What about Jason Johnson?" Harkins asked.

"Douglas and I will work with Johnson. We'll have to get the justice nominations through Congress and on the bench as soon as possible. Of course, we'll make it look like a good faith effort to appoint a balanced Court, but we'll be counting. You and Johnson will get the Court you want," Bucks said.

Harkins smiled slowly. "Good. Thank you, Mr. President. You know Emily wants this whole nightmare over as soon as possible, and she'll be pleased the decision will likely go in our favor."

TWO BLOCKS AWAY in a little corner coffeehouse surrounded by Secret Service agents, Emily Harkins sat alone, sipping black coffee with a blank sheet of plain stationery on the table in front of her. She stared down at the page, contemplating the right words, how she could say the things she wanted to say. How could she pour her thoughts onto this 8 × 10 inch sheet of paper? Would the words make any difference anyway? Emily took another sip of coffee and touched her pen to the paper. Her hand shook a bit as she wrote, *Dear Jessica.*

Chapter 9

Meagan Sullivan woke suddenly from a deep sleep, frightened by her dream. Her eyes wildly searched the room, looking for a hint of where she had fallen asleep, until she saw Elizabeth's shirt lying on a chest at the foot of the bed. Meagan rolled over and found Elizabeth still asleep, half-reclined on a stack of pillows with a copy of *The Last of the Mohicans* creased open on her chest. She studied Elizabeth for a moment, admiring the smooth curves of her face and strong line of her jaw.

Two weeks had passed now since the long flight home from DC. Meagan filled the daytime hours accepting condolences from friends and neighbors and kind people she didn't even know. There were also arrangements to be made, bank accounts and bills to be gathered, and legal documents to sort through. The business and visits kept the days passing in their own agonizing time, but the nights were unbearable. Finally last night she called Elizabeth at twelve-thirty, half crazy and empty. Elizabeth helped her pack a few clothes and brought her here, and then held Meagan in her arms until Meagan finally fell into the first restful sleep since the last night she slept with Chris.

Now the morning sun broke full through the bedroom windows and Meagan reached to lightly brush a tuft of hair away from Elizabeth's face.

Elizabeth slowly opened her eyes to the touch and rolled toward Meagan with a sleepy half smile. "Good morning." Her voice was thick and drowsy. "How are you feeling this morning?"

"Much better," Meagan replied, with another light stoke across Elizabeth's forehead. "Thanks for rescuing me last night."

"Of course. I'm just glad you called me," Elizabeth said. Holding her last night Elizabeth was certain she meant something to Meagan. Meagan needed her, and for now, that was enough.

Blown Away
© 2006 by The Haworth Press, Inc. All rights reserved.
doi:10.1300/5706_09

Meagan picked up the book from Elizabeth's chest and read the title, "*The Last of the Mohicans,* huh? I never knew you were into Cooper," Meagan said. She looked over the cover and put the book back on Elizabeth's chest.

Elizabeth picked up the paperback and studied the dark painting on the front. "Well, if you can't fall asleep with Cooper," she said with a subtle smile, "you can't fall asleep." She put the book on the headboard and rested on an elbow, studying Meagan's eyes. "No, seriously, I like the stories of the noble savage. Seems kind of familiar," Elizabeth said. "I wonder how many people in our community are like that—truly noble people who are detested by the nutcase conservatives of society. Once a person is openly gay, no amount of good deeds will make them morally worthy to half the fools in this country."

"I suppose," Meagan said. "Nobility counts for squat in this world."

Elizabeth watched Meagan's sad eyes drift across the shadows on the ceiling and wondered if she really meant what she just said. Meagan Sullivan—the eternal optimist—had plenty of reason to be angry and cynical, but had she given up? No, the Meagan Sullivan she had come to know was a fighter. She just needed time to regain her strength, and optimism, even her joy.

"Meagan, why don't you stay here for a while?" Elizabeth said. "I have the extra bedroom. It's not very big, but it's yours as long as you want to stay," she said. She reached over to gently brush through the soft red hair falling on Meagan's pillow. "I wouldn't think you would want to be alone right now."

Meagan kept her eyes on the ceiling, thinking as she said, "That's true, but I'm not sure yet if I'll stay in Birmingham. Are you planning to stay here?"

"I think for a while," Elizabeth replied softly, still stoking Meagan's hair. "I've already had a couple of good offers to keep me employed until I take the bar, and after if I want to stay with them. The Southern Poverty Law Center called me, but I don't want to go to Montgomery. Maybe if I could set up an office here—I don't know," Elizabeth said, knowing in truth that as the lone survivor of the Jessica Thompson defense team she was one of the hottest young commodities going in the world of civil rights law.

Meagan shifted closer to Elizabeth's touch, needing the security and faithful protection of her hands. "Well," Meagan said, turning to face Elizabeth with a sad smile, "before I move in, don't you think we should ask Rico first?"

Rico's big tail thumped against the floor. He stood and bounced across the room to rest his chin on the bed, his tail swinging wildly as his brown eyes fixed on Meagan.

"I think he'll be okay with it," Elizabeth laughed. She scratched Rico behind the ear and rolled out of bed. "How about some breakfast, you two?" she said as she pulled on her robe and headed toward the kitchen.

"Sure," Meagan said. "Believe it or not, I'm actually hungry for a change."

THE DARKNESS OF WINTER magnified Meagan's misery, and some days she only endured. Elizabeth watched her patiently, letting most days pass with little conversation, but staying close by. Occasionally, though, Elizabeth would coax Meagan out for the day, going for a long drive or a hike together. Over time Meagan began to laugh again, and Elizabeth knew the bond between them grew more solid with each passing day.

Spring finally came to Birmingham, arriving with particular magnificence. The streets of Birmingham burst in color with azaleas, dogwood, irises, and daffodils. Slowly, the season's magic lifted the dark veil that had covered their spirits.

THE MONDAY AFTER EASTER Elizabeth pulled her Outback into their duplex drive and caught something new in the shine of the car lights. She backed up for another look and saw the flower bed by the doorway planted with a rainbow of annuals—red, orange, yellow, green, blue, and violet. Elizabeth smiled as she shut off the engine and grabbed her gym bag and a sack of groceries.

As usual, Rico greeted her at the door, but the apartment was dark and empty. "Meagan!" Elizabeth called out. There was no answer. "Meagan!" Elizabeth called out again, still with no answer.

Rico nuzzled Elizabeth's hand and led her to the back door. Out the window Elizabeth spotted Meagan's silhouette kneeling beside a newly planted tree. "Ah, there she is," she said to Rico. "Thanks, buddy."

Elizabeth stood at the door and watched Meagan work, wondering how much longer Meagan would stay. The lease on the apartment would be up soon, and they may want to move to a place with more room. But what would it mean if they moved to a new place together? Elizabeth had not been out much since Meagan moved in, and she had not yet brought a date home to the apartment. She convinced herself it was to spare Meagan's feelings of being alone, even though she knew there were plenty of rumors as to why a woman as attractive as Elizabeth would be spending so much time at home with a widow. But those were just rumors. She knew exactly where she stood with Meagan. Or least, she thought she knew. As she watched Meagan walk toward the door, she wondered if after tonight she would know at all.

"I see you've been busy," Elizabeth said as Meagan crouched at the door to pull off her dirt-covered shoes. "The flowers in front look great." Elizabeth reached into the refrigerator for a beer. "You want one?" she asked, holding up the beer.

"Yeah, I think so," Meagan replied as she walked barefoot to the sink. "How was the game?"

"We kicked their ass," Elizabeth smiled. She twisted off the top of Meagan's beer and set it on the counter. "What've you got going in the back?"

Meagan turned on the faucet and scrubbed brown dirt from her hands. "I'm building a flower bed around the tree I planted for Chris." Meagan dried her hands and took the beer from the counter. She took a swallow and noticed Elizabeth looking at her in the way she always did when she wanted to say something to her, but was not sure how. "You look like you have something on your mind. What is it?"

Elizabeth leaned against the refrigerator and took a long swallow from her beer, "You're right," she said. "I do have something on my mind." She looked over to Meagan. "It involves you, too."

Meagan eyed Elizabeth warily and swung herself onto the counter. She picked up her beer. "I'm listening."

Elizabeth looked up at the ceiling and said, "Annette Peters with Lambda Rising called me today. She wanted to know if I would come to DC to give a speech at Pride. She wants me to speak about the Thompson case and what it means to the gay community. We should have the Court's decision by Pride week."

"Uh-huh," Meagan said. "And where do I fit into this picture?"

Elizabeth shoved away from the refrigerator walked next to Meagan. She looked at her sincerely, "I want you to go with me."

Meagan's face filled with a sudden flush of anger. She shook her head slowly, "*Why*, Elizabeth? You know that place is haunted for me. Forever."

Elizabeth had expected resistance. She edged closer, lightly leaning against Meagan's thigh. "I know it will be hard, Meagan, but I know you can do it," she coaxed. "I think you are strong enough now to face the demons you left in DC. And I believe people need to see you to know that something good has survived all of this. Look, right now it would be easy for us to give up on our community. Chris and Colton are gone and, with the new Court, I don't see any way we will win the case. We need *something* to show they haven't beaten us."

"And how is my being there supposed to show *that*?" Meagan snapped, glaring up at Elizabeth.

"When King was killed, what did his wife do? Conveniently drop out of sight so everyone could forget he ever lived? No, she didn't disappear," Elizabeth argued. "She was out there, reminding people that there is survival when a great person dies. Someone lives to remind people of who that person was and what they stood for."

Meagan quickly turned away from Elizabeth's intense gaze and stared at the floor. She knew Elizabeth was right. Chris deserved to be remembered, and if she had to stand as a human reminder, she would have to find the courage to do it. "Okay," she whispered. "I'll go with you."

Chapter 10

The afternoon sun of the third Sunday in June scorched through the humid air of Washington, DC, leaving the city in an unusually slow mood. In a sweltering line of more than twenty Elizabeth and Meagan waited to buy a three-dollar pint of water. They passively watched the parade of passersby, but neither of them really felt like celebrating Gay Pride. Meagan had been restless with the city from the minute the plane landed Friday night, and as the Sunday crowd swelled Elizabeth's mind was increasingly preoccupied with the speech she would be delivering at four p.m. today.

Elizabeth peered out on the mall and the sea of people stretched out in every direction. She guessed there must be at least fifty thousand gathered in clusters of blankets and deck chairs crammed across the lawn. Every few hundred feet a rainbow flag or a pink triangle on a black banner flapped gently in whatever breeze managed to make it through the city. Under different circumstances Elizabeth would love being here—if only she didn't have to speak in front of the whole lot of them.

Elizabeth looked at her watch and said, "If we ever make it through this line we won't have much time left. I have to report to the stage in about an hour."

"Are you ready, then?" Meagan asked. She reached for Elizabeth's hand and held it tightly to quell the apprehension she saw in Elizabeth's active eyes, "It's a good speech, Elizabeth. I should know since I've heard it five times already. But I'm still anxious to hear you knock 'em dead."

"Thanks, but I'm just ready to get it over with," Elizabeth replied after a nervous sigh. She looked down to Meagan's reassuring smile before turning to the huge stage in the center of the mall, the stage where she would be standing in just a couple of hours.

Blown Away
© 2006 by The Haworth Press, Inc. All rights reserved.
doi:10.1300/5706_10

Elizabeth reached out and wrapped her arms around Meagan. "Don't leave me up there alone now. I need to know you'll be behind me."

"I'm always behind you, baby." Meagan tightened her arms across Elizabeth's back, "And so is every person here. You just remember that."

"I will. Thanks for reminding me."

The next two hours ticked by slowly, but at the same time passed all too soon. At four p.m. Elizabeth and Meagan stood behind the stage, Elizabeth now wearing freshly pressed light golden slacks and a loose white shirt, and Meagan in navy blue and a cream blouse. The back breeze from several huge stage fans blew across their faces.

Elizabeth watched the rock band on the stage playing with encore abandon, checking her watch every thirty seconds and tapping her foot against the beat. At 4:06 the last note faded across the lawn and the band disappeared behind a makeshift wall. Elizabeth shifted nervously, watching the stagehands hurriedly move the instruments and pull a podium onto the center stage.

After a couple of minutes the stage manager found Elizabeth. "Okay," he said as he descended three steps toward her. "Are you ready?"

"Yeah, let's go," Elizabeth replied. She followed him to the top stair and got the first glimpse of the stadium-sized crowd. She stood motionless, watching the afternoon master of ceremonies walk across the stage and take the microphone in his hand, as if in slow motion. Her mind went blank and her mouth dry.

"As you all have heard by now," the MC said, "the Supreme Court recently upheld the lower court's decision on *Roe versus Idaho*." Immediately the crowd fell silent as every eye turned to the stage. "Now I know most of us have followed the case closely, but I'm proud to announce that today we have someone with us who knows as much about *Roe versus Idaho* and what it means to our community as anyone on the planet. Elizabeth Nix served as an assistant to the first Roe defense team, and she has an intimate knowledge of the case, but more important, she knows what this case will mean to us in the coming years and what we can do now about the Court's decision. So here she is. Let's welcome Elizabeth Nix."

The applause that roared forward sent Elizabeth's heart wildly hammering. As always, her physicality took over. She walked to the podium in long, apparently confident strides and set down her notes. *"Roe versus Idaho,"* she said into the microphone. Her own voice boomed across the lawn, seeming to carry for miles. The boldness of it startled and her she looked out to the thousands of eyes looking directly at her. For a moment Elizabeth just gazed back at them, a sea of human faces, silently waiting for her to speak.

From the back of the stage Meagan desperately waited for the next word. She took an anxious step toward Elizabeth, ready to cue her on the first line.

But then Elizabeth spoke again. *"Roe versus Idaho* gave me the opportunity to meet and work with two great and noble Americans. Their names were Colton Rice and Chris Landry." Elizabeth paused as applause erupted.

In the front row just to Elizabeth's right was one man who could not bring himself to join the adulation. He was satisfied with the *Roe versus Idaho* decision and had no interest in seeing it overturned. His name was Nicholas DuBose, a senior staff assistant to Douglas Whitman.

Here at this Gay Pride Celebration Nick DuBose was the minority, something he knew little about. As the only child of a privileged family from New Hampshire, Nick DuBose always felt superior to most people. He graduated from the right schools, met the right people, married the right woman, and had two perfect children—Michael and Rebecca. But in this crowd of proud and confident gay people DuBose felt odd and out of sorts, and right now he hated his boss for this lame-brained assignment.

Douglas Whitman's instructions to DuBose had been simple: attend Gay Pride, report on impressions, and find out who among the newcomers were headed for leadership roles in the movement. So far DuBose had been unimpressed, but he watched Elizabeth Nix intently, noticing something in her the others lacked. Maybe it was a natural air of integrity. Just by the passion of her voice she could have led *him* to agree with the words she spoke. DuBose studied her face. Elizabeth Nix was young—very young—but her demeanor held a maturity beyond her age. She was confident but not cocky, and sure of her convictions without being self-righteous. Her voice was bold and steady and her words were eloquent and lively. A leader like Elizabeth Nix could be a problem.

Elizabeth's words boomed from the speakers. "In the memory of my friend Chris Landry and our communities' friend Colton Rice, I'm asking you to support our efforts to find all those responsible for their deaths as well as the others who died that day. I will never believe Philip Norton Taylor was a lone assassin who suddenly decided to strike."

Philip Norton Taylor, the mere mention of the name rushed adrenaline through Nick DuBose's veins. DuBose could agree with Elizabeth Nix on one thing: he never believed Taylor acted alone either.

"I only knew two of the people who died that day, the others I never had the opportunity to meet," Elizabeth continued. "But I can tell you that when this country lost Chris Landry and Colton Rice we lost two great citizens we will never replace. You see, for them, justice was more than just a word or an abstract concept of the way things should be. For them justice was the primary purpose, the basic reason for law, and they believed the law, like justice, should be applied equally to *all* people. They knew that justice is the only road to real peace in our society." Elizabeth paused as applause again interrupted her words. "But a part of Chris Landry did survive that day," she continued. "Her name is Meagan Sullivan and she was Chris Landry's spouse. I would like you to meet her. So, Meagan, will you join me?"

Meagan walked toward Elizabeth as growing applause began to rumble through the crowd. In a moment, though she hadn't planned to, Meagan found herself speaking. "I want you all to know how much Chris would have liked to have been here with us," she began. "Elizabeth and I have been here all weekend and we have met some wonderful people. We really appreciate all of your generosity. I know how much we were all disappointed with the recent Court decision, but as Elizabeth said, this is not the end, folks. I guarantee you Chris Landry would not have given up and we cannot either. In these past two days I've seen moments of brutal hatred out there from people who want to keep us from our rights, but I hope you will remember that violence is not the way of our people. In the memory of Chris, I ask that you never use violence as a way of change. Violence has hurt us enough and we must never condone it. I believe through diligent, persistent efforts, every citizen of the United States will one day be free to love and marry the person that fate brings them. We must all act together, and we must all be willing to sacrifice. Remember, the next generation depends on us. Again, thank you all."

Elizabeth wrapped her arm across Meagan's shoulder as they walked across the stage. The applause of the charged crowd rolled as Elizabeth reached the bottom of the steps and whirled around to take Meagan into her arms. She pulled Meagan tight, lifting her off the ground as she spun her around.

"We did it, we did it!" Meagan exclaimed. She took Elizabeth's face into her hands and quickly kissed her.

"Yes we did," Elizabeth said, laughing as she eased Meagan back to her feet. "Now I finally feel like celebrating." She grabbed Meagan's hands, "My God I'm glad that's over with. You know, we've been invited to some big parties around town. I think I wanna go to every one of 'em. How about being my date for the night?" she said, looking down into the renewed joy of Meagan's dancing eyes.

"Why Ms. Nix, I thought you would never ask," Meagan said with a sweet Alabama accent and a teasing smile.

Chapter 11

President Bucks hung up the phone and rubbed his bloodshot eyes, paying no attention to the four men waiting silently in the Oval Office. The four faced each other, Chief of Staff Whitman and his assistant Nick DuBose on one sofa, and Attorney General Perez and John Harkins on the sofa opposite. Bucks stared out the window and loosened his silk tie, still pondering his phone conversation. "Governor Stewart said it's quiet for now," Bucks said. "Apparently, the mounted police had the necessary effect. They were able to confine the arson to a few blocks and the looting is under control. But Stewart thinks this is just the beginning. California is in for a long summer."

And so was the rest of the United States. The conservative right now controlled Capitol Hill, and once in charge, and backed by a sympathetic court, they quickly pushed through quiet legislation that at first seduced the country under the guise of "commonsense solutions"—until the people realized what had happened to them. Suddenly latent emotions burst into a social unrest like the country hadn't seen since Vietnam. The first major riot broke out in Los Angeles thirty-six hours previously and there was promise of more to come. The entire state of California was a social tinderbox waiting for a spark, and California was just a blueprint for the rest of the country. America now carved itself into unyielding factions identified by race, sex, religion, morality, environmentalism, gun ownership, or corporate ambition. And they were all mad as hell at each other.

The press mercilessly hammered the administration, and the president wanted solutions, but so far his staff had come up with nothing innovative. Bucks turned to the men and let his piercing blue eyes sweep all four before settling on Salvador Perez. "Sal, what do you have from law enforcement?"

"We've been in touch with our state attorney general contacts," Perez answered. "They all say they have hot spots that may piggy-

Blown Away
© 2006 by The Haworth Press, Inc. All rights reserved.
doi:10.1300/5706_11

back if Los Angeles breaks out again. It's possible we could have simultaneous riots in at least twenty cities if LA loses control again. We don't have the law enforcement to handle that kind of outbreak. Mr. President, the National Guard should be put on full alert. This whole thing hinges on southern California."

Bucks stared at Perez for a moment and then turned to Whitman. "Douglas, what do you think?"

"I don't think we have any other choice," Whitman replied. "Calling the Guard in is the only way to ensure law enforcement doesn't lose control."

Bucks frowned and rubbed his eyes again. "Call out the Guard, huh," he began. "You guys are supposed to be the country's best political minds, and this is what you came up with? Just how long do you think your half-assed solution will last?"

The president again shifted his nerve-rattling glare from one man to the next. "Well, let me give you gentlemen some advice. Ever since that bomb went off in February and we appointed the new Court this country has been like a powder keg. I've got every alligator in the swamp coming up to bite my ass. The blacks and Hispanics are mad as hell about the possibility of losing affirmative action, brawls are breaking out at abortion clinics, and two weeks ago this city was filled with a bunch of queers demanding we recognize their rights to marry for God's sake! Now, I'm trying to hold the line here, but John and his CMA friends are telling me I need to do more to return the country to its people!"

Bucks's glare fell on Harkins as he continued. "All of that might not be so bad if it was all I had to worry about, but it's not. I've got a budget that needs more trimming while at the same time I've got governors calling and asking for help because they can't afford to keep things going without the Uncle. I've got the damn environmentalists yelling that I personally am trying to destroy the world, and I've got to keep an eye on Korea and the kings of that big sandpit in the Mid-East to make sure they don't beat me to it!"

The president turned to his chief of staff. "Douglas, in one week I want ideas on how we can fix some of this mess. I'm gonna be expecting something that will blow my shorts off. I want something bold.

And don't get bogged down in bureaucracy. I'll even give you an easy one to start with. Give me a roll-out strategy for gay marriage rights and give it to me in one week."

Whitman nodded uneasily, but sending DuBose to the Pride celebration now seemed like a stroke of genius. "Who will I have, Will?" Whitman asked.

"You name them," Bucks answered. The office again fell silent and Bucks looked gravely at his hapless staff. He said, "The buck doesn't stop with you, does it, gentlemen?" Bucks looked at them be sure he was understood. "That's it. Thank you, gentlemen."

IN SEVEN DAYS Whitman sat across from the president's desk, giving his final brief before Bucks's ten-day trip through Europe and the Middle East.

"Before I go I want to hear what you guys have on gay marriage," Bucks said as Whitman finished the foreign relations briefing.

"Yes, Sir," Whitman said. "Do you want Harkins in here?"

Bucks thought before answering. "Yeah, I want to keep him fully informed. I don't want his paranoia jumping up again. He'll swear we're trying to undermine him."

Bucks buzzed his secretary. "Jo Ann, we need John Harkins in here, right away."

"And Nick DuBose," Whitman said. "He's here today. He was in my office when I left."

"And Nick DuBose," Bucks said to Jo Ann. "He's in Douglas's office."

In less than ten minutes Nick DuBose and John Harkins walked into the Oval Office and sat down on the sofa. Bucks walked to his chair and sat down with them. "Gentlemen," Bucks began, "I've asked Douglas to brief me on the gay rights strategy he has been working on for the past week. I have a schedule to keep so I want to keep this brief for now." Bucks turned to Whitman, "Where are we going with this, Douglas?"

Whitman shot a glance at Harkins and noticed no visible signs of emotion, except a slight flare of the nostrils. "Sir, the way things are right now, we don't see how we will ever be united across the states on gay issues anytime soon," Whitman said. "The public views are either deeply seeded in religious conviction or the belief in the validity of human rights. Leaders in the gay movement are saying, quite convincingly, that they pay federal taxes but are not regarded equally by the law. I don't think we can get by the Fourteenth Amendment again if the right case comes to the Court." Whitman paused and unconscientiously shifted away from Harkins. "What we want to propose, Sir," Whitman continued, "is to offer a compromise. Our alternative is to give gays the rights and protections they want, but only in a certain area. We are proposing to develop a territory with the goal of sovereign governmental control. The idea is to offer gays a choice to live in a state that offers them rights, relocate to this territory, or stay in the closet."

A brief silence fell over the Oval Office as Whitman paused to let Bucks and Harkins digest the bizarre idea.

The president's jaw dropped slightly as he stared at Whitman, seeming to be waiting for a wink, or anything to indicate he was only joking.

Harkins's reaction wasn't as subtle. "Are you insane?" he challenged as he sprung from the sofa and stalked over to Whitman, glaring down at him with his fists clinched tightly.

"John, sit down!" Bucks commanded. "Get ahold of yourself. I'm not having any fistfights break out in this office." Bucks glared at Harkins until he sat back down, and then said, "I want to hear what Douglas has to say here."

The president sat back comfortably in his chair with his hands folded in his lap, looking at Whitman with a faintly amused expression. "Go on, Douglas," Bucks said.

"We're looking at several areas of the country where we have blocks of land we can set aside into something like a reservation-type of ownership," Whitman began. "Right now it looks like the most viable alternative is northwest Florida."

"*Florida!*" Bucks exclaimed with a caustic laugh. "Now *I* think you are insane, Douglas." President Bucks stood and walked across the office, mockingly gesturing as he spoke. "Let's say for a moment we actually try to do this. There's no way we could do it in Florida.

Governor Reed would never agree to it. What about some place like Nevada or Wyoming; we own half of those states already," Bucks said with an amused smile.

"A western state was our first choice too," Whitman replied seriously. "But it would cost too much to get water into any of the places we looked at, not to mention we would never be able to redistribute the water rights. We wouldn't have those problems in Florida. There's an air force base we're in the process of closing and a national forest adjacent to the base. The base has an existing infrastructure we can build on, and we can convert and develop the national forest land as needed."

Bucks studied Whitman for a moment, realizing his chief advisor was truly dead serious about this. Maybe he owed it to Whitman to at least hear him out. After all, he had told him to be creative. With cautious interest he sat back down and looked at Whitman. The whole idea was so improbable, but it began to intrigue him nevertheless. Bucks gave Whitman a sly half smile and said, "You still haven't told me what you plan to do about Governor Reed."

"Governor Reed is on board with us already," Whitman replied confidently.

Bucks returned a long, doubtful stare. "How did you manage that?"

"We took the liberty of reminding the governor that we are trimming the fat from the federal budget and that we spend billions of dollars on Florida's hurricane season. He didn't budge—until we reminded him that the American taxpayers underwrite the insurance for developments along the coast—a little fact that the environmental community has been harping on lately. We told the governor that this administration really needs to score points with the environmental community, and that in light of the green versus development conflicts going on in his state it would look good to the greenies if we made sure Congress left Florida unfunded for coastal development insurance this year and for the rest of the administration's term."

Bucks looked at Whitman thoughtfully, "Interesting, Douglas. How many people do you think we could put on this reservation, or territory, or whatever you called it?"

"We estimate between four and five million with careful planning."

"And how many gay people do we estimate are in the United States?" Bucks asked.

"No one really knows, but estimates range between seven point eight and twenty-six million, nationwide."

"Doesn't that leave us a few million short of a solution?"

"Yes Sir, but several million of those people live in states where same-sex marriage or civil unions are already law. We anticipate most of those people will not want to move. Mr. President, the objective of this strategy is to satisfy the average American—not the gays. We believe this proposal will splinter and fragment the power of the gay rights movement as they debate the idea among themselves. As soon as that happens we've diluted their political strength. Giving up a few thousand acres of swampland in Florida is a damn small price to pay to get them off our backs."

"I see," Bucks said. "Even with the base and national forest, Florida is a highly populated state. Do you anticipate any need for condemnation?"

"About two hundred families may want to move," Whitman replied. "But I think we could make an offer sweet enough to get them to move. I don't think condemnation will be necessary."

"Condemnation!" Harkins again leapt from the sofa and took a couple of defiant steps toward Whitman. "Come on, this is the most absurd thing I have ever heard! You're asking two hundred good families to move from their homes so we can give their land to a bunch of *homosexuals?* Well, I for one will not stand for it, and neither will the American people!"

Bucks looked up and gazed assuredly at Harkins. "Yes, John, yes you will stand for it," he said calmly. "In fact, I think if we decide to go with this you will be the one to sell the idea to the CMA and the rest of our friends on the right."

"No way, Mr. President," Harkins said, his voice reined in only subtle control, "I'll never agree to this, and neither will Jason Johnson."

Harkins's words were just the challenge to convince Bucks. He was president of the goddamn United States and no one, especially his vice president, was going to tell him what he would and would not do.

"John," Bucks said, almost patronizingly, "a president has to do a lot of things he doesn't want to. You know that. This will be a good exercise for you. You do want to be president one day, don't you?" he asked, meeting Harkins's cold stare dead on.

A tense, silent moment passed between them before Bucks turned again to Whitman. "What about the other side?" he asked. "Do you think this territory thing will sell in the gay community?"

"Yes, we think it will if the right person sells it to them," Whitman answered.

"I assume you have that right person in mind?" Bucks asked.

"We do have someone in mind," Whitman replied, turning to take a small stack of files from DuBose.

Whitman opened the top file, took out two 8×10 photographs, and handed them to Bucks. "The photograph on top is Elizabeth Nix," Whitman began.

"Isn't she the one involved with *Roe versus Idaho?*" Bucks asked skeptically. "Why do you expect she will work with us?"

"That's part of the plan, Sir," Whitman answered, avoiding Harkins's icy stare by focusing directly on President Bucks. "If we can get Elizabeth Nix and Meagan Sullivan on board they will be the ideal representation with the gay community. These two have plenty of reason to distrust, even hate this administration. If gays see them willing to support this idea, they'll be more willing to buy into the idea themselves. Elizabeth Nix could make an excellent spokeswoman for us."

Whitman pointed to the photographs and said, "The woman in the second photograph is Meagan Sullivan, who was the partner of Chris Landry. Apparently she is a close friend of Elizabeth Nix. If we can sell the idea to both of them, then we've got a strong tie to the gay community."

Bucks looked over the photographs again. "They certainly have the looks. What do we know about Elizabeth Nix?"

"Ms. Nix is intelligent and articulate," Whitman began. "She graduated number four in her class at the University of Georgia School of

Law. The gay community greatly respects her, and from what we can find she has a clean personal life. She's interested in politics and was quoted as saying she would like to be a senator but doesn't believe any state will ever elect an openly lesbian senator in her lifetime. She's high profile in the gay community, and she's been featured in both gay magazines and law journals. She will be a major player in a couple of years."

"What are the negatives?" Bucks asked as he handed the photographs back to DuBose.

"She is young, Sir; she just turned twenty-eight," Whitman answered as he pushed an uneasy finger against his lips.

"You mean to tell me your proposal to make this thing work rests in the hands of a twenty-eight-year-old *woman?*" Bucks asked sharply.

"You have to remember, Mr. President, she is just our liaison with the gay community. For the first few years we propose to control the purse strings of the territory and to control most governmental affairs until the people there ask for sovereignty, and until we believe they are ready for it. By then their leaders will be defined," Whitman speculated.

"Yes, I suppose that's true," Bucks said thoughtfully. "I assume you've worked up a report for me."

"Yes, of course," Whitman said and handed Bucks a folder. "It's on DVD and hard copy."

Bucks took the folder and flipped through it, saying, "If I decide to pursue this I'll want to present it to the cabinet when I get back. Douglas, I want you and Nick to keep working on this thing, but I want specifics. The leadership on both sides of the aisle will have plenty of questions if we take this to them. In the meantime keep a lid on it. If we decide to go with it we'll talk to the gay community and the right on the same day we go to the Hill. If this leaks out before then you'll all be looking for a job. I'll talk to Governor Reed about it also. I assume you asked him to keep quiet."

"We did," Whitman answered.

"Good. I'll make a decision on whether we go forward by next week. Thank you, gentlemen," Bucks said, and turned to Harkins. "John, I'd like a minute with you."

DuBose nodded to the president, wished him a safe trip and walked to the door with Douglas Whitman.

"John," Bucks said as he casually took a couple of cigars from his humidifier, "I know you don't like this whole territory idea, and right now I'm not sold on it myself. But we've gotta do something to heal this country. I believe it will take bold steps to do it. We must have the courage to try new and innovative solutions."

Harkins took the cigar Bucks offered, knowing that right now he had no choice but to follow the president. "Sir, you are the president and this is your administration, your legacy," Harkins said in a deep, contrary voice. "But I'll not make any promises about the future and what my administration may do if this ridiculous idea of a gay territory ever materializes. If eight years from now the people of the United States elect me to be president they will know exactly what they are getting, and it's not a man who panders to every bleeding heart who thinks the world is unfair, especially not when these ungrateful blowhards are living in the greatest and strongest country on the face of the earth. Right now, I won't promise you that I'll protect gay rights *or* preserve a gay territory under my administration. You just remember that when you make your decision."

Chapter 12

For the fifth time in the hour Elizabeth walked to the window and anxiously looked out to the street. A lone pickup passed by slowly.

"Meagan," Elizabeth called as she turned from the window. "What are you doing?"

"Reading," Meagan replied from her bedroom.

"How can you be calm enough to read at a time like this?" Elizabeth asked as she picked up the TV remote and began flipping channels.

"It's better than watching you incessantly flip channels," Meagan replied coolly.

Elizabeth hit the power button and threw the remote on her chair. She pushed her arms in an overhead arc, stretching tense muscles while she walked in deliberate steps to Meagan's room. She stopped in doorway and leaned against the frame, admiring the sight of Meagan stretched lengthways across the bed flipping through a magazine.

Meagan looked over and gave Elizabeth a quick, welcoming smile and then went back to her reading.

"What do you suppose they want to talk to us about?" Elizabeth asked as she stretched out on the bed next to Meagan.

Meagan smiled at Elizabeth's impetuousness and dropped the *GQ* onto the floor. She rolled on her side to face Elizabeth. "Well, like I told you yesterday, I think it's probably either about the case or about the bombing. I doubt they want to talk to us about our thoughts on the U.S.–China policy," she teased patiently.

Since Thursday afternoon, when Nick DuBose called Elizabeth at work, she had been like a caged animal. That night Elizabeth skipped her workout to rush home and tell Meagan that the president's *freakin' chief of staff*, Douglas Whitman, would like to come by and speak to them as soon as possible, preferably Saturday afternoon.

And now Whitman was scheduled to arrive in less than ten minutes. Meagan doubted Elizabeth would make it until then. She reached over and lightly trailed her fingers the length of Elizabeth's arm. "Just relax, girl. They'll be here in a few minutes."

"Yeah, you're right," Elizabeth said, staring solemnly at the ceiling as her mind raced from one possibility to the next, until Rico's bark jarred her from her thoughts.

"Who is it, Rico?" Elizabeth asked as she jumped from the bed and rushed to the front window. She slowly pulled back the curtains and looked out to the street.

The scene unfolding in front of the apartment seemed surreal, almost comical. It was just like Elizabeth had seen hundreds of times in the movies. A fleet of three cars—two sedans and one black SUV—stopped on the street in front of the apartment. Two men from both the front and back sedans leapt out and swept the street with their eyes, looking everywhere for the threat of evil.

The entourage unfolded from the cars and moved in a tight formation toward the door. With the ring of the doorbell Rico launched into his deep bark.

"Please remove the dog," one of the men said from the opposite side of the door.

Elizabeth grabbed Rico's collar and pulled him back. "Meagan, will you let them in, please?" she said, retreating through the kitchen with Rico.

Meagan strolled to the door and pulled it open, "Good afternoon. Please come in," she said with her best Southern charm.

"Good afternoon, ma'am," one of the agents said. "You are expecting Mr. Whitman and Mr. DuBose."

"Yes, we are."

Douglas Whitman held out his hand as he walked through the door. "Ms. Sullivan," he began, "I'm Douglas Whitman, and this is my assistant, Mr. Nick DuBose."

Meagan took Whitman's hand and shook it firmly, then DuBose's, and closed the door. She noticed Whitman and DuBose's casual dress, as if they just got off the golf course, though it was way too hot outside for golf. Apparently, it was an effort to seem informal.

In a moment Elizabeth emerged from the kitchen, looking totally relaxed, though inside she was as tight as a cork.

"Please, have a seat gentlemen," Elizabeth said, pointing toward a rocking chair and the winged chair next to it. "Would you like a drink?" she asked casually. "We have iced tea, sweet and un, beer, orange juice, Coke—I mean soda—and water. I'll make coffee if anyone wants it in this hundred-degree weather. Oh yeah, we have Jack Daniels, Absolut vodka, and dark rum."

"I think I'd like a beer," Whitman said. "Light, if you have it."

"Water for me," DuBose said.

"I'll get it," Meagan offered. "Do you want anything, Elizabeth?"

"Just water, thanks," Elizabeth replied and sat down on the couch opposite the two men.

"Birmingham has really grown," DuBose offered in an early attempt at small talk. "I was stationed at McClellen back in my army days and we'd come to Birmingham on weekends."

"For anything in particular?" Elizabeth asked politely.

"Just the clubs." DuBose smiled back.

Meagan returned from the kitchen carrying the drinks on a flowered metal tray. "Here we are," Meagan said, politely casual, as if she did this every day.

Amazed, Elizabeth watched June Cleaver serve the drinks. She didn't even know they owned a tray. She waited until Meagan finished before she said to Whitman, "Now, Mr. Whitman, what is it you wanted to speak to us about?"

Douglas Whitman took a sip of beer and eased back in the rocking chair. "Ladies, I've come here to ask for your help," he began casually. "President Bucks knows this country has deep wounds to heal, and he has innovative—some would even say radical—plans to address our domestic problems, but he needs help from our best and brightest citizens—people such as the two of you. The president and I would like to ask you to serve as liaisons between the administration and the gay community."

Elizabeth realized all eyes were on her. "I'm not sure I'm following you," she said. "Do mean you want us to serve in some sort of advisory capacity to the administration?"

"Not exactly," Whitman said. He shifted in the rocker and flashed a glance at DuBose. "The administration is in the process of developing plans to provide more opportunities for our gay citizens. When those plans are ready we'd like for you to help us sell them to your community."

"What kind of plans?" Elizabeth asked cautiously.

"Well," Whitman began slowly, "What I'm going to propose to you today is the most radical plan any administration has come up with since World War II, but we think the plan has a chance to work, given the right combination of people." Whitman paused and set down his beer. "We believe the two of you could be just the type of people we need to make our plan work. What we want to do," he said carefully, "is to develop a territory for gay people, probably in Florida."

Dead silence fell over the room. Elizabeth shot a look over to Meagan. Her blank, shocked expression confirmed Elizabeth had heard Whitman correctly. "Excuse me, Mr. Whitman. Did you say a territory for gay people?" Elizabeth asked at length.

"Yes," Whitman replied, again shifting anxiously in the rocker, realizing he had about three seconds to throw his best sales pitch. "What we have in mind is to set up a protected territory where gay people living under antigay partnership state legislation can relocate and be free to live according to their own rules. Of course, others could also move to the territory if they wished, and if the people of the territory agreed to it. What we have in mind is to build the infrastructure and work with the people of the territory to set up the laws and regulations and to eventually grant sovereignty to the territory, much like the American Indian reservation system."

"Uh-huh. I see," Elizabeth said slowly, looking at Whitman with a disbelieving stare. "And I suppose you think it's perfectly all right for gay people to pull up their careers, families, and homes, and move to this territory—probably some swamp you've found out in east hell— so they can have their basic liberties, their basic *rights?*"

"Oh, I can assure you it will not be a swamp," Whitman countered, quickly reverting to damage control. He motioned to DuBose for the file and held it out to Elizabeth. "Look, this is the entire plan for this proposal. The plan shows our proposed location, what we want to do and what we would like for you to agree to do."

Elizabeth stared for a moment before she reached for the file.

"I can assure you we only have your best interests in mind," Whitman said.

Elizabeth passed the file to Meagan without opening at it and turned her indignant, angry eyes to Whitman. "You can assure us, Mr. Whitman? Well, you sure couldn't assure Chris Landry, or Colton Rice, or even the Supreme Court justices, could you Mr. Whitman?"

Whitman said nothing.

"No, Mr. Whitman, I'm not sure you can assure us of anything!" Elizabeth stopped before going too far.

Whitman stared back without a trace of reply.

"I'll tell you what," Elizabeth said coolly. "We'll look over your proposal here. We'll consider it and let you know in the next few days, but I wouldn't get my hopes up if I were you. I have a little problem trusting your boss after what he did to us with his Supreme Court appointments."

Elizabeth turned to Meagan. "Anything you want to add?"

Meagan shook her head slowly.

Elizabeth stood up and walked over to Whitman. "Is there anything else we can help you with, Mr. Whitman?" she asked sternly.

"No, I don't think so," Whitman said solemnly as he stood. He looked past Elizabeth to Meagan and said, "The numbers where you can contact either me or Mr. DuBose are listed in the proposal. Please remember most everything in the proposal is negotiable. We really are trying to find a solution. I hope you will consider our proposal in the manner it was intended."

Elizabeth eyed him with thinly veiled disdain as she turned to lead him to the door.

Whitman nodded amicably to Meagan and then followed Elizabeth. At the entryway he extended his hand. Elizabeth considered refusing it, but took it with one firm shake.

"Thank you both for your time," Whitman said. "Let me know as soon as you decide."

Two secret service agents were now at the door with them. "Good day, Ms. Nix," Whitman said and waited for the agents to file out first.

Elizabeth made sure of their departure, watching their taillights disappear before slamming the door. "Those bastards!" She stormed to the den and found Meagan sitting on the couch with her legs crossed, leafing through the pages of the proposal. Calmly, Meagan looked up at her, refusing to feed Elizabeth's fierce temper. She understood Elizabeth's indignation, but she had never seen Elizabeth burn a political bridge before, especially for something as immediately benign as this proposal.

Elizabeth looked at Meagan incredulously. "Can you believe that shit? They just want to lock us away somewhere—take away what rights we do have, and forget about us. I can't believe anyone would even suggest such an asinine idea! What kind of idiots do they think we are!"

Meagan sat silently, letting Elizabeth fume without interruption—or response.

"Where have I heard this before, Meagan? Was it Germany? Was it Hitler? Yeah, Whitman says it will be set up like a Native American reservation. Well there's something positive," Elizabeth ranted sarcastically. "The American Indians got a great deal, didn't they?"

Meagan kept her silence.

Elizabeth looked at Meagan, realizing that Meagan was not going to endorse her anger. After a moment she sat down opposite Meagan and leaned toward her with a slight hint of regret. "Okay, I'm sorry I lost it," she said. "What do you think?"

Meagan took a deep breath before she answered. "Well, I think we ought to at least read this," she said, looking down at the file in her lap. "It won't hurt to look through it."

"I can't believe you're even *considering* trusting them," Elizabeth snapped.

"I didn't say I trusted them. I just said we should read it," Meagan replied firmly, matching Elizabeth's determination. "I'm going to. It's up to you to decide what you want to do."

The proposal obviously intrigued Meagan and Elizabeth knew it was not fair to stop her from exploring it. The *why* was not important. Whatever Meagan's motivation, she was right about one thing: it wouldn't hurt to read the plan. Reading it was a long way from accepting it. And, to be sure, Meagan was determined.

"Okay, I'll read it too," Elizabeth surrendered. "I suppose we may as well get started tonight."

THEY AGREED TO DEBATE Tuesday night, and by Wednesday morning they would come to a decision.

The next two days passed quietly in their apartment. Once in a while they met in the hall, but the air between them hung as thick as between quarreling lovers. Elizabeth took to the den with her documents spread across her desk, and Meagan stayed in her bedroom, meticulously studying the maps, papers, and drawings that blanketed the floor.

Tuesday afternoon at four-thirty Elizabeth drove home, knowing that Meagan wanted to accept the offer, and determined to do everything possible to change Meagan's mind. She pulled into the drive and found Meagan already home from her seven a.m. shift at the ER. Inside, Meagan sat at the kitchen table with three neat piles of papers and two folded maps stacked neatly in front of her. She held a loosely bound document in her lap, highlighting words and sentences here and there as she read.

"It looks like you're ready to get started," Elizabeth said, looking at Meagan with an earnest smile, but knowing that the evening may very well end in real anger.

Meagan looked up from her reading, returned her own guarded smile, and went back to the document.

Elizabeth noted the defiant tilt of Meagan's chin and walked to the refrigerator for a beer. She twisted the cap as she threw a long, cavalier leg over the back of her chair. "No way you're gonna convince me to dance with these clowns," Elizabeth said as she sat down. "I've always said I wouldn't help the Republican party off the *Titanic,* and now they want me to help them sell all us queers down the river."

Meagan deliberately sat the document on the table. "You're in a good mood for a lawyer who is about to lose a debate. I know how you legal eagles hate that," she said coolly, taking a measured sip from her wineglass.

"Well, I would hate it if I did in fact lose," Elizabeth replied with a self-assured smile that tailed off with just a hint of doubt.

"I see you're confident," Meagan said. "So why don't you go first. Convince me once and for all that we should tell them no." She sat back and defiantly crossed her arms over her chest.

"All right," Elizabeth began. "I'll start with what I see as the best-case scenario. Let's just assume for a minute that we agree with this proposal and Bucks follows through, and for the sake of argument, we'll believe they'll actually do the things they say they are going to do. I still don't think this territory would be some kind of gay utopia. In the first place, the territory would be small in geographic terms, but population-wise it would be huge. You know what happens when you cram a bunch of people in one small area—sooner or later all kinds of social problems will crop up and we'll be faced with the same problems of all the major U.S. metropolis areas."

Meagan looked at Elizabeth evenly, keeping her arms crossed on her chest. "I don't expect a gay utopia, Elizabeth, where everyone lives in peace and harmony. Of course there will be problems. I don't assume for a minute that there won't be, but this is an opportunity. Opportunities never come with guarantees. There's no such thing as utopia."

Elizabeth began to feel a slow erosion of power. She stood up and walked over to the counter, putting some distance between herself and Meagan. "Well, I don't see how all these people will make a living. Who do you think is gonna buy our products if we have to compete with already established companies?"

"So you don't think gay people have talents, salable skills?" Meagan asked with her brow furrowed curiously. "The plan says the feds will cover all of the major costs of developing the infrastructure. For the first few years capital investments will be largely paid for. That leaves a lot of room for innovation and development of ideas, not to mention how the outlay of capital investment gives us a huge competitive advantage. We'll find plenty to fuel an economy."

"Yes, I understand how federal money could be a big advantage, Meagan, but I'm not convinced we can trust the Bucks Administration to follow through. Most of all, I can't see taxpayers being willing to support this thing. I don't think the average taxpayers will go for spending government money to set up a little paradise for queers," Elizabeth argued.

"Since when do you think the taxpayers get what they want?" Meagan countered. "This is a Bucks Administration thing. You know what that means, they control the House and Senate. They'll zip it through Congress and it's done."

Elizabeth did not respond right away. She studied the resolve in Meagan's face, her steady eyes and the straight lips that turned down just slightly at the corners when she was this serious. "You really want to do this, don't you?" she said.

"Yes. I really do," Meagan replied. "Probably more than you don't want to."

Elizabeth nodded and looked out the window to the square frames of the neighbor's windows. She considered the people living there—a young couple with a newborn who only spoke to Meagan and Elizabeth in short, necessary phrases of greeting. On the other side, just across the drive lived a thirtysomething couple with three children and a key to their apartment. This was the reality of their America—a nation split by a conscience of dated morality on one side, or a true sense of fairness on the other. Elizabeth still believed those who despised them would fight harder and dirtier than those who believed in fairness. *Fairness and equality are of little consequence—until it's personal,* she thought. It seemed intolerance and hate, masquerading behind some sort of perceived threat, was always personal. Their detractors would never give up, and neither should she. The protection of laws not the protection of space was the only way to affect the American conscience. It would take time, but change would come, and not by taking the gay fabric out of society and forcing it away to some secluded territory. Chris Landry would know that, Elizabeth thought, and Chris would never agree to run from *this* fight for civil rights.

Elizabeth turned back to Meagan sincerely, speaking in slow, determined words. "Meagan, even if we think this territory plan will actually work, I just can't get past the idea that we are giving up the fight for our full rights—that we will just be running and hiding instead of staying and fighting." Elizabeth paused, and then said carefully, "I don't think Chris would ever agree to do this."

Meagan fell back in her chair, stunned. "How do you know what Chris would have done?" she challenged. With a seething glare she dared Elizabeth to answer.

Elizabeth turned her eyes down, knowing she had gone too far. She said nothing as Meagan stormed to her bedroom, slamming the door behind her.

Elizabeth grabbed her basketball from the utility room and stomped out to the driveway. The heat of the August evening surrounded her as she pushed herself with the quick dribbles and short shots, moving at a furious pace, pushing through the rage in her body. William Bucks, Douglas Whitman, even Nick DuBose—the men she had held with such contempt—had somehow managed to bring her to hurt the one person she promised herself she never would.

Elizabeth was too lost in her fury to hear the door opening. She spun around for a rebound, and Meagan was there.

"Elizabeth, I'm sorry," Meagan said.

Elizabeth stopped and moved the ball to her hip and draped her arm across it. Her breath came in winded pants as she drew her thumb across her forehead to sweep away the sweat.

Meagan walked across the drive to stand closer to Elizabeth. She looked up at her and said, "Elizabeth, I know you and Chris shared a fighting spirit I never completely understood. But there was another side to Chris that she wouldn't let you see, a part of her that was vulnerable and weary. She once told me she felt like she spent her whole adult life swimming against the current, taking refuge on occasional islands of time when she was alone with me or surrounded by other gay people. She said that those were the only times when she felt she was really free to be who she was. The rest of the time she just went through the motions, waiting for another island." Meagan tightened her jaw to catch her shaking voice before she continued. "Chris hated not being able to touch me in public places, or having that nagging feeling in the back of her mind that when she wrapped her arms around me while we watched a sunset that some redneck might come up and kick our ass."

Meagan's voice caught again, but she talked through it. "Chris wanted to have freedom everywhere, not just in private places. She knew she would probably never have it in her lifetime, but she hoped that somewhere, some fortunate generation would not have to face the same prejudices. It was freedom she wanted, Elizabeth, simple human freedom. That's why she fought so hard."

"So why don't you think we should stay here and continue the fight?" Elizabeth questioned cautiously.

"What I'm trying to say is that I believe Chris would have taken this chance to have a place where we can be free to make our own rules—a place where we don't have to swim against the current all the time," Meagan replied. She reached over and took the ball from Elizabeth's hip and held it between her hands. She studied the burnt orange dimples, avoiding Elizabeth's gaze. "This can be our place," Meagan said softly, but ardently. "I don't know how to make you see what I see—how it would be to live in a place where we never had to watch over our shoulders, a place where justice for gay people is expected—not hoped for, but *expected*."

"And what makes you think we will have justice in this territory? What makes you believe that it will be like this free, just society you envision?" Elizabeth asked.

Meagan stood silently for a long moment, again studying the brown dimples of the basketball. She ran a finger across the smooth black ridges of the seams and said, "I believe it because I have faith in you." She looked up at Elizabeth. Her voice was now strong and certain. "It amazes me that you still have no idea how rare you are. You have something that is so unique—this natural force that seems to draw people to you, and connects you to them. . . ." She searched for the right words. "Elizabeth, there is a boldness in you that is obvious even when you just sit quietly. You give people confidence, and they believe in you. If you decided to march into hell, I swear people would follow you. You have that gift. You—Elizabeth Nix—can make the difference. Right here, right now, you have it in your power to affect the future. How many people have the chance to do that? *You* will make this work. I believe this is your time. It's what you were *born* to do."

Elizabeth looked again at the house of her intolerant neighbors. *What would they want me to do?* Elizabeth wondered, keeping her eyes on the house. She determined to do just the opposite.

"Even if what you say is true, Meagan, don't you believe I could best use my skills right here, putting my energy into pushing for federal protection?"

Meagan looked at Elizabeth for a moment before she answered. "Maybe so Elizabeth, but there are hundreds of gay activists across this country, and that many more organizations fighting for the cause. This is our chance to go in another direction, to shape something different, something unique."

Elizabeth nodded thoughtfully. Meagan was slowly wearing her down. "So you believe Whitman is being straight up with us? You really believe Bucks will do what he says he'll do in the plan?"

Meagan nodded. "I think you are right to be skeptical," she began, "but I believe we can use that to our advantage to keep us sharp, always one step ahead. We just have to be smarter than they are, at least at first."

Meagan stepped closer and lightly pushed the ball against Elizabeth as she looked up at her. "*We* can make this place, Elizabeth. We can shape this territory to become our own vision, but we are going to have to seize this chance to take control. This is our time, and I don't believe it will come again."

Meagan was right. This was a lifetime chance, the kind you had to take or forever regret. Elizabeth smiled to herself, realizing the intriguing appeal of a gay-owned, gay-operated, major freakin' queer metropolis.

"Okay," she said as she took the ball and shifted it to her hip. "We'll do it. I'll call DuBose tomorrow."

THE NEXT MORNING Meagan sat at the kitchen table and watched Elizabeth dial the numbers. On the second ring, DuBose answered from the back seat of Douglas Whitman's limo.

"Nick DuBose."

"Good morning, Mr. DuBose. This is Elizabeth Nix."

DuBose switched to the speakerphone. "Yes, Ms. Nix," he said. "I'm here with Mr. Whitman. How can we help you?" DuBose glanced over at Whitman, and by habit he grabbed a pen and legal pad.

"I'm calling to let you know we've made our decision," Elizabeth said.

"And what decision have you made?" Whitman asked.

"We've decided we would like to work with you," Elizabeth replied.

"Excellent!" Whitman said. "Can you come to DC for a meeting with the president?

Meeting with the president. Elizabeth disliked Bucks, but her heart jumped anyway. "Yes, just give us time to arrange our schedules," she said evenly.

"Good. I'll have Mr. DuBose set up the date and time and make the travel arrangements. Don't worry about expenses. We'll cover everything for you. Mr. DuBose will get back with you on the details. Do you have any questions I can answer right now?"

"No. We'll wait to hear from you," Elizabeth replied.

"All right then, we'll be in touch soon. Thank you, Ms. Nix," Whitman said, and hung up.

From the side window Whitman watched an aging 737 climb slowly toward the sky. "Well, Nick," he said as he settled back against the polished leather of the limo, "It looks like the time has come for all those radical gays to either sink or swim."

"Yes, sir. It looks like it has," DuBose answered.

"In my opinion, Nick, there isn't a decent swimmer among them."

Chapter 13

Just as Douglas Whitman promised, he arranged for Elizabeth Nix and Meagan Sullivan to meet President William Bucks. They were to be received at two p.m. in the White House Oval Office for a short meeting followed by tea and an informal chat.

The president's assistant showed Elizabeth and Meagan into the Oval Office at exactly two.

"Come in, ladies," Bucks said graciously, standing behind his desk. He walked around and extended his hand to Elizabeth first. She grasped it, and though she never liked the man, she was still in awe. After all, he was the president of the United States.

For the next fifteen minutes President Bucks coolly, softly, and humbly sold them on his vision for the country, and how they were the perfect people to bring a new future to gays in America. By the time the teacups were empty and the tea cakes were eaten, President Bucks had heartily convinced them of his sincere appreciation for their effort and his own genuine dedication to making certain the territory project would work.

FIVE WEEKS LATER, on a breezy September day, Elizabeth and Meagan began the tour of the chunk of Florida that President Bucks proposed in his territory legislation to congress. Nick DuBose met them at the airport in Tallahassee the evening before, and said he would be their guide for the next three days.

Now Elizabeth and Meagan sat in the back seat of a Lincoln Navigator, riding over mile after mile of sandy dirt road, looking out the windows and hoping to see something other than the thick green wall of dense, tangled vegetation that lined both sides of the road. Once in a while Elizabeth would spot a break in the vegetation ahead, but as they drove to it she realized the ground was actually covered by brown stagnant water surrounding gnarled cypress trees that dripped with Spanish moss.

When they stopped for lunch Elizabeth grilled DuBose as to what they might see in the afternoon. She warned DuBose she didn't like what they had seen in the first four hours, and DuBose quickly assured her that the land they would see in the afternoon was better. Soon, he assured her, she would begin to realize the possibilities. But by three-thirty, Elizabeth knew that the afternoon tour would be no different than the morning. She surveyed the callous landscape as they drove, feeling all of her remaining hope gradually slip into a slow burning anger. Elizabeth had never really wanted to do this, never wanted to trust William Bucks, and never wanted to give up the fight in the states. But she agreed to it because Meagan wanted it. She remembered the night in the driveway, when Meagan had looked up at her with those convincing, beautiful green eyes and made her believe that they could trust Bucks. Meagan had played her so well, and had gotten what she wanted.

Elizabeth flashed a resentful glance at Meagan and tried to shake away the harsh feelings growing toward her. As another mile of swamp passed outside the window Elizabeth leaned back and closed her eyes. In two days the leaders in the gay rights movement would be expecting a full report from her. Since the meeting with Bucks, Elizabeth had managed to convince most of them that this would work, that William Bucks was earnest and the territory concept had true merit. Now she would have to call them, one by one, to tell them she had been wrong.

Elizabeth opened her eyes and looked again at Meagan. Meagan looked back with a hesitant smile, but Elizabeth turned away and closed her eyes again. If she ever found a way to gain back an ounce of the political credibility she had lost, she would never again take Meagan's advice.

At six thirty the driver dropped them off at the Tallahassee Radisson. For three hours Elizabeth had said nothing to Meagan, and whenever she could she avoided looking at her. In thick silence they walked to their suite. Without a word Elizabeth unlocked the door and went in.

Meagan followed right behind, letting the door slam. She stormed across the room and grabbed Elizabeth's arm. "Goddammit, Elizabeth!" Meagan jerked Elizabeth around. "Quit being so fuckin' hardheaded. Do you think it's going to help anything if you don't talk to me?"

Elizabeth yanked her arm away and glared back as her hot, rapid reply spilled out. "All right, Meagan, you want me to talk? Well, what do you want to hear? Would you like to hear how you made me believe all that bullshit about changing history? You saw what was out there today, Meagan. Nothing, that's what's out there—absolutely nothing but swamp and jungle, and we're supposed to all pull up our stakes and move down here to live happily ever after? I don't think so, sweetheart!"

Meagan stood firm. "Oh, come on, Elizabeth. More than half of what we saw today can be developed. Most of Florida looked like that at one time. And what they show us tomorrow will look better. You know that."

"No, I don't know that, Meagan," Elizabeth argued. "I would think they would show us the best on the first day. I'm ready to call Bucks and tell him to shove the whole idea up his ass."

"No, you're not," Meagan retorted. She pointed a rigid finger down and leaned forcefully toward Elizabeth. "You're going to finish this tour before you tell Bucks a damn thing!"

Meagan matched Elizabeth in a fierce stare, until Elizabeth finally spun away. "I'm going for a ride," she said as she stomped toward her bedroom. "And don't wait on me for dinner." Elizabeth snatched open the closet and pulled out a pair of faded jeans and a white T-shirt, putting them on in quick, determined yanks. Grabbing her keys from the dresser she stalked past Meagan. "I can't believe I let you talk me into this," she said at the door, and walked out. In long strides Elizabeth walked down the hall, feeling only a brief sting of regret.

At the bottom floor Elizabeth shoved open the door to the back parking lot. Her shiny new Harley—a token of appreciation from her grateful president—sat on a trailer across the lot. Elizabeth stared at the bike, questioning the motives of the people who came to the thousand-dollar-a-plate dinner that paid for it. She looked down at the key, contemplating telling DuBose to come get the damn thing, she didn't want it. She looked again at the bike and wrapped her fingers around the key. Yeah, she'd ride it. All she wanted right now was to burn pissed-off energy.

The four-lane in front of the Radisson was still packed with evening traffic, but a quarter mile away Elizabeth found an open side road. She turned onto it and rode south, roaring on the power as her mind flashed through memories of the Oval Office, a smiling President Bucks, and an agreeable Douglas Whitman. Had she sold herself out because of her weakness for Meagan, or the hope of some oddball power, or the price of this Harley? Had she just been naive?

Elizabeth cursed her own judgment and felt her heart twist as she remembered the look on Meagan's face when she left her in the hotel room. Elizabeth turned the throttle for more speed. Tight rows of pine trees became a green blur as she flew past them, looking for the next curve. She rode past fields and pastures and more rows of planted pines, turning down every back road that held the hope of leading to nowhere. Darkness fell, and she followed the moon until she found a beach road—a long, straight, black slab of indifferent openness. Elizabeth felt the power build beneath her again as she turned the throttle open, pushing for enough speed to escape the bounds of her own skin. She glanced down as the speedometer pegged past 100, and she pushed for more. Six more miles of gray-black pavement passed under her wheel before she saw the guardrail ahead fixed firmly across the road. Waiting until the last possible moment Elizabeth swung to a stop and killed the engine.

In long, angry strides Elizabeth stalked down the stark white sands of the deserted beach, still searching for escape. Heavy, salt-laden air blew strong across her face as she walked toward the black line of a jetty that stretched out well beyond the swell of the surf. Early autumn waves crashed and swirled at her feet as she walked, fast but without destination, blind to the scurry of sand crabs and silver blanket of the evening tide. Her turbulent mind snapped from anger to disgrace and back to anger. She kept moving, past the jetty and on, covering more than a mile before she stopped suddenly and turned to face the night sky. Her eyes scanned the early stars that filled the black dome above her, peaceful, distant—and sterile. Where was the God she had once found in this distant peace, in those stars? Was there even a God out there? Why did this God let Chris Landry die? Why did this God give power to men like William Bucks and John Harkins? Did he really favor men like Jason Johnson? Would *she*—Elizabeth Nix—ever be good enough for *this* God?

Enraged tears filled her eyes, "You *Bastard!*" she yelled at the darkness above her, swinging her fist against the hollow wind. *"Why do you let them win? Do you even know justice?"*

She stared at the sky, defiantly waiting. No answer came in the callous wind that blew steady against her face. No answers came in the pound of the surf or the cry of a passing gull. There was nothing, nothing but empty sounds, distant light, and the heartless mist of the ocean. Elizabeth fell on her knees as a heavy void cloaked her mind, leaving her weak and hollow.

The moon tracked across a quarter sky before Elizabeth again found the strength to move. She sat up quietly and again looked up to the sky, feeling the unexpected comfort of a subtle peace. For now, the controlled and combative thoughts that constantly filled her mind were gone, replaced by answers that seemed to arise from the depths of her soul. Slowly, one by one, the answers came, filling her mind with bold clarity.

Growth requires adversity. Seeing the world through unique eyes, you will learn justice. Your adversity will become your strength.

Elizabeth kept her eyes on the sky as she began to understand that every joy and tragedy that had happened to her in the last year—meeting Chris Landry, working on a national profile case, mourning the loss of her dynamic mentor—had prepared her for this calling, and led her to this moment. For whatever reason, the fates had fallen to her, and the future of thousands depended on her decision. Elizabeth knew she had to go through with it.

"Okay, you win," Elizabeth said softly, looking to the stars above. "Wherever you are, whoever you are, this must be what you want from me. So let's get on with it, huh? But you know you can't leave it all to me. I'm gonna need your help."

This time Elizabeth didn't wait for an answer. She knew she already had it. She stood up and looked out to the sea. The endless water crashed onto the shore in a gentle rhythm, inviting her in. She peeled off her clothes and walked to the surf, feeling an ever-growing strength fill her body and mind. The cool spray of the evening surf splashed onto her skin as she walked on, pushing past the forceful waves and into the sea. The sand beneath her feet slipped away, and she began to swim toward the silver light of the waxing moon.

TWELVE YEARS LATER

Chapter 14

Katherine Hopkins sat tense and motionless in the backseat of the county prison van, looking down at the shackles around her wrists as she battled surging emotions, desperately working to appear unaffected by a body on full alert and heading toward system overload. Her chest pounded harder and faster as her mind raced through chaotic thoughts of what the next few hours would bring.

The prison van took a sharp right, slamming her shoulder against the metal side. She pulled herself upright and heard a faint roar, at first barely audible over the hum of the engine, but growing steadily louder. Two more turns to the right and the van slowed, now barely moving above a steady crawl. Katherine lifted reluctant eyes to the window just in front of her. Through the gray of darkened glass Katherine saw her nightmare: a sea of people packed together in an angry mob, filling the lawn and lining the sidewalks, waiting for her.

At just after sunrise they began gathering on the lawn outside the Fairfax County Courthouse. A few overzealous radicals arrived before dawn, but since daybreak the crowd grew steadily into the mass that now spilled out onto the streets and sidewalks of the blocks surrounding the courthouse. It was a scene that had lately been repeated hundreds of times around America. Impromptu chants, flags, handmade signs bounced and waved in the air; blacks, whites, Hispanics, men, women, children, media, satellite trucks, FBI agents, and local curiosity hounds crammed together in a throng of elbow-to-elbow anger and emotion.

Katherine never expected to actually be part of such madness, much less to cause it. She turned from the window and caught her breath. The past twenty-two hours were the most horrifying of her life, and the next twenty-four would be worse. She kept her eyes down until the van stopped in front of the courthouse. Two uniformed officers from the escort cruiser rushed back and slid her door open. The hysterical pitch of the shouting voices hit her head on; she barely heard the officers ask if she was ready. Katherine nodded slightly and leaned forward as each officer took an arm. From twenty feet inside the crowd something flew at them, barely missing the officer on her right. A large iron cross fell at her feet. Maybe the bulletproof vest she wore was a good idea after all.

Only seventy feet of sidewalk stood between Katherine and the courthouse stairs, but it looked like miles. The police barricades and human wall of officers lined against the crowd seemed to offer little protection.

Determined to keep her head up and her eyes forward she began the brisk walk to the courthouse as the front lines surged toward her, shouting and gesturing with clenched fist and angry faces. A few offered support and encouragement, but most shouted self-assured declarations of where she would spend eternity.

Inside the courthouse Katherine found little relief. Reporters packed the halls, pushing and jumping to shout their questions before rushing inside the standing room only courtroom. Above the tumult the click and flash of aimless cameras filled the air. Halfway through the corridor Katherine paused to search the crowd for a familiar face, but the officers tightened their grip on her arms.

"We need to keep moving, ma'am," the tall one said.

The two officers moved her quickly down the corridor, finally pulling Katherine inside the service elevator. The elevator doors closed slowly to sudden silence. Katherine leaned against the cold metal of the back wall and tightly shut her eyes. *How could I let this happen?* she thought. *Why didn't I see it coming?* Others had faced prosecution on the same charge with scarcely more than a byline on the back page of the statewide news. But she was different. She was Dr. Katherine Hopkins.

On the third floor the elevator doors slid open, this time to a quiet, deserted corridor. The officers tightened their grips on Katherine's arms and silently led her into a small room. Inside, the bailiff tossed his magazine on the desk and stood next to her. Cold metal bit into her wrist as he twisted each cuff and unlocked it. Katherine swung her arms forward, mindlessly rubbing her wrists as she stared at the heavy oak door that opened into the courtroom. On the other side of the door, in courtroom one, she would meet her fate.

The bailiff took Katherine lightly by one arm and moved forward. She took a deep breath as he swung the door open. Hundreds of eyes turned their focus to her, and her legs turned to stone. A quiet buzz of whispering voices filled the air as she walked on shaky legs to the defendant's table and stood next to her counsel. Her attorney smiled nervously at her, vanquishing the little nerve she had left.

In the corner of the courtroom the clerk banged his gavel and said, "All rise. This session of the Court for the Commonwealth of Virginia, January twelve, in this year of our Lord is hereby called to order. The Honorable Justice Calvin Marshall presiding."

A tall, broad man walked through the door of the judge's chamber and took his seat at the bench. Judge Calvin Marshall was a solemn man of sixty-two years who commanded respect in his courtroom, mostly through effective use of his cold, gray eyes. He shot a quick glare at Katherine and then turned to the clerk. "Mr. Gillman, may I have the first case on the docket, please."

The clerk approached the bench and handed Judge Marshall a small stack of papers. Marshall slid on reading glasses to briefly read the top page, and then raised his eyes squarely on Katherine. "This case number one-two-oh-one-six-five, *Commonwealth versus Hopkins*. Mrs. Hopkins, you have been charged with acts considered threatening to the well-being of the commonwealth, specifically adultery in the form of homosexual sodomy. These acts are in violation of the laws of the commonwealth of Virginia," Marshall said, his commanding voice rolling across the worn wood of aging walls and floors. He pulled off his glasses and again focused on Katherine. "Before I ask for your plea, I want to be sure you understand your options and your rights in relation to this charge. I want you to understand that in the commonwealth of Virginia the crime of sodomy-adultery is considered a sexual offense. Therefore, if you plead guilty, or if you are found guilty of this charge following a trial, your conviction is subject to the laws and regulations of the commonwealth regarding crimes of a sexual nature. The commonwealth will require that your name and conviction be added to the commonwealth's register of sexual offenders. Now, with that in mind, how do you wish to plead?"

Katherine stared back at Marshall. Intellectually, she expected everything Marshall said, but hearing the words out loud slammed home the reality that she would be forever known as a sex offender, publicly regarded the same as a rapist, a child molester—a monster.

How did she wish to plead? Katherine could hardly think right now, much less plead. She looked behind her, searching for a bit of strength from her husband of sixteen years. Desperately she searched his face for some bit of encouragement, perhaps a slight smile, or even a nod. She did not find it. He towered above her, expressionless, holding the hand of their daughter Ellen on his right and son Jacob on his left.

For the most part, Thomas was a good husband. He was a few years older than Katherine, and she sometimes wondered if her initial attraction to him was from love or from her youthful desire for a strong protector. Thomas was very much like Katherine's own father, who had died suddenly when she was eight years old. A quiet, methodical man, Thomas often ignored his own ambitions to take care of his family. He earned his degree in political science and dreamed of one day becoming a member of Congress, but by the time Katherine finished medical school he realized he had waited too long to get into politics. Now, he found himself torn between his obligation to her and his job as the chief in-house-council for the Christians for Moral Accountability.

Thomas looked down at the floor, unable to look at Katherine. How could he reassure her? He was the one who had called the authorities, putting this horrible scene in motion.

The anxious voice of Katherine's court-appointed attorney snapped her attention back to the front of the courtroom, "My client pleads not guilty, Your Honor."

Katherine looked over at her attorney. She doubted the frail boy had been out of law school more than a week. But he was all she could get on short notice. Thomas controlled most of their finances and refused to pay for better representation. It made little difference. Anyone could handle entering her plea. Katherine and the rest of the country knew this proceeding was nothing more than a farce.

Marshall turned to Katherine's attorney. "Have you informed your client of her right to suspend the charges through acceptance into the Apalachicola Territory?"

"Yes, Your Honor. And we intend to submit the application. We would request a stay at this time while we await the decision from the Territory," her attorney said as he cleared his throat and nervously tried to return Marshall's gaze.

Marshall ignored him and turned to Katherine, "I'm granting you a thirty-day stay pending the Territory's decision. If citizenship is not granted this case will be continued in thirty days. Mrs. Hopkins, I hope you now realize your immoral acts will be taken seriously by this court. Adultery causes serious repercussions to the integrity of America's family structure. I hope you realize that our efforts to stem the tide of these threats to the sanctity of marriage are not only good for our society as a whole, but require our vigilance for the good of your own children."

Marshall banged his gavel once. "This court is in recess for thirty minutes."

Katherine watched him step off the bench and turned again to her family.

Ellen looked up at her mother with large, innocent eyes. "Where are you going, Mommy?" Ellen asked. "Will you be home tonight?"

Katherine knelt by her daughter, holding back tears. "No, baby, I won't be home for a long time, but your father will take great care of you. Your grandma will help take care of you too, but you know what, she will need you to help her. Will you do that for me? Will you help her take care of Daddy and Jacob?"

Ellen nodded and threw her arms around her mother. Katherine squeezed her daughter tight for a brief moment, and then gently pushed her back. She couldn't afford to lose it now.

The bailiff moved behind Katherine and tapped her shoulder. She stood and put her hands behind her back and waited for the cuffs. The metal bit her wrists again and the bailiff motioned to the oak door. She turned for one last glimpse of her family.

Jacob waved politely. "Bye-bye, Mommy." He was much too young to understand this.

Outside the courthouse the knowledge that Katherine would apply for Territory citizenship refueled the angry shouts. To them, it was a guilty plea. The officers shielded Katherine for the walk back to the van, but this time the crowd did not frighten her. Really, she felt nothing toward them. Her thoughts were of her two small children who would be raised without her. They would never understand this or forgive her. The van pulled away from the courthouse and Katherine looked down at her shackled hands, wondering if she had just made the biggest mistake of her life.

ELIZABETH NIX LEANED forward in the desk chair of her office, staring at the solemn face of the on-location news correspondent. "And that's the story here in Fairfax County, Virginia," the reporter said sternly.

"Television—Power off," Elizabeth said and watched the screen go blank. "Well, it looks like we will be receiving an application from Dr. Katherine Hopkins. What do you think?" she asked Meagan, now her most trusted political advisor.

"We'll need to think about this one carefully," Meagan said after a long pause. She sat in an antique rocking chair just to the right of Elizabeth's desk, cradling her chin in her hand.

In a moment, Elizabeth turned troubled eyes to Meagan and said, "I tell you, Meagan, this is not what we built this Territory for—to be some dumping ground for the poor souls one of the states wants to make an example of. Lately it seems we're getting one of these cases every few weeks, somebody that the military goes after, or someone that one of the backward ass southern states drags through the court system to get the churches stirred up and scare the hell out of everybody just so the local gays don't get too sassy and powerful." Elizabeth stood and looked out to the Gulf of Mexico. "But this case with Dr. Hopkins I just don't know about. This is a major story. She's a respected physician. Why would the Virginia prosecutor's office go after an adultery case that was certain to generate this kind of heat? I'm not sure what's going on here. What are those instincts of yours telling you?" Elizabeth asked.

"I'm not sure yet," Meagan answered. "I'd like to do more background research on Dr. Hopkins if we had the time, but I can tell you we could really use her talents as a pathologist. As you know, she has an outstanding reputation in the research arena." Meagan paused, looked out the window to the Gulf and continued. "On the other hand, I'm not sure we should be approving her application based on a single incident. As far as I know she has never come out publicly and admitted that she is a lesbian. Not to mention she has two children and, I'm assuming, she's still legally married."

Elizabeth didn't respond. Her eyes were fixed on the water, watching the waves swell and crash against the shore.

"Okay, Elizabeth, you're not listening to me," Meagan said. She walked over and stood by the window, across from Elizabeth. "Something else is on your mind. What is it?"

"I'm not sure you want to know," Elizabeth replied, glancing at Meagan, then back out to the Gulf.

"I wouldn't have asked if I didn't want to know. Obviously you have more on your mind than Dr. Katherine Hopkins."

Elizabeth watched two more waves roll onto the white sand below. "*Roe versus Idaho*," Elizabeth said finally.

Hot blood flushed to Meagan's face. "*Roe versus Idaho*—what does that have to do with anything? It's history, Elizabeth," Meagan said sharply.

"Meagan, I'm sorry," Elizabeth said. "I know you don't like to talk about that case but sometimes when I think of everything we are doing here it just overwhelms me that we wouldn't be here if it weren't for that case. We wouldn't be here, and Chris would still be with us." Elizabeth turned an ironic smile and said, "Chris would know what to do about Dr. Hopkins."

Meagan turned her eyes down to the floor. "Chris was never slow to make a decision," she said softly.

Elizabeth eased over and cautiously wrapped her arms around Meagan. "Hey, beautiful, what do you say we take a break," she said softly. "Dr. Hopkins can wait. I'll buy you dinner and we'll come back to this later. We have plenty of time to meet Virginia's timeline. What do you say?"

Meagan nodded.

"All right then," Elizabeth said. She leaned back and looked down at Meagan's down-turned eyes. "Are you okay?"

Meagan nodded and said, "Yes. Let's go." She looked up at Elizabeth with a sad smile. "This is going to cost you, though," she said, and playfully elbowed Elizabeth's ribs. "In case you haven't noticed, I'm not a cheap date."

Elizabeth held the door open, waited for Meagan, and turned out the lights. A gray darkness fell across the room and across the fading photograph of Chris Landry placed on the corner of Elizabeth's desk, the photograph taken long ago on a Sunday afternoon in north Georgia when Chris perched playfully over Meagan's shoulder and smiled for the camera, before *Roe versus Idaho* became part of a national conscience and the lives of Meagan, Elizabeth, and Dr. Katherine Hopkins were set on a collision course.

Chapter 15

Elizabeth stood on the beach at just after midnight, watching the approaching silver clouds of a winter rainstorm. The beauty and power of the night begged her to stay, so she settled onto the sand and watched the mounting waves crash against the shore.

There was an odd irony in the fact that there was now an application for Territory citizenship, she thought. She remembered the struggles of the first few months after the Territory legislation passed. She spent endless days traveling from state to state, trying to recruit enough adventurous men and women to build the territory. Oddly enough, late baby boomers were the first to come in mass. Many retired early from their first career, and having amassed small fortunes by age fifty they hungered for a new challenge. They were smart and ambitious, with enough business savvy and real-world experience to make things happen fast. They were opinionated too, though few had the desire for the trials and uncertainty of political office. Instead they pushed the younger ones with political challenges that tested the young leaders' metal. Elizabeth grew from every battle, and when the time came, her challengers realized her potential and backed her run for governor.

In the early, formative years, Elizabeth represented the people of the Territory to the governor of Florida and to the White House. President Bucks appointed her and four others to an advisory panel responsible for planning construction and development projects. At times the panel faced difficult conditions as they dealt with thousands of acres of wild, godforsaken land, but they found just as many prime acres suitable for development. Some places, like the white sand beaches and the crystal clear springs, attracted gay tourists by the thousands. In four short years the Territory began to thrive. By the fifth year the citizens demanded sovereignty, and by the seventh year they had won it.

Blown Away
© 2006 by The Haworth Press, Inc. All rights reserved.
doi:10.1300/5706_15

The people elected Elizabeth Nix to her first term as governor in a close race against the mayor of Liberty Beach, the Territory's largest metropolis. Then, just three months ago, as the incumbent from her first five-year term, Elizabeth was reelected by a landslide. The constitution allowed only two terms, and in her second term Elizabeth was discovering great clarity in the freedom to govern without a second thought of what her decisions might mean to reelection.

Elizabeth was grateful for that freedom as she considered the decision to grant asylum to Katherine Hopkins. The buzz throughout the Territory had reached fevered proportions since Dr. Hopkins's arrest. The opinions varied. Some people wanted no part of the wife of a man so strongly connected with the CMA, some people felt sorry for her, some thought she had gotten what she deserved, and some people were merely amused—but everyone was talking about it.

Tomorrow the people would know Elizabeth's decision, and like it or not, Katherine Hopkins would be one of them.

"LOOK, JESS, I KNOW you don't like it," Elizabeth said to Jessica Thompson, now the Territory attorney general, sitting across from Elizabeth at the breakfast table on the back courtyard of the governor's mansion. "But that's my decision and it's final." Elizabeth fixed a gaze on Jessica long enough to deter rebuttal. "However, you'll be pleased to know I'm not going to drop it at that."

The governor leaned back, but kept her commanding eyes on Jessica. "According to her application, Dr. Hopkins doesn't know anyone here in the Territory. She'll arrive in a few days without any contacts, no friends, no relatives, basically no support group whatsoever. It's my intention to fill that void for her. What I want you to understand is that Meagan and I will be making it our business to spend time with her, try to befriend her, get to know what she's like. We intend to be among the first people she meets. I want to know who she knows, what she does in her personal life, if she might be dating."

Jessica crossly stared back at Elizabeth. "Now you think you have time to run a dating service for her?" she asked with an edge of sarcasm.

Elizabeth again narrowed her eyes on Jessica and slowly sipped her coffee, using her silence to convey that she was in no mood for an argument—or any sharp comments. Methodically Elizabeth sat the mug down before she continued. "Dr. Hopkins's trial in Virginia was one heck of a show, but it was not enough to convince me that it was time to send her to the Territory. We don't even know who she supposedly had the affair with. I just want to keep an eye on her for a while."

"Elizabeth, if you're not sure she's a lesbian then why in hell did you approve her application?" Jessica asked sharply. "If you hadn't, then you damn sure wouldn't be spending the next few months playing nice face to some woman who's husband works for the goddamn CMA for chrissakes."

"Yeah, you are right about that, Jess," Elizabeth replied evenly. "The nice face wouldn't be necessary, but you know her reputation as a medical researcher, and quite frankly, we don't get that many applications from research professionals. We very rarely get applications from anyone of Katherine Hopkins's caliber."

Jessica ran an agitated hand through her short blonde hair and crossed her arms. She turned away from Elizabeth, squinting against the morning sun as she looked down to a distant tree line. "I know we need her, Elizabeth," she said with a slight shrug. "It just gripes the hell out of me that we've worked so hard to make this Territory thrive, and here someone who has worked against us for years can now just walk in here and take advantage of everything we've built, everything we've sacrificed for. That is, if she's even gay now. If she is, she can have it all," Jessica said. She turned back to Elizabeth sincerely. "If she does belong here she ought to have to pay her dues, Elizabeth. That's the way I see it."

"She will pay her dues," Elizabeth assured. "If we find we can trust her, Meagan plans to assign her to a classified research team as soon as possible. You know that's not easy duty. If she provides a catalyst for a breakthrough, one pharmaceutical patent would be worth millions—maybe billions—of dollars."

"And if you find you can't trust her, then what?"

"Then she becomes the commonwealth of Virginia's problem again."

"In the meantime she's our problem," Jessica countered with a final glance of warning. "But I'm willing to play it like you want. At this point, I'll bend over backward to be nice to the woman. I can assure you that Dr. Hopkins will think Sharon and I are the greatest people she ever met."

"Good." Elizabeth picked up her coffee and cradled the mug between her hands. "I'm fully aware that this goes against your nature. I appreciate you're making the effort. Who knows, in time you might actually like the woman."

Chapter 16

The governor's office occupied the top floor of the tallest building in Liberty Beach, a sprawling four-wing structure that stood six floors over the coast of the Gulf of Mexico and housed all government administrative offices. Elizabeth walked into the staff conference room and stopped next to Meagan, leaning down to whisper. "Jess doesn't like it, but she'll do it."

Meagan nodded without reply, and Elizabeth moved to her chair in the middle of a long, oval-shaped cherry table designed to seat twelve. Today, only six were present.

"Good morning," Elizabeth began as she opened her notepad. Michael DuBose, her public affairs director, sat in the chair across from her, swiveling slightly left and right with a trace of a smile across his lips. Meagan sat on her right, talking to Jessica, who was at the end of the table. Joe Pattilo, Elizabeth's chief of staff, sat on her left, scribbling notes in his daily planner. Elizabeth's executive assistant Linda Sanders sat opposite Jessica, waiting with her usual air of equanimity.

"Okay, folks," Elizabeth began. "Glad to see we're all here. This will be a busy day for all of us, because," she paused to take a long breath, "I've made the decision to accept Dr. Katherine Hopkins application for citizenship."

Elizabeth made a quick look around the staff for reaction before she continued. "We all know there will be repercussions of this decision throughout the Territory, and I want to keep the effects to a minimum." Elizabeth turned to her chief of staff. "Joe, today I want your full attention to this matter. Monitor the situation and keep me informed of anything I need to know. Michael," she said, shifting to DuBose, "I'm counting on you to get this decision out to the public and make sure it plays right. As usual, I'll trust you with the press release so you can quote me saying whatever you want, but make sure I

Blown Away
© 2006 by The Haworth Press, Inc. All rights reserved.
doi:10.1300/5706_16

see a copy before it goes out." The bright blue eyes of Michael DuBose sparkled even through his sincere nod.

Elizabeth looked to Jessica. "Jess, I expect Dr. Hopkins to be here in a couple of days. Between today's announcement and her arrival I would anticipate a few protests to pop up here and there. I don't see any real law enforcement problems, but if we have public protests that get ugly, I don't want arrests made. Have the police do everything they can before they get to that point. As we all know," she said, glancing around her staff, "the press gages the potency of protests in terms of arrests, so the last thing I want is an arrest count on the evening news." Elizabeth paused and irritably turned her pen from end to end. Despite all the years of seasoning the press could sometimes still get to her, especially those from the states.

"More important," Elizabeth said as she again focused on Jessica, "I don't think it's any secret that quite a few of our police officers don't like the idea of Katherine Hopkins coming here. I'm counting on you to make sure she is treated with the same respect from law enforcement as any other citizen would be. Also, there's a possibility that she may need protection for the first few weeks she's here, so arrange extra patrols near her home once we determine where she'll be living. The same goes for whatever hotel she checks into when she arrives."

Elizabeth looked down to her notebook, checking her notes for anything else. "That's it for now. I'll be in all day today," she said. The staff pushed back their black leather chairs to leave.

"Jess," Elizabeth said before Jessica stood up. "I'd like to speak to you for a minute. You too, Meagan. Don't leave yet."

Michael and Joe went out the door first, and after gathering up her notes, Linda followed them, closing the door behind her.

"Jess," Elizabeth began as the door clicked shut, "I was thinking about the presidential election on the drive in this morning and I was wondering—how good is your line of communication with Emily Harkins? Are you still in touch with her?"

"Somewhat," Jessica answered pensively, surprised by the question. "It's been more difficult since Harkins became president. My aunt Tommie only sees Emily once in a while, and you know I haven't been able to write her since they moved into the White House, but

Tommie says Emily still asks about me when they speak. I suppose if something's important I could still get in touch with her. Why do you ask?"

"It's nothing urgent," Elizabeth answered, "but with the election starting up it would be helpful to have a heads-up if Harkins has something cooking for us. I'm betting he'll come after us in the primaries of the conservative states and I'd like an early warning. We're going to have to be ready, especially here in north Florida."

"I agree," Jessica said as she leaned back and folded her hands behind her head. She looked at Elizabeth shrewdly. "But keep in mind that Emily Harkins isn't privileged to the inner workings of the campaign. Harkins and his people handle everything. Emily is just window dressing. In fact, I don't think she and Harkins even talk much anymore."

"What a shame," Meagan deadpanned. "What she's trying to ask, Jess," Meagan continued, turning to Jessica, "is if there's any way we could find out if John Harkins and his reelection campaign had anything to do with Katherine Hopkins's arrest."

Jessica nodded slowly and looked back to Elizabeth.

"Yes," Elizabeth confessed. "That is what I had in mind. With the primaries taking off, Harkins may be playing to the conservatives with the arrest and trial of Dr. Hopkins, showing how squeaky-clean he is by demonstrating that the rules apply even to his own cronies. Or, what's of more concern to me is that he may be using her case to focus the country's attention on the Territory, and then somewhere down the road he'll make a campaign issue out of us. We all know we don't need that. Then there's what we discussed this morning." Elizabeth turned the pen end to end again, studying their reflection in the shine of the table as she thought out loud. "The timing of this whole damned thing is just a little too convenient to believe John Harkins has nothing to do with it."

KATHERINE HOPKINS PULLED her white Volvo into the first available spot in the parking deck of the Apalachicola government building and shut off the engine. She wrestled the keys from the ignition and checked her hair in the rearview. Tired, bloodshot eyes reflected back at her.

Her day started at six a.m. in room 158 of the Ashley Inn, feeling even worse than she did last night, having arrived to the Territory late and exhausted from the twelve-hour drive from Charlotte, North Carolina. The night before she finally dozed off sometime after four-thirty, and at six came the wake-up call, a cup of coffee, and a shower, a bowl of cereal, and some fruit. Then there was the forty-five minute battle through morning traffic to make a fifteen-mile drive. At eight sharp she joined 249 others in the orientation session required for all new citizens of the Apalachicola territory. Tomorrow, she heard, there would be another 250. The territory was still growing fast.

Katherine quickly discovered the pace of the orientation class was geared for the 99.9 percent of new citizens who knew they would be moving here and had the benefit of many weeks of preparation. Throughout the day Katherine nursed cup after cup of strong coffee, absorbing what she could about every aspect of Territory life, including pertinent laws, employment, travel, commerce, real estate, government, and the political process. By the lunchtime break all she longed for was a quiet night and early bedtime back at the Ashley Inn. Instead, she walked out the door of the auditorium to find a young woman dressed in a sharp blue business suit approaching her with an invitation from Governor Elizabeth Nix to please drop by the governor's office following orientation.

"I hope this doesn't take long," Katherine muttered to herself as she pushed the buttons on her keypad and locked the Volvo. Quick, tight steps of her purposeful gait clicked along the brick pavement as she walked toward the bright orange and white signs leading to the elevator and stairwell. She opted for the elevator and impatiently watched the lights of four floors tick off. Raised black letters on a sign of flat silver chrome pointed her to the bank of six glass doors at the building's entrance tunnel.

Katherine marched through the tunnel, keeping her busy pace, her footsteps now muffled by the thick carpet beneath her. At the end of the tunnel the door handle hit her with a static pop. Damn, she hated this day. When she reached the information desk, her mouth had turned down into a tense scowl.

The beautiful young man sitting behind the desk didn't seem to notice. "May I help you?" he asked pleasantly.

"Yes, I have an appointment with Governor Nix," Katherine answered without a hint of returning his amiability.

"Sixth floor, Suite Six Hundred," he returned pleasantly. "Take the elevator to your right, and when you get to the sixth floor, turn right off the elevator. You'll see the doors to the governor's office just down the hall. You can't miss it."

"Thank you," Katherine said as she turned on her heel marched off. She stepped alone into the elevator, hit button six, and rode up without interruption.

"I'm here to see Governor Nix," Katherine said to the cheerful receptionist she found perched behind the raised station just inside the doors of Suite 600.

"Dr. Hopkins?" the young woman asked before Katherine could offer her name.

"Yes," Katherine replied coolly.

"The governor is expecting you," the young woman said with a sweet smile that actually seemed honest. "It will just be a moment. Can I offer a drink while you wait?"

"No, thank you," Katherine replied, and followed the receptionist across the room to the public waiting area. Katherine made a quick sweep of the office décor. Traditional furnishings with rich colors, deep wood tones and solid, classical accessories suggested power without intimidation. An office like this could be quite inviting, if it weren't for the quick and frequent glimpses from the curious receptionist now sitting back at her station. Katherine had to hand it to her, though, the glances were barely noticeable in comparison to the looks she'd caught when she walked into the auditorium at eight this morning.

"Dr. Hopkins?"

Katherine looked up as a tall, lean woman walked toward her from a side hallway. "Dr. Hopkins, I'm Linda Sanders," the woman continued. "I'm Governor Nix's assistant."

Katherine made a quick look up and down Linda's body. By physical appearance there was little wonder the governor chose Linda to be her assistant. Linda Sanders was as beautifully put together as anyone Katherine had met. Short, closely cropped hair surrounded a beautiful, dark brown face highlighted by golden brown eyes, a round nose, and full, red lips. Crisp, tailored clothes flowed from a body that moved with the grace of a dancer.

"Nice to meet you, Ms. Sanders," Katherine said, offering her right hand as she stood.

"Thank you, and you as well. Governor Nix is anxious to meet you also," Linda said. She held her arm up and pointed down the hall. "I'll show you to her office."

Katherine followed Linda to end of the hall and the deeply grained door labeled with bronze letters: GOVERNOR'S OFFICE. Linda tapped once and held the door open for Katherine. "Go on in," she said with a slight smile. "She'll be with you in a minute."

Just inside the door Katherine hesitated, struck by the informality of protocol. She turned around and saw Linda was gone, so she walked to the center of the office. In front of her a large window was set in the middle of the back wall, just behind the antique desk that spanned the length of the window. Between the desk and window the back of a large brown leather chair swung slightly from side to side, and a single finger pointing upward from a strong, smooth hand reached up from the chair.

"Give me just a minute," Katherine heard from the woman sitting in the chair.

"Give who a minute?" an impatient voice pierced from speakers on the governor's desk.

"I have a guest," the voice from the chair answered patiently.

Katherine moved slightly to her left, just far enough to get a view of the computer monitor and the person on the other end of the videophone. As best Katherine could tell it was a woman, probably about forty years old, with wild, windblown, graying black hair and a wrinkled, deeply tanned face. Whoever it was, she was no beauty.

"Now Henri, I know you're worried about Rico, but Meagan's birthday party will be in two weeks and I need to know you're going to have the grounds in good shape. I think you'd best forget about that gator you claim is wandering into the yard and get busy. Rico is too old to do anything but lie around anyway, and even if there is a gator that close Rico's not going to let it come up and just drag him off. Rico knows about gators," the voice from the chair said.

"But," Henri protested.

"No," the governor interrupted firmly. "Look, I'll talk to you tonight. I've got to go."

"Okay," Henri replied in a huff. She turned away and began to walk off.

"Henri," the governor called loudly.

"What?" Henri turned back with an annoyed glare.

"Hang up, Henri."

"Oh." Henri replied. Her hand reached forward and the screen went blank.

"Disconnect, monitor down," the Governor said. In a single motion Elizabeth swung around and stood up, now directly facing Katherine. "I'm sorry to keep you waiting," she said, extending her right hand across the desk. "Dr. Hopkins, it's a pleasure to meet you," she said with a warm smile.

Katherine reached to take the Elizabeth's hand and looked up into the gaze of Elizabeth's commanding, dark eyes. As their hands touched, an odd, hot rush surged through Katherine's body. Her face flushed red. "How do people address you?" Katherine asked as she dropped Elizabeth's hand and turned from her eyes, trying to recover from whatever the hell had just come over her.

"Formally, Governor Nix; informally, just Elizabeth," the Governor replied with a smile. Elizabeth pointed to a small couch and chairs arranged in a horseshoe just to the right of her desk. "Please, have a seat," she said, walking from behind her desk.

Elizabeth waited for Katherine to take a seat at the end of the couch and settled into the single chair next to her. "Dr. Hopkins," she began.

"Please, call me Katherine."

"Okay, Katherine." Elizabeth looked at her cordially and continued. "I won't keep you long. I know orientation can be a long day and you still have all the personal business you need to do to get settled in."

Katherine nodded, though her mind was still stuck on Elizabeth's eyes.

"As a matter of fact, that's what I wanted to see you about," Elizabeth continued. "We know that you've been through a lot in the past few weeks with the trial, leaving your children and family, your job, and everything else you've suffered through lately. So we want to make your transition here into the Territory as simple and comfortable as possible."

Katherine nodded again, trying to keep her expression from revealing anything of the peculiar anxiousness building in her mind and the knot tightening in her stomach. Elizabeth leaned toward her, and Katherine glanced down at Elizabeth's hands. She questioned her relief in seeing Elizabeth's left ring finger vacant.

"My staff and I would like to offer our assistance wherever we can," Elizabeth said. "I've asked one of our best real estate agents to help you find a place to live, and Meagan Sullivan secured a position for you at Bayside Medical Research Labs. In fact, the staff at Bayside is thrilled at the prospect of having you come on board." Elizabeth paused and waited for Katherine's response.

Katherine nodded through her blank expression, but said nothing.

"Of course you don't have to accept the Bayside position," Elizabeth offered. "And certainly you're welcome to choose your own real estate agent."

"Oh no," Katherine replied quickly, breaking from her daze with a faint smile. "I appreciate all of your help. After this morning's orientation I realize I'm going to need all the moving assistance I can get. And I couldn't be happier about Bayside. They were my first choice." Katherine looked up at Elizabeth, for the first time braving another meeting with her eyes. "Really, I do thank you. I haven't had much kindness lately."

Elizabeth studied Katherine for a moment, seeing the weariness in her eyes. They were kind, green eyes, the color of jade, with faint creases etched beside them, the sign of a woman that smiled often— in better times. There was a latent confidence in her eyes, too, a remnant of the self-assured woman she had been just a few short weeks ago, before her life had been so horribly thrown out of balance. Whether Elizabeth's suspicions about Katherine were true or not, there was no doubt that the woman had been through a private hell.

"We'll do what we can to help you," Elizabeth offered kindly. "As a matter of fact," she said with a smile, "I'd like to start by buying you dinner tonight. Will you join me? Or do you have other plans?"

The tired ache of Katherine's body reached to the bone. Twenty minutes ago all she wanted to do was to go back to the hotel and take a good long bath and try to relax. Yet, right now she had no desire to leave the company of Elizabeth Nix.

"I am rather tired, so I can't promise to be much with conversation," Katherine began, "but I do have to eat. So, yes, if you can put up with me, it would be a pleasure to join you for dinner."

"Good," Elizabeth said. "There are several excellent restaurants close by, so I promise not to keep you late."

Katherine smiled back at her, a little disappointed by the promise.

ELIZABETH UNLOCKED THE PASSENGER side of her BMW convertible and waited as Katherine got in, discretely watching Katherine's nicely toned legs swing into the car. She pushed the door closed and walked around, knowing it wouldn't be long until they knew if Katherine was truly gay. A woman like Dr. Hopkins could have plenty of dates, if she wanted.

"What do you have a taste for?" Elizabeth asked as she pulled over the seat belt and turned the ignition. "Just about anything you could want is within a few miles of here."

"How about seafood?" Katherine answered. She caught Elizabeth's eye as she looked around to back out.

Elizabeth slid the gear into first. "Seafood sounds good. Do you want Cajun, or Southern? We also have a place that specializes in Carolina low country seafood that's about ten minutes from here," she said with a cordial smile.

"Low country, I think," Katherine replied, for the first time with a hint of levity in her voice. "My husband and I love. . . ." she began, and then her voice abruptly trailed off. She sat perfectly still, realizing the words that had rolled off her tongue for years had little value here.

Elizabeth caught her struggle, and without losing a beat she said, "I understand. It's okay if you'd rather—"

"No, low county's fine," Katherine interrupted. She looked down and her eyes drifted over to Elizabeth's hands, gracefully cradling the shifter as she moved it through the gearbox.

"Low country it is," Elizabeth said as she took a right and accelerated. "Do you mind if I ask where you are staying?"

"At the Ashley Inn," Katherine replied as she cautioned another look at Elizabeth. Her eyes lingered there, studying Elizabeth's profile, the line of her jaw and the dark brown eyes set deep above the wide cheekbones from a Cherokee ancestor, the small, round ears that held back thick black hair. Governor Nix was a handsomely beautiful woman, Katherine thought, the product of good genes, a healthy lifestyle, and a confident mind.

"Ah, yes. The Ashley," Elizabeth smiled. "It's the first hotel we built here and still the best."

Katherine nodded and turned to her window, watching the buildings pass and trying to condition herself to the sight of the occasional couple holding hands as they casually walked down the street.

"I'm really surprised you don't have a driver," Katherine blurted suddenly, looking back at Elizabeth. "Do you always drive yourself? And what about bodyguards? Don't you have bodyguards?"

"I'm not completely alone," Elizabeth replied with an indulgent glance. "I have my personal emergency alert system and my cars are constantly monitored at the police station by a GPS tracker. When I'm driving in the Territory there's always someone within a block of wherever I am," she said, leaving out the fact that her frequent motorcycle rides were a different story. "I'm well enough protected, I can assure you," she said, looking over to Katherine as they stopped for a traffic light. "I don't like bodyguards. I just don't like being surrounded by people all the time. Besides, I'm only an administrator. Where's the glory in knocking off a government bureaucrat?" Elizabeth said with another slow smile.

Katherine didn't answer. She knew at least ten people in the states who would just as soon see Elizabeth Nix dead.

The driveway to the Taste of Charleston was the next right. Elizabeth pulled in and stopped for the valet.

"Hello, Sarah," she said as she handed over the keys. "How's it going tonight?" she asked.

To Katherine's surprise, Elizabeth actually waited for the answer, and, fortunately, Sarah was either too disinterested or too polite to take notice of Elizabeth's dinner companion.

Inside the restaurant Katherine wasn't so lucky. She felt the eyes of every patron turning to watch her as the maître d'—a man Elizabeth called Rex—led them toward the back corner of the restaurant.

Will it always be this way? Katherine wondered as she followed behind Rex. At least Elizabeth walking behind her deflected the stares that were surely streaming to her back.

"Here you are," Rex said, stopping in front of the curved bench of a spacious leather booth.

Elizabeth waited for Katherine to slide across the seat before taking the opposite side.

"Governor, your usual?" Rex asked.

Elizabeth nodded and Rex turned to Katherine. "And you Dr. Hopkins?" he asked cordially, verifying that he, and probably every other person in the place, knew exactly who she was.

"Just water with a lemon slice for now," Katherine replied awkwardly.

After a nod, Rex left them.

"I'm sorry about the stares," Elizabeth said. "I know people in the Territory are curious about you, but I thought this restaurant would be fairly safe." Her eyes swept the tables around them. A silver-haired man two tables over held his condemning stare, but Elizabeth's return glare sent him back to his own business. Elizabeth looked to Katherine again, smiling apologetically. "But, then again, after all you've been through in the past few weeks, you of all people know that being queer is not for sissies."

A waiter returned with their drinks in record time. Saying nothing, Elizabeth watched him carefully set the drinks on the table, and sensing the possibility of the governor's wrath, he quickly walked away. When he was gone Elizabeth said, "I guess I really didn't think about how people would react to seeing you here with me. Are you okay with staying?"

"Yes. I'll be all right," Katherine replied. "I understand that I'll have to get accustomed to the looks, at least for a while."

For a moment Elizabeth studied her, realizing that Katherine Hopkins was one of the most attractive women she had met in years, not so much traditionally beautiful, but in her manner, in a confidence that was revealed in ways like the security of intelligence and the assurance of character. Dr. Hopkins's physical traits were striking, too. Her sandy blonde hair stopped just above her shoulders, and she pushed it away from her serene eyes. Her face was rather normal, but all of her features were pleasing, so that when it was all put together the total of it was quite handsome. Today she wore small, silver-rimmed glasses, probably because of fatigue, but still her eyes were steady. Elizabeth focused on Katherine's mouth, and in the lines of her lips she noted a faint strain that couldn't be faked. If the doctor was acting, she was damn good at it.

"It will get better," Elizabeth offered sincerely. "People will get used to you being here. Your fifteen minutes will be up before you know it."

Katherine tilted her water glass toward Elizabeth, "Here's hoping," she said, and took a sip. "Let's talk about something else," Katherine offered as she set the glass down. A trace of a smile crossed her lips. "Tell me something about yourself."

"Okay, what would you like to know about me?" Elizabeth asked.

Katherine's mind hummed. There were many things she wanted to ask, but decided to stay away from personal questions—at least for now.

"What are the most difficult issues you are dealing with right now as governor?" Katherine asked.

"Urban sprawl and custody," Elizabeth replied without hesitation.

"Custody?" Katherine asked curiously.

"Yeah, custody," Elizabeth replied. "You see, here in the Territory the life partners of both the biological mother and father sometimes have legal custody rights to a child. In most cases where the preconception agreement is for joint custody, one of the couples has primary care custody and the other couple has whatever secondary custody rights are agreed to before conception. The problems come if there is a divorce of the primary care parents. We're seeing a significant increase in cases where the partners having secondary custody rights are suing for primary custody, arguing that the child is better off being raised by a two-parent household rather than by a single parent."

"Wow," Katherine said with a rise of her brows. "As if normal custody cases aren't complicated enough."

Elizabeth looked back at her evenly, noting Katherine's use of the word *normal*.

Katherine braved another look into Elizabeth's eyes. "And what about urban sprawl?"

"That I can do something about," Elizabeth replied and launched into a brief history of the Territory's planning and development, explaining details here and there. Katherine listened intently, welcoming the diversion from her own thoughts.

The next hours passed quickly as they talked easily, lingering over she-crab soup, shrimp and grits, and key lime pie. Once, Elizabeth asked Katherine if her lover intended to relocate to the Territory. Katherine replied that her lover, too, had children and would not leave them by choice. Elizabeth filed the information away in her mind.

At just after eight o'clock, following a second cup of coffee, Elizabeth glanced down at her watch and said, "As much as I hate to say it, I've got to get back to the office for a few hours tonight. I suppose we should get going."

"Oh, I'm sorry to keep you so long," Katherine replied as she reflectively glanced at her own watch. She tried to smile, but the disappointment still showed. The empty walls of the Ashley Inn would be even more unbearable now that she knew the pleasure of being in the company of Elizabeth Nix.

ELIZABETH DROVE UP the garage ramp and pulled into the space next to Katherine's Volvo. She turned off the engine and leaned against her door, facing Katherine. "Thank you for joining me, Katherine," she said with a warm smile. "I've had a lovely night. Everything I knew about you was something I read in your application package or heard from the news media. I enjoyed the opportunity to get to know you a bit more personally."

"And you, too, Elizabeth," Katherine replied with a reserved smile. "Thank you for dinner. Again, I'm sorry I kept you. I guess I'm just in no hurry to get back to an empty hotel room. I'm not used to that much quiet."

"I understand," Elizabeth replied. "These next few weeks are going to be hard. In fact," she said, reaching into a dash compartment and pulling out a small stack of business cards, "I want you to take one of these." Elizabeth pulled a card off the bottom and leaned next to Katherine, looking at the card as she said, "My office phone and home phone number are listed on here." Elizabeth handed the card to Katherine. "I want you to feel free to call me anytime if you need anything, or even if you just want to talk. And I'd like to invite you to a little get-together we are having for Meagan Sullivan's birthday in a couple of weeks. I'll send an invitation to your work address at Bayside. I hope you'll consider coming."

"I'd love to," Katherine replied. "I'll see you then." After a quick smile Katherine opened the door and got out. She settled into the Volvo and lifted her hand for a placid wave as she watched Elizabeth drive away.

Driving back to the hotel Katherine replayed her evening with Governor Elizabeth Nix, recalling the strange physical rush of the first meeting, followed by the hours of easy conversation, and then the drive back from the restaurant, sitting comfortably next to Elizabeth, feeling nothing of the rush of sensation that had hit her the first time they touched.

It must have been the fatigue and the caffeine, she thought, *nothing more.*

Chapter 17

Katherine closed the door and leaned against it, looking blankly into the emptiness of her hotel room. After a private pep talk she gathered the resolve to walk across the room, shedding one shoe and then the other. She sat down heavily on the king-sized bed and looked up at the ceiling, void of thought, until laughter from a group walking through the hotel corridor interrupted the silence. Katherine listened as they passed, her loneliness deepening. She reached into her jacket pocket and pulled out the small card she slid in earlier tonight. She studied it, knowing few citizens of the Territory would have ever been given the Governor's personal card. Katherine slowly traced the raised black letters with her fingers. She focused on the name. GOVERNOR ELIZABETH NIX. There was a nice ring to it, she thought, though she had never thought so before. Probably because every time she had ever heard Elizabeth's name spoken aloud there had been a thick tone of contempt hanging there, but that contempt had always come from people like her husband, people who had never met or even spoken to Elizabeth Nix, never encountered her graciousness or the sound of her laughter.

There was a phone number and e-mail address listed in the corner of the card. Maybe she would call Elizabeth, just to thank her again for dinner, just to talk to her for a few more minutes, but then, she reminded herself, *that's not what you're here for.* With an odd sense of creeping guilt Katherine slid the card back into her pocket and looked around the room. Her mind wasn't ready for the *North American Medical Journal* just yet. A hot bath and silk pajamas might help.

As usual, the bath settled Katherine's spirit, and she slid between the sheets with the November edition of the *Journal.* She turned to the feature article and read the first sentence. Then she read it again. By the third sentence her concentration slipped further, and by the next paragraph wandering thoughts had taken over. She stared at the *Journal*'s words, for now just as sterile and meaningless as to a layman.

Katherine tossed the *Journal* aside and leaned back. She closed her eyes to find the memory of Elizabeth standing up from behind her desk and extending her hand. Katherine blinked hard and rubbed her eyes to erase the image, then closed her eyes again. There was Elizabeth again, still smiling, but now with that deep boldness manifested in her eyes. Katherine's startled eyes flew open and she stared across the room. *Stop thinking of her!*

Katherine picked up the *Journal* again and read the first paragraph, this time focusing with the same mental discipline that pulled her through endless nights of medical school.

At just after nine o'clock Katherine put the *Journal* away and reached to the nightstand for her laptop. Her children should be asleep by now and she could see them. Although Katherine had longed for this moment since waking, the thought of having to speak to Thomas was stifling. She had dreaded the sight of her husband since leaving yesterday's secret rendezvous with him at the Holiday Inn in Charlotte, North Carolina. Thomas had kept her there until the noon checkout, pushing himself onto her again and again. Katherine did not share his passion yesterday—in fact, she had not for quite a while. Years had passed since Katherine shared the physical desire Thomas felt necessary for their marriage. But she was his wife, and she believed it her duty to oblige him often enough to keep him satisfied.

"Did I call too late?" Katherine asked dryly as Thomas's image appeared on her laptop screen.

"No," Thomas replied. "I wouldn't have answered if you'd called before now. How are you?"

"Okay." Katherine replied, suppressing the urge to curse him. "Are they in bed yet?"

"Yes," Thomas said. His eyes were distant and bare, as if he knew her anger with him but refused to regard it as legitimate. "I'll switch over to the mobile camera if you'd like to see them."

"I would."

"Any preference for order?"

"It doesn't matter," Katherine replied coolly, though her heart was in her throat, anxious with the anticipation of seeing her children for the first time in days, even if it was only while they slept.

Her laptop screen went blank, but in a moment the image of Jacob appeared. He slept soundly in his bed, his favorite cowboy blanket tucked under his chin. Katherine watched him breathe, feeling every inch of the miles that lay between them. She touched her fingers to her mouth and lightly placed them on his forehead.

The laptop went blank again, and in a few moments Ellen flashed onto the screen. Her daughter made a quick restless turn and mumbled something in her sleep, so Thomas eased out of her bedroom, sending jumbled images bouncing across Katherine's screen.

In a few moments Thomas appeared again. He studied Katherine for a moment, reading the tension in her face and the slight quiver that ruled a corner of her mouth. "Kate, I'm so sorry for all of this," he said earnestly. "But we had no other choice."

"I know, Thomas," Katherine said bluntly.

"How did it go today?" Thomas asked. "What's it like down there?"

"It went quite well, actually," Katherine said as her mood lightened. "I even managed to meet Governor Nix."

Thomas looked at her, a bit alarmed. "Really—your first day? How did you manage that?"

"She summoned me to her office," Katherine said in a brief, ironic laugh. "And later I had dinner with her."

"Oh," Thomas said curiously, though his eyes filled with disdain. "And what is Ms. Elizabeth Nix like, pray tell—the queen of the queers?"

"Come on, Thomas," Katherine rebuked. "I found her to be very pleasant, actually. After spending time with her it was apparent how she's been able to do everything she's done here. She's an intelligent and dynamic woman—very capable," Katherine said. A slow, sly smile crept across Katherine's face. "And, she's invited me to a party."

"Don't be absurd, Katherine," Thomas countered. "Bad enough you have to live with them; you don't have to resort to going their parties. No telling what they'll be doing."

Katherine's expression hardened with determination, "Oh, I'm going, Thomas," she assured him. "How do you think I'm going to make it down here if I don't? If you'll think for a minute you'll realize how fortunate this is. This party is for Meagan Sullivan, who we know is the closest friend *and* chief advisor to the governor. The guest list will probably include everybody who is anybody in the Territory. I can't think of any better opportunity to make contacts than with the people at Meagan Sullivan's party."

Thomas sat back, thinking. "I guess you're right, Kate," he said finally. "I just don't want you getting too familiar with those people. Just get in there and do what you have to do and get out. Jacob doesn't have too much time, you know."

"Not a second goes by when I'm not thinking about that. All I want is to put my arms around both of them again and tell them how much I love . . ." Katherine's voice broke and she turned away. "This is not easy for me, you know—you do know that, don't you?"

"Yes. I do know," Thomas sympathized. "I want you to know I think you are the most courageous woman in the world."

"No, you're wrong, Thomas." Katherine turned her face back to him, "I'm the most desperate woman in the world." She looked at her husband for a moment and said, "Good night, Thomas. Please get the cameras up in their rooms as soon as you can. And talk to Jason about setting up the monitoring system."

"I will, Kate. You'll be watching them play by the end of the week. Good night, babe."

Katherine clicked Thomas off line and closed the laptop. It was still early, but the last two days had been brutal. She turned out the bedside lamp and lay still in the darkness with her mind racing through images of the day—orientation; the landscape of Liberty Beach; Thomas, Jacob, and Ellen sleeping in their beds; and disturbingly, and too often, her first few hours with Elizabeth Nix.

KATHERINE WOKE BEFORE the sun from another restless night, a barrage of disturbing thoughts running through her mind. Last night's image of Jacob sleeping soundly would have been comforting, if she didn't know exactly how sick he was.

Katherine pushed the covers back and walked to the window. Nightlights from the hotel cast dim shadows on the white sands of the beach below, forming fading outlines of ever-darkening gray that finally faded to solid black. Her spirit felt just the same as those shadows—struggling islands of faint light surrounded by immense darkness. She remembered the day just four months ago, two days before his third birthday, when Jacob was diagnosed with multisymptom infectious cirrhosis, commonly known as MIC, the latest deadly disease to come from the rain forests of South America.

Just as the AIDS virus decades ago, no one forecasted the invasion of MIC into the human race. And, just as the AIDS virus, it was a slow but sure killer. For over a year the disease quietly existed in the United States before the first deaths occurred. Then, rather quickly, the death toll passed a hundred and the medical community and federal government began to take notice.

Researchers quickly discovered the infecting agent to be very sophisticated bacteria with an alarmingly high rate of mutation, but as a bloodborne disease the vector to humans remained a mystery. In a stroke of pure luck a Florida veterinarian researching canine heartworm incidence discovered the bacteria on the mouthparts of mosquitoes. Confidence for a cure ran high within the medical community, in spite of the mutation rate. Spokespersons for pharmaceutical companies assured the public that their immense knowledge of genetics would provide a foundation for the development of an antibiotic very soon, but two years had passed without a single treatment making it to even the primate trial stage.

In time researchers discovered that the MIC bacteria made its passage from South American forests to North America by way of neotropical birds, the small creatures that made a yearly migration from north to south and back again. For years the birds had taken flight and then rested near the brackish waters along the coasts of both continents, but recent coastal development pushed the birds takeoff and resting sites farther inland, toward the rain forests of South America and the fresh still waters in stagnant pools and swamps of the lowlands of North America.

The reason for the sudden explosion in MIC bacterial growth in the coastal rainforests was still uncertain, but now traces of the bacteria could be found in almost every freshwater pool along the northern coast of South America. The migrating birds took flight from the pools of the coastal rain forests with the bacteria coating their feathers and feet, and landed on the coast of North America with most of it still attached. As the birds took their first drink or bath after the long flight, the bacteria washed off the birds and right into the choice breeding grounds for thousands of mosquitoes.

Injection into humans came by way of the bite of a mosquito, and in the human host the MIC bacteria found its most welcome habitat. As a bloodborne pathogen the bacteria traveled everywhere. Symptoms could manifest first in the muscles and joints, or in the nervous system, or the immune system. Most patients eventually suffered a multiplicity of symptoms, often intermittently and sometimes all at once, but in the end, most every victim died a slow and merciless death from aggressive liver cirrhosis.

In Jacob Hopkins's body there were no signs yet of the onset of cirrhosis. So far his case had manifested only in intense muscle spasms, frequent headaches, and intermittent chills and fever.

As Katherine stared into the black darkness beyond the beach she prayed a prayer for the protection of her son's health. *It's in God's hands now,* she thought. She had done everything she could to give her son access to the best doctors in the States, but there were no documented cures, or even long-term treatments, for MIC. Death was a certainty—except in the Apalachicola Territory. Reports to the Centers for Disease Control showed one of the highest rates of infection among the citizens of the territory, but for the past six months there were no reported deaths.

In a desperate, last-ditch effort to save her son, Katherine was determined to find out why.

Chapter 18

"She's here," Meagan said into the phone of her office at Bayside Research Center.

"You'll let me know how it goes?" Elizabeth asked with a trace uncharacteristic anxiety creeping in her voice.

"Of course. I'll call you as soon as we're done," Meagan replied and hung up.

"Dr. Hopkins," Meagan said, extending her hand as her secretary escorted Katherine into the office. "Welcome to Bayside."

"Thank you," Katherine replied. "This is a beautiful facility. I'm excited to be joining the staff here."

"We're so glad to have you," Meagan replied earnestly. "Would you care to join me for breakfast?"

"Sure," Katherine replied.

From Meagan's door they walked through a long corridor that eventually opened into one of Bayside's garden lobbies, a large, open affair with windows of tall smoked glass arched twenty feet above them. Katherine walked beside Meagan, her eyes darting around to take in every detail of the gardens. With a subtle smile Katherine looked through the clear glass wall separating the lap pool of the staff fitness facility.

"Not bad, huh?" Meagan smiled. "This area is shared by research and hospital staff. The staff spends so much of their time here we felt we should give them a decent place to relax." Meagan opened the door of the cafeteria and held it for Katherine. "Elizabeth mentioned you joined her for dinner last night," she said.

"Yes," Katherine replied with a faint smile. The heavy darkness that enveloped Katherine's mind slowly began to scatter in the lively presence of Meagan Sullivan—and the mention of Elizabeth Nix pushed it farther away. "I think Governor Nix took pity on me last night. I must have looked quite disconcerted by yesterday afternoon,

Blown Away
© 2006 by The Haworth Press, Inc. All rights reserved.
doi:10.1300/5706_18

after spending all day in orientation." They each picked up a tray at the beginning of the line and slid them past the bacon and eggs. "But Elizabeth managed to salvage at least part of the evening for me," Katherine continued. "She was especially gracious. Elizabeth must be very popular with the people here."

"Yes, she is. Of course, there are those who attack her policies, many of whom have no obligation to the truth—which is the one thing Elizabeth has always used as her political moral compass, even when it wasn't advantageous to do so. I'd say her most fierce critics are those who insist she's a socialist," Meagan said, and glanced up for Katherine's reaction.

Katherine looked unfazed, or at least unconcerned.

Meagan turned to the fruit section as she continued. "There's a very vocal faction in the Territory that maintains Elizabeth is socialist—as if there's nothing worse in the world." An edge of irritation crept into Meagan's voice. "And we have a small group of physicians here at Bayside who are among the nastiest." Meagan pulled a couple of bananas from a bunch and put them on her tray. "The conservatives may see things that way, but when Elizabeth and I made the decision to give this Territory a shot we decided we would do everything possible to pursue policies that would not leave any of the people behind. We thought we owed that to them, especially after they put enough faith in us to come here and start their lives over."

Katherine put a bowl of mixed melons on her tray. She nodded occasionally as Meagan continued her Elizabeth Nix sales pitch. Katherine supposed it was now just a natural habit. After all their years in the Territory, Meagan just sold Elizabeth to others by instinct. Katherine understood. In her husband's world of high-stakes politics the lines of friendship and political promotion were usually blurred, though she remembered coming home from more than one A-list party, plotting a way to avoid the next one. She didn't really like most of the people, and the conversations always bored her, but Katherine never showed it. From Meagan, though, the sales pitch seemed genuine.

Meagan filled a glass with skim milk and set it on her tray, still pitching, "Elizabeth has an ability to connect with people as individuals. I swear that woman can talk anybody into doing anything, or at least into giving it their best shot. And she's just as comfortable talking with the guy in the doughnut shop as to the governor of Florida." Meagan turned to Katherine with amused eyes. "She says the guy in the doughnut shop has a better story to tell anyway," Meagan said with a quick wink.

"I can understand that," Katherine smiled and nodded. "After spending time with the politicians my husband worked with I would say I feel the same way."

Meagan set her tray on the checkout counter, paid for both breakfasts, and led Katherine to a table in the corner. They sat down, and Katherine spoke first, "Last night at the restaurant Elizabeth spoke to so many people I would believe she knows everyone here by first name."

"Well, she does. And it helps," Meagan joked. She picked up one of the bananas and peeled it thoughtfully. "Knowing everyone—and living on about four or five hours sleep a night," Meagan grumbled. "I've told her she needs more sleep, but she swears she doesn't. As long as I've known her she's been that way. But, with her schedule, I suppose it works out." Meagan sliced the banana onto her cereal, frowning as she focused on the knife-edge she moved quickly down the fruit. "Unfortunately, long hours are nothing unusual for many of us here in the Territory. And we probably expect the most from our people in the medical field," she said glancing at Katherine. "As soon as you're settled I'd like to talk to you about placing you on a research rotation."

"Yes," Katherine replied. "What can you tell me about the rotation concept? Yesterday's briefing at orientation was sketchy."

"Well, let's see. I suppose I should start with the basics," Megan answered. "As you know, all medical professionals work for the Territory, so the Department of Human Health will assign your workplace and schedule, as we've already done. In addition to that, as a research professional you'll be asked to work on a six-week rotation once a year. During those six weeks you'll be working on either a new or ongoing project. Either way you'll be focusing totally on one project. Many of those days you'll be pulling fourteen- to sixteen-hour shifts." Meagan paused to gage Katherine's reaction.

Katherine returned an undaunted nod.

Meagan continued. "Once you're in a rotation, the only leave you'll be allowed is for emergencies. And," she said with a smile, "if you want more, for a nice bonus you can voluntarily be reassigned to another rotation of four to six weeks. With your skills, I'm sure several rotation team leaders will be after you."

"Lucky me," Katherine deadpanned. She looked down and pushed her fork into a bite of melon. "It's not as if I'll have anything else to do." Katherine's distant eyes fixed on the honeydew at the end of her fork. "As a matter of fact, the sooner you get me on a project, the better." She chewed slowly as her eyes flashed a trace of anger.

Meagan read Katherine's anger exactly. "Have you heard from your family?"

"No," Katherine replied. She stabbed another piece of melon. "Thomas doesn't want me to talk to my children. In fact, he doesn't want me to have anything to do with them now," she said and bit the melon forcefully. Though her words weren't totally true, the effect of the separation was the same.

Meagan studied Katherine for a moment, checking her sincerity, and then she said, "I understand. It must be very hard. I'm sorry."

"Thank you for saying so," Katherine replied. "But there's nothing I can really do about it, except to stay busy."

"All right, then," Meagan said. "There is a liver cancer project I'd like to have you working on in about six weeks, if you're ready."

"I'll be ready," Katherine said. "I know the Territory has had a number of very successful cancer projects in the past few years. I'll be looking forward to it."

"Good," Meagan said. "Elizabeth will be pleased to hear you'll be on that project team. Cancer research is one of her priorities. Although we've made a lot of money off the cancer treatments we've developed, it's more personal for Elizabeth. She lost her partner to ovarian cancer."

Katherine suddenly looked up at Meagan. "I'm sorry to hear that," she said sincerely. "You said she lost her partner? Were they married?" Katherine asked cautiously, still uncertain of the terminology.

"Yes. They were married five years before Virginia died," Meagan replied. "And that was three years ago. It nearly killed Elizabeth. After Gin died Elizabeth buried herself in her work like never before. She's still not completely out of it."

"You said her name was Virginia? What was she like?" Katherine asked, now deeply curious of the woman who captured Elizabeth's heart.

"She was several years older than Elizabeth," Meagan began softly, "and as independent a woman as I've ever met. Her full name was Virginia Avalon, and she made a living as horse breeder and trainer. She even worked with a few of the thoroughbreds down in Orlando. Elizabeth met Gin one morning when I dragged her out to the stables to go riding." Meagan's eyes grew distant and her lips turned into a melancholy smile. "Virginia was standing at a stall at the front of the stable and Elizabeth said good morning to her. Virginia turned around, and, *by god*, she was so beautiful. Gin smiled, returned the good morning, and picked up a shovel to muck a stall. I knew by the look on Elizabeth's face that she was *gone*. Virginia was still at the stables when we got back from riding. Elizabeth is not one to beat around the bush when she wants something, so she went up to Virginia and introduced herself. Ten months later they got married."

"And then she lost her," Katherine said.

"Yes, she did. Elizabeth hasn't been on a horse since the day Gin died. In fact, she won't go near a stable. She says even the smell of a barn still bothers her."

Meagan sat quiet for a moment, and then smiled to move on from the memories. Her eyes were warm as she looked back to Katherine. "Speaking of horses, do you ride?"

"Yes," Katherine replied. "As a matter of fact I do ride a little. Virginia is horse country, after all."

"Yes, I suppose it is. Well, Jessica Thompson and I are planning to ride in a park near her place this Saturday if you would like to join us."

"It sounds nice. I'd love to," Katherine replied

"Good. And," Meagan said with a teasing smile, "you will get to meet the notorious Jessica Thompson."

Chapter 19

Katherine drew the slow horse—a big bay gelding quarter horse named Zack. At the stable Jessica warned Katherine that Zack would have to be pushed to stay up, but after a couple of rounds with him Katherine simply decided to give in. It was far too beautiful a day to have to work at anything, and Zack instinctively knew to follow the white path that meandered through a green carpet of grass spreading in all directions below towering columns of longleaf pines.

Eventually, the structured order of the pines melted into the thick tangle of vines and shrubs that lined Alligator Creek. Katherine reined Zack onto the bridge across and reveled in the relaxing rhythm of the solid clop, clop, clop, of Zack's hooves echoing up from wooden boards. From the height of the bridge Katherine searched the dense, snarled vegetation along the edges of the creek bank for a glimpse of an alligator, or a heron, or the stark white feathers of an ibis. She spotted a young gator sunning at the end of a fat, hollow log just as Zack stepped off the bridge.

Katherine rode on, and in a moment heard the unmistakable sound of Meagan's laughter. She nudged Zack into a trot to cross the field and join Meagan and Jessica where they waited by a small lake with the horses.

"There you are," Meagan said as Katherine dismounted beside them. "We were just discussing whether we should double back for you."

"Oh no," Katherine said. "I was enjoying this beautiful country. This is very different from the mountains of Virginia."

"Or Idaho," Jessica offered pleasantly, coolly covering her annoyance that Katherine Hopkins had somehow ended up on one of her horses.

Katherine smiled back and noticed Jessica's jeans were deeper blue from the knees down.

 doi:10.1300/5706_19

Jessica looked down to her wet pants with an aggravated grin. "I guess you're wondering how this happened," she said. She reached around the neck of her chestnut mare and gave her a pat. "Well, Trump here has a nasty habit of taking me for a swim every time I ride her to the water for a drink. So I was showing Meagan how I had trained her not to do that anymore." Jessica grabbed the wet pants just below her knee. "As you can see, I still have more training to do."

"It was quite amusing," Meagan offered. She held the back of her hand to her mouth to suppress her laughter and said, "Jess said, 'watch this' and reined Trump right up to the edge of the lake. Trump hesitated, stomped twice, and then walked proudly into the water." Meagan's laughter spewed out in a burst. The rest of the story came in barely discernible spurts. "Jessica is yelling and cussing and trying to get her feet out of the stirrups and by that time Trump is practically up to her shoulders, steadily walking deeper and deeper. Jess finally stopped her just before the water got to her withers."

"She wasn't *that* deep," Jessica protested.

Meagan's eyes furrowed in doubt. "Darn close," she teased. She rubbed a tear from her eye as she looked back at Katherine. "If it's okay with you, we'll stop here for lunch." She nodded toward Jessica. "The great horse trainer here needs to let her pants dry or she'll get chapped," Meagan said with a quick, playful wink.

They settled on a blanket under the ceiling of a giant live oak, and after wrestling with water-soaked boots, Jessica wiggled out of her clinging wet jeans.

Katherine watched Jessica casually walk sans pants around the tree, searching for a sunny branch to hang her jeans. She noticed there was total freedom in Jessica's manner, and realized Jessica's freedom arose from the same freedom she had felt since being with these women today, the kind of freedom she hadn't experienced since she was a girl, the freedom that came only from being totally uninhibited by the sexual mores shaped by the presence of men, or even the thought or concern of them. Today there were no deep, overpowering voices, insisting on command of the conversation, nor any wives holding back their true opinions to avoid their husband's judgment, or obsessive concerns centered on trying to please someone else. In this place, a woman could be just who she was, and speak and think and act just for herself. In fact, it was expected of her. Her opinions, her choices, were totally her own. She was—equal.

"DID YOU FIND a place to live?" Jessica asked Katherine before taking a bite of her lunch apple.

Katherine smiled slightly as she shook a handful of cereal into her hand. "Yes. Tim Littleton helped me find a place in just a couple of days," she replied. "It's a condo right on the beach. I'll be renting, but I have the option to buy later."

"Yeah, that's a popular deal for folks here in the Territory." Jessica took another bite of the apple and watched a Frisbee game that was starting down at the lake. "Gays seem to want to keep their real estate options open. We tend to move around a lot. I don't know if that's because it was what we were used to doing in the States or because we're just born restless. My personal belief is that it's a weird cultural pattern left from years ago, when people subconsciously moved around to avoid being outed."

"Or to try to accommodate two careers," Meagan offered. She leaned back on the blanket and looked over at Katherine. "The woman I'm seeing is a mining engineer in Arizona," she said before lazily turning her eyes back to focus on the cloudless sky. "Jill snuck into her father's mine when she was a little girl, and hasn't really left since." Meagan smiled for a moment, thinking of Jill. "She won't leave her career and I won't leave the Territory—so we rack up a lot of frequent flyer miles."

"Jill is coming for your birthday, right?" Jessica asked.

"Of course," Meagan said. "She's staying a few weeks after, too. The mine she's at now is winding down before shifting to reclamation, so she'll have a few weeks break before she has to go back."

"Maybe you can change her mind and get her to stay this time," Jessica said with a suggestive smile. "A lot can happen in a few weeks."

JESSICA'S JEANS DRIED to a tolerable dampness and she slid them back on. Still barefoot she walked back to the blanket to take up the challenge of putting on wet boots. She rolled on her back and tugged at the sides of each boot, her face twisted and grimacing with the effort.

Meagan watched with an amused smile, and then sat up to look around. "I've got to be at a meeting at four," she said to no one in particular. "We'd better start back."

At the picket line they untied the horses and turned them toward the trail. Jessica swung her leg over Trump and looked back to Katherine. "By the way, be sure to call if you need any help with moving into your condo," she began.

"I won't," Katherine interrupted sharply. "My husband saw to that. I'm lucky he let me keep the few things I have with me. I'll have to start over with everything. I just wish I could figure out a way to make him pay for it all."

Katherine reined Zack toward the trail and swiftly nudged his side, moving the big bay out in a trot. A hundred yards down the trail Jessica and Meagan caught up and the three horses slowed to a walk.

"I'm sorry if I touched a nerve," Jessica offered.

"No, it's okay." Katherine returned an apologetic smile. "I shouldn't have been short with you. I do appreciate your offer."

And Katherine truly did appreciate it. Jessica's open hospitality had not been what she expected. Before today Katherine had never actually met Jessica Thompson, but she thought she knew her well enough. A few months ago Thomas brought home a fifteen-page briefing on Jessica, including the history of her Supreme Court case, her political activism, and a list of the criminals she had defended in private practice back in Oregon. Jessica Thompson—militant liberal against all that was good and wholesome. Katherine understood propaganda, but until now she found no reason to doubt what she had read.

It wasn't only Jessica that was not as Katherine expected. She could say, in fact, that the entire Territory was not as she expected. From all she had been told before coming here she felt certain that everyday life in the Territory would linger on the edge of bizarre, the product of a culture lacking necessary restraint or order, ruled primarily by personal whims—mostly the libido- of individuals. The "gay world" was never familiar to her in the least, even through popular culture. In her life there was little time for television, and if there had been Thomas would not watch *those* shows. She knew of no gay friends or relatives, and all she knew of the "gay lifestyle" she had seen from news clips or had been told in her briefings before coming here.

In medical school Katherine studied a number of clinical theories about homosexuality, but as a pathologist she never really made true connections to any patients or their lives. Her biggest adjustment since being in the Territory was getting accustomed to seeing men hold hands with other men as they walked casually down the street, or watching two women kiss briefly before they parted. For a few days her gut reaction had been to quickly turn away, but she had gradually grown quite used to the change.

"We'll be coming back into my property just around the next curve," Jessica said after they had ridden a couple of miles. "Meagan and I have a little tradition of racing from here to the paddock gate. If you don't want to run, you may want to wait here. Otherwise Zack will want to take off with you. He doesn't hang back when there's running involved."

"I'm game," Katherine said. "It sounds like fun. And," she said boldly, with a pat to Zack's thick neck, "I'm betting Zack and I will be the first ones home."

"You're on," Jessica said with a challenging smile.

They turned into the pasture and Jessica made the first move. "Hyaa!" she yelled with a swift kick to Trump's side. Sand flew from Trump's hooves as Jessica gave her full rein.

Zack threw up his head, pranced once, and jumped into a full gallop as Katherine dug her heels into his sides. With three more quick kicks she pushed him for the speed to catch Trump. In a determined squint Katherine threw herself forward and lowered her body over Trump's neck. Pounding hooves churned furiously beneath her as her racing mount stretched his long body in an all-out run for the lead. One hundred and fifty feet from the gate, Katherine leaned her full weight onto the stirrups. Closing in on Trump, she looked ahead to plan her pass. Then she caught a distant glimpse of Elizabeth casually leaning against the fence rail ahead. For a brief moment Katherine's eyes stuck on Elizabeth, and in that second Katherine missed seeing the small ditch ten feet away.

Without breaking stride Zack made his jump, landing solidly on the other side—and sending Katherine flying. She spun across the grass and sand, throwing out a cloud of dust that grew with each head-over-heel tumble. On the third roll she stopped flat on her back and lay dead still for a long moment before she shook her head and sat up, leaning on an elbow to catch her breath. Her shoulder burned with pain.

"Are you all right?" Katherine heard Elizabeth ask.

Katherine swung around to see Elizabeth kneeling beside her. Her face flushed red. In the distance Katherine heard the faint pounding of feet as Jessica and Meagan ran toward them.

"Yes. I think so," Katherine said as she rubbed her shoulder and tried to stand.

"Wait. Don't try to get up just yet," Elizabeth said. "You landed pretty hard." She reached toward Katherine's collar. "Mind if I take a look at that shoulder?"

"No!" Katherine replied hastily. "I'm sure it's fine," she said softly as her lips turned up slightly in an awkward, apologetic smile. She shifted again to try to stand.

"Wait a minute," Meagan said as she walked up from behind them, still breathing hard to catch her wind. "Let me take a quick look at you before you stand up."

Katherine looked over as Meagan kneeled beside her. "Really, I'm okay, but it doesn't look like you're going to let me go anywhere until you do."

"You're right about that," Meagan replied. She ran her hands down Katherine's legs and across her back, then pulled back Katherine's shirt collar and let out a low whistle.

"That one's gonna need ice," Meagan said, gently pulling the shirt back over Katherine's shoulder. She lightly moved her hands across Katherine's arms and ribs to finish the check for fractures. "Well, it looks like you escaped this one intact," Meagan said. "But you'll want to get that shoulder X-rayed as soon as you get a chance. You've already got a mean bruise there. There may be a hairline fracture. Other than that, everything appears to be all right."

Elizabeth held out her hand to help Katherine up. Katherine looked at the hand, and then her eyes followed the arm up to the warm smile and dark eyes looking directly at her. Katherine reached up and grabbed Elizabeth's hand, and just as the first time they met, Elizabeth's touch sent an unsettling wave rushing through Katherine's body. Katherine's eyes fixed on Elizabeth's as she pulled her up, and Katherine's face filled with a hot flush.

Damn. *Why?* Katherine rebuked herself. Using one hand Katherine dusted the sand from her shirt and pants and walked with the other three to the paddock. She led Zack around the paddock to cool him off, and then into a stall to brush and feed him. She knew Elizabeth was watching her, and though her shoulder throbbed with pain she said nothing and tried not to favor the arm as she worked. Still, the pain slowed her down.

"Sorry it took me so long," Katherine said ten minutes later as she emerged from the stall. She walked toward the tack room door where Elizabeth waited with Jessica and Meagan. "I was enjoying being in a barn again. It's been a while."

"Just let me know when you want to come back," Jessica offered kindly as they walked out of the barn. "You're welcome anytime. My horses need to be ridden and I haven't had much time to ride lately. Between my job, my spouse, and Elizabeth's demands, I don't have time to breathe."

"Hey," Elizabeth protested. "You can resign. . . ."

"Yeah, like you'd let her," Meagan interrupted. She nudged Elizabeth with a cool smile.

"I'll keep the offer in mind," Katherine said to Jessica as they reached the driveway. Katherine walked to the Volvo and smiled as she pulled open the car door, pushing down the pain to keep it from showing on her face. "Thanks again for today."

"You bet," Jessica replied.

Elizabeth watched as Katherine gingerly eased into the Volvo. After a quick smile Katherine turned the car around and drove up the drive without looking back. She turned left out of the driveway and disappeared down the road.

"So, you've decided to visit the stables again? You're taking this buddy-up-with-Katherine thing pretty seriously, huh?" Meagan teased, rubbing Elizabeth's shoulder. "I'm going to take a shower. Don't worry, I'll fill you in on what I think about Ms. Katherine on the drive to Tallahassee," Meagan said, and turned for the house.

Elizabeth smiled and slid her hands into her pockets. "Well, what about you, Jess? I know you have an opinion of Dr. Hopkins. What do you think? Are you still of the opinion that Dr. Hopkins shouldn't be in the Territory?"

"It's hard saying," Jessica said. She looked back at Elizabeth with eyes squinted to the afternoon sun and her forehead furrowed in serious thought. "I spent most of the day absolutely convinced that she should go back to the States. She didn't seem to want to interact with Meagan and me at all. Most of the morning she hung back and rode by herself, and when we talked about our pasts in the States she didn't have anything to say. It would seem that after all she had been through she'd want to talk about it. Once she did say something derogatory about her husband, but she never mentioned anything that would indicate she had a gay past." Jessica paused and intensely fixed her eyes on Elizabeth. "But then I saw the way she looked at you when you reached down to help her up."

"So you noticed it?" Elizabeth asked.

"I couldn't help but notice it," Jessica replied. "The look in her eyes, the way her face flushed—you can't fake that kind of reaction. I don't even know if she's even aware of it, but there's definitely something there."

Elizabeth looked down and nodded slowly, lightly kicking against the gravel.

"And the way you looked back at her, I think maybe there's something there for you, too." Elizabeth abruptly looked up and saw Jessica's eyes flash their familiar warning, but then her face softened as she continued. "Look, Elizabeth, I'm not suggesting anything. If you want, ask her out, fall in love, whatever, it's fine with me. I'm just asking you to be careful. If she's not legit and she gets you, she's got all of us."

ON THE DRIVE back to the hotel the pain in Katherine's shoulder subsided to a dull, throbbing ache, but as she tried to lift a stack of medical journals from the front seat of the Volvo the sharp pains again shot down her arm.

Five thick stacks of journals already covered the desktop in Katherine's hotel room. Every night since she had been in the Territory she brought home another year's volumes of the Territory's inch-and-a-half thick quarterly medical research journals and worked into the late hours, sipping hot tea and poring over every article. So far she had found two MIC articles, but both of them discussed methods for early diagnosis rather than treatment. Each night her break from the journals came at just after nine o'clock when she would call Thomas for her fifteen hollow minutes of watching her children while they slept.

Today, though, that was to change. Thomas promised that by tonight high resolution cameras would be hidden in every room of their house and every corner of the yard, giving Katherine the ability to watch her children whenever she wanted. No longer would her secret visits be limited to those few minutes after nine p.m. when her husband would slip into Ellen or Jacob's room with the Web camera. From today on Thomas had said, she could go to a restricted Web site anytime, 24-7, to watch the daily activities of her family.

"The next best thing to being there," Thomas had reassured her.

Katherine tossed the journals onto the hotel bed and reached for her laptop. She flipped up the screen and pushed the "Home" icon. "Hello, Thomas." She smiled as her husband appeared. She gently swung her aching legs up and leaned against the headboard. "Have you got the cameras working? Is the Web site ready?"

Thomas turned his eyes away. "No, Kate, I'm sorry. They're not ready yet," he said solemnly.

Katherine's eyes narrowed into a glare. "The children are at your mother's?"

"Yes," Thomas answered. "She picked them up this morning."

"How's Jacob?"

"He's had a couple of really good days. No headaches or fever."

Katherine breathed out a sigh and turned a slight smile. "Good," she said. "What about Ellen?"

"She's doing well. Her schoolwork is good and she's playing with her friends. She was excited about going to her grandmother's today."

"Does she ask about me?"

Thomas hesitated. "I think she's trying to be brave for her brother, but I can see that she misses you."

"In other words, she hasn't."

"Not yet."

Katherine's eyes again narrowed on her husband, "That's exactly why those cameras are so important," she said. "When I come back home I'm going to have to convince Ellen that I didn't abandon her. She's got to know that I was with her every day, and the only way I'll be able to do that is to share things I saw her do, and she'll know that I was there, watching over her."

"I agree," Thomas replied.

"You agree?" Katherine questioned. "If you agree then why didn't you keep your promise to have the cameras ready by this weekend?"

"I tried, Kate." Thoma argued. "Jason promised me he would have a couple of technicians here yesterday to install them, but there was a problem setting up a global videoconference that Jason started at eight this morning. The technician crew ended up working at the studio all night. They just couldn't free anybody up."

"And what about this morning?" Katherine asked coolly.

"No one's working today. As I said, most of them worked all night."

"Most of them?" Katherine asked, her voice growing hard. "There weren't two available who could do it today? Or doesn't Jason think it's worth the overtime?" Katherine asked sarcastically. "What's with him anyway, Thomas? The way he's been acting lately, you'd think I really did have an affair."

"Don't be ridiculous, Kate," Thomas retorted. He looked back at her with the condescending expression Katherine knew all too well and could never stand. "Jason just has a lot going on right now. Presi-

dent Harkins keeps him busy, not to mention everything else he has
to deal with."

Katherine silently stared at her husband. *Everything else he has to deal
with.* She was in no mood for excuses, or conversation about Jason
Johnson, or any further conversation with Thomas about anything for
that matter.

"Look, Thomas, I'm just going to go for now," she said. "I fell off a
horse this afternoon and I need a hot ba—"

"What? You fell off a horse!" Thomas interrupted.

"Yes, I fell off a horse. And it was no big deal, so don't get so upset.
The horse jumped and I didn't; that's all. I'm not injured, just a little
sore."

"Look, Kate," Thomas possessively began, "you know I don't like
the idea of you socializing with that crowd. The idea of you getting so
friendly with them bothers me—a lot I should say."

"Thomas, we've already discussed this," Katherine said calmly, refusing to argue. "Every contact I make is one step closer to finding
what they have and getting Jacob well and me back home. You're just
going to have to learn to deal with it. Now, if you and Jason can find
the time in your busy schedules I'd like for you to get those cameras
up in the children's rooms at the least."

"I'll be sure it's done Monday," Thomas grunted.

"Good. You can tell Jason that if those cameras aren't up by Monday night, I just might come home," Katherine warned him.

"They'll be up," Thomas assured.

"I'll call later," Katherine said, and clicked off without a good-bye
or an I love you. The throbbing in her shoulder pounded incessantly,
and her body ached from the first horseback ride in six months. She
could ice the shoulder later, but for now she wanted warmth. She
brewed a mug of tea and filled the bathtub with streaming water and
bath salts. She winced as she slowly took off her shirt and checked the
bruise on her left shoulder. The deep purple of it was as big as a fist
and ragged margins of blue and brown radiated to the center of her
back.

"Nasty," she whispered and turned from the mirror. She slid off her
pants and stepped into the tub. Sore muscles relaxed as she leaned

back into the chest-high water. Resting her neck on the cool porcelain rim she closed her eyes. There was Elizabeth, standing over her, looking down with haunting eyes as she reached down to lift Katherine up from the sand and grass of Jessica's pasture.

Katherine sat up and she grabbed the sides of the tub, clutching onto anything to keep from falling further into the hole of confusion that suddenly seized her. She forced her mind to Thomas, her one true security, but she only remembered his hollow promises. She swallowed hard and leaned back into the warmth of the water with a deep, steadying breath. Again she closed her eyes.

There was Elizabeth again, looking down at her, but now with such assurance, her dark eyes telling Katherine to take her hand. Then two fingers of Elizabeth's hand slowly twitched twice, assuring Katherine to grab hold. Their fingers touched, and Katherine eased down into the water, a contented smile slowly turning on her lips.

ONE FLOOR DOWN and two rooms over in the Ashley Inn two men sat in a quiet room, watching iridescent colors in the shape of a human body flowing over a computer screen.

"It's really amazing how the infrared of her body goes up when she lays in the bathtub," said the man with the plump round face, round wire-rimmed glasses, and thinning brown hair. His name was Larry Robinson, and he was one from the legion of Exit for Life, an organization with the sole purpose of torturing homosexuals with promises of a "cure." Larry sat in a roomy office chair with a bag of Double Stuf Oreos wedged beside him.

The man with him, Paul Harman, was a few years older, but his sparse beard and smooth, olive skin disguised his age. Paul leaned up to take a closer look at the screen over the shoulder of his partner, "Yeah, it got more intense in the last few minutes. I wonder what she's thinking about." Paul stood straight and walked over to the wet bar to pour Canadian whiskey over ice.

"I'm guessing it's the cameras," Larry offered. "She's pretty steamed about that. I'd better let Jason know he needs to be sure they get installed on Monday," he said and pulled a cookie from the bag and stuffed it in his mouth.

"Call him tonight," Paul said. "How are we doing for space on the drive?"

"We probably need to download before she goes to bed," Larry replied as he pulled out another cookie. "I wanted to ask you if I could take night shift tonight," he asked before taking a bite. "I want to go to church in Tallahassee tomorrow."

Paul took a sip of his drink. "Yeah, whatever." He looked across the room at the monitor before turning up the whiskey, taking the rest down in one healthy swallow. He reached for the bottle again and poured another finger. "This place getting to you?"

Larry swallowed and reached again into the cookie bag. "Yes, it is bothering me a little bit. I mean, when I see these people, it just makes me ashamed of all the things I used to do and the way I used to live before I got saved."

"I guess it's tough for you," Paul said reflexively, though he really couldn't care less. He swirled the whiskey around his glass and took another sip.

"It is. But when Jason explained everything to me, I just had to do this. He told me you guys needed someone to help you navigate the gay community, and I guess he thought I was the right person for the job. And it's just *so* important—what Jason and President Harkins are doing. I mean, if all these gay people can come down here and do whatever they please and feel so comfortable about it, they'll never get saved."

KATHERINE LINGERED NEARLY an hour in the tub. She felt steady again as she dried her freshly sunned skin. She avoided another look at the bruise as she pulled on her robe. She brushed wet hair away from her face as she considered dinner. There was enough in the refrigerator to put together a salad. She was mixing the greens when the doorbell rang.

"Who is it?" Katherine said as she crossed the floor and pulled her robe tighter.

"Delivery," a woman's voice answered.

Katherine lowered her eye to the peephole and saw a young woman patiently standing in the hall, holding a towering bouquet of purple and white orchids mixed with flowing fern fronds. Katherine smiled and swung open the door, thankful that Thomas had been thinking of her—wanting to apologize for his broken promise, for everything.

"Dr. Katherine Hopkins?" the delivery woman asked with a polite smile.

"Yes."

"These are for you."

"Thank you. Would you mind bringing them in?"

Katherine held the door as the woman walked into the room. "Just set them on the counter," Katherine said. She grabbed her purse and took a five from her wallet as the delivery woman set up the bouquet and rearranged a couple of stems shuffled in the drive over.

"Have a good day," Katherine said as she handed the woman the bill.

"You too, Dr. Hopkins," the woman said and walked out the door.

Katherine lightly fingered through the ferns, looking for the small card that would have the message from Thomas. She found the card and pulled it out. There was no florist insignia, but Katherine thought little of that as she opened the card.

The note wasn't from Thomas. It was a plain white note, handwritten in a script she did not recognize.

Dear Katherine,
   I thought you might need a lift after the nasty fall you took this afternoon. I hope these will help you to feel a little better. If you need anything, don't hesitate to call. I am looking forward to seeing you next Saturday.
Until then, my best regards,
Elizabeth.

Chapter 20

A steady rain fell on the balcony awning of the condo Katherine had moved into less than a week ago. The condo wasn't bad. The kitchen glistened with new tile and shiny chrome and black appliances, and there was a spacious home office that was wired to the hilt. The den and bedroom opened to a view of the gulf, but the selling point for Katherine was the full-length balcony, half of which was a screened sleeping porch.

At seven-thirty Katherine flipped on the coffeepot and settled onto to the couch to watch a few minutes of the Saturday morning routine of her children.

True to his word, Thomas had the cameras and Web site up and running by Monday night. Katherine came home from her first real day at work, anxious to spend the entire night watching her family. When the images appeared on her monitor she sat in the lonely quiet of her den, watching her children play, laugh, scream, and sometimes cry with no way to talk to them, or to touch them. Katherine quickly found long sessions of watching her family to be unbearable, but the Web site was all of them she had, so she kept the sessions short, but frequent.

Katherine sipped her coffee as her laptop flickered to life. Immediately an urgent message flashed onto the screen. Katherine clicked on the icon and waited through a two-second panic for the message to appear.

"Good morning, Kate," Thomas said. "I'm sorry for the message. I didn't want to wake you. Listen, I have to catch an early flight to California. There's an abortion battle brewing in the California legislature and Jason needs me out there. I'll probably be gone most of the week. The children are at my mother's. I'll call you tonight."

Katherine watched him disappear and stared at the screen. If she could find a way to pull Thomas through the screen and choke him to death she would have. They had a deal. As long as Katherine was in the Territory Robert agreed to never leave the children. Now there was no way for Katherine to watch them, not for six days.

Katherine slammed the screen down and tossed the laptop onto the couch. She walked to the window and watched the dark clouds rolling in from the gulf. "Don't bother calling me tonight, Thomas," she said in a tight, angry whisper. "I won't be here."

BY ONE O'CLOCK the rain had cleared and Elizabeth strolled out onto the porch of the governor's mansion, looking over the final preparations for Meagan's birthday party. Jill Akers followed, sipping a beer from the bottle.

"Forty-four," Elizabeth said. "And she's never looked better."

"I don't see how she could have," Jill replied with a smile. Jill's dark brown hair flew about in the steady wind that blew away the morning's cold front.

"I'm happy to hear you're staying a few weeks. Meagan needs a break," Elizabeth said. "I told her that after tonight I don't want to see her for at least a week. I'm counting on you to make sure I don't."

"Gladly," Jill said as they walked, their footsteps clipping across the green painted boards of the porch that wrapped around three-quarters of the mansion. "She's looking forward to this party this afternoon." Jill stopped and looked down with a slight smile as she studied her beer label. "She made me leave just so she could get ready."

Elizabeth returned an understanding nod. Meagan had left Elizabeth waiting plenty of times, and sometimes the first sight of Meagan would still rock Elizabeth unexpectedly. After all their years together, on certain days Meagan walked into a room and stirred Elizabeth in ways she would force herself to ignore. Surely if a love affair between them was to have ever been, that time had passed.

"I'm sure it will be worth the wait," Elizabeth said as she turned her eyes up to the sky. "And it looks like the weather's going to cooperate. It'll be a good night for a celebration."

"Meagan tells me Katherine Hopkins may be coming," Jill said cautiously.

"Yes. She's been invited." Elizabeth sifted uneasily and looked out across the lawn. "Hopefully she won't cause too much of a stir. A lot of people are still troubled by her."

"Maybe they should be," Jill replied.

Elizabeth flashed questioning eyes at Jill. "What makes you say so?"

"Meagan told me about the difficulty you two had with the decision to accept her application," Jill said. Her eyes narrowed on Elizabeth with the steady gaze of a certain opinion. "I personally don't see any reason to take the risk. Let the States deal with her."

"We did seriously consider that," Elizabeth assured. "In the end it was purely an economic decision. We need her research skills."

"Ah yes, skills and economics. That's why she's living in the Territory and I'm not."

KATHERINE DROVE THROUGH the tunnel of trees lining the winding drive to the governor's mansion. Her heart kicked hard with the thought of seeing Elizabeth, and pounded harder as she drove through the final sweeping curve to the first sight of the mansion. Slowing to a near stop Katherine stared at the antebellum structure standing boldly on the highest hill to be found for miles, overlooking a sea of green grass, and flanked on one side by a meandering river. She drove on through the final alley of live oaks, their branches arched together to form a graceful ceiling that ended at the brick front drive.

Katherine stopped at the valet and handed her the keys. Immediately Katherine felt the staring eyes of the fifty or so people gathered on the porch of the mansion. Though her body urged to take flight, Katherine set her mind and walked steadily toward the porch. Grabbing onto a single, fading thread of resolve she walked across the porch and into the house, returning the looks to as many as she could.

"Makes you feel like a piece of meat, don't it?" a loud voice screeched as soon as Katherine walked through the door.

Katherine turned on a heel to the smiling face of the woman she had last seen on the governor's computer screen. The woman looked much better now. Salt-and-pepper hair was brushed back in a short ponytail, and her face was scrubbed clean from dirt or tobacco. A crisply pressed light blue shirt was tucked into a new pair of tan Carhartt work jeans.

"Don't pay any attention to them rude bitches. Just act like they're cruisin' you." Henri's eyes danced as she smiled at Katherine, obviously pleased by her own advice.

Katherine smiled back, "You must be Henri."

Henri's jaw dropped and she stared at Katherine in bewilderment, "How'd you know?"

Katherine smiled again. "I saw you a couple of weeks ago when you were talking to Elizabeth," she answered, feeling her anxious heart begin to calm.

"Oh," Henri said. "Well, no need for introductions then. I sure know who you are. Let me show you around the house, and where the alcohol is, too," she said with a quick grin.

Katherine nodded as she looked around the foyer. A vibrant ceramic tile mosaic of the Seal of the Territory covered the floor directly beneath her feet. In front of her a grand staircase curled down to the polished hardwood floors of the hallway that connected open double doorways on her left and right. The doorway to the left led into a formal sitting room complete with a baby grand piano and three clusters of antique chairs, couches, and love seats covered in rich gold, red, and blue tapestries. The doorway to the right opened into the thirty-guest dining room. Floor-to-ceiling windows lined the walls and looked out onto the wraparound porches that encircled both the top and bottom floors.

"Come on; this is the boring stuff." Henri took Katherine lightly by the arm and whisked her down the hall, speaking rapidly, but as bored as a burned-out tour guide. "It's obviously Louisiana architecture. God, this place was a pain in the ass to renovate. When we found it, it was in shambles. We had to strip all the walls and floors and replace half the studs and joists, and the roof leaked like a sieve." They walked around the right side of the staircase into a short hall. Henri pushed through a full-length swinging door. "Here's the kitchen."

Katherine quickly peeked into a commercial kitchen swarming with caterers piling silver trays with hors d'oeuvres, pouring champagne, or emptying tubs of dirty plates and glasses.

"Over here are the restrooms and a little sleeping quarters for caterers. There's a library and sunroom through there," Henri pointed. She
walked to a hidden door at the back of the stairway and opened it.
"Come on, I'll show you the good part."

Katherine looked at her warily, but sensed Henri was harmless. She
followed her down the narrow stairs and into a basement.

"This is my little cave," Henri said with pleasure. "Most people
don't get to see this part of the house 'cause Elizabeth says it's her
hideaway, but I don't think she'd mind you seein' it. I think she likes
you a good bit. She doesn't send her best orchids to people she doesn't
like."

Katherine felt her face flush, wondering what else Henri knew.

At the bottom of the stairs they turned left into a fully equipped
gym, complete with free weights and weight machines, a treadmill,
aerobic cycle, climbing machine, and a short resistance lap pool. On
the far end was a sauna and whirlpool hot tub.

"This is all Elizabeth's stuff. I don't need this shit. I work enough
during the day." Henri waved a dismissing hand at the gym and led
Katherine to the door on the right. "Here's my room," she said with a
wide smile as she opened the door.

Near the door an eight-seat card table and a pool table were centered in front of the cypress wood wet bar that filled the back wall. In
the far right corner a bank of electronic control panels stretched to the
ceiling. A semicircle of thickly cushioned reclining chairs and deep
couches faced the giant screen at the far end of the room.

"This is the best room in the whole damn territory," Henri smiled
as she looked around, taking in the wonder of it all. "And it's the only
reason I put up with Elizabeth's ass." She walked to an end table next
to the center recliner and picked up a remote control. "Check this
out." With the push of a button and the room suddenly filled with the
booming voice of Johnny Cash.

Henri smiled widely and flipped the music off. "I love Johnny
Cash," she said as she carefully put the remote back on the table.
"Maybe one day you can come to one of our real parties, like the one
we just had to watch the Super Bowl."

"Maybe so," Katherine smiled. "It sounds like fun."

"Yeah. Well, I guess we ought to get back to the one going on now," Henri said. She led Katherine out a back door and across the lawn toward the courtyard.

"Well, I want to thank you, Henri," Katherine said. "It was so nice of you to show me the rest of the house."

"Well, that's not really all of it," Henri said. "There's Elizabeth's living quarters upstairs. Maybe one day you'll get to see that, too," Henri teased with a genial wink.

Katherine returned an uncertain glance, finding the thought both thrilling and terrifying.

"Hello, Katherine," Meagan said as Katherine and Henri walked into the courtyard.

Katherine did not recognize the woman loosely holding Meagan's hand.

"This is the woman I told you about, Jill Akers," Meagan said. "Jill, this is Dr. Katherine Hopkins, and you know Henri."

Jill flashed a critical eye up and down the length of Katherine's body, and then held a steady gaze on her. "Good afternoon, Dr. Hopkins," Jill said coolly. The indifferent glare of Jill's icy blue eyes tore away the last twenty minutes of Henri's goodwill.

Meagan nudged Jill and smiled apologetically, "Jill and I are going for a walk down by the river. We'll catch you later?"

"Sure," Katherine replied.

As they strolled away, Henri looked at Katherine awkwardly, "Would you like something to drink? I was just going—"

"No. I'm fine," Katherine confidently reassured Henri, all the while repressing the urge to ask her to please stay.

Henri nodded amiably and walked away, sliding through laughing and talking groups of three or four before she melted into the crowd.

Katherine turned her attention to the decor of the courtyard, trying to ignore the condemning gazes and covered-mouthed whispers of the group of five that had just noticed her. She looked down to the aged bricks laid in circular patterns that formed the courtyard's foundation, and then followed the patterns up to the brick posts and the intricate wrought iron designs that adorned the post corners. Hanging pots of thick, trailing flowers hung from iron hooks above her, and curved railings outlined the clover-shaped terraces that rose six feet above a yard green with winter grass. Beyond the grass a hedgerow of mature trees lined the broad-banked river that flowed in the distance. Katherine wondered what it must be like for Elizabeth to be alone here in such a beautiful place. She imagined how it must have once been for Elizabeth and Virginia. Did they relax in this courtyard at night, or walk along the river at sunset? After Virginia was gone, how did Elizabeth endure such a place? How did she live in the immense solitude?

Katherine shook away the thoughts and cautiously turned back toward the curious five. They, like everyone else, had moved on to other interests. She felt safe enough now to brave another pass through the crowd, maybe to find Jessica, or an acquaintance from work, or maybe to see Henri again. Forcing a faint but assured smile, she walked back through the courtyard, allowing her eyes to wander just enough to search for a recognizable face. Once in a while she caught someone's eye and found a quick smile or a cool, aloof nod in return. She pushed on through the crowd and made her way up the side stairs toward the upper porch of the mansion. Topping the last stair, she spotted Elizabeth.

Three men stood in a circle with the governor. One of the men looked up and noticed Katherine, and then leaned in and said something to Elizabeth.

Elizabeth looked up and caught Katherine's eye, nodded once, gave her a weak half smile, and turned back to her group.

Katherine stood still, unsure of whether to even approach Elizabeth. It seemed apparent that Elizabeth had no desire to speak to her. Perhaps the governor believed Katherine was a political liability, that being seen again with Dr. Hopkins was a risk that Elizabeth would not want to take. But Elizabeth *had* invited her to this party. Katherine took a step forward. Elizabeth noticed and returned an indifferent glance before turning back to the three men.

The coolness in the glance left no room for doubt. Katherine spun around and hurried back down. She stopped on the bottom stair, desperately looking through the crowd for a familiar face, but found no sign of Henri, or even Meagan and Jill. She grabbed a glass of cham-

pagne from a passing waiter and weaved her way through the courtyard to the terrace rail. Grasping the wrought iron tightly she fixed a
distant stare out toward the river.

This was misery like Katherine had never known, confined to a
place where she'd never fit in, her children only an image on a computer screen, her husband more concerned about the needs of Jason
Johnson than her own. Now the people who had been so kind just
days ago would barely speak to her. What kind of cruel game were
these people playing anyway? She turned up the champagne glass and
took down a great gulp.

"You'd better take it easy on that stuff or you'll be spending the
night here."

Katherine whirled around to the voice that had haunted her mind
since the first moment she heard it. She smiled uneasily as Elizabeth
walked over and stood beside her, close enough to brush her shoulder.
Elizabeth rested her hands on the rail and turned to Katherine. For a
brief moment Katherine returned her gaze, before she realized that
for now they were quite alone. She turned away awkwardly, focusing
on the black rail and the empty champagne glass in her hand.

"I'm sorry about a little while ago," Elizabeth said earnestly. "I tell
people I don't like to spend too much time at parties talking business,
but it always happens. Seems like the only time people respect my
personal time is when I'm in church."

Katherine turned a puzzled look to Elizabeth. "You go to church?"
she asked. She had seen a few churches in town, but she had not yet
thought of Elizabeth in a spiritual way.

"Yes," Elizabeth said. She smiled at Katherine's surprise before she
continued, "But I'm guessing it's nothing like the churches you're
used to. Whenever my travel schedule allows I attend the Church of
the Good Shepherd." Elizabeth looked to the evening sky and casually
lifted her foot to rest it on the bottom rail. She thought for a moment
before she said, "I generally take the big picture view of the God
thing, but if you need a label I guess you can call me a liberal Christian." She looked back to Katherine. "If you'd like, I'll be happy to
have you attend church with me sometime."

"Sure," Katherine replied. "I would like that." Katherine had wondered what they must be like, the churches here. It had never occurred to her to attend on her own, probably because she had never stopped to really question her husband's convictions—that surely these people were not worshipping the same God.

In a comfortable silence they watched the last of the orange and silver-blue sunset disappear. As the sky gave way to the deep blue of early night Elizabeth said, "Can I show you the mansion?"

"No," Katherine replied too quickly, uneasy with the thought of being alone in Elizabeth's upstairs rooms with her. She realized her reply had come too hastily and she looked up at Elizabeth, raising her brows with a playful smile, "Henri graciously showed me around when I first arrived. She even showed me the media room downstairs."

Elizabeth laughed heartily and shook her head. "Henri's not much on keeping secrets, but I'll bet she didn't show you everything. Would you like to see the grounds?"

"I'd love to," Katherine replied.

Elizabeth stepped away from the rail and looked at Katherine with a smile as she held out her arm.

For a brief moment Katherine looked strangely at the gesture, unaccustomed to taking the arm of a woman. Her movements felt strange as she moved beside Elizabeth and wrapped her arm beneath Elizabeth's, finally resting her hand lightly on top of her forearm.

Elizabeth tucked her arm in and held it close to her side as she led Katherine across the courtyard.

Walking beside Elizabeth Katherine felt unexpectedly at ease with the closeness of their bodies, and she finally relaxed under the protection of Elizabeth's attention. She leaned into Elizabeth's shoulder as they walked through the crowd, smiling to herself at her earlier unfounded assumptions—Governor Elizabeth Nix had no reservations about being seen in the company of Dr. Katherine Hopkins, and plenty of people were watching.

"This is our azalea garden," Elizabeth began as they strolled from the front porch and down a curved path of crushed white gravel lit by the reflecting moonlight and an occasional overhead lamp post. "In a few weeks, this garden will explode with the most beautiful display of blossoms that you've ever seen. The azaleas are bursting with reds and pinks and purples, and the dogwoods are everywhere. By then the jonquils have sprung up from the ground. Henri always has the annuals planted by then, too. You really do have to come back to see it."

"It sounds wonderful," Katherine said, for the moment just grateful that Elizabeth would care enough to offer her even a few hours of happiness, unlike her husband, who carelessly dismissed her needs simply to join another political battle.

They strolled in silence for a while, enough at ease to avoid forced conversation. The path led them toward a pond, laying still and soft below them, holding the reflection of the February night sky like glowing silk. At the path's fork Elizabeth turned left toward the first of the twin piers that stretched far out over the pond. They walked on to the end of the pier and Elizabeth leaned over the rail, peering with contented eyes at the reflection of the hundreds of stars held in the water below.

Katherine folded her arms and leaned on the rail next to Elizabeth. "Come here often?" she teased.

Elizabeth smiled, still looking out over the water. "Actually I do," she said as she turned to Katherine. "Water has always been my solace. It helps me find the answers I need."

Katherine propped her chin in her hand and looked back out to the water. She leaned in to softly press against Elizabeth's shoulder. "And what answer is the water giving you tonight?"

Elizabeth sincerely looked at Katherine for a moment, debating her answer. She decided on the truth. "That maybe you need me right now," Elizabeth said.

Katherine stood straight and looked at Elizabeth, meeting her knowing eyes that had somehow read Katherine's unspoken questions.

"That as beautiful and intriguing a woman as you are, what you really need is a friend you can rely on," Elizabeth continued. "So, I should put aside my own desire for more, at least for now, until you have time to adjust and heal from all that has happened to you. In the meantime, if another woman catches your heart first, then I'll just have to accept it."

Katherine stood speechless, letting Elizabeth's words sink in slowly. *Beautiful and intriguing . . . desire for more.* She hadn't wanted *that*, had she? No. Elizabeth had it wrong. Surely she had never done anything to lead Elizabeth into believing she wanted that kind of attention. How could Elizabeth have known that once or twice, when she couldn't sleep at night, she had thought of Elizabeth beside her, wrapping her arms around her as she drifted off to sleep—but those thoughts had come because she wanted Elizabeth's protection, nothing more.

It didn't matter anyway. For now Elizabeth was settled on friendship, and with any luck she would be gone before Elizabeth would ask for more. "And what if another woman catches your heart first?" Katherine cleverly teased, turning back to the water and the reflecting stars.

Elizabeth leaned her back against the rail to face Katherine. She looked up at her with a gentle smile and said, "Then at least you'll have friends in high places. And I'll probably keep more of my orchids."

Chapter 21

In the days that followed, Katherine's mind played Elizabeth's words over and over, battling the same conflicting emotions that rushed over her as she drove home from the party—the crushing guilt, the isolation of deceit, the uncertainty of her own desires. That night she had sped back to the condo, fighting the urge to turn around and go to Elizabeth to tell her everything: why she had come here, the sham of her trial, the schemes of President Harkins and Jason Johnson.

Katherine doubted she could resist telling Elizabeth the next time they were alone. Then she would remember her son's face, racked by the pain of a migraine as he cried out for her. *Elizabeth doesn't matter. Let it go. Stay with the plan. You know what you are here for,* she told herself.

In time the urgency of Jacob's needs eased Katherine's guilt, and the structure of her new routine overcame the pull of loneliness. Katherine spent most of her waking hours working, plowing through journals, or checking out other research facilities at Bayside. In the early evenings she roamed through the labs, chatting with research technicians and learning everything she could about each laboratory, who headed the research, and who worked for them. After a couple of weeks she could say a few of the second-shift technicians were friends. But neither they, nor she, had ever seen one particular wing of Bayside. This secluded wing was sealed off by a solid steel door and an ID system so secure that entry required an eye scan.

ON A WARM, early March Sunday afternoon Katherine accepted Elizabeth's invitation to visit the governor's mansion. As promised, magnificent grounds at the height of their bloom surrounded Elizabeth and Katherine as they sat in the courtyard, munching on sandwiches and watching the comings and goings of busy hummingbirds

Blown Away
© 2006 by The Haworth Press, Inc. All rights reserved.
doi:10.1300/5706_21

darting about among flowers and feeders. After lunch Elizabeth led Katherine through a tour of the greenhouses and her multitude of orchids, explaining that her passion for growing them had begun with a single plant given to her by Virginia, and now included somewhere around four hundred species.

As they strolled by the pond and along the river Katherine felt a subtle contentment in being with Elizabeth, realizing that they could be friends, at least for now. She admitted a pang of regret when they shared a moment of laughter, or when Elizabeth's eyes regarded her kindly as she spoke, but there was no use in such sentiments. When the time came to leave the territory Katherine couldn't give Elizabeth Nix a second thought.

Chapter 22

They called it the R&R Blowout, and everyone invited knew it was the last good time before a short stint in the hell of a research rotation. Katherine found the Blowout invitation in her rotation assignment package, a thick white envelope delivered to her door containing a roster of the team members by specialty, the team leader, date, time, and place to report, and a twenty-eight page document to be read before arriving for the first day.

Katherine finished the research report the afternoon of the Blowout, and, though it wasn't MIC, she still found the research fascinating. The next six weeks could be quite stimulating, she thought, if she set her mind to research. By focusing on her work she could overcome any idle thoughts of Elizabeth, or any lingering remorse about her own deceptive mission.

After taking an hour to get dressed Katherine drove the fifteen minutes down the beach to the Green Tide restaurant. She pulled her Volvo into a space in the fifth row and looked into the rearview mirror. The Florida sun had been good to her. Her skin was lightly tanned and her hair a lighter shade of blonde. As she got out of the car she looked up to the restaurant's crowded deck and the row of men standing on a long bench, lifting their beers and swinging their hips to the beat of the reggae drums, their free hand wrapped around the next man's waist, linked together in a chain of carefree rhythm that only alcohol would allow. Katherine took a deep breath, gathering the needed attitude to walk into the restaurant and what she imagined would be a crowd of drunks.

Under a bright pink and teal striped awning a six-foot tall sparkling young man dressed in full cabana-boy garb checked her invitation. With a smile he opened the door and Katherine walked into one of the greatest displays of garish décor she had ever seen: vibrantly colored fake parrots perched on neon glass were attached to teal and pink columns, gaudy tropical flowers and miniature palm trees were scattered among the tables, and bright wall murals, a rainbow painted sailfish, and a faux rock face rushing with electric blue water decorated the Green Tide restaurant.

Katherine smiled at the whole carnival of it all as she walked toward the front bar, searching for a familiar face. Halfway through she spotted Jill Akers leaning against the polished wooden bar, waiting for drinks.

"Hello, Dr. Hopkins," Jill said indifferently.

Katherine stopped next to her, realizing now that Jill had been watching her from the minute she walked in. "Good afternoon, Jill. Nice to see you again," she said in a pleasant but careful tone. "Is Meagan here yet?" Katherine asked as a harried waiter carrying a full tray rushed by them, forcing Katherine to take a side step toward Jill.

"Yeah, she's out on the deck. If you'll wait, you can follow me out there," Jill said dryly.

Katherine turned from Jill and looked around the bar, searching the oddities for something, or someone, to occupy the next uncomfortable minute of waiting.

"Would you like something?" Jill asked after a moment.

Katherine turned back to her with a quick, hesitant smile. "Ginger ale, please," she said. She reached for her handbag.

"I've got it," Jill said.

"Thank you," Katherine said uneasily.

The bartender pushed three tall glasses across the bar and Jill signed a piece of paper.

"The food is free tonight," Jill said, handing the ginger ale to Katherine. "Drinks from the bar are half price, but if you get anything you have to sign for it."

Katherine took a sip of her ginger ale and followed Jill toward the back door, looking over the three long buffet lines of fresh boiled shrimp, crab claws, gumbos, crawfish, corn, and snapper, grouper, and amberjack grilled or fried to order. There were salads and slaws and hush puppies and desserts, too.

Jill pushed open the backdoor leading to the deck and the shoulder-to-shoulder crowd of boisterous men, dancing and shouting conversations above the music. Katherine walked out first but waited for Jill, then stayed close as Jill shouldered their way through the crowd.

Just ahead the deck dropped off to a lower level and a short stack of bleachers that faced the beach. Katherine scanned the three lines of butts and backs before spotting Meagan's long red hair, blowing softly in the breeze that drifted across the top bleacher. Meagan shouted something to whomever it was she was watching, heard a reply, and then threw her head back with a hearty laugh.

Climbing onto the bleachers Katherine settled beside Meagan and looked out to the volleyball net stretched out perpendicular to the deck and the makeshift lines uniformly marking a sand court. Two women stood on either side of the court. The two to the left were crouched slightly in a ready position, and on the right another woman stood close to the net, intently looking at her two opponents. At the serving line Elizabeth stood with the ball in her hand, checking her partner for ready.

The sight of Elizabeth caught Katherine unguarded, and for a moment she just stared. Katherine had never imagined Elizabeth like this. Smooth bronze skin glistened beneath a thin film of sweat that covered her body. Her shoulders sat square and smooth above the curve of her chest, the line of her back separated into two perfectly symmetrical waves of muscle that opposed the slight indentation of her abdomen. Close-fitting shorts surrounded a rounded butt that tapered into solid, muscled legs. Elizabeth was also barefoot.

Elizabeth tossed the ball into the air and with an easy stroke sent it flying across the net. On the other side the back player lunged to dig the ball up, and her partner pushed it into a soft set. The spike that followed screamed down. White sand flew up from under Elizabeth's feet as she hustled to dig the ball up. Her partner scrambled to make the set but managed a beauty, and Elizabeth leapt from the far corner to smash the ball down. Skimming over outstretched hands, the ball slammed just inside the near corner. Elizabeth pumped a fist into the air, grasped high hands with her partner, and then turned to shake hands with the players on the other side.

Katherine's eyes locked on Elizabeth as the four women laughed and talked for a moment, then grabbed their towels and water, quickly waved to the bleachers, and disappeared below the deck.

"The old girl's still got it," Meagan smiled as she stood and stretched. "I think she's lost a inch or two on her vertical jump, though," she said. "I'll have to remind her of that."

Jill stood up and looked over to Katherine, "We're heading to the chow line. Would you like to join us?"

"Sure," Katherine replied. "Lead the way."

There was only a short line at the buffet, and Katherine filled her plate with small samples of shellfish, slaw, and potatoes. She took a chair at the table where Meagan and Jill already sat munching salads, waiting for their fish orders to cook. Katherine sipped her ginger ale and glanced around the restaurant, not conscious that she was looking for Elizabeth until she saw her walking toward them.

"Hey y'all," Elizabeth said to Jill and Meagan, taking a seat across from them. She casually leaned her arms on the table and turned to Katherine, flashed a quick smile and said, "Good to see you again, Katherine. Have you been here long?"

"Just long enough to see the last play of your game," Katherine said, glancing back. "It looked exciting. I wish I'd seen more of it."

"Maybe next time," Elizabeth smiled again, and looked up to the buffet. "I'll be right back." She stood quickly and walked toward the food line.

Katherine watched Elizabeth walk with determined strides and breathed in the lingering light scent of Elizabeth's freshly showered skin, taking it in over the sharp aroma of fish and beer. In a few minutes Elizabeth was back with a plate of jambalaya and a mug of Sam Adams. She put the plate on the table beside Katherine and sat down.

Katherine patiently peeled her shrimp as she watched Elizabeth shake a generous portion of Tabasco over her jambalaya and pick up her fork. Before the first bite reached Elizabeth's mouth the hearty voice of man cried out from behind her: "There you are!"

A tall, round man slid in the chair next to Elizabeth as he kept talking. "Meagan told me you would be here."

Elizabeth put her fork back down. "Hello, Frank," she said, turning to Dr. Frank Mozingo. "What can I do for you tonight?"

"Oh nothing, girl." His words, like his voice, were cheerful and animated. "You go ahead and eat now. I just wanted to talk to you about a few things," Frank said with a light touch to Elizabeth's arm.

Katherine cautioned a look over to Frank. Rosy spots dotted his pale skin, most of which was covered by a thin gray beard that trickled from a full head of steel-gray hair. Multishaded gray eyebrows sprung from his forehead, leaping in all directions above gray-green eyes that sparkled as he spoke in an aberrant tone of seemingly unbridled joy.

Frank said, "I was just talking to Dr. Steele. She is really concerned about her budget this year, and I understand it's not expected to get any better in the next year or two. Elizabeth, we've got to do something about this soon."

Elizabeth nodded, or occasionally said yes as Mozingo talked on, again and again stating his concern about the increasing demands on the Territory's geriatric medical resources and the need for more money.

Katherine quietly munched on her shrimp, somewhat amused and somewhat marveled that Mozingo talked about such serious matters in such a lighthearted tone.

"Is this who I think?" Mozingo asked suddenly, looking directly at Katherine.

Elizabeth leaned away and looked over to Katherine. "This is Dr. Katherine Hopkins. Katherine, Dr. Frank Mozingo."

Mozingo's delighted eyes lit up as he held out his hand to Katherine. "Oh, it's so nice to meet you, Dr. Hopkins. I hope I get to work with you someday soon." Mozingo's cool, meaty hand shook Katherine's vigorously. "I know how good you are," he said with a sly wink.

"Thank you, I think," Katherine replied with a hesitant smile. "I'm sure I'll look forward to it as well."

"Okay, gotta go," Mozingo said to them. He stood up and left as quickly as he had come.

"Sorry about that," Elizabeth said to Katherine. "Believe it or not, he's one of our best project team leaders. Strangely enough, he's organized, and blessed with a mind that never forgets a thing, and at the same time he's creative."

"What project is he working on now?" Katherine asked.

"This and that," Elizabeth answered lightly. "I'm not exactly sure what he's working on right now." Elizabeth pushed her fork into a shrimp, wondering if Katherine noticed the hesitation that always crept into her voice when she lied. Dr. Frank Mozingo, in reality, was the eccentric but gifted leader in charge of all MIC research.

"Do you know, Meagan?" Katherine asked.

"Know what?" Meagan said, looking up from a plate of fresh grilled snapper.

"What project Mozingo is working on?"

Meagan turned back to her fish and picked up a lemon slice from her plate. "He's coordinating and scheduling projects and making staff recommendations to me. Right now I don't have him assigned to a research project." She focused on the lemon she squeezed onto her snapper. "Why do you ask?"

Katherine turned a lighthearted smile. "I was just wondering what research labs I should avoid."

Meagan returned an understanding smile and said, "I understand, but Frank's really not that bad. You'll get used to him."

In a while, the food was finished and the plates were cleared. Elizabeth turned up the last of her beer and set down the mug. "I think I'll go for a walk on the beach. Would you like to join me?" she asked, looking over to Katherine.

"Sure. After all this food, I can use a walk, and the beach is beautiful tonight."

THE SUN HAD set a half hour before, leaving the beach lit by only a bright half moon and the lights from the hotels and restaurants lining the beachfront. Katherine followed Elizabeth through the Green Tide kitchen and down a narrow staircase that opened into a storage room filled with lounge chairs and umbrellas, sports equipment, and stacks of liquor. Through a side door they stepped onto the white sand of the beach and quickly walked south, away from the restaurant and the crowds. A hundred or so yards from the Green Tide they found a dark spot and Elizabeth stopped, untied her shoes, and pulled them off. Katherine sat down on the sand beside her and slipped off her suede loafers too, then buried her feet into the sand to ward off the chill of the March night.

Elizabeth guarded their privacy as they walked, staying high on the sands, just inside the gray shadows and away from the couples and packs of friends who strolled along the ebb and flow of the gulf.

"So, do you like Jill?" Katherine asked as they walked slowly on the soft sand.

"Yes. I do," Elizabeth replied. "She's a solid person—dependable, decent, straightforward—and she's good to Meagan."

"Are they serious?"

"I believe they love each other," Elizabeth replied. "Time will tell how it will turn out. Meagan wants Jill to move to the Territory, but so far Jill hasn't decided to take that step."

"Meagan told me as much when we went riding," Katherine said.

"It's a hard decision for many people to decide whether to come here or not," Elizabeth replied. "I know of other couples who have faced the same situation Meagan and Jill are in now. Some of them keep a long-distance relationship up for a while before they eventually break up, and sometimes one partner will give up a higher-paying job to come here and do something less rewarding careerwise. But, either way, sacrifices are always made. I can't say as I blame Jill for not wanting to give up a job she loves and is so well suited for."

Elizabeth looked over at Katherine. The gulf wind blew Katherine's dark golden hair around on her shoulders, contrasting the silver glow that lit her face. Katherine grew more beautiful every time Elizabeth looked at her.

"But would you like to see Jill move here?" Katherine asked, keeping her eyes away from Elizabeth's gaze.

"I'd like to see Meagan happy," Elizabeth replied. "She's had a rough go of it at times, and in spite of everything that has happened to her, she stays positive. It would be nice to see things work out for her. And if Jill Akers can make that happen, then yes, I'd like to see her move here."

"Meagan means a lot to you, doesn't she?"

"Yes, she does. I can't even begin to tell you how much."

Katherine had seen it once or twice, the way Elizabeth would look at Meagan with eyes that said she would always honor her.

Katherine stopped walking and turned to Elizabeth to ask, "What about you and Meagan? Have you ever been involved with her, or would you like to be?"

Elizabeth turned a melancholy smile, "I'd be lying if I said I wasn't sometimes attracted to her." She was quiet for a moment before she continued thoughtfully. "A long time ago Meagan lost the one woman I believe she will love until the day she dies. When we buried Chris Landry I knew we buried a part of Meagan with her. Since then, every time I thought of Meagan in a romantic way, I immediately knew that it should be Chris Landry with her, not me. I've never been able to put myself in Chris's place, and now I think that Meagan and I have moved past the point of romance anyway."

"I see, but what about others?" Katherine asked cautiously. "I know losing Virginia must have been very hard for you, but you haven't mentioned if there has been anyone else. Was she your last love?"

Elizabeth looked out across the beach to the rolling gulf, alone in a world of her own, and for the moment, she wanted it that way.

"Yes, she was. I haven't been in a serious relationship since then," Elizabeth replied after a long moment, keeping her eyes on the distant waters. "I don't know if it's really a good idea to bring someone else into my life right now. Virginia was different from any woman I've ever known. She didn't need me; she always had her own life, even after we were married. Ninety-nine percent of the women in the world aren't like that. They want an equal partnership, and that's how it should be, but that's more than I can give anyone right now. It's hard to hold onto a relationship when you sometimes see your partner for only four hours, once or twice a week."

Elizabeth's face lightened as she turned to Katherine and continued. "I wonder sometimes if I'm destined for a single life. I was the same damn way in college. I can't seem to put anyone else ahead of the work I do."

"I don't know if you have a choice, really," Katherine said.

Elizabeth raised a single eyebrow in a silent question.

"You are one of a rare breed of driven people," Katherine continued. "Your ideals are your life, and seeing them through is the most important thing you do. Virginia's independence allowed you to follow your drive, but until you find someone else who understands and accepts that part of you I guess you'll just be single until you retire," Katherine said with a perceptive smile.

Elizabeth smiled back, but raised another skeptical eyebrow.

"I know because in that way you remind me of Jason Johnson," Katherine said.

"What!" Elizabeth swung around indignantly. "I'm nothing like that son of a bitch."

"Yes, you are," Katherine replied with a quick, lighthearted smile. "Of course you're nothing like Jason Johnson in the obvious ways. I just mean you are both driven by your ideals. I'm not saying that's a bad thing." Katherine waited until Elizabeth's expression relaxed before she continued. "You know before all this mess happened I was friends with Jason's wife, Brittany. She always complained that Jason was so preoccupied with his work that she could never get him to concentrate on their family. He apparently spent more time worrying about family values than his real family."

"So Jason Johnson's family is not perfect, huh? Could have fooled me," Elizabeth said sarcastically. She turned back to the Gulf and pushed her hands into her pockets.

Katherine sensed Elizabeth wasn't angry, just perhaps a bit stung from the truth. "The Johnson's are far from perfect," Katherine said. "Jason is so worked up about telling other people how to raise their families that he doesn't take time to raise his own—just like you're spending so much time trying to make sure people have a place to live and love freely," Katherine now felt Elizabeth's penetrating eyes directly on her, "that you don't have time for your own love," she finished softly.

Katherine looked up and met Elizabeth's eyes, and though there was a full four feet between them, a hot jolt rushed through her body, just the same as the first time Elizabeth had grasped her hand. What happened next Katherine did not understand. She had never in her life acted on instinct alone, without thought, or calculation, or hesitation. She would think of it later and still not understand the force that pulled them together, without effort or barrier, as if drawn by a power free from logic or control. A sweet void took over her mind, and the four feet disappeared as their lips met and lingered, forming together in a slow, soft dance that they both somehow already knew.

For that moment there was nothing else, nothing but Elizabeth. Serene warmth flowed through Katherine's body and she reached up and buried her fingers in Elizabeth's thick black hair—hair that was soft and full, and not at all like Thomas's. Not at all like—*Thomas's!*

Their bond suddenly shattered. Katherine pulled away and looked down at the sand as guilt rushed in.

Elizabeth stared at her, for the moment speechless, perplexed. She reached for Katherine's hand, but Katherine stepped back.

"I'm sorry," Katherine stammered as her mind reeled. "It's just. . . ."

"It's okay, Katherine," Elizabeth offered. "It doesn't matter here. You know you won't be arrested again."

"I know. I'm just not ready yet," Katherine replied, turning her eyes toward the gulf. "I'm so sorry. I just can't do this right now." She glanced back up at Elizabeth. "Can we just go back?"

"Sure. Katherine, I know I said I wouldn't," Elizabeth began.

"No," Katherine interrupted. "It wasn't just you. I'm sorry," she said again. "I think I need more time, that's all."

Elizabeth looked into eyes that were near to tears. "All right, I know I'm a lot to take on," she joked lightly. "I think you're entitled to a few weeks out of the newspapers."

Katherine braved a quick smile at her.

"Let's go back, then," Elizabeth said.

They walked back through the shadows in thick, confused silence. Elizabeth offered a light comment, but Katherine had no appetite for small talk. In truth, she was battling an overwhelming desire to grab Elizabeth's hand and run into the darkness.

Chapter 23

Katherine turned from Elizabeth when they came to the Green Tide volleyball court. Fortunately no one was in the parking lot, and Katherine managed to slip off unnoticed. She drove down the beach trying to convince herself that the kiss was just another part of a passing phase, that it was all just a result of her loneliness and her growing familiarity with seeing women with women and men with men. It was just curiosity. She only needed to focus on who she really was and what she believed in. She would go home and watch her children, she would talk to Thomas and tell him that she loved him, for a change. She would get over Elizabeth Nix and regain control of her emotions. She had to.

Katherine parked the Volvo and hurried up her condo stairs in quick strides, anxious for the solace of her own place. She opened the front door and immediately saw the "urgent message waiting" blinking across the screen of her home monitor. She threw her purse on the counter and grabbed the remote.

Instantly the recorded message of her husband appeared, "Katherine, we're on the way to the hospital with Jacob," Thomas said in a repressed monotone. "He's got a severe headache and his left hand and arm have been numb since this morning. I'll get back to you when we know something more."

Thomas's face disappeared and Katherine helplessly watched the screen go blank. Her legs begin to shake, and she slowly walked over and crumbled onto the couch. She stared at the ceiling, listening to the roar of waves breaking against the beach.

Twenty blank minutes passed before Katherine wearily pushed herself up and walked onto the balcony. The wind blew against her face as she leaned against the railing, staring without expression at the sea as her mind filled with a quiet rage, thinking of John Harkins, the man whose political ambition took her away from her family, of Jason

Blown Away
© 2006 by The Haworth Press, Inc. All rights reserved.
doi:10.1300/5706_23

Johnson, and her own husband. They had no notion of the depth of
the sacrifice she had made to leave a sick, dying child. She thought of
Meagan Sullivan and Elizabeth Nix, unable to comprehend that they
held a secret that would keep her son alive but refused to share it.
Katherine no longer knew who to believe, and she never felt this
alone. She turned to her faith, but as she watched a compassionless
ocean beat against the shore she felt nothing. God must be like the
ocean, she thought, just an indifferent eternal, nothing more. Surely it
was foolish to believe otherwise.

"DO YOU MIND if I come over for a while?" Meagan's shaky voice
came from the speaker of the bedroom telephone at the governor's
mansion. Elizabeth laid down her reading and picked up the handset.

"Hey, baby. Of course I don't mind. Are you all right?"

"Yes." There was a long pause before Meagan finished, "I just need
to talk."

"Do you want me to come over there?"

"No, I want to get out of this house. I'll be there in fifteen minutes."

"If you're sure, then. I'm upstairs reading. Let yourself in and come
on up." Elizabeth hung up and looked at the clock. It was a few minutes after ten p.m.

At ten-thirty she heard Meagan climbing the stairs. As she turned
into the bedroom, Elizabeth knew it was Jill.

"Jill?"

Meagan nodded.

Elizabeth put away her briefing and waited as Meagan walked to
the bed and fell onto it. She rolled over to rest her head on Elizabeth's
shoulder, and Elizabeth pulled her close and cradled her in the crook
of her arm. "What happened?"

"We're taking an indefinite time-out," Meagan said after a moment. "She said our relationship didn't seem to have much possibility
of going further, so we should cool it for a while and just see what happens. She says it's starting to hurt too much when she has to leave."

"I see," Elizabeth said as she stroked Meagan's hair. "How do you
feel about that?"

Meagan took a moment before she answered. "I understand why she feels we have to do this, but I wish it could have been different. I know I'm as much a part of it as she is. I won't leave the Territory—at least not now."

"You know you can go if you want," Elizabeth said.

"You'd let me go that easily?"

"Of course not," Elizabeth replied and pulled Meagan closer. "But I don't want to stand in your way, either."

"You know how I feel about what we're doing here. I can't deny it's what matters most to me right now. We've been blessed to have the opportunity to affect as many people's lives as we do."

"I'll have to admit I'm glad to hear you feel that way, though I know it's not good for your relationship with Jill," Elizabeth said. "I wouldn't want to lose you right now. With the election coming up in the States, things may get interesting in the next few months."

Meagan was quiet for a moment before she asked, "Speaking of things getting interesting, what happened with you and Katherine last night? You came back from your walk alone."

"I'm not exactly sure what happened. I kissed her," Elizabeth began, and then she paused. "Well, I should say we kissed each other."

Meagan sat up suddenly and looked squarely at Elizabeth, "Is this some new way to figure out if she's legit?"

"No," Elizabeth replied. "I didn't plan to kiss her. It just happened."

"Well, since it did, it makes me more curious that you came back alone. Women usually don't run away from you. So, do you think maybe it was the first time she actually kissed a woman?"

"That question has crossed my mind several times today, believe me. But I just don't know. It happened very unexpectedly, and when it did, I can assure you I wasn't thinking of it as a test."

"No, I suppose not."

"She did pull away suddenly, though," Elizabeth continued. "It was like one second she was completely there, wanting it as much as I did, and then the next second she pushed away from me, and I have no idea why." Elizabeth thought for a moment. "Maybe it was the re-action to her first kiss, or it may have been what I told her at your party—that I was attracted to her but I wanted to give her some time to regroup. I meant that too, Meagan. In spite of our reservations, in spite of our original plans, you know I think about Katherine more than I'd like to admit. But she's got so much in her head right now. Her trial was traumatic, and worse, she's been torn away from her children. She needs time to work all that out, without any emotional pressure from me. Whatever kind of relationship I eventually have with Katherine I wanted to take things slow, but then I go and kiss her."

"Well, whether you're ready to admit it or not I think you truly want her, and I've never known you to take things slow when you want something." Meagan rolled to her back and leaned against the stack of pillows at the headboard. "But the problem is, based on her reaction, we still don't know if we can trust her."

"No, we don't."

"God, I wish we did," Meagan said. "We desperately need Katherine working on MIC research. We're still having major problems with side effects from the synthetic compound, and our natural fruit source is being depleted faster than we can create habitat for new plants. Katherine headed a research team a few years ago that solved the side effect problems for the Alzheimer's treatment. With the expertise she could bring to our team, we might have a marketable product in two, two and a half years."

"And I would have a quarter billion a year more in the budget," Elizabeth said. "We need that kind of money to fund the convalescent homes that we're going to need in the next five years or so. A bond issue could be risky, and I damn sure don't want to go to President Harkins to ask for the capital investment money, especially now. You know how Harkins loves to throw our budget requests out as a campaign issue."

"Yes. I know all too well," Meagan replied.

Chapter 24

Katherine reported for the first day of rotation and fidgeted through two hours of boring bureaucratic instructions. The lectures were as dry as August grass, leaving her mind free to wander back to Saturday night, the beach, and the moment she kissed Elizabeth. She opened her instruction notebook and skimmed the material to keep her mind from the memory. Flipping through the pages she wondered how Thomas could stand being a lawyer. Just when she was certain she couldn't stand another sentence about subparts, rules, or codes, she and the twenty five other doctors in the room were asked to sign an agreement releasing all research and patent rights to the Territory. For this they were rewarded with a photographed and fingerprinted pass to the section of Bayside that housed all research rotation projects.

Katherine signed her agreement without reading it, picked up her pass, and joined the other nine of her research group. Dr. Prescott, the physician in charge, led them through the halls, only briefly stopping at the entrance to the wing sealed by a six-inch thick steel door and three armed security guards. There Dr. Prescott unceremoniously explained that the high-security wing housed research facilities for highly infections diseases, and therefore required the utmost security. Katherine knew the economics of research for rare disease treatments would not add up to profit for the territory, and she knew the information she wanted had to be on the other side of that door. She would find a way to get there.

Katherine knew, too, that Elizabeth was her way to the secrets of the Territory, but right now her emotions were too uncertain. Before she could face Elizabeth again Katherine would have to overcome the strange fever that left her weak for a woman. Katherine would, in fact, have to vanquish all of her distracting emotions. From now on, every move would be calculated, every lie would be planned, and her

Blown Away

doi:10.1300/5706_24

life would be free from the sentiments that lead to mistakes and delays she could not afford.

AS THE DAYS passed, Katherine found the structure and long hours of the rotation perfectly suited for banishing thoughts of Elizabeth. The work required a clear focus of mind that left no room for idle sentiments. By the second week of rotation Katherine was free of distracting thoughts and daydreams. She also found less time to look in on Ellen and Jacob, and, with some remorse, less desire to do so. The nightly talks with her husband became a draining burden, and she resented his ranting monologues, full of self-pity and useless causes, complaining about the lives of people he never even knew. Katherine was working to save lives, and he was working to destroy them.

By the third week the research consumed Katherine's days and nights. She brought clothes and cosmetics to her locker and left them there, often finding a bed in the residents' quarters for sleeping. After her first night away Thomas asked why she hadn't been home. She told him it was the traffic, though she felt no need to justify anything to him.

In the final five days of Katherine's rotation she pondered volunteering for another six weeks, but so far she hadn't heard so much as a single word mentioned about MIC research, and she couldn't allow herself to become diverted from her son's needs. Now, Katherine decided, was not the time for another rotation. Now, it was time to return her attention to Elizabeth.

ALL ROTATIONS ENDED just before May Days, the annual celebration that marked the beginning of the Apalachicola tourist season. Three days of festivals, glowing nighttime parades, street parties, and raucous carnivals that pounded into dawn attracted tourists by the thousands. The May Days celebration culminated at Liberty Beach Park with the Third Night Festival, the final extravaganza before life turned to the busy routine of the summer season. Elizabeth would be delivering a speech at the festival, and Katherine knew she could find her there.

Liberty Beach Park was an easy walk from Bayside, so Katherine drove to the hospital garage and parked in her space. She checked her look in the mirror and swung out of the Volvo, straightening the shorts and shirt she picked to catch Elizabeth's attention. Her steps were quick and light as she walked out of the garage and melted into the tide of people heading for the festival.

Katherine walked in the middle of the crowd, avoiding the tangle of people gathered around the beer booths and the street-side vendors who hawked their half-price wares to anyone who still had a dollar left to spend. Still, it took her nearly twenty minutes to walk the half mile to the park entrance, and another fifteen to clear security. Inside the park entrance the throng of people finally dispersed. Katherine saw a great green field ahead, now covered by families and packs of friends lounging on blankets and lawn chairs, facing a covered stage. On the stage a country band played, but most people still moved about, paying little attention. Katherine spotted the governor's tent at the far end of the field. She took a steadying breath and walked toward it.

Still thirty feet away, Henri greeted her. "Hey, Katherine!"

Katherine lifted a subdued wave and picked up her pace, hoping to reach Henri before she yelled again.

"Hello, Henri," Katherine said as soon as she was close enough for normal conversation. Katherine took a second look at the can cooler hanging from a thick canvass strap draped over Henri's neck. A beer was snuggled inside the aging foam rubber.

"Hadn't seen you in a while," Henri said. "Where you been?"

Katherine stopped next to Henri and glanced through the tent, not recognizing any of the twenty or so people sitting at the tables underneath the canvas. "Research rotation," Katherine answered.

"Oh," Henri said. She smiled suddenly. "Ain't you glad that shit's over?"

"The hours, yes." Katherine replied. "The work, not really. I miss it already."

"Damn, you're a dedicated woman."

"Or bored, maybe."

"No need for that," Henri said. "Elizabeth can keep you busy," Henri said with an eager smile.

"I'll keep that in mind," Katherine answered patiently. "Is there anyone I know here?" she asked, again looking around the tent.

"Yeah, somewhere. Meagan and Elizabeth are both out politicking. Have you met Michael DuBose?"

"I don't believe so," Katherine answered.

"Come on, he's over here," Henri said with a tilt of her head.

Michael stood as they approached his table. "Dr. Hopkins, so nice to finally meet you," he said. Michael took Katherine's hand and cradled it in his own, looking into her eyes as he shook her hand graciously. He pulled out a chair for her.

"I was going for a drink," Michael said. "Would you like one?"

"Yes, but I'll go with you. I'm not sure what I want yet," Katherine said. She waited for Michael to move past her and followed him to the bar at the back of the tent.

Katherine ordered iced tea and waited patiently as the bartender set up drinks for three others. In a whirlwind he set a too-full glass on the counter before making his way to the next customer. Katherine sipped off the top of the glass as she backed away from the bar. Without looking, she turned—right into Elizabeth's chest. The tea flew straight up in the air, and straight down Elizabeth's white shirt.

Katherine stared in disbelief at the tea soaking into Elizabeth's clothes. "I'm sorry; I'm sorry," Katherine said. She looked up to Elizabeth's eyes, "Oh, Elizabeth, I really am sorry."

"It's okay, Katherine. I have to change before my speech anyway." Elizabeth gave her a quick, reassuring smile and reached for a napkin. "I should have been paying more attention myself."

Katherine watched Elizabeth's hands patiently dab her shirt, feeling a sudden ebb in the facade of control she had so carefully constructed.

"Have you been here long?" Elizabeth asked. She threw away the napkin and reached for the bottled water the bartender handed across on the counter.

"Not really," Katherine answered. "Henri just introduced me to Michael."

"Good," Elizabeth said as she twisted the cap off the water bottle. "Then I know you've been in good hands. Will you be staying with us the rest of the night?"

"Yes, if I won't be in the way. I mean you must have a lot of people you need to speak with tonight, and I know you have a speech." Elizabeth's steady gaze drew Katherine in. It was everyone else who was in the way, Katherine thought, she wanted Elizabeth to herself, to talk for hours, or maybe go for a drive down the beach together.

"You won't be in the way, Katherine," Elizabeth answered kindly. "I'd like for you to stay. My speech will be short and I'll be hanging around the tent the rest of the night. I've made the rounds with everyone I needed to see, and now there's nothing more I'd rather do than spend time with you. I'd like to hear what you think of rotations, among other things."

"I actually enjoyed the experience," Katherine replied.

Elizabeth raised her brows inquisitively, "Well, you must tell me why," she said with a slow smile. "Let's find a quiet place to sit down, and you can explain to me how six weeks of nonstop work can be an enjoyable experience."

Elizabeth led Katherine to table in the corner of the tent and deliberately sat down with her back to the rest of the guests. Katherine settled into a chair beside her and took an anxious sip of tea, knowing that for now Elizabeth intended to devote her total attention to her. She looked up from the glass and saw Elizabeth's eyes focused directly on her, and all of the rehearsed words Katherine had planned to say disappeared from her mind.

"So tell me about your rotation," Elizabeth inquired as she leaned toward Katherine.

"It was fascinating," Katherine began.

Elizabeth listened intently as Katherine explained the work of her team, the progress they had made, and the problems they had encountered. After a time the conversation turned from the research rotation to politics, and then to ambitions, and to childhood, and to dreams for the future. The late evening sun waned toward the horizon when Meagan came over to the table, apologized for the interruption, and reminded Elizabeth her speech would be in half an hour.

Elizabeth nodded and stood up. "I'll see you in a bit," she assured Katherine.

Katherine watched Elizabeth walk away with Meagan and wondered if she would ever earn a fraction of the trust that existed between the two of them. Then she remembered that one day she would have to break Elizabeth's trust. Katherine sat alone, struggling against her desire to leave, to run home and again close off the world, away from her husband, her children, her work, and especially Elizabeth.

WHEN KATHERINE SAW the governor again she wished she had fled. Her eyes fixed on Elizabeth, standing in front of the microphone, patiently waiting for the applause to die. Elizabeth looked magnificent. Dark skin contrasted against her white linen shirt and pants that billowed in the light breeze. Her thick black hair was pushed behind her ears, highlighting the assurance of her eyes. Katherine felt her chest pound, and she knew there was nothing she could do to stop it. She concentrated on the words as Elizabeth spoke about the first days of the Territory, the progress of the last twelve years, and her vision for the coming years of her administration. Without notes Elizabeth thanked a list of people for their efforts in the May Days Festival and ended the speech with praises for the Apalachicola Symphony Orchestra and the Territory Choir. Their performance, Elizabeth said, would begin in a few minutes.

Katherine sipped a glass of wine and watched the stagehands busily set up chairs for the orchestra and risers for the choir. The music, Beethoven's ninth, in particular the choral, was her favorite, the most stirring piece of music she knew, and she had never heard it performed live. Tonight she would hear it performed by the best choir in the country. Katherine looked above at the tent, considering the acoustics. She decided to move out into the night air, away from any interference.

"Mind if I join you?" Elizabeth asked, now standing next to her, holding a chair in one hand and a carafe of wine and a glass in the other.

Katherine smiled up to her. "Not at all. Please do."

Elizabeth set up her chair and poured a glass of wine and held it up, "To tonight," she said.

"To tonight," Katherine replied.

They sipped the toast as the orchestra conductor walked onto the stage and took his bow. Silence fell as he lifted his wand and in one quick movement, put into motion the ebb and tide of the music that swirled through the night air like the sweet aroma of early spring.

The orchestra rolled the ninth into the flurry of the finale, the last note leading to a trail of fire that streaked toward the sky and exploded into a burst of shimmering green. The fire and light that followed filled the skies with burst after burst of brilliant color until at last the final flicker faded into the night sky.

"So I'm guessing you enjoyed it?" Elizabeth said over the whoops and applause of the charged crowd.

Katherine nodded with a contented smile, but said nothing.

Elizabeth reached over and filled Katherine's empty wineglass. "You may as well relax here for a while. You won't get far in that crowd," she said, looking out to the mass of people heading toward the gates.

Katherine looked toward the gates and said, "No, I guess I won't." She turned to the empty stage for a moment and then back to Elizabeth. "That was incredible."

"The Territory is blessed with so much talent," Elizabeth said. "But then again, did you ever doubt a gay territory like this wouldn't have the best damn choir ever?" she said with a smile.

Katherine laughed. "No, I guess not."

"Do you have any plans for the rest of the night?" Elizabeth asked. "If you'd like to come to the mansion, I've got some great desserts left from last night's party."

Katherine looked at Elizabeth for a moment, considering an excuse. But her senses were too peaked to go home just yet. "Yes," she nodded. "The back terrace of the mansion with you and a great dessert sounds wonderful."

"Good," Elizabeth said. "I'll be glad to drive you, but I'm on my motorcycle. You may want to drive, or if you're willing we can get out of here faster if you ride with me."

"Okay," Katherine said. "But I'll have to warn you, I've never been on a motorcycle before."

"There's nothing to it," Elizabeth assured. "Just hang on, sit back, and enjoy the ride."

Elizabeth held out her arm and Katherine wrapped her hand around it as they walked to the Harley. At the bike Katherine waited as Elizabeth took a thin pair of pants and a jacket from a side box and pulled them on, then reached into the box again and took out a neatly bundled jacket. She shook out pants from the folds of the jacket and handed them to Katherine, and then unfastened the extra helmet and handed it to her too.

The rising rush of wind blew against Katherine as Elizabeth turned from the parking lot and picked up speed. Katherine tightened her grip as the big engine roared beneath her, leaving her at the same time terrified and elated. Her fear slowly slipped away as she began to feel the pure joy of an open ride: the air filled with the aroma of cookouts and spring flowers, the moonlight reflecting off the pavement, the whipping wind against her body. Katherine smiled as they rode. A year ago the idea of riding on a motorcycle with a full-blown lesbian would have been unthinkable. Yet, here she was, riding through the heart of the queerest place in America with the woman they had elected as their leader. The bike roared on, and Katherine reached up and put her hands around Elizabeth's waist, knowing for the first time in her thirty-eight years her life could be her own.

Elizabeth turned onto the beach road and opened the bike up to sixty. Katherine tightened her grip and looked out to the beach and the silver lapping of the gulf, pulling herself closer to Elizabeth to block the wind's force. Thick sea air filled Katherine's lungs as they passed miles of beach, and then with a sweeping left Elizabeth turned inland.

The air changed with the terrain: at first thick and repugnant as they passed decaying swamps, then cool and crisp as they drove into the open pines of sandy forests. Katherine breathed it all in, the thrill of the speed, the span of the beach, the fragrance of the air telling the story of the land. She would never know this pleasure in the safe, air-bagged, seat-belted, comfort-controlled compartment of her Volvo.

Elizabeth pulled up to the gate of the mansion and took off her helmet. She looked over her shoulder to Katherine. "I'd like to show you something," she began. "It's about another ten minutes from here. Would you mind?"

"Not at all," Katherine replied. "You have my curiosity piqued now."

They rode toward an ever-darkening forest, and soon there was no light except the moon's reflection from occasional patches of bare sand. After a few miles Elizabeth turned onto a road that was nothing but hard-packed dirt. Spanish moss hung low over the road that was lined on both sides by loosely strung fence. A faint glow of light wavered in the distance. They rode to the light and stopped there, just in front of a small white house.

Elizabeth shut off the engine and threw her leg over, taking off her helmet in the same motion. "This is it," Elizabeth said, watching Katherine's blonde hair fall around her shoulders as she took off her helmet. "My escape," Elizabeth said with the sweep of her arm across the landscape. "My sanity."

Katherine looked up at the house. A long, screened porch ran the distance of the front, and an open deck lined the opposite side. Dozens of rich green plants filled the rails and floor of the porch, and a hammock and chairs sat in the spaces left among them. "This is your place?"

"Yes, it is," Elizabeth replied. "Would you like to come inside?"

"Yes, very much."

On the porch Elizabeth stopped among the blooming pots of flowers and looked out to the night. "You'll have to come back in the daylight. There's a beautiful spring just down the hill. The water is so clear it's like looking into an aquarium—the fish, the dark green and brown plants swirling against white sand—it's incredible, and it's one of the reasons I bought this place. That, and the remote location." She reached out and took Katherine's hand and, as if they had done it a hundred times, together they walked to the front door.

"Any preference for music?" Elizabeth asked as she walked across the den. "I can't match what we heard tonight, but I have at least a disc or two of every kind of music you could want."

"No preference," Katherine answered. "Anything's fine."

Elizabeth picked Billie Holiday, and with the push of a button her haunting, silky voice filled the room, and Katherine nodded in agreement.

"Billie is never wrong," Elizabeth smiled as she walked back to the door to take off her riding clothes.

Katherine watched Elizabeth pull the jacket over her head, noticing the sensuality of Elizabeth's movements.

Elizabeth hung the pants and shirt on a peg and looked back at Katherine. "Would you like me to hang yours? You may get warm."

As Katherine stripped off the pants and pulled up the jacket, she felt a dangerous pleasure in knowing Elizabeth was watching. She handed Elizabeth the clothes, studying her as she shook them out. The helmet had slightly mussed Elizabeth's hair, and the fatigue of three days drooped her eyes just slightly, somehow making Elizabeth even more gorgeous.

Katherine turned away quickly to the antique hutch centered between the two front windows. She walked over to focus her attention on the collection scattered across it. One of the books, *The Turn of Time* by William Bucks, caught her eye. Katherine opened the cover and saw it had been autographed, with a personal message to Elizabeth.

Elizabeth walked over beside Katherine, and in their closeness Katherine heard the slow rhythm of Elizabeth's breathing, even as she felt her own breath become quick and shallow. Katherine focused on the book to steady her mind. After a moment, she turned a puzzled look to Elizabeth.

"President Bucks and I actually get along quite well," Elizabeth answered. "I never voted for him and he knows that, but I like him. I have since we first started the Territory. I attended the opening of his presidential library last fall, and while I was there he gave me a signed copy of his book." Elizabeth leaned against the hutch to look directly at Katherine. "Believe it or not, his wife, Susan, and I have played golf together a couple of times," Elizabeth said, and then her eyes narrowed as she looked down to the floor. "It's John Harkins I can't stand. Arrogant bastard."

For weeks now, Katherine couldn't stand him either.

"With any luck he won't be reelected," Elizabeth said as she walked across the room and disappeared into the kitchen. She opened the refrigerator. "I've got sliced strawberries and shortcake," Elizabeth said, "and peach cobbler and ice cream. I've got chocolate cake, but I'm not sure how fresh it is. What would you like? I've got all kinds of fruit, too, or I can make you a sandwich if you don't want dessert."

Katherine didn't answer. Instinctively she walked into the kitchen and stood behind Elizabeth, waiting as her heart began to pound with anticipation, for what she wasn't sure. Frozen still she watched Elizabeth casually pick up the bowl of strawberries, look at them, and put them back on the refrigerator shelf.

Then Elizabeth stopped, sensing Katherine watching, and she turned around. For a moment they stood perfectly still, and then the moment broke. Elizabeth took Katherine into her arms with a kiss as soft as their first, but more urgent, as if finally being released from a tight binding.

Katherine fell against Elizabeth, wanting to touch nothing else in the world but her. In a quick motion Elizabeth pulled Katherine tight against her body, holding their slow and deepening kiss until she knew that this time, Katherine would not break it in shame, or fear.

Seeing the surety in Katherine's eyes Elizabeth took her hand and led her through the house and into the bedroom. Elizabeth lowered Katherine onto the bed, looking at her with intense but still inquiring eyes.

As if to answer Katherine reached up and pulled Elizabeth in, closing her eyes in pleasure as Elizabeth's gentle, deliberate lips moved across and down Katherine's neck. Katherine sighed as slow-moving fingertips reached under her shirt, moving lightly in discovery of the smooth skin beneath.

Elizabeth pulled her hand from beneath the shirt and rose up to look at Katherine. "I won't let you go again after this," she whispered honestly. "Are you sure?"

Katherine answered without words. She sat up, pulling off her shirt as she rose, returning the desire in Elizabeth's eyes as her clothes fell to the floor. The touch of Elizabeth's fingers lingered against the bare skin of her shoulders as Katherine deliberately unbuttoned Eliza-

beth's shirt and pulled it slowly down her arms, for the first time seeing the total beauty of her body, the golden brown skin of her smooth,
taut stomach, and the round, firm breasts centered just below the
strong curves of her shoulders. Elizabeth's body was fully feminine.
The desire to touch every inch of it, to hold her body tightly as Elizabeth made love to her took Katherine over. Her hands reached to
grasp Elizabeth's shoulders as she rose to meet her kiss, and then sank
into the strength of Elizabeth's arms, taking her in as they fell together against the bed.

The soft touch of Elizabeth's hand now moved across Katherine's
skin with the perfect balance of tenderness and passion, and Katherine knew the intention of that hand—of Elizabeth's entire body—
moved with the sole purpose of bringing her pleasure, of making love
to her. She wrapped her arms across Elizabeth's back and pulled close
the warm softness of her lips, now moving in lingering caresses down-
ward to Katherine's breasts. Katherine's breath came in short sighs as
Elizabeth kissed over the curve, and her back arched in impulsive
anticipation.

Waves of pleasure pulsed through Katherine's body as Elizabeth's
tongue gently circled her firm nipple, sending the first moans of desire rising from Katherine's throat. Elizabeth's body tightened and
Katherine opened her legs to the rhythm of Elizabeth's slowly moving
hips, pushing full against her until the pounding between Katherine's
legs begged for relief. Katherine slid her hand past the bare skin of
Elizabeth's back and down, wanting nothing to interfere with the
joining of their bodies.

They came together again, soft skin forming together in rising
heat. Elizabeth's hand traced slowly down to Katherine's thighs. A
soft cry met the touch of Elizabeth's two fingers sliding gently over
Katherine's wetness. Katherine's breath now came in rhythmic sighs
as her body trembled with each stroke.

Silver moonlight filtered through the bedroom window, lighting
their bodies as Elizabeth's lips trailed down from Katherine's breast,
across her stomach and down to push her tongue where her hand had
been.

At the first stroke an electric stream shot through Katherine's body and rushed into her brain, sending a clear cry rising from her throat. Katherine clutched the sheets as her body shuddered, and Elizabeth's arms encircled her thighs, pulling Katherine closer as her tongue alternated between light twists and forceful stokes. Katherine cried out as the ecstasy of Elizabeth's strokes built a pounding need inside her. The strokes came faster and the need more urgent until, at just the moment Katherine's trembling body converged on the edge of orgasm, Elizabeth slid two long fingers inside her. The fingers moved in and out, and then pushed powerful and steady with the rhythm of the tongue. Katherine lifted her hips to meet Elizabeth's rhythm as moaning cries rose. The intense ecstasy filling her body shook Katherine wildly and Elizabeth drew her tighter, turning the force of one finger slightly forward to push against constricting muscles. The sensations of every nerve in Katherine's body converged, and with one long unrestrained cry her body exploded with the flow of ecstasy.

FOR A LONG WHILE Katherine lay quiet in Elizabeth's arms, her body numb but her breath returning as she felt Elizabeth's fingers roam across her shoulders, through her hair, across the soft skin of her face. In time Katherine's strength returned, heightening her burning desire to touch Elizabeth, to taste her skin, to know the power of making love as she filled Elizabeth's body with the same pleasure she had just known. Katherine looked up at Elizabeth and saw a welcoming smile, answering her silent question. Their bed again became a tangle of flesh and body, sweet moaning of pleasure, and innate cries as the convulsing shudders of orgasm escaped their bodies, each time with a fresh power, until at last they collapsed together, breathless and spent.

They rested quietly as Elizabeth's hand roamed across the damp skin of Katherine's back. Katherine lifted her head from the shoulder of her lover. "My love," she began with a tranquil smile, reaching up to brush back tussled hair from Elizabeth's brow. Katherine realized that was enough and again rested against Elizabeth's body.

Elizabeth tightened her arms around Katherine and rolled to her side, enveloping Katherine's body inside her own. "I am yours, Katherine," Elizabeth breathed softly against her neck as she took Katherine's hand and pulled her closer.

In the peaceful silence of the room Katherine listened to the steady breathing of her sleeping lover. She took Elizabeth's hand to her lips and delicately kissed each finger. Her eyes lazily drifted to the clock: 3:09 in the morning of the night she finally realized who she was.

WHEN KATHERINE LOOKED at the clock again it was exactly eight-thirty. She stretched with a smile and rolled over to kiss her lover. Instead she found a single purple orchid nestled on Elizabeth's pillow. Katherine reached over, picked up the orchid, and found a note attached to a yellow ribbon.

My Dearest Katherine,
    It took the power of a hundred horses to pull me from you and this bed. I am sitting beside you as I write this note and my body aches to hold you, to touch you—but I will not disturb your sleep. Tomorrow is the first day of the legislative session, and I will be spending today in meetings with members. Henri will bring you a car to drive home. It should be here by the time you wake. I will call you later this morning. I so want to hear the sound of your voice. Be assured my thoughts will be with you every minute. I'm afraid you will be quite a distraction for me today, but I find myself energized by thoughts of you. I hope tonight will not leave me longing. Please see me if you can. Until then, my love goes with you.
    Elizabeth.

Katherine held the note to her lips and fell against the bed, elated, joyous, and desperate. What she had done last night was against everything she thought she believed, and yet she lay in the sweet fragrance of her lover's bed, feeling a change mounting inside of her, as if a long-exiled spirit was emerging from her dogmatic confinement. She would not go back; she would find a way to save her son and keep the love of the woman who had set her free.

Chapter 25

Katherine idly looked into her refrigerator, recalling the previous night when she watched Elizabeth do the same thing. She smiled, remembering the look on Elizabeth's face when she turned around.

Katherine picked out two eggs for a cheese omelet. It was just after ten a.m., and she supposed she had experienced every possible human emotion since she woke up. Cautious joy now remained.

After the omelet Katherine went for a shower, only begrudgingly washing the smell of Elizabeth off her skin. She lingered under the warm water, grateful for the day off, and stepped out of the shower just when the phone rang.

"Good morning," Elizabeth said pleasantly. "Am I forgiven for leaving you alone this morning?"

Katherine smiled. "I'm still thinking about it. I think you're going to have to make it up to me somehow."

"Hmmm," Elizabeth replied. "I know this place on the beach. It's amazingly quiet. I could pack a picnic and we could have dinner with the sea gulls."

"I don't think I want to share you. How about if you come here for dinner? There's a stuffed shrimp recipe I've been waiting to try. And then after dinner. . . ."

"Or before," Elizabeth enticed.

"Or both."

"Or both. I'll be through here by about seven o'clock tonight."

"How's seven-thirty?"

"I'll be there," Elizabeth said and hung up.

Elizabeth made it by seven-twenty. Katherine pulled Elizabeth through the front doorway and locked her into a long, deep kiss.

"Hello," Elizabeth said, pulling back slightly from the kiss but still holding Katherine tight. "I can see you don't mind that I'm a few minutes early. I ducked out before anyone could corner me. One of my better efforts, too, I should say."

"I'll have to make it worth your while," Katherine replied. "But I think it's the least you could do seeing as how you were gone when I woke up this morning."

"I know—nasty habit of mine—loving and leaving. You'll get used to it."

"How about we get to the loving part again?" Katherine said, and led Elizabeth into the bedroom.

They finally got to the stuffed shrimp a little after ten.

"Why did you decide to become a doctor?" Elizabeth asked, now standing in a too-small robe in Katherine's kitchen.

Katherine took two plates from the corner shelf as she answered, "My fascination with the human body, how it works. Ever since my father died I've been in awe of the nuts and bolts of it all, you know. Like, what made my father die? What happened in him that made him suddenly just cease to exist? I spent years terrified that the same thing would happen to me, that one day I'd just cease to exist. My mother's only comfort and advice was that I should be ready for death whenever it comes, no matter what happened to my body. Of course, my strict Christian upbringing taught me that to overcome death I should prepare for my day of judgment. So I went to church every time the door opened."

Katherine set the two plates on the kitchen bar and opened the silverware drawer, "The other thing that was going on in my adolescent mind was this drive to take the mystery out of the workings of the body, so I began to read everything I could get my hands on about anatomy, physiology, even cellular biology. No one doubted that I would become a doctor, but it was in my internship that I decided to go into research. I wanted to figure out how we could make the blood and bones work better, how we could keep people from dying suddenly, and how we could make life easier when death came slowly. I never really wanted to save people. I accepted the fact of death at an early age. I just wanted to place death in its own time—not before we've all had the chance to live."

Elizabeth moved in behind Katherine and pulled her close.

"And what about you, Governor?" Katherine asked, looking over her shoulder at Elizabeth. "What in the world made you decide to take on something like building this Territory?"

"Meagan," Elizabeth answered. "And the Force of God."

Katherine again looked over her shoulder into Elizabeth's eyes, "Meagan and who?"

"The Force of God," Elizabeth replied earnestly. "I was once foolish enough to go up against Her," she said, smiling with the memory. She leaned against the counter. "It was the first night Meagan and I were here. We'd spent the entire day on a tour of what was to be the Territory, and we'd seen nothing but swamp. I was certain that the Bucks administration had cooked up the whole territory idea just to divide the gay rights movement, and that Meagan and I had played right into Bucks's hands. I had had a fight with Meagan, one that I had started. I was so angry, and I took it out on her. But fighting with Meagan wasn't enough. I was furious, at Meagan, at William Bucks, at the whole world. I wanted someone to fight, so figured I would take it to God."

"Wow," Katherine said. She moved next to Elizabeth and put her hand on her chest. "What happened?"

Elizabeth turned a trace of a smile as she remembered. "God took up my challenge, and She kicked my ass. That night She led me out into the ocean. I don't know how long I swam that night, or how far I went from the shore, but when I came back, something inside me had changed. I realized that my whole adult life I had been motivated by the need to take on the challenge, to conquer and win. I was always willing to be the one to wade in, take the challenge, and fix everything. I thought that drive, that motivation to fix things, to always right the wrongs, was the source of my power."

"And what did God show you instead?" Katherine asked.

"How wrong I had been," Elizabeth answered. "Until that night I had been relying on my mind and my body for everything, my heart and my soul were nowhere to be found. I had thought the heart and soul held no power, that they only confused things and made me vulnerable, but that night after the swim I sat on the beach for a long while, and I realized that the mind and the body are actually weak, that the heart and soul are the source of real, true power."

"What did you do to change?"

"I began to listen more and more to my deep, inner voice, and the more I did, the more I felt this new source of power growing within me. After a while it was as if I had shed my skin and I was walking in a new body."

"What was that like?"

"Unsettling at first. I had to learn how to find that quiet voice within me when the world is going crazy all around. But once I learned I found more than ever that people were willing to follow my lead, but not like they had before, not because I was willing to lead the fight. They followed me because they trusted me."

"And because you trusted yourself?" Katherine asked.

"Because I trusted myself," Elizabeth said, lifting her glass up, "and Her."

Katherine leaned into Elizabeth and smiled up at her. "So God is a woman?" she asked.

"Sometimes," Elizabeth replied.

In an apartment building across from Katherine's condo, Larry Robinson's face twisted in disapproval. God, female? No way. Never. "Whoever your god is," Larry whispered to the empty room, "you're going to need her soon."

"Did you say something?" Paul said as he walked into the room for the night shift.

"It seems our Dr. Hopkins has a new lover. Governor Nix, if you can believe it," Larry replied. "And we have to notify her husband right away. This is *serious*."

"No. You won't call her husband," Paul commanded. "And you won't tell Jason anything, either."

"I have to," Larry protested.

"Don't be an idiot," Paul began. "Thomas Hopkins is not going to hear a word of this. If he finds out he'll be down here tomorrow and blow the whole thing. You just keep your mouth shut and let me take care of this."

Chapter 26

For the fourth time in ten minutes Elizabeth walked from the window to her desk and sat down. This time she dialed up Meagan, tapping her fingers for the five seconds it took for the video connection.

"Yes ma'am," Meagan said with a smile as the plopped down in her office chair. "What's on your mind?"

Elizabeth stood again and leaned next to the window, watching two sailboats race across the gulf. "I need to talk to you about Katherine," she said. "Have you got a few minutes this afternoon? This has to be in person."

"Yes. My afternoon's flexible," Meagan replied. "You say you need to talk to me about Katherine? Is everything okay?"

"Yeah, everything's fine—great, in fact. That's why I need to talk to you. What time can I expect you?"

They agreed on one-thirty, and Elizabeth pulled up a budget file and skimmed the charts and tables in the executive summary. The Territory was barely staying in the black, not including capital investments, and she knew the demands of the next five years could blow the expected revenues by more than ten percent. There was little Territory-owned land left that she would recommend to sell, and any increase in taxes would never pass the legislature. She wouldn't sign a tax bill anyway. But someway the Territory had to collect another 300 million just to keep up with current expenditures.

Elizabeth closed the file and glanced at her watch. Meagan would be another forty-five minutes—just enough time to burn off the pent-up energy twisting through her body. She headed downstairs for the gym.

Despite a thirty-minute workout Elizabeth was pacing when Meagan walked into governor's office. Meagan patted Elizabeth on the back as she walked to the rocker. "Wow," she said as she sat down and pulled

Blown Away
© 2006 by The Haworth Press, Inc. All rights reserved.
doi:10.1300/5706_26

her knee up to her chest. "You really are wound up. What's going on?"

Elizabeth stopped the pacing and leaned against her desk, "When does the next MIC rotation start?"

"The second week in July," Meagan replied. "You're thinking about asking Katherine, aren't you?"

"Yes, but I haven't made my mind up yet. What do you think?"

"How long have you been working on this?" Meagan asked.

"I started tossing it around a couple of weeks ago. I've been working on a decision for about three days."

"And you're concerned that you may not be separating your personal feelings from your professional judgment."

"That's about the sum of it," Elizabeth replied.

"Have you been to the beach?"

"Yeah. Twice."

Meagan's brows furrowed. "Huh, you are stuck. But in your gut you're leaning toward asking her, because if you weren't, you would wait."

"That's true. It's just I'm not sure this time I can trust my gut. And it's not just about the rotation, Meagan, or I probably would wait until this fall. The problem is I think Mozingo is right. We need Katherine heading up the pathology team, right away. Her expertise and her ability to focus a research team are exactly what we need to get to a breakthrough. You don't have to be in love with her to know that." Elizabeth paused, realizing that she had, for the first time, admitted to Meagan that she was in love with Katherine.

Meagan said nothing as she looked up at Elizabeth with a slight pang of anxious insecurity. She took a deep breath before she said, "You're right about everything you have said. She is the best person in the Territory—well, probably even in the country, to head the pathology team. And you're right that the sooner we get her in the rotation system the sooner we can move her up to lead the team. What I don't hear you saying is that you are absolutely confident that she can be trusted, even though you're in love with her."

Elizabeth went back to the window. "Do you remember when we stood right here at this window, just this past January, trying to decide whether to accept Katherine's application to the Territory?" Elizabeth asked.

"Of course I remember," Meagan replied. "We struggled with that one, too."

"And there was less at stake, then," Elizabeth replied. "We knew from the outset that we had questions about Katherine, whether she belonged here in the Territory, and we decided how we were going to try to answer those questions. And it worked," Elizabeth said with an ironic smile. "I never expected it to work this well, or to get caught up in it, but still, here we are, certain of her sexuality, and I still don't know if we can trust her totally. I trust her love. I trust her friendship. I just can't get to trusting her with this. You know we can't afford to be wrong. There's no going back if we are."

Meagan rocked a bit as she said thoughtfully, "That's very true. While there is no doubt about where she is right now, the question of her past and why she came here obviously remains in your mind."

"Yes, in spite of the past few weeks, that question still lingers. What has happened since Katherine's been in the Territory is a matter of certainty. What happened in the weeks before she came here is not."

"Well, it seems to me that we've got two questions here, Elizabeth," Meagan said thoughtfully. "One, did Katherine actually have an affair before she came here? We've never really been able to verify or refute her story. And two, does it matter anyway? What we really need to know is whether your current relationship with her is based on love or seduction. If she truly loves you there is less chance of betrayal, regardless of her original motives."

Elizabeth took a deep breath and folded her arms over her chest. She narrowed her eyes thoughtfully. "How would you answer those questions?"

"I think you're the best one to answer them, Elizabeth," Meagan replied. "The answer to one should help to answer the other."

"How so?"

"I think you have to go back to that first night you slept with her. Did she seem at all uncomfortable or unsure—in any way did she in-

dicate that you were her first lesbian lover? Was there anything in her
manner that seemed contrived?"

Elizabeth glared back at Meagan, feeling a sting in her questions.
"Shit, Meagan, I don't know," she snapped. "The way you ask me that
all the time you would think I had planned what happened with
Katherine, like I was acting out some grand concocted scheme to try
to figure her out, like I was taking goddamn notes all night. I'm telling you it just happened, and I can promise you at the time I wasn't
thinking about Katherine's motives either."

Meagan looked back at Elizabeth, matching her glare. "You need
to calm down," she said coolly. "In the first place, I don't ask you that
all the time. Maybe you ask yourself that question all the time, but I
believe it's only the second time I have asked you anything remotely
similar. I never said you planned anything. In fact, I defend your relationship with Katherine to quite a few people," Meagan said firmly.
She stood from the rocker and walked over to the window. "I tell you,
Jessica still isn't comfortable at all with your relationship with Katherine," Meagan said with her eyes out on the Gulf. She stood silently
for a moment before she turned back to Elizabeth. "So you need to
quit being so angry and listen to me," she said, unperturbed. "I'm just
trying to help you think through this. Isn't that what you wanted?"

Elizabeth walked to her chair and sat down heavily, turning up a
guilty shrug. "Yeah, you're right, that *is* why I wanted you to come
over," she said. She looked at Meagan with a vague, apologetic smile.
"Look, I'm sorry. I do sometimes replay that first night with Katherine in my mind, and I always end up wondering if there was something there that I should have seen but was too swept away to notice."
Elizabeth picked up a pen and reflectively pushed it end to end, thinking aloud. "Or maybe I overreacted because I'm wrestling so much
with the decision of whether we should ask her to serve on the MIC
team. I want to, you know, but the reservations we had when she first
came here keep popping up in the back of my mind. I want to trust
her, but I don't know how I'd ever recover if she betrays me, not to
mention the damage she could do to the Territory. I think the bottom
line is that I'm not ready to allow her enough freedom to find out

what she will do. I'd rather just keep things the way they are right now. No risk, no pain."

Meagan walked behind Elizabeth and rubbed her shoulders hard. "It's a huge decision, Elizabeth, and once you've made it there's no going back. Ultimately you're going to have to make it yourself. You are the only one who knows what's going on between you and Katherine and whether we can trust her, but maybe I can help you figure it out, if you're ready."

"Yeah. Go ahead. I'll keep it calm," Elizabeth said evenly.

Meagan walked back to the rocker and sat down again. "I know you weren't taking notes, but do you remember anything about your first night together? Was she coming on to you at May Days? Whose idea was it to go for a drive?"

"That was me," Elizabeth replied. "I'd spent most of the afternoon with her, and I wasn't ready to leave her yet. I invited her to the mansion for dessert. But I think she did come to the tent looking for me that afternoon."

"Uh-huh, so that one's a toss-up. What about that night at your house? Mostly, what about the sex? Who initiated it?"

Elizabeth smiled with the memory. "I'm not sure who initiated it," she said. "I just turned around and she was standing there looking at me, and then boom! The next thing I know she's in my bed and she's undr. . . ." Elizabeth stopped and looked out the window. "Well, let's just say I made love to her."

"So you made love to her first?" Meagan asked.

"Yes."

"And then what? What did she do?"

"You mean did she make love to me that night?"

"Not just that, but did she seem comfortable in knowing what to do? Did she seem to . . . to desire you?"

"You mean did she have experience and did she want to touch me in the same way I touched her," Elizabeth replied. She leaned back, thinking. "There was one moment before she made love to me when she looked hesitant, like she wasn't sure I wanted the same thing from her. But there are some women like that, you know. Maybe her lover in Virginia was." She looked back at Meagan. "But the way she accepted me and the way she made love to me, it wasn't contrived. She wanted to."

"What about since that night?" Meagan asked. "Has there been any indication that she seemed to be having trouble accepting you sexually? Has she ever pressed you for information or wanted to meet anyone in particular?"

"No," Elizabeth replied. "Our sex life is great. She's very open to me physically. Our conversations about the Territory have been mostly general. She's never asked about anything that struck me as out of line or peculiar. I know it has only been about a month, but I've been around long enough to know when things feel honest."

"Do you believe she loves you?" Meagan asked.

"Yes, I do."

"So where does that leave you?" Meagan asked after a moment.

"I think I'm getting there," Elizabeth replied. "Give me a couple of nights to think about it, and I'll let you know. Right now I'm leaning toward asking her."

"Whatever your decision, it's good enough for me," Meagan replied. "Who knows, maybe Dr. Katherine Hopkins will one day indeed be our savior," she said with a slow smile.

Chapter 27

"Hello, beautiful," Elizabeth said as soon as Katherine answered her mobile phone. In the background the smooth voice of a NPR commentator was interrupted by the sharp insolence of a blaring horn. "You must be driving home."

"You got it," Katherine replied, her voice wavering between smoldering frustration and renewed expectations. "When are you going to do something about this traffic?"

"As soon you start using public transit," Elizabeth returned blithely. "But I would like to make that awful commute up to you," she said. "You know, I still haven't shown you that beach place I told you about."

"You mean the magic place you claim holds all the answers to the world?"

"That's it."

"There are a few questions I would like to have answered by those mysterious forces that speak to you there," Katherine said lightly, her mood lifting.

"Maybe tonight they will reveal their secrets," Elizabeth teased. "And while we're waiting I'll grill a couple of chicken kabobs." Elizabeth hesitated, deciding on her next words. "I want to get away because there is something I need to discuss with you, and I don't want any interruptions."

"Well, how could I possibly say no to that?" Katherine laughed. "Once again you have my curiosity. But I'm sure you know that, don't you?"

"I thought I might get your attention. Pick you up at seven?"

"I'll be ready, if I ever get through this traffic. Good-bye, babe."

ELIZABETH SPEARED A SLICE of bell pepper onto the skewer, followed deliberately by a healthy chunk of onion, and then a quarter to-

Blown Away
© 2006 by The Haworth Press, Inc. All rights reserved.
doi:10.1300/5706_27   *207*

mato. She studied her fingers sliding the tomatoes down shiny steel, distracted from conversation by the thoughts churning in her mind.

Beside her Katherine sat on their blanket, tolerating Elizabeth's silence and the taunt draw of her lips. Katherine first sensed Elizabeth's detachment as they swam. Her usual playfulness seemed reserved, or subtly forced, giving way from time to time to solitary sprints of quick, forceful strokes, leaving Katherine to stand alone in the surf, appreciating the grace of Elizabeth's body moving through the water, but wondering. Now Elizabeth may as well have been alone, though as they sat close on the blanket they had never been more aware of each other's presence and the thick tension filling the salty air that blew between them.

Elizabeth lowered the ends of the skewer over the grill, avoiding Katherine's eyes as she reached for her wine. She took a healthy swallow and looked out to the gulf before she spoke. "Katherine, I've told you that I love you, and I do, very much. But I haven't yet told you that I trust you." Elizabeth turned and looked steadily into Katherine's eyes. "And I do believe the two are separable."

Katherine nodded, but said nothing.

"I believe sometimes we have to consciously decide whom to trust," Elizabeth continued, studying Katherine's eyes and finding only appropriate curiosity. "I'm telling you this because the Territory needs your help soon, but I've got to know that I can trust you. Right now the only thing I know to do is to ask: can I trust you Katherine?"

Katherine looked back blankly. Of course Elizabeth could trust her. She took a deep breath and reached for Elizabeth's hand, answering with a reassuring smile. "Yes, Elizabeth, of course you can trust me."

Elizabeth held her eyes for a moment and nodded, and then looked out to the gulf again. "What do you know about MIC?"

The pace of Katherine's heart suddenly quickened, but she kept her expression unaffected. She answered calmly, "A little. Most of what I know I've read in journal articles."

"That may be good," Elizabeth said. "You'll be more likely to have an open mind."

Katherine's brow furrowed curiously. "An open mind about what?"

Elizabeth wrapped her arms around her knees and pulled them to her chest as she looked out to the open sea, a little more relaxed, but still a bit distant. "Katherine, we have a classified MIC research rotation," Elizabeth began. She turned again to the eyes of her lover. "The MIC research needs you. I would like for you to consider serving on the next rotation."

KATHERINE FOUND MEAGAN waiting in her office. "You ready to go?" Meagan asked, looking up.

Katherine nodded assuredly. "Oh yeah, I've been waiting for today since Elizabeth asked if I would do this rotation."

"I have been curious as to how she convinced you to commit to another rotation so soon," Meagan said. "You haven't had much of a break since your last."

"You know how persuasive Elizabeth can be," Katherine said with a light, knowing smile as she walked with Meagan to the corridor.

"I was very happy to hear she talked you into it. I believe your skills will be exactly what we need to push the research to the next level," Meagan said.

Katherine followed Meagan into the short corridor leading to the high security wing. Ahead, three armed guards stood ready to verify identification through a series of eye scans and voice codes. Just in front of the guards Meagan turned into a small conference room.

Dr. Mozingo was waiting there. "Oh my lord!" Mozingo said loudly as he sprung up and approached them with a delighted smile. "You actually did it, huh?" he said to Meagan. He reached for Katherine's hand, shaking it vigorously as he spoke. "I told Dr. West I didn't think you would take on another rotation just now. Especially since you and Elizabeth got it going on."

"She hasn't signed on just yet, Frank," Meagan reminded him.

"Oh, she will. She will," he said eagerly. "We're so glad to have you on board."

"Thank you, Dr. Mozingo. I'm looking forward to working with everyone," Katherine replied politely.

Dr. Mozingo talked on as they waited for a troupe of doctors to slowly drift into the room. A few of them Katherine had met, but most she had never seen before. She was certain the majority of them were not from Bayside.

In fifteen minutes the door closed and Katherine looked around to the other nineteen curious doctors gathered around a long table in the center of the windowless room. Slim, triple-sealed notebooks sat in front of each of them, taped with strict instructions not to break the seal unless directed to do so. In a moment a tall handsome man of about fifty years strolled into the room and spoke briefly with Mozingo, nodded to Meagan, and walked behind the podium at the head table. Katherine recognized him right away—Dr. Charles Winston, Chief of Research at Bayside.

Winston looked around the table, taking a silent role. He took reading glasses from his suit pocket, opened his notebook, and began speaking in his proud British accent, "As you all know, the Apalachicola Territory has recently made significant strides in the treatment of multisymptom infectious cirrhosis. We are certain, in fact, that we are on the verge of a major triumph in the treatment of this insidious disease. However, the costs to the Territory of multisymptom infectious cirrhosis research have been very high, and therefore we are not yet in a position to share the benefits with the rest of the world. We cannot risk losing a patent to an outside company, thereby losing the financial benefits of the tremendous economic investment we have made so far. Furthermore, in light of our recent successes, we feel it is vital to the economic interest of this Territory to press on with this research. In fact, one single MIC drug patent could fund our projected medical budgetary shortfalls for the next twenty years."

Winston grasped the podium as he paused and leaned forward, reviewing the faces of the new recruits with the intensity of a hungry hawk.

Katherine felt a shiver as she looked into the blue paleness of his commanding eyes, reminded of the same look in the eyes of Judge Calvin Marshall as he stared at her across the Virginia courtroom just six short months ago.

Winston's eyes darted from one doctor to the next as he continued, "Now, any of you who wish to work on this research effort will be required to sign a contract of confidentiality that you will find in the sealed notebooks in front of you. If you agree to this contract and then break it, you will be arrested and tried before a panel of judges in a court of law. If you are convicted, you may very well spend a good number of your years in prison. If our research efforts are successful, for your tireless and dedicated efforts you will see all patents or other financial benefits resulting from your research become the property of the Territory. Of course, you may expect generous financial bonuses for significant contributions, but nothing else. If you do not believe this is something you can do, you may leave immediately."

A thick silence fell over the room, and Katherine wondered if anyone could hear the hammering of her heart.

"I see you all have great confidence in your convictions," Winston said after another slow scan of the room. "While I admire your assurance, I'm not certain of its legitimacy. In front of you, you will find a notebook with a confidentiality contract inside. In a few moments, Dr. Mozingo, Ms. Sullivan, and I will leave you alone to read over these contracts. You may leave this room without question at any time before you sign the contract, but once you have signed the contract, you have agreed to its terms, including all confidentiality clauses. Leaking of research findings will likely result in criminal conviction, including the possibility of treason charges. You will be given thirty minutes to make your decision. As I said, you are free to leave without penalty or question at any point up to your signature. Any questions before we continue? Good. We will return in precisely thirty minutes."

Katherine watched them disappear behind the closing door, and turned to the notebook in front of her. Treason. Years in prison. She never expected the stakes to be this high. She broke the seal on her notebook, skimmed through the confidentiality clauses, and signed it.

MEAGAN WALKED BACK into the conference room first. Just inside the door she stopped for a quick count, noted that all twenty doctors remained, and walked up to the front of the room. Dr. Mozingo and Winston followed, collected the contracts, inspected the signatures, and placed them in a locking steel box at the front of the room. Katherine sensed a change in their air, as if a separation of trust was now gone.

Meagan moved to the podium and turned up her disarming smile. "I'm glad to see you are all still here. I think you'll find your work in the next six weeks to be some of the most exciting and rewarding of your career. With your skills and a bit of luck we just might get there."

Meagan looked over to Dr. Winston. "Did we get them all?" she asked. Winston nodded. "Okay, good," she said. She looked back to her audience. "I want you all to know what Dr. Winston just told you was only partially true. The final truth is that we believe we have a cure for MIC."

Katherine stared back at Meagan, ignoring the low murmur of whispers suddeny swirling around the room. Could the woman she loved and this friend she trusted be so cold and calculating, holding back critical medical advances for the sake of money?

Meagan answered her right away. "I want to say on the outset that we are not withholding research advances for the sake of money." Meagan pushed a button on a remote control, bringing up the image of a small yellow flower shooting up from a clump of grass onto a large screen behind her. "This is *Harperocallis flava*, commonly named Harper's beauty," Meagan began. "It is an extremely rare plant known only to occur in isolated pockets of the Apalachicola Territory. As some of you know, when we established this Territory twelve years ago we conducted extensive inventories to find and preserve any rare plants and animals that occur inside the boundaries of the Territory. At the same time, we inventoried the properties of each of our rare plants to determine potential benefits of each of them. During our inventory we discovered a highly acidic compound found in the fruit of Harper's beauty, but due to the rarity of Harper's beauty and the difficulty in domestic cultivation of this particular plant we did not actively pursue uses for the compound." Meagan moved from behind the podium and slowly walked around the table. "Now, fast-forward to the present and we discover that the compound is a highly effective antibiotic, one that preliminary results have shown will completely destroy the MIC bacteria. Our early trials indicate total elimination of the bacteria in the bloodstream, and follow-up tests on all patients treated have not presented indications of reoccurrence."

Meagan stopped and stood directly behind Katherine. "Unfortunately, we haven't yet been able to successfully synthesize the active compound, and therefore we have been forced to limit drug trials to Territory residents. Our primary problem with the synthesized compound is a history of severe side effects, primarily consisting of a multitude of digestive illnesses. When presented in a patient with a compromised immune system these digestive illnesses can be life threatening. We feel that we could obtain an accelerated approval from the FDA for the naturally derived compound, but of course, due to the rarity of the fruit source, we can't produce the amount necessary for mass distribution. Therefore, the goal of this research effort is to resolve the side-effect problems with the synthesized compound before we go to the FDA." Meagan paused and looked around the table. "Any questions so far?"

No hands or voices were raised, so she continued. "Okay, Dr. Mozingo will fill you in on the details of how this rotation works."

Meagan sat down next to Winston as Mozingo took the floor. "Good morning, everyone," he said in an unusually subdued manner. "I want to thank you all for volunteering your time and skills for this rotation. Without a doubt this is the most important medical work being conducted in the Territory, perhaps even in the country. Now," he said matter-of-factly, "this rotation is a bit different from most rotations. Each of you will be assigned to an existing team according to your specialty. Each team has two permanent members in addition to the team leader, so your role is to provide fresh thinking, new ideas to your team."

Mozingo pushed the remote control to replace the image of Harper's beauty with an organizational chart. DR. FRANK MOZINGO appeared in bold letters across the top slot, and underneath were a series of boxes labeled according to specialty: pharmacology, pathology, chemistry, genetics, internal medicine, and so on. "As you can see, I am the MIC research team leader. Whether you knew it or not, I recruited each of you to work on this rotation. From now on, until we find a marketable cure for MIC, each of you will work only on MIC rotations. When your rotation comes up again, you will be reassigned to your MIC team."

The Mozingo twinkle returned to his eyes and with a wry smile he scanned across the stern faces of twenty physicians. "From now on, you are mine, my pets," he said slyly. Five or six faces smiled back before Mozingo continued seriously. "I should also mention there will be two permanent positions opening up very soon, one on the pharmacology team and one on the pathology team. If you accept a permanent position you'll still work long hours, but the schedule isn't as tortuous, and you will be relieved from any and all rotation schedules. I hope some of you will consider joining one of these teams in a permanent capacity," he said, looking directly at Katherine.

Katherine returned a cool, acknowledging nod. *Oh, yes,* she thought, *I'll be there. You can bet your crazy ass on that. And, one way or another, my Jacob's going to get this treatment.*

Chapter 28

Elizabeth toweled off her hair as she walked into Katherine's kitchen. "How about ordering out tonight?" she asked, wrapping an arm around Katherine's back. She lightly kissed Katherine's neck and walked over to the couch.

Katherine kept her eyes on the orange she was peeling, lost in her thoughts, and said nothing.

Elizabeth lazily fell on to the couch. "Katherine—hello, are you here tonight, or should I just go back home?" she said, nestling in and dropping a pillow behind her back.

Katherine abandoned the orange and leaned against the counter, focusing her eyes intently on Elizabeth. "Harper's beauty—why doesn't cultivation work?"

Elizabeth returned a puzzled shrug. "Well, as I understand it, the wetland conditions Harper's beauty prefers are hard to mimic. Given enough time we might be able to do it, but it would likely take years to determine the exact growing conditions needed to make the plant flourish. After all, most rare plants require unique conditions, otherwise they wouldn't be quite so rare, would they?" Elizabeth said with a light, puckish smile.

"No. I guess not," Katherine replied seriously. She picked up the orange again.

Elizabeth watched Katherine for a moment. The intense lines on Katherine's face were much too serious to have accepted her flippant answer. Elizabeth got up and walked back into the kitchen, "I'm sorry, babe. I shouldn't have blown you off like that. I guess you have a lot to sort through after what you heard today. Do you want to talk about it?"

Katherine set down the orange but kept her eyes on the peelings piled on the counter. "I'm not sure," she said before looking at Elizabeth. "It is a lot to deal with, you know, to find out there is a cure for

MIC and then at the same time to find out the cure is only available to the people of the Territory. And even *they* don't *know* they've been cured. In fact, we don't even know for sure that this antibiotic kills the bacteria permanently. She paused for a moment, still trying to sort through her thoughts. "Remember how you felt the first day Meagan told you about the breakthrough with Harper's beauty?"

Elizabeth nodded, saying, "Yeah, you're right. I've never really thought much about the psychological impacts all this must have on you guys in research. Meagan has never talked to me about it, but I'm sure she's counseling the staff on how to deal with this kind of secret. You may want to talk to her, and I'm always willing to listen."

"I know," Katherine said. She took Elizabeth's hand, lacing their fingers together as she looked up at her. "I think what I really need to-night is a long walk on the beach."

"Do you want me to go along?"

"No. I feel like I need to go alone."

Katherine didn't need to say it; Elizabeth knew she needed the en-tire night. She wrapped her arms around Katherine and held her closely for a moment. "Maybe it would be best if I go on back to the mansion. I think you need the space to sort out what you're feeling right now."

Katherine looked up at her, "Do you mind?" she asked. "I'll be fine tomorrow. This is really on my mind tonight."

"Of course I don't mind."

After a quick kiss Elizabeth headed back to the bedroom. In ten minutes she was dressed and standing at the door. "I'll call you later tonight," she said, and left for the night.

KATHERINE'S WEEKS OF MIC research were passing with the amaz-ing speed of purpose, and tonight her mood was unusually good, in spite of the August heat that had settled over the Territory with op-pressive certainty. Even Elizabeth's energy had waned as she ner-vously spent the day monitoring the maddening track of Hurricane Belinda, a category three predicted to go north into Louisiana, but a couple of models still predicted it could turn east.

Right now none of that mattered to Katherine. For the past four weeks her lifeblood had raced through her body, and her mind focused with single-minded clarity. It was about more than saving Jacob now. Through her work she could possibly save thousands of lives. Just this morning she talked to Mozingo about the permanent position on the pathology team and he assured her that if she wanted the job, it was hers. So tonight her senses heightened with reenergized passion. She seduced Elizabeth twice, the first time as soon as she walked through the door and again after dinner. Now she rested on Elizabeth's bare shoulder, teasing her with fingers sweeping across her stomach and warm breath blowing lightly across her skin. She pondered more, but as she saw Elizabeth's eyes slowly closing she decided to let her go. In a moment she heard the familiar, slow rhythm of Elizabeth's sleeping breath.

Katherine rolled over and smiled as she closed her eyes and gathered the sheets around her, for the first time in months feeling completely peaceful. Soon enough, her nightmare would be over.

Chapter 29

Ed Zytowske called himself a military man, but as he crawled through the hot, mosquito-filled muck at the edge of the governor's estate he was thankful he never saw any real combat. He was as miserable as he figured a man could be, covered with sweat and mud, gnats swarming at his nostrils, trickles of blood seeping from the cuts on his arms—the result of an unseen line of barbed wire fence he had hit on the way in. All he wanted now was the beer and shower he would have within the hour, after this little job was over.

His instructions were simple enough. Go to the location set in his GPS system, dig up a couple of plants, put them in the bag, and be back at the road for pickup in an hour. For this simple job he'd make twenty thousand. For that kind of money his wounds would heal fast.

Zytowske waved vaguely at the gnats swarming his ears and nose as he again checked his GPS. Sixty-seven feet, two o'clock, read the LCD display. He turned his body slightly right and crawled another five feet. He checked again. Right on course with only sixty-two feet to go.

A puff of breeze filtered through the trees, followed by the rumble of a low growl. Zytowske hoped to God the rumble wasn't what he feared. Another bellow rose in the air, and Zytowske knew it was in fact an alligator. By the sound of the bellow he imagined it was at least a fourteen footer, waiting right in the path he planned to backtrack to the road. Zytowske swore as he grabbed the grass in front of him and pulled himself forward.

Now the GPS-LCD read only five feet to go. Zytowske stopped to pull night-vision glasses from his hip pack. He slid them on and fished out the photograph of Harper's beauty. After a good look he stuffed the photograph under his shirt and moved toward the grassy clump just ahead. Sweat dripped from his face as he pulled out the folding trowel from his pack, followed by two sealable paper bags and again

Blown Away
© 2006 by The Haworth Press, Inc. All rights reserved.
doi:10.1300/5706_29

the photograph. In four quick motions he dug one plant for each bag and carefully replaced the dirt and leaves. They would never know it was gone.

Now there was the little matter of the gator. Zytowske slowed his breathing, listening carefully through the sounds of the night, waiting for the familiar roar of his new nemesis. Clouds cleared from the glow of the half moon and he heard the bellow again, verifying his fear. The gator had not moved. Zytowske checked his watch. Only twenty-five minutes to pickup, and if he was not there he would be left. He had to find another way out. He reached to his hip pocket for the map. Studying the coordinates he saw he could be in timber only 200 feet ahead. The trees would provide enough cover for him to stand, making movement faster, and then, circling back, he could get behind the gator for a clear path back out to the road.

Zytowske hastily folded the map and put it back in his pocket. In quick side-to-side motions he slid on his belly through the muck of the swamp, making his way toward the safety of the tree line. He made it there clean, and at the edge of the trees Zytowske stood up. Suddenly a crash of breaking tree limbs cracked behind him.

"What the hell are you doing!" the voice of Henri DeVaul pierced the night air. "Get your hands in the air, boy, and don't bother lookin' around! I've got a twelve-gauge pointed right at your head."

Zytowske slowly reached his hands upward.

"Now you do what I tell you or you won't see tomorrow," Henri commanded as she walked toward him.

Zytowske decided not to test her. He stood quietly, keeping his hands above him.

"All right now, let me see what I've got here," Henri said in her loud, chafing voice. She stood behind Zytowske with a pump shotgun to her shoulder, aiming the barrel at his back. "I want you to turn around, real slow and easy now—and keep your hands up."

In deliberate, clockwise quarter steps Zytowske turned around, his hands straight above his head. He peered through his night glasses at his captor, his eyes immediately going to the shotgun. His blood ran cold as he stared down a barrel that looked as big as a cannon. Then his eyes slowly lifted up to the face of his captor. Henri stared back at him, peering through a pair of ancient military night goggles.

Staying stone still Zytowske measured up Henri. She didn't look like much, a slim five and a half feet, wearing worn army fatigues and a dark T-shirt that read VEGETARIANS TASTE BETTER. Zytowske considered an overpowering move, but the look on Henri's face told him she would use the shotgun.

"You don't have a gun on you, do you?" Henri asked suspiciously.

Zytowske shook his head.

"Well, I don't know what your doin' here but I'm gonna let the police figure that out for me."

Henri kept the gun on him as she barked her commands. "All right, mister, you and I need to take a little walk. Now I want you to turn to your right and get goin' up the path there, and keep your hands up. I'm gonna be right behind you, and don't think I won't shoot your ass off if you try to run."

Zytowske believed her. He started up the path.

JESSICA THOMPSON WALKED up to the fifth precinct's desk sergeant within thirty minutes of being awakened by a 1 a.m. call. "I'm looking for Detective Brimmer," she said.

The desk sergeant escorted her to the small corner office Detective Brimmer shared with four other detectives, none of whom were in tonight. Brimmer sat at his desk, playing blackjack with Henri.

"Looks like you guys have everything under control," Jessica said lightly as she walked into the office. She held her hand out to Brimmer. "Detective Brimmer, I'm Jessica Thompson. Thanks for calling."

"'Bout time you got here," Henri interrupted.

"I had to get dressed, Henri," Jessica replied. "Did this guy have anything on him?" Jessica asked, turning back to Brimmer.

Brimmer pointed to a small, black mud-covered pack and two clean paper bags on his desk, "That's all we found," he said. "In the pack is a fairly sophisticated GPS unit, a pair of high-tech night-vision glasses, and a map. I found these two bags with a couple of plants in them, too," Brimmer said. He looked up at Jessica and shrugged, "No signs of any bombs, biological or chemical agents, poisons, or anything, really, to do any damage; not even a gun. Best I can tell, all's he wanted was those plants. I figure they could be on the protected list. I thought I'd call the folks in natural resources tomorrow to see if they want to charge this guy with anything. From what I've seen of this stuff, though, it looks like that's all we can do. He didn't do anything dangerous or threatening to the governor, and it looks like he didn't intend to. Maybe he's just some whacked-out botanist wanting to enhance his plant collection."

"I suppose that is possible," Jessica agreed casually. "I know we do have a few species of rare and protected plants in the Territory. Chances are that is what's in the bags."

Jessica opened one of the bags and looked inside. Right away she recognized Harper's beauty. "Well, I'm no botanist so I can't tell the difference," she said, putting the bag back on the desk with a sharp glance to Henri to keep quiet. "Go ahead and process his equipment and the plants as evidence, and I'll go have a little talk with this guy. Is he a Territory citizen?"

"He wasn't carrying any ID, and so far he hasn't given us a name," Brimmer said. "Maybe you can get something from him. He's in interrogation room two. You want me in there with you?"

"No." Jessica said. "But I might want Henri to come in with her shotgun after a bit," she continued with a wink. Jessica shot another quick glance to Henri, again assuring her that yes, she knew exactly what was in the bags. "Anything else?" she asked.

"Only a hunch," Brimmer said. "I really don't think this guy is family."

Jessica shrugged. "Huh, a straight guy with a dangerous obsession for plants—kinky."

Two doors down Ed Zytowske waited quietly in the interrogation room, one arm and one leg shackled to the metal table in front of him. Jessica walked in and closed the door behind her. Immediately she turned off the two monitor cameras aimed at Zytowske.

"Good morning," Jessica said as she sat down in a gray metal chair across from Zytowske. "Damn awful way to spend the morning, isn't it—wet, filthy, and chained up to a cold table?"

Zytowske shrugged indifferently.

Jessica leaned back in her chair and relaxed. "Of course," she began slowly, "it's not nearly as bad as hearing that steel door slam shut behind you."

Zytowske glanced up at Jessica to assure his apathy, and then returned his vacant stare to the handcuff around his wrist.

"Well," Jessica began again, "I suppose in time you may get used to the slam of that steel door. But I know I never did. That whole time I was locked up I never got used to it." Jessica paused, reflecting on the memory. "It's an awful thing, being in prison," she said softly. She turned her gaze straight on Zytowske, "You ever been locked up—I'm sorry, what was your name again?"

"Zytowske," he said. "Ed Zytowske."

"Ed Zytowske," Jessica repeated. She tipped her chair into a casual rock. "So, Ed, have you ever been locked up?" Zytowske didn't answer. "God, I hated it," Jessica said, speaking to him as if they were sharing a beer and war stories at the local bar. "They just treat you like shit, man; it doesn't matter where you are. The guards mess with you. They don't give a damn if you get yourself in a scrap and get your ass kicked. I remember the first few weeks the girls all wanted to either fight me or fuck me, you know what I mean, Ed?" She watched as Ed began to twist in his chair, keeping his eyes down at the cuff around his wrist. "I'm betting you don't know what I mean. I'm betting you've never been in jail. Shit, you've probably never even been arrested."

Zytowske stiffened, but still said nothing.

"Well, you're arrested now, Ed." Jessica leaned toward him with steady eyes, "Are you aware of your rights?"

Zytowske faintly nodded.

"Good. And you're aware you were arrested for trespassing on restricted property?" Zytowske nodded again. "Yeah, that's gonna be a misdemeanor, but you can be sentenced to up to six months in jail if you are convicted," Jessica said. "And since you were on the governor's property, I'll recommend you get the full time."

Zytowske shifted nervously, but kept up his front.

Jessica stayed on him, "It's the plants you had on you that's got me worried, Ed. You know, if those two plants are on the protected plant list I'll have to charge you with a felony. It'll be a class one felony that will get you five to twenty-five."

Zytowske's face flushed. "What?" he asked incredulously. "You're saying you're gonna put me in jail for digging up some damn plant?"

"That's the deal," Jessica replied calmly. "Or you can go home tonight and we may let you get by with a fine and suspended sentence, depending on how serious the offense is and what we at the prosecutor's office decide to recommend."

"I need to speak to my lawyer," Zytowske grumbled.

"Okay," Jessica said. "We'll assign you one or you can call your attorney in the morning, but it usually takes a day or two for lawyers from the States to get here. We'll pick up this conversation then." Jessica pushed back her chair and stood up. "In the meantime we'll hold you here in the fifth precinct jail. I'm sure I can convince the magistrate that you're a flight risk, so I wouldn't count on bail."

"Wait a minute," Zytowske said as Jessica turned for the door.

Jessica looked back at him.

"You said I might just pay a fine and go home tonight. Maybe I want to do that."

"Oh," Jessica said, walking back to the table, "I thought you wanted to talk it over with your attorney."

"Maybe I don't need him."

"How so?"

Zytowske looked up shrewdly. "Maybe I can tell you things you'd want to know."

"Like what, Ed? What could I possibly want to know from a guy caught crawling around the governor's estate swiping some plants? It looks pretty cut and dried to me."

"Maybe there's more to it," Zytowske offered.

Jessica let her silence play him a bit longer before she said, "You don't know much about plants, do you Ed?"

"No, not really."

"That's what I thought. I'll bet that you didn't even know that mere possession of the plants you had in your bag is a felony."

Zytowske swallowed hard. "No, I didn't know that," he said. "Misdemeanor trespass, yeah, but a felony? No way."

"Okay," Jessica said. She paused to let Zytowske's expectant mind run free, then she said, "Now, Ed, I could see right away that you don't know a damn thing about the plant you had in those paper bags, but there is no jury in the world, much less this Territory, that I can't convince that you clearly, intentionally set out tonight to steal that particular plant. And the only reason I can figure you did that, Ed, is because somebody is paying you for it."

"You might be right about that."

"And if I am I suppose you would rather tell me than risk twenty-five years in prison."

"You're right about that, too," Zytowske said.

"So, Ed, who was it? And just for kicks, how much was it going to cost them?"

Zytowske took a long, measured look at Jessica before asking, "Am I gonna walk out of here tonight?"

"If I believe you, there's a good chance of that."

Zytowske leaned his chest onto the table and glared cunningly at Jessica. "The person you want is Dr. Katherine Hopkins."

"IT CAN'T BE TRUE," Meagan said. She sat at her kitchen table with Jessica, nursing a strong cup of fresh-brewed coffee. She ran her fingers through her hair as she vacantly stared out the window into the black of the early morning.

"Whether he's lying or not, we've got to investigate it," Jessica replied. "And before we start the investigation, Elizabeth has to know." Jessica took a sip of coffee. "When is she coming in?"

"The fund-raiser for the congresswoman in Atlanta was last night, so she's taking the first flight into Tallahassee this morning. She should be here by about eight-thirty."

"Can you meet her at the airport?" Jessica asked. "You're the one who has to break this to her."

Meagan's face grew tense and she looked down in her coffee. "Of course," she said softly.

"What time does Katherine report to work?"

"She's still on the rotation, so she'll be at the hospital by six," Meagan said. She turned her gaze out the window. "You know, Jess, the timing of this whole thing seems out of line to me. Katherine's team was making real progress in finding the causes of the side effects. She told me the other day she thought it was just a matter of months until they had most of the problems resolved. Why she would do this now doesn't make sense."

Jessica nodded. "Maybe the investigation will turn up something. I'm going to head it up myself. First thing in the morning I'll get a warrant to search Katherine's apartment, but I want to be certain Elizabeth knows before we go in."

"She will," Meagan said. "As soon as I get her alone I'll tell her."

ELIZABETH STEPPED OFF the Jetway, surprised to find Meagan waiting. The solemn look on Meagan's face said it was bad news. "What is it?" Elizabeth asked after a quick hug.

"Not here, Elizabeth. You know Tallahassee has ears. Wait till we get to the car."

Meagan stalled until they were merging onto Interstate 10. She accelerated into the traffic and said, "Elizabeth, a man was arrested last night on the governor's estate. Henri caught him near the edge of the property, right off Highway Eight Thirteen."

Elizabeth looked at Meagan strangely. Estate trespassers were not totally uncommon, and certainly didn't constitute a special trip to the airport.

"He had two Harper's beauties on him," Meagan continued. "It looked like they'd just been dug up."

Elizabeth nodded and turned to watch the traffic ahead. "So it seems our secret may be out," she said calmly. "Did Jessica talk to the guy?"

"Yes, she did," Meagan replied. "She quickly determined that he didn't know what he had. Apparently someone paid him to do the job." Meagan drove on, keeping her intent eyes on the light mid-morning traffic.

"And was Jessica able to find out who hired him?" Elizabeth asked.

"Yes. She got a name out of him," Meagan answered, her eyes still intense on the road ahead.

"Okay, do we know this name?" Elizabeth asked, growing impatient.

Meagan looked back at Elizabeth uneasily. "Baby, the guy said Katherine hired him."

Elizabeth recoiled like she had been punched, but Meagan held her eyes as she looked back, assuring Elizabeth that she had heard correctly.

"No! I don't believe it!" Elizabeth protested. "No way she would do that. Not now!" Elizabeth's jaw clinched tight as her hands drew into fists. After a severe, silent moment, she slammed her fists onto the dash. Her wounded eyes filled with tears. "We were talking about her moving into the mansion soon—was that all a lie, too?" Elizabeth slammed her fist again, and then fell silent.

Two miles outside of Tallahassee city limits Meagan decided Elizabeth had calmed enough to hear the rest. "Jessica is obtaining a search warrant for Katherine's condo this morning. I've got to call to tell her, you know. She said she wouldn't go in until you did."

"Go ahead," Elizabeth said quietly. "And tell her to come to my office as soon as they're done. I want a full briefing on what they find."

JESSICA WAITED WITH TWO natural resource agents in a paneled van tucked in the back corner of Katherine's condo parking lot. "Are we clear?" Jessica asked.

"Yes," Meagan said. "She knows, and she wants you to report to the governor's office as soon as you're done."

"Okay, I'll see you in a few hours. We'll make sense of this yet, Meagan," Jessica said confidently, and hung up.

"Let's go," Jessica said to the agents.

In just a few minutes Jessica would come face to face with the secrets of Dr. Katherine Hopkins.

Chapter 30

Elizabeth stood vacuously at her office window, waiting for Jessica, who had called a few minutes ago to say the situation was more complicated than they expected, and that yes, they had taken Katherine into custody.

"Hey chief," Jessica softly said as she walked into the governor's office. "You doing okay?" She walked over to lightly squeeze Elizabeth's shoulder.

"Yeah, buddy, I'm okay. Thanks," Elizabeth replied with a weak smile.

"Is Meagan here? I think she'll want to hear this."

Elizabeth nodded. "Yeah. She's across the hall. I'll call her over."

Elizabeth made the page and sat down with Jessica. They avoided each other's eyes as they waited, turning instead to the window and the sailboats on the gulf. Their attention snapped gratefully to the door when Meagan walked in.

Meagan settled into her rocking chair and Jessica began. "We took Katherine into custody this morning. They picked her up at work, very discretely, and we have her under house arrest at a secluded cottage we keep inland. She's shaken, but doing okay."

"What were the preliminary charges?" Elizabeth quietly asked, wincing slightly as if stifling a latent pain.

"Right now we're holding her on conspiracy to defraud the government."

"We're not to treason yet?" Elizabeth questioned.

"Not yet. And I'm not sure that's where we want to go," Jessica replied. "Elizabeth, did you know Katherine's son Jacob is infected with MIC?"

Elizabeth incredulously stared at Jessica, "*What?*"

"That sounds like a no," Jessica replied.

Blown Away
© 2006 by The Haworth Press, Inc. All rights reserved.
doi:10.1300/5706_30

"Hell no I didn't know!" Elizabeth bolted from her chair and stormed into a perturbed pace. "How did you find this out?"

"By the things we found in her apartment," Jessica replied, rubbing her palms together anxiously. "Elizabeth, we found some very damaging evidence at Katherine's apartment, but nothing of the nature that would corroborate Ed Zytowske's story. We found evidence that appears to indicate she was trying to cure her son and then separate from the States, evidently to be with you." Jessica looked up at Elizabeth, hoping her last few words would soften the blow of the past few hours.

They did not seem to. Elizabeth stopped the pacing and set a skeptical stare on Jessica. "What the hell kind of evidence did you find to make you believe that?"

"The first thing we found was a vial of antibiotic powder. It appears that Katherine had been collecting bits of the antibiotic, gathering enough to send to Thomas Hopkins. Apparently she intended to send the meds to cure her son without revealing that it is actually a cure, and stay here in the Territory."

"And how do you deduce all of that?" Elizabeth challenged.

Jessica reached for her briefcase and pulled out a single sheet of paper. "I made a copy of a file we found in her computer. By the date on the file it appears she wrote the letter several days ago," Jessica said. "I want you to read it, but I want you to sit down first."

Elizabeth kept her doubtful glare, but moved to her chair anyway. She sat down and Jessica handed her the paper.

Dear Thomas,

I have come to a decision that was the toughest of my life. I would give anything not to have to come to this, but time and circumstances have led me to a place where I believe I must act. I have decided to stay here in the Territory. I believe my research here is the best hope we have for saving our son. But more than that I have developed affections for people here that I cannot deny and will not betray. My love for Elizabeth Nix is sincere and intense, and I will not sacrifice her trust. I know you will probably never understand why I am doing this, but you know me well enough to know the hours of agony and tears that passed as I battled with my heart and mind. I have no interest in helping John Harkins in his mission to discredit and ultimately destroy this Territory, and I will no longer be a part of his plan. Now, saving Jacob's life is the most urgent concern of my every waking hour. If we are to find a cure the best place for me is here, working with these research teams. Please, Thomas, do nothing to expose me or our original mission as I make my way in this Territory. I will continue to work for Jacob and all other people infected with MIC.

The contents of the vial in this box will give Jacob at least another two years, maybe longer. You must trust me on this. Be most careful with the powder in the vial. Jacob will need 25 mg of the powder per night, given on eight consecutive nights, just after dinner. There is a pharmacist scale in my office that you can use to measure the 25 mg. Dissolve the powder in water and have Jacob drink it. Don't let him have anything but water for the rest of the night. Once you start with the medication, DO NOT MISS A NIGHT. On Jacob's next examination the MIC bacteria will not be traceable in his blood. It is still there, only in a latent state. The blood test should give you the opportunity to publicly claim a miracle. I will continue to be in touch. I am hoping you will find it in your heart to allow me to continue watching Ellen and Jacob as I have every day and night. Give my best affection to both of them. We will address the future of our marriage after the election, when we both have the focus to deal with those matters. I pray you will find it in your heart to forgive me.
Love,
Katherine

The stagnant silence that filled the room shattered when Elizabeth finished the note. "Goddamn it . . . goddamn it!" she screamed at the ceiling, slapping the note against her knee. Her cynical eyes shot to Jessica. "How do you know she ever intended on sending this? Huh? This letter could have easily been written to try to deceive us into believing she had nothing to do with Zytowske. She could have written this last night! She's smart enough to manipulate the file date."

"You're right, she could have done that," Jessica replied evenly. "But why would she go after the plant when she has the antibiotic in her possession *and* she knows the name of the source of the antibiotic? She didn't need to take that chance. She has everything she needs to go to Harkins right now."

Elizabeth looked at Jessica for a long, silent moment. "I suppose she does," she said finally. "But what if she already has and Harkins wanted more. He may have insisted on a sample of the plant as well."

"She hasn't gone to Harkins yet," Jessica replied.

"How do you *know* that?" Elizabeth asked.

"I don't know it, but I believe it," Jessica replied. "She's had plenty of chances to take the antibiotics, grab a Harper's beauty, and get the hell out of here. She has the necessary access. In fact, she could have easily obtained everything she needs in one day and left the Territory before we knew what hit us. But she's still here. Do you think she would have taken all this time to get the meds for her son if she planned to leave the Territory?"

Elizabeth thought for a moment, and for the first time her eyes softened. "I guess you're right about that." Elizabeth stood up again and walked to the window.

"I want to talk to her," Meagan offered. "I've seen Katherine almost every day since she's been in the Territory and I know her moods. I'd like to see if I can sense anything by talking to her."

"Jess, what do you think?" Elizabeth asked as she stared out over the gulf.

"Not a problem, if she wants to do it," Jessica replied.

Meagan nodded and walked over to Elizabeth. She lightly rubbed Elizabeth's arm as her soft green eyes studied Elizabeth's face. "Any messages from you?"

Elizabeth looked down at Meagan and thought for a moment. "Tell her I'm sorry to hear about Jacob," she began, "but tell her I would have rather have heard about it from her."

Meagan nodded, "Okay, baby. Remember I love you." She gave Elizabeth a reassuring smile and walked out of the office.

The click of the closing door again left Elizabeth and Jessica in a strained silence. Elizabeth kept her eyes on the water below as she began dimly, "I have no idea why you want to believe her now, Jess. You were the one who always said she shouldn't be trusted." Elizabeth shook her head slowly, her eyes still on the water. "This whole damn thing was a setup, just as we suspected, and I still let myself fall right into it. Every move I made was exactly what she wanted. I'd think you would be proud that you have been right all along."

"I don't think I have been right all along." Jessica replied. "I was right at first. We know now that the trial in Virginia was a setup, but I also believe that Katherine fell in love with you. Her whole world changed when that happened, and she was working on a way to save her child and protect you and this Territory from John Harkins. What we need to focus on now is how this clown Zytowske found out about Harper's beauty and who else knows about it. Zytowske gave up Katherine too easily. He wasn't working for her."

Elizabeth nodded. After a moment she turned to Jessica. "So you believe Katherine's feelings for me were sincere? You believe she loved me?"

Jessica replied earnestly, "Yes, I do. And I believe she still does."

Chapter 31

Meagan startled at the sight of Elizabeth, tightly curled into the deep blue of the porch hammock, an empty beer bottle beside her. She had never seen Elizabeth look so small while she slept, and she had never known her to drink when she wasn't relaxed. Worse, it was eight-thirty on a Tuesday morning and no one had yet heard from the governor.

Meagan closed the screen door lightly and walked across the porch. Kneeling quietly beside the hammock she pushed the dark hair away from Elizabeth's face.

Elizabeth's eyes reluctantly opened and she reached up to wrap her fingers in Meagan's. "Good morning." Elizabeth slowly sat up and rubbed an eye. "What time is it?"

"About eight-thirty."

"Oh shit," Elizabeth whispered. "I thought the sun would wake me up."

"Are you okay?" Meagan asked with a quick glance at the beer bottle.

"Yeah," Elizabeth replied. She looked out to the white sand and sparse grass of the yard below and squinted in the morning glare. "For a person who's just had the shit kicked out of her, I'm okay."

"Why don't you stay with me for a while? Let me take care of you till you feel stronger," Meagan said, and then a sparkle of mischief lit her eyes. "Bring a big suitcase and we'll start a rumor," she said with a wink.

Elizabeth looked back at Meagan's smile and the playful, dancing green eyes that she'd loved since the first time she saw them. "Or a U-Haul," Elizabeth said with a raised brow and a sedate trace of a grin.

"Or a U-Haul," Meagan laughed, losing herself for a moment before she remembered yesterday. The smile left her face and her eyes turned down as she took Elizabeth's hands in her own. "Katherine

Blown Away
© 2006 by The Haworth Press, Inc. All rights reserved.
doi:10.1300/5706_31

asked me to tell you she had nothing to do with Zytowske," Meagan said, measuring her words. She looked up at Elizabeth. "And she asked me to tell that you she loves you."

Elizabeth wearily stood up and walked across the porch, standing with her back to Meagan in a long, thick silence. The ring of Meagan's phone broke the air. It was Jessica.

"Are you with her?" Jessica abruptly asked as soon as Meagan answered.

"Yeah," Meagan answered cautiously. "What's up?"

"You two need to meet me in her office as soon as possible."

"Can it wait?" Meagan asked. "She's needs a little time. . . ."

"I know," Jessica interrupted. "But we don't have time. Thomas Hopkins just called. He says he knows we have taken Katherine into custody and he says he may be willing to offer information concerning Jason Johnson that we should be interested in. Hopkins thinks we may need this information if we ever have to go toe to toe with President Harkins, and he thinks we may have to do just that very soon."

"Whoa. Slow down a minute. You're saying that Thomas Hopkins just called to offer information that may in some way incriminate his boss and President Harkins? What does he want?"

Jessica hesitated. "Unfortunately, I think he wants his wife back."

ELIZABETH STUDIED THE FACE staring solemnly back from the teleconference screen of her office. Thomas Hopkins clearly wanted something, but in the narrowing of his eyes, the way he held his chin, just tilted slightly up, he still held a superior air. For all Thomas Hopkins knew his wife had been faithful. He didn't know; neither Katherine nor anyone else had told him. Now Elizabeth knew Jessica was right. Katherine had nothing to do with Ed Zytowske.

Jessica was much less analytical. She'd been at war with John Harkins and company since she was twenty-one, and for the first time she sensed the possibility of advantage. Anxious for the hunt, she jumped in. "Okay, Mr. Hopkins," Jessica said, speaking directly to him. "Without getting into the charges we are considering against your wife, let me just say that they are serious, and if she's convicted she may be in prison for a very long time. I suggest that as we proceed you keep that in mind. We'll be needing something substantial to work a deal here."

Thomas Hopkins gave her a contemptuous glare before he remembered his position. His expression quickly relaxed. "Look," he began, "Jason Johnson is the architect of this whole thing with Katherine. It was his idea to set up the arrest here in Virginia to try for a citizenship petition to the Territory. We devised the operation because we believed you were conducting covert MIC research, and it was Katherine's job to crack into that research. She agreed to it because our son Jacob is infected with the MIC bacteria. Anyway, Jason worked with John Harkins to set up the arrest in Virginia and make sure we got the right court and the right judge. Since day one Jason has been briefing Harkins on Katherine's progress. But lately there hasn't been much, and Harkins is getting impatient. He wants something he can use in the election if he needs it, in which case you'll need counter information to back him down."

"And you think you can provide this counter information," Elizabeth said.

"I don't have anything on Harkins directly, but you can keep him honest through his connections with Jason and the CMA."

"So, I'm assuming you know a few secrets Jason wants to keep out of the public eye?" Elizabeth asked.

"Jason has plenty of skeletons in his closet, believe me, but the only one I have personal knowledge of happened some time ago, about two years before William Bucks was elected."

"Go on," Elizabeth said.

"There was a young man named Steve Eddleton who was arrested outside of an abortion clinic with three pipe bombs on him. After he was arrested the police linked Eddleton to an explosion that happened at a clinic a few weeks prior but had only done minor property damage. During the investigation the police discovered that Eddleton was involved with an underground group called the Guerillas for God, who, of course, disappeared as soon as Eddleton was arrested. For some reason Jason took a personal interest in Eddleton's case. Jason believed Eddleton could be rehabilitated and didn't want to leave him hanging, so he decided the CMA should help Eddleton out with his legal defense. Of course, Jason is savvy enough to know that there could be no appearance that the CMA was in any way involved with this kind of a lunatic, especially since some people were throwing the *terrorist* label on him. Jason made sure you'd never find any direct ties from the CMA to Eddleton's legal team, but we were heavily involved in defending him in several ways. Jason laundered money to pay for his defense, including expert witnesses, attorney's fees, jury experts, the whole deal. He also had a few of the CMA legal counsel team, myself included, working on research for the case. In the end our lawyers beat their lawyers and Eddleton was declared mentally incompetent. Just before the trial a deal was made and he was sentenced to an Ohio state mental facility."

Elizabeth crossed her arms as she looked at Hopkins. "Interesting story, but that happened, what, thirteen or fourteen years ago? If we decide to work this kind of lead it will be difficult to follow a money trail that cold. If we get lucky, and that's a big if, I doubt something that happened so long ago would have any impact on public opinion. Johnson could easily spin his way out of it, unless there was something more to his motivation than helping some poor bastard stay out of the state pen. Where is Eddleton now?"

"I don't know what happened to him except that he was sentenced to do a stint in the mental ward. I had no reason to follow him after the sentencing."

"What was Johnson's motivation in helping Eddleton?" Elizabeth asked. "I don't see what the CMA could possibly have to gain in this, and I've never known your organization to take unnecessary risks."

"I've wondered the same thing myself," Hopkins answered. "The only thing I ever got from Jason was that he felt some obligation for these guys that go off the deep end, like they just take our message and lose their moral radar. Jason believes it's up to us to try to rehabilitate these people and help them refind their way. Besides that, he says we have plenty of money and resources."

Elizabeth studied Hopkins for a moment. "I'm aware that money isn't an issue with your organization, but I do find it interesting that Johnson says he feels some obligation here," she said thoughtfully. "He's so much as admitting his hard-line tactics are partly responsible for extreme radical behavior, which he's always succinctly denied. If we have any luck finding evidence of the CMA supporting Eddleton our real leverage will be in exposing Johnson's justification. Admitting his tactics may incite violence should set Jason back. If we time exposure close enough to the election it may have a ripple effect to Harkins."

Jessica interrupted them. "Look, this is all real interesting, but it's softball stuff. I don't see a thing here that would be more than a flesh wound to Jason Johnson *or* John Harkins." She looked over to see Elizabeth nodding. "Mr. Hopkins, if you want us to go easy on Katherine you're going to have to give us something more than this."

Hopkins loathingly turned to Jessica. "That's all I've got, Ms. Thompson."

Their eyes locked in a cold stare before Elizabeth interjected. "I don't want to leave it here. Mr. Hopkins, we'll look into this. Let's keep the line of communication open. We're going to start with an investigation on this Eddleton guy, so we'll be needing information from you."

"When can I speak to my wife?" Hopkins asked.

Elizabeth's blood rushed hot in sudden resentment. *My wife.* She detested the sound of those words coming from his mouth. "We'll let you know," she said abruptly. "Anything else?"

"No," Hopkins said.

Elizabeth clicked off the call and stared at the blank screen. His fucking wife. Yeah, the bastards had done it. Just as they suspected the first day Dr. Katherine Hopkins arrived, the whole deal in Virginia was nothing more than a grand farce. But her lover had played the part so well. How much of it was a lie?

Chapter 32

Elizabeth closed her office door and walked to the conference table. The four people waiting, Jessica, Meagan, Michael, and Joe, knew their boss was back. She had finally slept last night, drifting off in the comfort of Meagan's lap and waking up an hour after sunrise in bed.

"Good morning," Elizabeth said as she sat down. "We've got work to do, folks. Jessica, I'll let you start with the investigation angle. What have you got?"

Jessica began immediately. "Thomas Hopkins agreed to provide information about the security systems for the CMA computer network. I'll be bringing in our best cyber agent this afternoon to brief him and begin initial work. I want to take a look at the financial records of the CMA at the time of Eddleton's arrest and see if we can pick up any patterns of money laundering used to pay for Steve Eddleton's defense. If we have time while we're in we'll see what else we can find."

"Good," Elizabeth replied. "I want any communications on the investigation to be verbal only, preferably face to face."

"Sure," Jessica replied. "And Governor, I don't think we should disregard any information Katherine may be able to give us."

"Of course," Elizabeth replied dimly. "I expected you would interrogate her as well."

Michael DuBose spoke up quickly. "So far we've kept Katherine's custody under wraps," he said. "Mozingo and the research team are aware that she's being questioned, but they don't know she's been taken into custody."

"We've talked to most of them," Jessica offered. "No one on the team noticed any suspicious behavior with Katherine, but then again none of them noticed she was squirreling away the meds we found in her apartment."

Blown Away
© 2006 by The Haworth Press, Inc. All rights reserved.
doi:10.1300/5706_32

"She was good," Elizabeth said dryly. She turned to DuBose, "Michael, we'll be looking for you to keep Katherine's custody out of the press, and for that matter, out of the rumor mill."

"I'm working on it," Michael replied. "But there's only so long I can keep the lid on since you're involved. I figure we've got a week before the rumors start. Three weeks is the absolute best we can possibly hope for before it hits the press."

"Two weeks should be ample time to determine formal charges," Jessica offered.

Elizabeth nodded. "We've also got the problem of protecting the rest of the plants."

"We took care of that yesterday. We have an officer assigned to each location twenty-four seven," Jessica replied.

"Good. Joe," Elizabeth looked at her chief of staff, "I need you to take up the slack for me. Make sure the Territory's business stays on track until we get through all of this."

"No problem," Joe said. "You know you may need to disappear for a few days. Maybe a trip to the States or to the Hill could get you out of here without raising suspicion."

"I can do that, but only if I see I need to. Start a few inquiries just in case." Elizabeth swept her eyes through her staff. "Okay, I don't need to remind any of you how important these next few days will be. John Harkins and Jason Johnson sent Katherine here to do a job. We all know they won't stop simply because we stopped Katherine. You can bet John Harkins doesn't intend to quit until this Territory is just an experiment of the past."

ELIZABETH HAD NOT heard Meagan come in, so she checked Meagan's bedroom on her way out the door to the office. She found Meagan asleep on top of the bedcovers, fully dressed under the cotton throw draped across her legs. Elizabeth smiled contentedly and backed out of the room.

It was four hours later when Elizabeth saw Meagan again. She reported to Elizabeth in the governor's office with a large cup of coffee in hand.

"Last night was pretty amazing," Meagan said as she walked toward her rocker. "Those computer people scare the hell out of me, but damn if our man—Agent Terry Vogel in case you hear the name—didn't get in. Thomas Hopkins gave us the name of the security system and a few other details, and by three a.m. Vogel was downloading the financial records we need. Fortunately they had been archived, or it would have been much harder to get in without being detected."

"So Vogel thinks he got out clean?" Elizabeth asked.

"Yeah, with the records we needed for both years."

"Have you been able to find anything yet?"

"Hardly," Meagan said with a slight laugh. "There are thousands of records in those files. Jessica's planning to call in more agents today, but finding evidence of laundering will be like a needle in the haystack."

Elizabeth nodded and said, "And who knows how much time we have. I'm guessing the Harkins campaign will start to leak whatever they have in mid-October."

"So you're thinking we have six weeks?"

"Six weeks at the most," Elizabeth replied.

Meagan took a sip from her coffee and was silent for a long moment. Then she said, "Katherine wants to see you, Elizabeth. She asked again last night. She says there are some things she wants you to know."

"Like what, Meagan?" Elizabeth said crossly. "Look, I know she may not be the one that hired Zytowske, and I want to believe everything she wrote in that letter, but none of it changes the fact that she lied for so long. Do you really think I could see her now, not knowing if she will be filling me up with more bullshit lies? I doubt it has even occurred to Katherine how much damage she has done to us and the Territory. She opened the door and let those bastards in. Now we're in for the political fight of our lives. We may not survive this, Meagan."

"Maybe you should talk to her then. She may tell you something we can use."

Elizabeth shook her head slowly, "Not now, Meagan. Not now."

AT 8 P.M. Meagan gave Elizabeth her evening briefing. Jessica had two teams fully at work with ten agents assigned to dissect financial records and a detective team of four tracking down anything they could find on Steve Eddleton. So far there had been nothing, but they knew the trail of laundering would be difficult to follow, and with the CMA's resources behind him Steve Eddleton could be anywhere in the world.

"WHERE ARE YOU NOW?" Meagan asked as soon as Elizabeth answered her cell.

"I just got back to the office," Elizabeth answered.

"I'll be there in ten," Meagan said and hung up.

Elizabeth closed the file of her morning briefing and switched on to CNN. She propped her feet on her desk and watched a bearded correspondent spill through his in-depth report on the Harkins administration's environmental record. Two minutes in the report flashed to the tape of the previous day's press conference from Harkins's Idaho ranch. *Harkins played this part so well,* Elizabeth thought, his cowboy image and down-home style selling his words like ice cubes in hell. The report broke for a commercial just as Meagan flew into the office.

"Better than we could have hoped for," Meagan said excitedly as she closed the door behind her and briskly crossed the floor without a thought of sitting down.

"Okay," Elizabeth said slowly. She clicked off the television. "You want to settle down and tell me what's going on?"

"I won't settle down," Meagan said as she paced. "But I will tell you that we may have something bigger than the laundering thing. Forget Jason Johnson. We may have something that could tie directly back to Harkins."

"I'm listening."

Meagan kept pacing. "How about illegal campaign contributions?" she said. "First William Bucks campaign—the September just before the election—all of a sudden we start to see money go from CMA accounts down to the local church level. This keeps up through the end of November, and then just as suddenly, it stops." Meagan finally took a breath before continuing. "There were these things called community aid grants—several million dollars worth—sometimes tens of thousands and sometimes even hundreds of thousands, doled out to local churches and religious organizations for about two months. This short time period of only a couple of months for a grant program got our agents' attention. Then one of the agents noticed the grants weren't awarded in every state—in fact, they were granted to just a select few states. Jessica had a hunch to compare those states with the poll numbers for the presidential campaign, and sure as shit every one of the churches that got a grant was in a state where the poll numbers were within a three percent margin." Meagan stopped pacing and planted her palms on Elizabeth's desk, leaning in. "Now you tell me that's just a coincidence."

Elizabeth smiled slowly. "If it is, it's a hell of a coincidence." She picked up her pen and turned it end to end, thinking aloud. "But something like this will be difficult to prove. Where does Jess want to go from here?"

"She's not sure yet. She's thinking she may talk to her aunt Tommie on the outside shot that Emily Harkins may be able to tell us something."

Elizabeth raised her brows with a low whistle. "That's an outside shot all right, like half-court."

"When time's running out, you take those shots."

Chapter 33

Emily Harkins walked onto the covered porch of Sutton's General Store, the dust under her feet spreading in brown puffs as she passed the mountain of horse feed and bundles of fence posts stacked high on gray, worn, wooden planks. Four Secret Service agents surrounded the first lady, mirroring her footsteps in practiced time.

In a somber rush four more agents posted themselves in each corner of Sutton's store as Emily greeted her old friend Tommie Sutton at the door with wink and a long hug. "They say you get used to them," Emily said in a whisper, "but I never have. They still aggravate the hell out of me."

Tommie Sutton laughed heartily and held the door. "Would you like some lemonade?"

"You bet. I'd love some," Emily answered graciously. They walked past the glass counter covering the block cheese, beef jerky, and fried pies, and into the kitchen of the living quarters Tommie shared with her husband for more than forty years.

"How was Japan?" Tommie asked as she took two glasses from white cabinets and opened the freezer for ice.

"Crowded," Emily answered plainly. "That's why I had to get back here as quick as I could. You know I like my wide open spaces," she said with a wry smile. She watched Tommie take a glass pitcher from the refrigerator and pour lemonade over the ice. "But I was surprised you called so soon," Emily said. "I don't think the dust had settled from my entourage when you called. I'd swear you were watching for me."

"Well, to tell the truth, I was," Tommie admitted as she handed Emily her lemonade. "And that fleet of black rigs following you around these days is hard to miss. It looks like the return of the dust bowl every time you come home," Tommie teased, walking to the

Blown Away
© 2006 by The Haworth Press, Inc. All rights reserved.
doi:10.1300/5706_33

kitchen table. "But I was waiting for you for a reason," Tommie continued seriously. "My girl Jess needs help, Em."

Emily sat down at the kitchen table and held her lemonade between her hands. "I'm listening."

"Unfortunately, it's about politics," Tommie said.

"Of course it is," Emily replied. "What else would she need from me?"

Tommie turned a quick, self-conscious smile, and said, "She called last night and told me they've got a serious political situation brewing with your husband. She said John's folks are planning to go after the Territory in the reelection campaign, you know, to make the future of Apalachicola an issue in the parts of the country where it would play well. Jess says the Territory can't afford the controversy right now, and they need something to keep John's campaign off their backs. Fortunately, they've uncovered something they believe may be a violation of campaign finance laws from way back in the Bucks campaign. They found expenditures in the CMA's financial records that look suspicious, but they need a bit more."

Emily nodded and looked down, focusing on the lemonade with a serious frown. "Let me make sure I understand you," she began. "Jessica wants me to give her information that will indicate that I know, and have always known, that my husband did something illegal? That he violated campaign finance reform laws? Now, why would I admit that, Tommie?" Emily said, looking up with narrowed eyes.

"I know, Em," Tommie replied in a nervous breath. "It is a lot to ask, but I don't think Jess intends to ever use any of the information with Congress," she said, pausing to decide her next words. "You know how this all works. She just needs something she can use to sit at the poker table with John's campaign. The Territory needs a bargaining chip, that's all."

Emily sat back and thought a long moment. "I do like to see the game played evenly," she said finally. "I overheard a few things about the time the Bucks campaign was getting into full gear. But to deter John, Jessica will need concrete evidence, not just something overheard twelve or thirteen years ago from some unnamed source." She thought again, and said, "Let me take a look at the note files John keeps locked away at the cabin. He's prolific with notes and he saves things forever. Maybe there's something there."

JESSICA THOMPSON STEPPED off the jetway in the Boise airport and looked around. Monty Weaver walked across the corridor, tipped his weather-beaten straw Stetson, and grabbed Jessica as she threw her arms around his wide shoulders.

"Good to see you, man," Jessica said as she tightened her arms around him. "I've missed you."

"You too, my friend," Monty said, letting her back down to her feet.

"We'll be heading out first thing in the morning," Monty said as they walked through the airport. "To ride into Dry Gulch by noon we'll have to spend a night on the trail. You know the closest trail into the gulch comes from John Harkins's ranch, but ever since that SOB made vice president nobody's been able to use it. I figure you don't want to been seen near Harkins's ranch anyway," Monty said with a dry smile.

"No sir," Jessica replied, remembering the last time she rode into Dry Gulch, the day she and Amanda Harkins breathed in the fresh aroma of the tall pines as they frolicked in their "secret" mountain stream, letting the ice cold water numb their bodies before climbing to dry, bare rocks to warm in the sun. The joy and ache of the memory was never more acute now, knowing that in two days she would see the place again. And she would be meeting Emily Harkins.

JESSICA AND MONTY pulled their horses to a halt. "This is it, Monty," Jessica said confidently.

Still a man of few words, Monty merely nodded and looked around. For the most part, the land was dry, rocky, and open, but just above them the trail switched back into a grassy meadow. Monty would wait with the horses there.

"There's an old cemetery across that creek," Jessica began, pointing to the stream below. "It has a wrought iron fence around it."

"I know the one," Monty replied.

"If I'm not back in three hours, come looking for me," Jessica said as she swung her leg across the horse.

Monty nodded again and took Jessica's reins. She watched until he disappeared behind the tree line, then she headed down to the creek. On a couple of stones she skipped across the stream, then scrambled up the steep gray rocks of the hill on the other side, making her way to the cemetery she knew lay hidden inside the tight circle of ponderosa pines a few hundred feet away.

A powerful gust blew the cemetery gate open just as Jessica reached for it. She looked west to a mounting gray thunderhead that looked like trouble. Twin bolts of lightening danced down to the line of a distant ridge as another powerful gust pushed against her. "Shit. Not now," she mumbled as she moved away from the trees for a better measure of the sky. "I hope to hell she's behind that." A whirlwind of swirling dust rose from the rocky slope below, sending Jessica running for refuge behind a gravestone. All she could do now was wait and hope Emily Harkins was still on the trail.

For the next two hours Jessica waited in the cemetery full of memories. Checking her watch again for the third time in twenty minutes she knew time was running out. Jessica pulled a branch from a cedar tree and vacantly snapped the twig into tiny pieces, losing faith with every snap. She reached for another branch, but then suddenly stopped dead still, her head cocked, struggling to filter all other noises but the faint click of what seemed to be distant horse hooves. Jessica moved to a clump of small trees for better cover, anxiously waiting as the clip of the horses, five, she figured, grew louder and clearer. A hundred feet from the cemetery the horses stopped.

"Just give me two minutes," Emily Harkins commanded from the trail just above. "I've got to go. I'll be down in that clump of trees. Well, you'd better make that five minutes, you never know out here," Emily said with a dry laugh, the same laugh of her daughter.

In a moment a single set of footsteps crushed against the dry duff of twigs and rosin near the cemetery gate. The footsteps stopped as the gate squeaked open. "Jessica, are you here?" Emily asked softly.

Jessica stood slowly. "You bet," she said quietly as she walked out from the cover of the trees.

Emily's face lit with a proud smile, but she kept her distance as she spoke. "My god, girl, you look terrific. Florida's been good to you."

"Most of the time," Jessica said. "I miss this country, though, Miss Emily. It doesn't look like this in Florida," she said, turning her eyes to distant snowcapped peaks. "We've got no mountains there."

"No," Emily said. "I suppose not." She kept her eyes on Jessica, as if trying to read ten years of history in the lines of her face and the way she held herself now. "I'd like to come over there and give you a hug, but I've got to keep my distance," Emily said. "Can you believe they monitor the heat surrounding my body to tell if anyone is close? If you get within five feet of me, there'll be four men down here in the blink of a gnat's eye."

"I understand," Jessica said, focusing on Emily's eyes, eyes that were the exact color of Amanda's. "I got your letters," she offered.

"Good," Emily ardently replied. "You know I'd still be writing if I thought we could get it by John. It wouldn't be worth his wrath on you if he found out we'd been keeping in touch."

"You were right," Jessica said. "But I'm afraid I'm against his wrath anyway."

"Yes. Tommie told me as much. That's why I wanted to see you, Jess. I have something here that I think will help," she said as she reached into her pocket. She held up a single page folded into fourths. "I'm going to leave this here. John wrote this note, just over twelve years ago, just before Bill Bucks announced John would be his running mate. The date is on it, in John's handwriting. The day before John wrote the note Bill had asked for financial help from the CMA. Keep that in mind, Jess. This note will give you the defense you're looking for." Emily bent down and slid the paper under a rock.

"Thank you," Jessica said.

Emily nodded. "Tommie says this won't go to the press or Congress, right?"

"No ma'am," Jessica replied. "Not unless he leaves us with no choice."

Emily nodded again, gave Jessica one last look, and turned to go.

"Miss Emily," Jessica said, quickly. Emily looked back to her. "Why did you stay in touch with me, even so long after Amanda was gone?"

"Because I know how much you loved my daughter," Emily replied. "I saw your devotion to her. That's all any parent should ever ask for, that someone loves and cares about their child the way you cared about Amanda. I saw it every time you two were together. It was a fine love you shared," Emily said earnestly. "And after she was gone you helped me get through, Jessica, because I knew there was someone who missed her as much as I did, who hurt for her as much as I did." Emily paused and looked around, taking in a deep breath of the crisp mountain air. She looked back to Jessica with a kind smile. "Besides that, I've always liked your spunk."

Jessica nodded and smiled back, "You take care of yourself, Miss Emily. I hope we'll see each other again one day."

"We will, Jess. We will." After one last look Emily turned and walked back to the gate. In a moment, she was gone.

The clip of the horses faded down the trail and Jessica went for the note. Slowly unfolding it she read,

Jason Johnson—thirty minutes to return call. Tax exemptions. The Court.

Jessica's blood instinctively ran cold. *The Court*. The words stared back at her like the eyes of a cobra. The Supreme Court, the determinant of all of her adult life, was returning to haunt Jessica again.

ELIZABETH READ THE NOTE and handed it back to Jessica. "That should do it, Jess," she said. "I believe combined with what we have from the financial records, the note should provide reasonable suspicion that a deal was made, at least enough for a congressional inquiry, which the Harkins reelection campaign can't withstand." Elizabeth sat back in her chair on the courtyard terrace of the mansion and looked across the table to Meagan. "What do you think?"

"This election is so close," Meagan began. "You're right; clearly Harkins wouldn't survive a scandal of this nature, even if it did happen a long time ago. I think the only questions we have to answer are when and how do we let Harkins know we have this. We can't wait

too long, but at the same time if we expose ourselves too early
Harkins may be able to develop a strategy to deal with it. Timing is
critical."

Elizabeth nodded. "I'd rather not have Bill Bucks involved in this,"
she said reflectively. "And if we have to go public he will be."

Jessica suddenly snapped a stern gaze on Elizabeth. "Whoa, wait a
minute. I know Bill Bucks may be a friend of yours, Elizabeth, but
there is someone else we have to consider here, someone looking at
higher stakes than Bucks. Emily Harkins will have enough hell to pay
if her husband finds out we have that note," Jessica asserted. "She
shouldn't have to go up against the media as well. I don't want this to
go public. Ever."

"I don't either, Jess," Elizabeth replied evenly. "But if we get
backed far enough against the wall we might have to. Emily Harkins
is no neophyte. She knew her husband could find out when she gave
you the note."

"I'd still consider it a betrayal," Jessica shot back. She sat back and
looked away to the river. A thick, silent minute passed before she
turned back to Elizabeth. "I think we need to keep digging. John
Harkins has plenty of secrets still out there."

"Probably so," Elizabeth replied. "But when do we stop digging,
Jess? We still don't know how we are going to handle Katherine's
case, and it will take all of our brainpower to deal with Harkins. I need
you to stay focused on those two things, plus you have your job to do."

Jessica stood up and stalked across the courtyard, seething underneath, as angry as she had ever been with Elizabeth. Intellectually she
knew Elizabeth was right, that there was only so much they could do,
even with a team of investigators, and Emily Harkins had given them
enough to keep John Harkins off their backs. But in her gut Jessica
knew there was something more.

After a moment Meagan walked over and stood beside Jessica.
"You want to tell me what's going on?" she asked quietly.

Jessica glanced at Meagan and turned her eyes down toward the
river. "I don't know, Meagan. I know she's right; we don't have the
time, or money, for more investigations, but I've got to find a way to
keep Emily Harkins out of this." Jessica paused, remembering, then

she said, "There I was, Meagan, standing in the same cemetery I discovered with her daughter, looking into the same eyes, hearing the same laugh, and I just knew there was a connection between Emily and I that will never be broken. And then I read the note, and those words—*The Court*—they just hit me like a bolt—quick, and hard, and taking every bit of life right out of me."

Meagan nodded slowly and moved closer to Jessica. "Do you think Amanda was trying to tell you something?"

"I don't know," Jessica replied honestly. "You're the one who knows those things. What do you think?"

Without reply Meagan slid her hand through Jessica's arm and led her back to Elizabeth. "Give her more time," Meagan said as she sat back down.

Elizabeth read the certainty in Meagan's eyes and knew there was no use in debate. "Two weeks, then," Elizabeth said, turning to Jessica. "I'll give you two more weeks to see what you can find. After that, I'll need both of you back."

"Agreed," Jessica said. "I'm going to see Michael. I'll see you both later." She turned to walk away.

"Why Michael?" Elizabeth called after her.

"His father's contacts," Jessica replied over her shoulder as she hurriedly left them.

Chapter 34

Michael DuBose checked the sinker on his fishing line and added chunks of cut bait to twin hooks. The pier was crowded with couples taking strolls, fathers with their children, and the senior citizens who came to watch the evening's fishing. Michael quickly looked behind him before he flung the stout shaft of his fishing rod toward the immense blue-green water ahead. The sweet zing of heavy line spinning off the reel rang in Michael's ears as the bait sailed toward a school of tarpon rolling beneath the shallow waters of the Gulf of Mexico. Michael let the bait sink and picked out a shark or two cruising the surf for schools of fish not a hundred yards from a shoreline full of swimmers. On the beach his partner, who only reluctantly agreed to a beach trip outside the Territory, sunbathed in the last of the August afternoon sun. Across the pier an angler's pole suddenly bent to the great pull of a huge tarpon, and the show was on. The curious, and even a few of the other fishermen, rushed over to witness the first jump.

"Pretty exciting stuff, huh?"

Michael turned toward voice of Robert Stark, his father's closest Beltway associate and the man Michael had come here to meet. Michael was seventeen the last time he had seen him, but right away he recognized it was Stark walking toward him.

"Yes, it is," Michael said casually. "Maybe I'll get lucky today, too."

"Maybe so," Stark replied. Keeping his eyes out to the Gulf, Stark stood straight, like a man who had long been a soldier. "Your father tells me you like to fish," Stark continued. "He said I would find you here."

"Did he tell you why I wanted to see you?"

"No, he didn't," Stark replied. "But I figured it must be important since you paid for my trip down from Maryland, plus a seven-day cruise for Julia and me."

"Don't forget first class," Michael said with his disarming smile.
"That helped. So what is it you want?"

"Just a little information—about the day the Supreme Court blew up."

Stark rocked back and made a quick look around, then turned his eyes back to the gulf. "You don't pull any punches, do you, son?" Stark said, still not looking at Michael.

"Dad told me you were assigned as agent in charge the first day," Michael said.

"I was the agent in charge of the investigation outside of the Bureau, for about twenty-four hours. Then that son of a bitch William Bucks put John Harkins in command of the entire operation, Bureau and non-Bureau." Stark reached to his back pocket and pulled out a worn leather tobacco pouch and unzipped it slowly, then took a wooden pipe from his shirt pocket and buried the bowl into the tobacco. He packed the pipe methodically, his forehead furrowed in thought as his gray hair blew in the Gulf breeze. From his front pocket he pulled out a pipe lighter, turned his back to the wind, and after a couple of quick sucks, he had smoke.

"We'd been working nonstop for twenty-four hours," Stark said, the smoke tumbling out with his words. "I had already assembled my team and set up central command. We were moving. Then my boss, Attorney General Perez, called me to his office to tell me John Harkins would be taking over the investigation. He said my services were no longer needed, and without any further explanation he assigned me to another case, some minor Internet banking scheme. I was angry, I tell you," Stark said, finally turning to Michael. "I still am."

Michael nodded and focused on to the end of his fishing rod, "Were you able to keep up with the investigation?"

"I heard some things," Stark began. He pulled another draw from his pipe, thinking for a long moment before he continued. "Look, Michael, I don't know what you're looking for, or why after all these years you want to ask questions about that god-awful day, but your dad asked me to come down here and talk to you, so here I am. Just remember, I wasn't part of the investigation. I don't know much, really."

A rigid silence fell between them before Michael turned squarely to Stark and said shrewdly, "I know your brotherhood. I think you know plenty."

Stark stared back sternly, checking Michael's grit. Michael DuBose stood firm, and Stark turned around to lean against the pier, his eyes scanning through the crowd as he talked. "You know Taylor—the suicide bomber—his body was completely gone. They never scraped enough of him to even bury in a matchbox. But one of my agents found a thumb, most of it still intact, that he said didn't match up to the wounds of any of the victims. He said the general print pattern didn't match Taylor's prints, either. Later word was that finding a thumb was just an urban myth among the agents and cops, and Harkins never followed up on it, but I believe the agent who found that thumb. He told me the damn thing just disappeared and the folks at forensics claimed someone else had processed it. I believe someone knows exactly what happened, and anyone else who knew about the thumb lied to avoid the retribution of John Harkins."

Michael nodded and thought for a minute. "Is it possible Harkins knew the truth about it—that there really was a thumb?"

"It's possible, but I doubt it," Stark answered. "Harkins was thorough, and he ruled that investigation with an iron fist. If he knew about the thumb he would have tracked it like a bloodhound until it was matched with a corpse somewhere."

"Who would have taken it, then?" Michael asked.

"Somebody with a lot to hide," Stark answered, looking at Michael with suggestive eyes. "Or a lot of power."

"You mean William Bucks," Michael said.

"I never trusted the man," Stark replied.

"JESUS CHRIST, MICHAEL," Jessica reflected, speaking just above a whisper. "Do you think that could possibly be true?"

"I don't know why he would lie about it," Michael replied.

They were alone in Jessica's office at just after 11 p.m., the smell of fish and salt spray still lingering on Michael's skin.

"So Robert Stark believes Bucks may have been involved in some sort of cover-up of the court bombing?"

"He never said exactly that, but that's what he led me to believe," Michael replied.

Jessica shook her head slowly, thinking. "In my mind Stark was close," she said after a moment. "There may have been a cover-up, but I'd be willing to bet it wasn't William Bucks. It was John Harkins," she said. Jessica stood up and walked across the office, rubbing her forehead. "So, if there was this thumb, then whose thumb was it? If it wasn't Taylor's there may have been someone else in the Court that day—an accomplice to Taylor."

"Possibly," Michael nodded, "but before we assume too much the thumb may have been from a victim. As I understand, some of the bodies were really messed up."

"That's true, some were. But why did the thumb disappear, Michael?" Jessica stopped and leaned against her desk, looking at Michael incisively, "The agents would have known if forensics matched it to a victim. It was their evidence. Forensics would have told them." Jessica shook her head, "No, if there was ever a thumb, John Harkins had something to do with it disappearing."

"So maybe Taylor did have an accomplice, but how would he, or she, get access to the floor of the Court? Access is tightly controlled. I don't see how anyone could have gotten close enough without authorization."

"You can't," Jessica agreed. "But Harkins could have easily arranged access. He was the goddamn vice president, after all."

"Why would Taylor even need an accomplice? All the survivors said the explosion came from his body. There's no doubt that the explosives were strapped to him."

"Steve Eddleton!" Jessica exclaimed suddenly.

"*What?*" Michael asked.

"Steve Eddleton." Jessica replied in a rapid, excited clip. "Our investigators have been searching five days and we haven't found a trace of him. The man seems to have disappeared from the face of the earth. Thomas Hopkins said Eddleton was sentenced about a year before the

bombing. He could have been there. He could have been Taylor's accomplice."

Michael looked back at Jessica stoically.

"We've got to go back twelve years, Michael. I'd bet my life that
Steve Eddleton vanished the day of the Supreme Court bombing."

ELIZABETH SAT IN THE MANSION courtyard, surrounded by the
gray of predawn. Beside her Jessica sat silently, letting Elizabeth digest the magnitude of her theory.

"So let me be sure I'm understanding what you're saying," Elizabeth began. "You believe that Steve Eddleton, the man the CMA fi-
nanced to keep out of jail, had something to do with the Supreme
Court bombing?" Jessica nodded to Elizabeth's skeptical eyes. "And
therefore you believe that the CMA, or a small urban guerilla group,
was somehow involved in the bombing. Is that what you are telling
me?"

"Yes," Jessica said assuredly, "That's exactly what I'm telling you."

"And based on the note Emily Harkins gave you, you believe John
Harkins may have knowledge of the entire scheme?"

"That's why the thumb disappeared," Jessica replied. "John
Harkins knew it could be Steve Eddleton's, so he had the whole thing
covered up. And that's why we can't find any trace of Steve Eddleton
in the public records. We're going to have to go to archived media
files and hope we can find some record of him."

Elizabeth sat back and drew a deep breath. "If you're even close to
right about this, Jess, have you even thought about what this could do
to the United States? *This could be catastrophic.* I can't imagine how
long it would take the country to recover. Have you thought that far
ahead?"

Jessica looked at her oddly, "Frankly, no, I haven't thought that far
ahead. You're the politician; I'm the law enforcer. I just want to get at
the truth."

"Of course, of course," Elizabeth nodded, still trying to sort out
Jessica's theory. "What have you got in mind?"

"We've got to find out what happened to Steve Eddleton," Jessica
replied. "For now I'm going to shift all of the agents to that effort,

and," she hesitated and leaned in closer to Elizabeth. "I'm going to call Thomas Hopkins again. He may have access to records from Eddleton's trial prep."

Elizabeth's face fell as she nodded slowly.

Jessica reached over and grasped Elizabeth's shoulder. Squeezing it gently she said, "Katherine's okay. She's still at the cottage and I'm told she asks to see you every day." Jessica moved her had down to rest it on Elizabeth's arm. She looked up at Elizabeth earnestly. "She never betrayed you, Elizabeth. The more we find out about Harkins, the more her story will come together. They set Katherine up, and that mistake, my friend, will be their undoing."

LINDA SANDERS STOOD in front of Elizabeth's desk, holding a stack of papers for official signature. She handed Elizabeth the last one and waited as Elizabeth quickly signed.

Elizabeth handed the signed page back when Meagan walked into the governor's office, carrying two oversized mugs of black coffee.

"Good morning," Linda said as Meagan set one mug down on the governor's desk.

"Good morning, Linda," Meagan said on the way to her rocker.

Elizabeth looked over to Meagan and mumbled a vague thanks for the coffee.

"You look like hell," Meagan said bluntly, focusing on Elizabeth's bloodshot eyes.

"Thanks. I love you, too," Elizabeth replied dryly.

Linda sternly nodded. "She's right. You do look like hell," she said. She reached to the bottom of the paper stack and pulled out a blue sheet. "Here is today's schedule. There's not much on it, and by the look of you, it's a good thing." Linda handed Elizabeth the page. "You know, Elizabeth, the whole office is gossiping about you and Katherine. They've noticed she hasn't been in the picture lately and they're all speculating as to why. Some of them have even gotten their nerve up to ask me. I just tell them I don't know." Linda looked at Elizabeth, expecting an answer. She didn't get one.

"Good," Elizabeth replied without hesitation. "Then as it is you're not having to lie to them."

Linda returned an aggrieved smirk. "I'm just trying to help," she said impassively. "You'd think I'd deserve a little more consideration," she mumbled.

"I just can't tell you right now, Linda," Elizabeth said sincerely. "You will be the first to know when I'm ready."

"I bet you know," Linda said to Meagan as she turned to leave them. She walked out, her displeasure with the both of them obvious in the extra swing of her sway.

"You don't have to stay at the mansion, you know," Meagan said with the close of the door. "I told you that you should stay with me as long as you need to, and by the look of your eyes I'd say you could use a few more days."

"Come on, Meagan," Elizabeth replied. "It's not Katherine that's keeping me up all night. This shit Jessica's talking about, if she's right . . . if she's right," Elizabeth's words drifted off as she lightly rapped the desk with her fist, thinking. She stood up and walked over to the window. "Have you even thought about what we do if we find out Jessica's theory is true? What do we do with that kind of information? There's no way the morale of the country can stand to know the president was involved in any way. All the scandals of the twentieth century are *nothing* compared to this. If we ever prove any of it we'll have to find someone we can trust to deal with Harkins. Michael's father's connections may give us a start, but how can we keep this confidential? How can we know who to trust with this?"

Meagan stared at Elizabeth blankly.

Elizabeth started again, "Surely you've thought of it, Meagan. Justice has to come for what Harkins may have been involved in, that's true, but what damage will be done to the national conscience in the meantime? Lying to Congress, lying to the people, that's one thing, but *this*! Talk about your high crimes and misdemeanors! It will take the United States fifty years to recover, if ever. We've got to be thinking about the next step."

Meagan clinched her jaw and stared at Elizabeth as her body began to tense with anger. "You know, Elizabeth, I haven't given the next step or the freakin' morale of the country a whole lot of thought. To tell you the truth, I don't give a shit. All I know is that it's possible that the people who killed Chris are still walking around—heroes to half the idiots in the country. So, no, I don't feel one bit for the morale of the country. Don't you even care that they killed Colton Rice and Chris, and they almost killed you? Don't you think they should pay for that?"

Elizabeth stared back at Meagan, caught short for a moment. "Look, Meagan," she began. The intercom buzz interrupted her.

Linda's still-annoyed voice came through the speaker. "It's Attorney General Thompson, urgent."

"Okay," Elizabeth said and waited for the click. "Yeah, Jess."

"You've got to get over here," Jessica urged. "We found a photograph of Steve Eddleton."

Chapter 35

Elizabeth and Meagan sat next to each other in plain metal chairs along the back wall of a small, windowless room, solemnly gazing at the projected image of a young man's photograph. The man appeared to be about twenty-one, with an amiable face and a lanky body. He stood on a lake pier, holding a boat oar in each hand. The fashion of his clothes and hairstyle suggested the photograph was taken at least twenty years ago.

"This is Steve Eddleton," Jessica said calmly, standing by the projected image reflected three times life-size. "This is the only photograph we've been able to find of Eddleton, and we got damn lucky when we found it. So far this is the only evidence we have to prove that this guy ever existed. Our investigation showed that great effort has been taken to wipe any trace of Eddleton from the face of the earth, but when you see the next two photographs I think it will be abundantly clear why."

"One of our investigators noticed something in Eddleton that we hadn't considered," Jessica continued methodically. She walked to the projector's computer and zoomed in Eddleton's face. "Watch this closely," she said as the computer began ticking through a series of subtle changes. "We had the computer determine age projections, and then we added a simple nose enhancement that could be done by any decent makeup artist. We changed the color of his hair and. . . ." The computer finished drawing, leaving the final product in a clear, sharp image.

"Jesus Christ!" Elizabeth exclaimed. She fell back in her chair, staring.

Next to her Meagan doubled over, holding her stomach to suppress a sick urge. "I'll be back," she groaned. She stood quickly and stumbled from the room with her hand over her mouth.

Blown Away
© 2006 by The Haworth Press, Inc. All rights reserved.
doi:10.1300/5706_35

Elizabeth sat frozen, gawking at the image that was now the perfect twin of Phillip Norton Taylor. A full minute passed before Elizabeth could speak. "Steve Eddleton was not an accomplice to Taylor," she said slowly, "he switched identities with Phillip Norton Taylor."

"I believe he did," Jessica answered. "Which leaves us with the question, where is Phillip Norton Taylor now?"

"I'm sure you are working on that."

"You bet I am," Jessica replied. "Based on what we know about Phillip Taylor, quite a sum of money would have to be offered to entice him to give up his identity and disappear, not to mention to take the historical blame for blowing up the Supreme Court. There has to be a money trail somewhere that will lead us to him. Our agents pulled out the CMA's financial records again and they're checking for irregularities. They'll dig into anything that looks suspicious."

Elizabeth nodded sternly. "What do we do in the meantime?" she asked. "John Harkins is clearly tied to this, but proving it is going to be tough. He's got a hundred times the resources we have."

"You're right," Jessica replied, "but I don't believe he has a clue we know anything about Steve Eddleton."

"So you're certain Thomas Hopkins isn't cooperating with Harkins?"

"As certain as I can be," Jessica replied. "I believe Hopkins suspects President Harkins had Katherine set up. That's part of his motivation to help us. So I doubt Thomas Hopkins is in a mood to cooperate with Harkins and Jason Johnson. At the same time it appears that with Katherine out of the picture, Jason Johnson is trying to find a way to discredit Thomas Hopkins. We just found out that Jason Johnson sent Hopkins home for a two-week vacation, evidently to keep him away from the workings of the CMA. I will be surprised if Johnson doesn't fire him soon. My suspicion is they are using these two weeks to find something on him."

Elizabeth nodded, thinking through the angles. She looked over as Meagan walked back into the room and sat down without a word or look to either of them. For a moment Elizabeth watched Meagan battle her emotions, but decided to leave it for now.

"Is there any way we can prove this conspiracy without finding Taylor?" Elizabeth asked.

"Not well enough to bring down John Harkins," Jessica replied.

"So that's where we're going, then, nothing short of bringing down John Harkins?"

Meagan shot a hard look at Elizabeth. "There are no other options, Elizabeth," she said sharply. "He is *not* getting away with this."

DAWN BROKE IN a fire-red sky. Elizabeth turned onto the west loop of the mansion drive and broke into a sprint, running fast as if to chase the last traces of darkness from the night. Covering the last hundred and fifty yards in twenty seconds she leapt onto the porch, gasping for air as she walked the wooden floor with her hands gripped on her hips. The last two miles felt like glorious freedom, the endorphins clearing the weight of her worries. John Harkins, she knew, had crafted his own downfall, and neither she nor anyone else in the Territory would be responsible for what would become of the future.

Elizabeth cooled down and watched the sun push through the horizon before going inside for a shower and breakfast. Halfway through a bowl of cereal, Jessica called.

"I think we have it, Elizabeth," Jessica said in an oddly reserved voice. "Can you meet me in an hour in your office?"

"I'll be there," Elizabeth said and hung up.

In forty-five minutes Elizabeth walked into the office and found Jessica and Meagan already waiting. They gathered at the conference table and began with barely a "good morning."

"Have we found Taylor?" Elizabeth asked.

"We're not that lucky," Jessica replied, "but we do believe we know where to look."

"And?" Elizabeth asked.

"Belize," Jessica answered.

"*Belize. Just Belize?*" Elizabeth echoed doubtfully. "Jess, I know it's a small country, but we'd still be looking at a nearly impossible task. How in hell are we supposed to find one man in a country we know nothing about? And why do you think he's in Belize?"

"We went back to the financial records," Jessica began, "and we found something interesting there. According to their records, the CMA sponsors two church organizations in Belize. Think about that. Why would the CMA sponsor two Protestant churches in a predominately Catholic country of only about a quarter million people? There must be something more to the story. We looked further and pulled the annual budgets for both churches. One showed about a million a year and the other was over one point two million. That's a lot of money for a Protestant outreach ministry. Take that in consideration with Belize financial laws that would allow someone to hide large sums of money and you've got the perfect setup for Taylor. It doesn't hurt, either, that for a bachelor like Taylor a tropical paradise like Belize could be very enticing."

"It is an interesting possibility," Elizabeth nodded. "Have you thought about the next step?"

Jessica looked at Elizabeth, hesitant to answer right away. She shifted uneasily and said, "We've got to send someone down there."

"I'm guessing by your hesitation that you have someone in mind, someone I will have a problem with," Elizabeth alleged.

"It's me," Meagan spoke up from across the table.

Elizabeth's disapproving eyes shot to Meagan. "No way."

"I'm going," Meagan rebutted firmly. "Jessica and I have thought this out." Meagan counted off the logic with her fingers "One, we think a woman will have a better chance of finding Taylor. People tend to be less suspicious of a woman asking questions, and, if the need arises, I can use flirtation to get the access I need. Two," she said, raising another finger, "this case is too confidential to trust with just anyone. I'm one of the few people who knows everything involved here—the CMA, Katherine, President Harkins, the whole story. And, three," she said with a slight smile, "I hear Belize is beautiful."

"I still say no," Elizabeth demanded. "I can't allow you to go down there. Not by yourself. Not like this."

"I'm not planning to go alone," Meagan countered. "Katherine's going with me. Now, I know you don't like that, but hear me out. If you think about it, it makes perfect sense. The way Harkins set Katherine up she will have no loyalty to him, and whoever it is in the Territory watching her will believe she's still being detained, so there will be no suspicion as to her whereabouts. And, maybe, if she agrees to it, we can consider working a deal with her. "

Elizabeth stared back at Meagan without a word, and then finally turned to Jessica, "You've agreed to this?"

"Yes. I have. This is our best chance, Elizabeth. We know now that Harkins has had operatives in the Territory for some time, probably since Katherine arrived. We don't know who they are or how many are here, but you can bet they're watching us closely. If we do anything to tip them off, to let them know that we've got a line on Taylor or Belize, they'll cover their tracks and we'll never find the man. Our best chance is to keep this operation very small and to do it right away."

"Why Katherine?" Elizabeth asked. "She's clearly shown that we can't trust her. If we need another female we can call in an agent."

Jessica answered straightforwardly, without judgment. "Katherine's shown she can be damn good at deceit, not to mention she'll want a way out of her current situation. And most important, I believe she wants the chance to make up for what she's done. I believe this time we can trust her."

Without reply Elizabeth sat back and looked out to the Gulf, thinking it over. Jessica, the one who had never trusted Katherine, was now her champion. Jess had been right about Katherine in the early months. Maybe she was right about her now. And Katherine did know enough to expose the secrets of the MIC story to everyone in the Territory, and beyond. Perhaps giving her an out was the best option. "Okay," she said quietly. "Who's going to talk to Katherine?"

Jessica glanced over to Meagan and looked back at Elizabeth steadily. "We believe it has to be you."

ELIZABETH STOOD NERVOUSLY in the middle of the cottage den, looking over the décor. It not such a bad place, she thought, except for the steel bars on the row of windows at the back of the room. She never imagined that she and Katherine would have ended up in a place like this. Elizabeth had not seen Katherine since leaving for Atlanta, but now Katherine was just one wall away. Elizabeth heard the guard ask Katherine something, and Katherine answered. Her voice raced Elizabeth's heart.

Elizabeth stood still as Katherine walked into the room with her hands behind her back. Katherine stopped five feet in front of Elizabeth and turned her eyes down. Elizabeth looked at her for a speechless moment before their awkward silence forced a question. "Are you handcuffed?" Elizabeth asked.

Katherine looked at Elizabeth with hard, exhausted eyes. "Do you want me to be?"

"No, of course not," Elizabeth replied quickly. Elizabeth looked over to the guard. "In fact, I'd like you to leave us," she said, assuredly returning the guard's doubtful gaze.

The guard reluctantly nodded once and left them.

Katherine swung her hands from behind her back and folded them tightly across her chest. "I take it this is not a social visit," she began smartly. Elizabeth said nothing, so Katherine walked to the couch and sat down. "So why are you here?"

Elizabeth sat down in the chair closest to Katherine. She leaned toward her and spoke sincerely. "Why didn't you tell me about Jacob? I could have arranged. . . ."

"Arranged what?" Katherine interrupted angrily. Her eyes locked onto Elizabeth's. "You could have arranged what?" Katherine demanded again. Then her words spilled out with fierce frustration. "Could you have arranged for Thomas to let Jacob live here in the Territory so he could be treated? Maybe Jacob could have moved in with us, huh? Or maybe we could have just sent the meds to Thomas, but then what, Elizabeth? Do you think I could ask you to break your own Territory's laws while I just casually mention, 'oh, by the way, I wasn't really a lesbian when I came down here and that whole trial thing in Virginia was all set up so I could get accepted into the Territory. You see, I was going to try to steal your medical secrets.'"

Elizabeth sat back and glared at Katherine, wondering why she had even come. Katherine would be ungrateful for any offer, and the idea of trusting her again was insane. "I thought you may have just an ounce of remorse," Elizabeth began evenly, keeping her own anger in check, "but I see from your attitude that you haven't made it that far.

Maybe you never will. Maybe this will always be about you and how it all went wrong."

Katherine did not back down. "And what have you done to prove it isn't, Elizabeth?" she asked. Her lip quivered slightly as she glared at Elizabeth. She looked away to gather her emotions, then she turned back. "Twelve days ago I was taken in for questioning, and the next thing I know I'm being held here in the middle of god knows where, no charges, no opportunity to speak to an attorney, and you—you won't even give me the courtesy of returning my calls!" Tears of anger and frustration swelled in Katherine's eyes, but she forced them back. "Do you even care? Did my arrest even faze you?"

Elizabeth stood and walked across the room, moving as far away from Katherine as she could. Should she tell Katherine what the last few days had been like, like someone had cut a huge chunk from her soul and thrown it down a well so deep that the depth consumed the echo of all sound? No, she wouldn't surrender that power to Katherine again.

Elizabeth turned and looked at Katherine, using all of her will to keep from just taking her into her arms. "Katherine, if you want out of here, if you want to avoid facing charges, you can do something for us. It's risky, but if you agree to do it and you're successful, you can walk right out of here, just as if nothing happened."

Katherine looked up, doubtful, but listening. "Are you here to make some kind of deal with me?"

Elizabeth nodded. "Yes, I am."

Katherine thought for a moment. "You say it's risky? In what sense?"

"It involves John Harkins."

Chapter 36

Katherine leaned against the sink in the restroom of the Cancun airport running cool water across her wrists, barely recognizing the reflection in the mirror. The platinum blonde hair, the thick, cheap makeup, and the fire-engine red lips had solicited plenty of looks, and two or three offers she wished she could forget.

In forty-five minutes the flight to Belize would be leaving and Meagan still hadn't shown, but there were plenty of chances for a delay. Meagan was to fly out for a week of camping with Jill Akers in the Big Bend National Park. A canoe float down the Rio Grande would take them to a local burrito shack in Mexico, where they would buy a dollar burrito and part ways. Then there were three diverting connections for Meagan to make on her way to Cancun. If she missed any of them, she would be delayed for another day, adding to the risk of detection.

Katherine's movements were less complex, but still difficult. She had left the cottage in the trunk of an unmarked police sedan at two a.m., arriving in the garage of police headquarters forty-five miles later. Still in the trunk she waited for a sweltering hour, then endured another fifteen miles to the home of the lead investigator. She unfolded from the trunk under the cover of his garage, and then without a word they transformed her into a woman who looked like a hardened call girl. She was given two sets of documents: one to get her into Belize under disguise, and one to leave under her own identity. Even with all of this, Jessica wasn't sure Katherine and Meagan could make it to Belize without suspicion.

"Continuing boarding flight five eighty-seven to Belize City. All passengers in rows ten through sixteen may now board."

Katherine stood and grabbed her carry on, an overstuffed bag she would never carry under her own circumstances. She handed her ticket to the agent and found her seat on the aisle of row ten. She or-

Blown Away
© 2006 by The Haworth Press, Inc. All rights reserved.
doi:10.1300/5706_36

dered a martini and waited as thirty minutes and sixty-two passengers passed by without a sign of Meagan.

"Final boarding."

Katherine cursed Meagan under her breath and helplessly watched as the flight attendant made her way to the door. She reached for it, and then looked up as one last passenger bounded down the Jetway.

Meagan flew in the door and walked by Katherine without a glance.

KATHERINE RODE UP the elevator of the hotel in Belize City, anxious for the comfort of Room 312 and the opportunity to lose the disguise. Meagan would join her in a couple of hours to go over their story once more. Tomorrow they would begin a four-day search. At the end of four days they had to be on a plane back to the Territory, with or without the proof that Phillip Norton Taylor was still alive.

They knew they had only a minute chance of finding Taylor, and it was one hell of a long shot to filter through a country of a quarter million people in less than 100 hours, but a digital photograph of Taylor would slightly increase their chances. Their computer could instantly manipulate the photograph with combinations of facial hair, hair color, and minor changes in facial structure. In the morning they would sweep Belize City eventually to focus on the three-block radius surrounding George Street and the address of Christ the Redeemer Church. They would tell strangers that Taylor was Meagan's brother, and they were looking for him for medical reasons. A sister needed a kidney, they would say.

Katherine dropped her bags on the hotel bed and walked over to the window. She drew back the thick, smoke-filled curtains and looked out to the crowd milling up and down Cork Street, realizing the near impossibility of their mission. How would they find this one man? And how would they do it in just four days?

Exhaustedly Katherine walked to the bed and fell onto it. She pulled the pillow next to her chest, wanting Elizabeth. She needed her strength. She wondered if she would ever feel that again, the protection of her arms or the assurance that came from the wanting in her touch. Katherine cursed herself for having argued with Elizabeth at the cottage. Already there was little hope for trust between them, and the way she lashed out at Elizabeth may have destroyed that possibility. The next four days were her final chance for redemption, and she vowed to not leave Belize without doing everything in her power to salvage the Territory from the damage she had caused.

MEAGAN PULLED OUT the city map and unfolded it. Christ the Redeemer Church seemed to be a phantom.

"This is bullshit, Katherine," Meagan said impatiently. "This church has over a million dollar yearly budget and no one knows where it is. No one seems to have even heard of it," her voice trailed off as her eyes pored over the map and her GPS. "Of course, it is possible the place doesn't even exist," she fumed.

"Something exists," Katherine asserted. "Offshore financial laws can't be *that* lax. There has to be something down here to show the auditors; at least an office door." She leaned over Meagan's shoulder and peered at the map. "Mind if I take a closer look?"

Meagan handed Katherine the map and looked at her watch. "It's almost lunchtime. Are you hungry?" Without waiting for a reply Meagan surveyed the street. "There's a restaurant a half a block up. Maybe someone there knows the address."

"I'm following you," Katherine said, folding the map.

Katherine walked a step behind Meagan's quick pace as they twisted their way up the lunchtime crowded streets toward the Caye de Plenty restaurant. Meagan ducked into the door first.

"Good morning, ladies." A tall, broad, chocolate-skinned woman breezed through an aisle of tables and greeted them with a kind smile. "Welcome to the Caye de Plenty—table for two?"

Meagan nodded, and they followed the woman past rows of square tables covered by red tablecloths and thick white paper. The hostess stopped at an empty table near the back, her bright pink blouse and full, turquoise skirt brightly contrasting the dark walls of the restaurant.

"Our lunch special today is shrimp Creole with coleslaw and biscuits," the hostess said in a soft Creole accent. "Our beer and drink selections are listed on the back," she said, pointing to Meagan's three-fold menu. "Is there anything else I can help you with today?"

"Yes," Meagan replied. "As a matter of fact, you may." She pulled out the address card from her pocket. "Do you know where this address is?"

The hostess held the card at arm's length and read it. "Oh yes," she said, glancing at Meagan, then back to the card. "I know where this is. There is a row of offices and apartments in an alley two blocks down," she said, waving her large hand in the direction of Haulover Creek. "But if you are looking for a church, I wouldn't bother going to that address," she said. She handed the card back to Meagan as her expression grew somber. "That church helps farmers in the South country. They only have an office here. I haven't been, but if it is in that row of offices," she said, pointing to the card, "it must be very small." She grasped the chair in front of her. "Now, is it a church you want?"

"No, actually we're looking for a man," Meagan replied.

"Aren't we all," the woman said with a quick, hearty laugh.

Meagan and Katherine smiled and returned a polite nod. "What man are you looking for?" the hostess asked. "Maybe I can help you there, too."

Meagan pulled out the computer and turned it to face the woman. "This is my brother."

The woman studied the picture closely.

"I haven't seen him in over ten years," Meagan continued, "so I have this computer to show people what he might look like now."

The computer flashed through a couple of images, and the hostess's eyebrows rose as her lips pooched together. "Why do you need all this to find your brother?" she asked suspiciously, pointing a twirling finger around the computer screen.

"Well," Meagan began cautiously, "as I said, I haven't seen him in more than ten years, and unfortunately we didn't part on friendly terms, but now I need to speak to him. Our sister needs his help for medical reasons."

The woman nodded, but still eyed Meagan guardedly. "I don't know him," she said boldly, "but if you want to find a white man you should look at the docks. All the white men here have boats. Tomorrow you should go to the marina just north of the bridge. Ask for Benga. Benga knows everyone in Belize City with a boat, but he's out in the cayes today."

"Does Benga have a last name?" Katherine asked, taking out a pad to write.

"Benga doesn't need a last name," the woman said, turning up a wide smile. With that, she left them.

MEAGAN HELD HER HAND over her eyes to block the early morning sun. On the pier beside her Katherine stood looking over the clusters of fishing boats anchored in the creek downstream of the marina. The marina had not yet come to life, but up and down the pier a few mates scrambled about preparing their early morning charters.

"Can I help you ladies?" a deeply tanned white man asked as he passed by them heading for his boat.

"I'm looking for a man named Benga," Meagan said after him.

The captain stopped and briefly chuckled before he answered. "So am I, ma'am. He's late again, but I expect he'll be here within the hour. What are two nice looking ladies like you doing looking for Benga anyway?" he asked with a laid-back smile.

"Actually, I'm hoping Benga can help me find someone else," Meagan answered.

"Oh?" the captain said. "Maybe I can help you then. Is he a white man?"

Meagan glanced around the pier. Seeing only one other white man, she knew it would not be a good idea to ask him. "Maybe I'll just wait for Benga."

"Suit yourself," the captain said impassively. "There's coffee in the marina if you want it."

Meagan and Katherine found a table by the front glass of the marina to wait and watch for Benga. "God, that's rough," Meagan said with the first sip of her coffee.

"How long do we wait?" Katherine asked, pouring extra cream in her cup. "He may not even show."

Meagan looked out to Haulover Creek, searching for a man she had never seen. "I'd say we wait half an hour, then we start asking the fishermen. . . ." her words trailed off as her eyes focused on a distant figure walking toward the marina. The man was dark as midnight, with a full head of close-cropped white hair. A couple of young boys ran up to the man and he stopped, pulled something from his pockets for each of them and smiled widely as they scurried away.

"I bet that's Benga," Meagan said as she watched him continue toward the marina.

Katherine looked out the window. The man wore worn navy blue pants and a stark white-collared shirt. His gait still held the spring of a young man. "I think you're right," she said. "We should talk to him before he gets to the marina."

Benga stopped when he realized they were walking toward him. He turned and looked behind him, saw no one there, and turned back with a wide, white smile. "Hello, my ladies," he said as they reached him. "It is a beautiful morning here in Belize, would you not say?"

Meagan returned his smile with a bit of a flirt. "Oh yes," she said cheerfully. "It certainly is." She moved closer to him. "Are you Benga?"

"I am," he said proudly. "How did you know?"

"A woman at the Caye de Plenty said we should look for you here. She said you might be able to help us find someone," Meagan said warmly. "A white man."

Benga looked at Meagan expectantly, sizing up her potential for money. "Maybe I can help you," he said amiably. "What does this man look like?"

Meagan pulled out her computer and booted up the image. "I don't have a recent picture of him," she began, "but this is what I think he may look like."

Benga looked at the screen, his face still blank. Meagan clicked to add facial hair, and Benga thoughtfully rubbed his chin. "I don't know," he said, shaking his head as he studied the images.

Katherine intently watched his eyes. Benga knew something. She slipped fifty dollars from her pocket. "We need your help," Katherine said, turning her hand to show him the money. "This man's sister needs medical treatment," she said, pointing to the screen, "and he may be able to help."

"I see," Benga began gravely. "That man comes here sometimes. Not often, but sometimes. He has a boat." Benga watched the money in Katherine's hand.

"What does this boat look like?" Meagan asked evenly.

"A keelboat, very nice one—new," Benga answered. He looked to Katherine, and she pulled out fifty more. Benga reached over and took the hundred. "She's called *Lifetime Chance*."

"You say he doesn't come here often," Katherine began. "Do you know where he lives?"

Benga looked skyward and again rubbed his morning beard. "I am not sure I remember," he said, bringing his eyes down to Katherine's pockets.

Katherine slipped out another hundred.

"He stays in Punta Gorda," Benga said. "He keeps his boat at the Orange Point Marina."

Meagan slipped out a final hundred from her pocket and handed it to Benga. "I would appreciate if you wouldn't tell your boss who we are asking for."

Benga folded the money and shoved it deep in his pockets. "You ladies should be careful," he said, his generous face now deadly serious. "That man you are looking for can be harsh, and the people of Punta Gorda watch their own."

Chapter 37

Katherine crouched down the short aisle of the smallest airplane she had ever been in, grabbing each of the four backseats as she made her way to the tiny cockpit. She had been dreading this moment since they made the reservation at noon. Meagan assured Katherine it would be a short flight to Punta Gorda, probably no more than forty-five minutes, and time wouldn't allow for the twelve-hour bus ride.

Katherine buckled her seat belt and waited nervously for the buzz of the engine. The first try sputtered, slamming the propeller to an abrupt halt. The pilot hit it once again. This time the engine choked and groaned, but finally sputtered to life.

"Don' worry, ma'am," the pilot reassured Katherine as they taxied down the short runway. "That the way it always does. It will be fine."

The pilot made the U-turn at the end of the runway and pushed the throttle forward. Trees, grass, and asphalt rushed by in a blur. Katherine closed her eyes as the wheels left the ground, white knuckles gripping her seat. In seconds the small plane met the first air current, suddenly rocking the six seater down and hard to the right. Katherine's eyes flew open expectantly and she looked down to see what she was sure would be a fast-approaching earth. Instead the beauty below settled her. Higher and higher they climbed above the green-white reef, the mosaic turquoise-blue of the Caribbean, and the lazy white specks of the fishing boats dotting the water.

In just under the promised forty-five minutes the wheels of the plane hit the airstrip, bounced once, and jolted onto the ground. Katherine took in a deep breath as the pilot cut the power and touched the brake, slowing the plane to an acceptable speed. She sat back and looked out to the land around them. They had arrived in a place far different from Belize City, and Katherine saw right away that time passed differently here. A man could disappear, fading into the jungle if he needed or out to sea for days at a time. He would live a

Blown Away
© 2006 by The Haworth Press, Inc. All rights reserved.
doi:10.1300/5706_37

simpler life, but a good one. With money he could come and go as he
pleased, and buy a lot of loyalty. The one thing he probably wouldn't
see often was an American woman. And there, she realized, lay their
best chance of finding Taylor.

LIFETIME CHANCE BOBBED gently in the waters of the Orange
Point Marina. Meagan covered her mouth at the sick sight of the
boat. It was the biggest in the marina, a gleaming white forty footer
with polished rigging and neatly folded sails. On the forward deck the
mate, a stocky young native man, was busy scrubbing the deck.

Meagan and Katherine strolled by the boat, showing only the pas-
sive interest expected of wealth-struck tourists. "There it is," Katherine said, feeling the pace of her heart accelerate as the hair at the nape
of her neck began to tingle.

They walked to the end of the pier and looked out over the water-
front. "If Benga was right," Katherine said, and paused. Looking
down into the clear water she watched schools of fish dart about. "If
Benga was right, we're so damn close right now it scares me. But we
need more time."

Meagan nodded, but looked at Katherine uncertainly. "We don't
have more time though, Katherine. The day after tomorrow I've got
to meet Jill in Mexico and you have to be back in the Territory. We
have enough to take back already. Jessica can get a couple of detectives to pick up where we leave off."

Katherine kept her eyes down at the water, watching the fish as she
considered her next move. She would run if she had to. She could leave
Meagan tonight with a note telling her to go back to Mexico, somehow she would make it back to the Territory when she had the evidence they needed. She could hide until Meagan was gone.

"Well, in the meantime," Katherine said casually, "we need to
make the best of today. I think we should concentrate on the marina.
Taylor may show up yet. We can book a snorkeling trip for later on
this afternoon and hang around the marina until then."

Meagan thought for a moment and said, "I suppose we do have a
better chance if we stay here. I can check with all the captains on charter prices to waste time."

Meagan was talking to her third captain and Katherine lounged on a pier bench when he walked by, so quietly unassuming that Katherine didn't notice him until, by happenstance, she slowly opened her eyes and saw someone stepping onto *Lifetime Chance.*

Katherine squinted down the pier to focus. She couldn't yet know for sure, but from a distance it looked like Taylor. Katherine stood and stretched, then slowly strolled down the pier, stopping at each boat for a brief inspection. She reached *Lifetime Chance* and stopped again, casually curious.

Taylor stepped out from the galley. Immediately he spotted Katherine. He walked to the stern and sat down with his mug of coffee. "Good morning," he said casually. "It's another beautiful day in PG, isn't it?" Taylor looked at her quite expectantly, letting his eyes drift down her body, lingering for a long moment on her legs.

"Yes, it is," Katherine replied with a guarded smile. Behind the cover of her sunglasses she studied him closely. His skin was tanned from his years on the water and deep crow's feet lined each eye. His graying hair was thick and full, and his brown eyes stern and careful. But his face was unmistakable. He was Phillip Norton Taylor.

"Your boat is beautiful," Katherine said nonchalantly.

"I'm glad you think so." Taylor scanned his domain, and then looked back to Katherine. "Are you an American?"

"Yes, of a sort. Canadian, actually."

"You have a great tan for a Canadian," Taylor said.

"Thank you," Katherine replied modestly. "I used a tanning bed to get me started and I've been in Belize for a couple of weeks."

"I see," Taylor replied. "That explains how you've made it all the way down to PG. Are you alone?" he asked, taking another opportunity to let his eyes dart up and down her body.

"No," Katherine replied. "I'm with a girlfriend. She's looking for a charter for us. We plan to go snorkeling this afternoon."

"I see," Taylor said. "The reef here is good, though not as famous as that to the north." He took a sip of coffee and looked back at Katherine. "Maybe after snorkeling you girls would like to join me for dinner this evening. I was thinking I might sail out to one of the Cayes for a bit of fishing and a moonlight dinner. It gets lonely with just me and the mate. I was planning to ask a few friends along, but if you'll join me, I won't have to. I'm sure I would enjoy your company much better, and you two will have a beautiful night to remember on *Lifetime Chance*."

"That sounds lovely," Katherine replied. "I'd love to come, but my girlfriend may not be able to make it. She brought work and she has to fax some loan estimates back home by tomorrow morning."

"That's too bad," Taylor said. "I've never understood working vacations. Either you're on vacation or you're working, not both."

Katherine smiled to keep him happy.

"By the way, my name's Jim Mundy," he said, lifting his coffee mug. "Folks in PG will tell you I'm an okay guy."

"I'm Carol Richards," Katherine said, "I guess I'm an okay girl."

Taylor smiled with his eyes still moving up and down her body.

"What time should I be here?" Katherine asked.

"About four's good."

"Okay, see you then." Katherine lifted a flirting wave and casually walked off.

Katherine's mind was set: she would get everything she needed from Taylor, an eye scan, a fingerprint, and, possibly, his DNA.

KATHERINE CHECKED HER LOOK in the mirror, peering deep into the reflection of her own eyes for a sign of the steely resolve that had emerged in the Territory. It was the resolve of necessity, the resolve born in women as the layers of carefully constructed facades were stripped down to the bare core of primal instinct.

Katherine reached into her makeup bag and chose the deep red lipstick, the same shade she had worn on the trip over from the States. Katherine abhorred the color, but tonight she wasn't wearing it for herself or for her lover. She paused as she dabbed the edges of her mouth. The sight of her own face disgusted her, and she felt nauseous with the realization of what she intended to do. She steadied herself against the sink and closed her eyes, remembering Jacob waving good-bye from the courtroom, and then Elizabeth looking down into her eyes the first night they made love. Reluctantly she opened her eyes and again looked into the mirror. She could do this. She had to.

"Well, Katherine, you're going all out tonight, aren't you? You'll have the attention of every man around," Meagan said from edge of the bed, alarmed by Katherine's cherry red toenails, fingernails, and lipstick of the same color. The normally conservative makeup was gone too, replaced by light pastel eye shadow and slightly heavy rouge.

Katherine walked over and sat down on the bed beside Meagan. "I've got to tell you something, Meagan," she began calmly. "I'm going to meet Phillip Taylor tonight. He's taking me out. . . ."

Meagan leapt up and spun around to Katherine, "What! What the hell are you talking about?" she asked incredulously. "You mean you saw Taylor?"

"Yes," Katherine answered evenly. "He came to his boat while you were out shopping for a charter. I talked to him a few minutes and he invited us for a dinner cruise tonight, so I accepted his offer."

Meagan fixed a disbelieving glare on Katherine. Not once had Katherine given the slightest hint of knowing a damn thing. Iced veins, Meagan thought, but this was much too dangerous for even a woman as cool as Katherine. "You accepted his offer," Meagan replied. "Then I'm assuming I'll be going as well."

"No," Katherine said. "I want to go alone. I told him that you had business to attend to tonight, but that I would accept the invitation."

Meagan turned away and rubbed her forehead. "We'll just have to say I changed my mind," Meagan said as she paced. "I can't let you go out on that boat alone with him."

"You have to," Katherine replied.

Meagan stopped and stared at Katherine again. "No, I don't have to, Katherine. Don't you realize what he could do to you? You could just disappear. Taylor could easily kill you and you'd be gone—without a trace."

"That's why you should stay here," Katherine replied. "If I don't come back, you can go to the police and tell them I'm missing."

Meagan threw her arms up in exasperation. "Like they'll care!" she exclaimed. "Look, Katherine, this man can buy this whole town. I'm sure it won't be a problem to bribe a few police officers, if he hasn't already."

Katherine looked at Meagen defiantly, "I'm going to do this," she insisted. "We have one shot at this man. One shot to get the absolute evidence that the man who has always been blamed for blowing up the Supreme Court is still alive. One shot, Meagan. If I go alone, I've got a much better chance of getting the hard evidence we need, an eye scan, a bit of DNA, everything. Tomorrow morning we'll be on our way back to the States with enough evidence to literally bury John Harkins. This is a chance I'm willing to take. It's my life, and you won't stop me."

Meagan could see the hard line wouldn't work. She sat back down on the bed beside Katherine and turned to face her squarely. "At least let me go with you to the boat, Katherine. We'll have a drink with the guy and then I'll leave. I'll have a chance to check things out, and it will still match up with what you told him this morning."

Katherine thought for a moment. It would make sense that her friend would want to see his boat, and it would be consistent with what she had told him. Maybe between the two of them they could distract Taylor long enough to slip away something with his fingerprints and then make excuses for the both of them to leave. She could avoid the dinner cruise altogether. But that could put Meagan in danger as well. If Taylor caught them, they may both disappear. Even if he let them go tonight Taylor could make a couple of phone calls and they would never get out of Belize.

"No, Meagan," Katherine replied. "You have to let me go alone. He may get nervous with two American women. He made a point right away to ask me where I was from, and I told him Canada." Katherine walked over to her bag and pulled out the necklace that held a microscopic camera in the locket. She draped the necklace around her neck and fastened it carefully. "I expect to be back around midnight, but if I'm not back in time for the charter flight tomorrow morning I want you to go without me. I'll find a way out later."

"Wait a minute now," Meagan challenged. "What do you mean 'if you're not back in time'? You are not thinking of spending the night with this guy."

"I'm going to do what I have to do," Katherine replied calmly. "We have one chance to get the evidence we will need, and I plan to get ev-

erything from him I possibly can. Gather a few things at the store tonight just in case you have to take a scrape from me to get his DNA."

Katherine saw Meagan slowly shaking her head in disbelief. She sat
down beside Meagan and took her hand, squeezing it hard. "I've slept
with my husband many times when I didn't want to," she reassured.
"In fact, the last time we had sex it became rather brutal. I can do this,
Meagan. I know how to get by with men."

Meagan jerked her hand away and turned to Katherine, looking at
her severely. "And did you ever do that with Elizabeth? Did you ever
sleep with her when you didn't want to, just to get something from
her?"

Katherine met Meagan's angry eyes with her own indignation.
"No, of course not. Elizabeth is the only reason I am willing to take
this chance with Taylor." Looking up to the ceiling Katherine continued. "When I saw Taylor today, my body filled with absolute hatred.
I wanted to strangle the man with my own two hands. But I had to
play it cool. So I thought of Elizabeth. I thought of her while I talked
to Taylor this morning, and thinking of her will be the only way I get
through whatever happens tonight."

"But why do you think you'll have to go that far? Can't you just get
a hair or something else with his DNA?"

Katherine replied frankly, "If he gets what he wants, he won't be
suspicious. He knows any woman willing to come onboard alone with
him is willing to have sex. Who knows, having sex with him may be
what keeps me alive."

Meagan's eyes softened and she reached across Katherine shoulder
to pull her close. "You know you don't have to do this, and I don't
think you should, but I won't try to stop you. I'll wait here for you.
The charter back to Belize City leaves at nine. I know we'll both be on
it."

"There's something to look forward to," Katherine said with an ap-
prehensive smile.

HIS HANDS WERE LARGE—larger, in fact, than Thomas's—and
soft, but scarred, like the hands of a man who had once worked but no
longer cared for it. His breath smelled like that of a man who drank

every day without missing a turn. Katherine worked not to flinch the first time he touched her, which he did as soon as he could. Just out of sight of the marina he had his hand across her shoulder as they stood by the rail of the aft deck, looking into the clear blue water passing underneath.

"Care for a drink?" Taylor asked.

Katherine asked for vodka, the liquor she knew would most greatly alter her state of mind. She downed four drinks and kept him on the aft deck for as long as she could, letting him touch her just enough to keep him believing he would get what he wanted. Three hours out and far beyond the sight of land the cook emerged from the galley to announce dinner was served. Taylor put his hand across Katherine's waist, and she forced her legs to move forward, toward the galley and cabin of *Lifetime Chance*. She ducked into the galley with him, knowing that of all the long hours she had endured since her January arrest in Virginia, the hours until dawn would be the longest and most horrendous of her life.

THE FIRST STRONG ray of morning sunshine broke next to Meagan's foot. She stood at the window, desperately searching for a sign of Katherine. It was 7:28 of the morning that followed watching 943 minutes tick off one by one. She had kept herself occupied with Honduran television, or a magazine, or the pages of a half-finished book, trying anything to keep her mind from panic. Growing more desperate she passed the early morning hours listening to every sound from the hall, praying it would be followed by the click of the door key. But it never was.

Now Meagan knew it would soon be time for the shower, and then packing for the charter, and finally checkout. But she could not leave without word from Katherine. At least she could swing by the marina to look for Taylor's boat and know if he was back. But Taylor would be smarter than that. He could stay away for days. And if he were ever confronted, he would simply deny Katherine had ever shown.

Meagan cursed herself for not following Katherine to the marina as she paced back and forth from the window to the door, anxiously looking out to the streets below and listening to every sound coming from the hall. Ten more minutes passed and Meagan knew she could not wait any longer. She pulled out travel clothes from her suitcase and walked into the bathroom, turned on the water and mechanically took off the clothes she had worn all night. She stepped into the shower and went through the motions of washing her face and rinsing the shampoo from her hair as she thought of how she should tell Elizabeth that Katherine was missing. Then the suite door opened. Quickly Meagan turned off the shower and swung around for a towel. "Is that you, Katherine?" Meagan cried anxiously as she threw open the door.

Katherine stood across from her, slumped against the wall. "Did you get a kit?" Katherine asked in a dull, husky whisper.

"I bought everything I'll need."

Katherine pushed away from the wall and walked toward the bed. "Let's get this done," she said wearily. "I want to take a shower."

IT WAS THE SAME plane and the same pilot. He picked them up promptly at nine and went about his work quietly, sensing an awful change had come to both of them. The doctor seemed the most affected. Maybe she just dreaded the flight back to Belize City. He hoped he could make the flight better for her today, but a storm was blowing in, and he knew the currents would be meaner than usual. He offered Katherine a Coke before he started the engine.

Katherine smiled weakly and shook her head. Closing her eyes she silently waited for takeoff.

In the air the plane rocked violently, bouncing and dropping suddenly as the pilot fought with the streaming currents. Katherine kept her eyes forward with her hands folded across her seat belt, saying nothing and feeling nothing. She could not allow herself to feel. She had just spent the night with a man she despised to the core of her soul, letting him make love to her, using all the powers of her mind to respond to him. There was only one thing in the world she wanted now—the touch of Elizabeth's hand, and to fall asleep wrapped in the safety and protection of her arms.

Chapter 38

CNN broke the story first. A thick, expectant air filled the governor's office as the news anchor interrupted the evening broadcast to report the breaking news. Elizabeth leaned forward in her office chair, her brow deeply furrowed as her total attention focused on the television panel. Meagan sat close by in her rocking chair, sitting very still now as she waited. Jessica stood across from the governor's desk, running her fingers through the half-finished leather bracelet she had been mindlessly braiding for the past half hour, passing the time as they waited for this report. The three of them had not talked much since they met at the governor's office an hour ago. Right now, the everyday concerns of daily conversation meant nothing to any of them. The autopsy of President John Harkins, who had died yesterday from a sudden heart attack, had just been conducted in Bethesda, Maryland. To the people of the United States this report was merely an afterthought. They had not yet awakened from the numbing shock of watching their president suddenly collapse on a crisp, clear, late September afternoon, reaching to clasp a hand on the campaign trail in the Indiana heartland.

"There will be a full press conference in about an hour from now," the on-location reporter cautioned from outside the hospital, "but a source close to the investigation has confirmed that President John Harkins indeed succumbed to ventricular fibrillation, or what may be commonly known as a massive heart attack."

"Brian," the anchor asked the reporter, "What can you tell us about the president's recent physical condition. Had there been any warning of a heart condition?"

"No. There were no indications of heart disease," Brian answered, "though the president was known to suffer from chronic acid reflux disease, which often causes discomfort in the chest area. We have also determined that President Harkins had begun taking a common anti-

Blown Away
© 2006 by The Haworth Press, Inc. All rights reserved.
doi:10.1300/5706_38

biotic to treat a mild infection, but there were no indications of a serious medical problem."

Elizabeth had heard enough. "Television—mute," she said. She sat back in her chair, staring blankly ahead. "Those guys are good," she said solemnly.

"And scary," Jessica replied as she sat down in the guest chair opposite the governor's desk. "When they have to, they can kill the president of the United States without leaving a trace. I have to wonder what else they are capable of." She thought for a moment and looked up at Elizabeth. "Have you thought about that, Elizabeth? I mean, five people right here in the Territory know the whole truth, not to mention a few of Harkins's cronies who know about Phillip Norton Taylor. What's the CIA going to do about us?"

"Nothing, if we keep our heads down," Elizabeth answered. She thought for a moment before she spoke again. "As you said, five people here in the Territory know everything, and a few others know enough. That should keep the CIA honest as far as we're concerned. They know we *will* go to the press if we have to, but on the other hand, every one of us knows how detrimental that would be to the country. Right now we have a healthy balance. They took care of our problem for us, and we stay silent for them."

"Are we even sure it was the CIA that was involved here?" Meagan asked. "After we fed the information and evidence back to Robert Stark we don't really know who he contacted from there."

"That's true," Jessica replied. "We'll probably never know who Stark went to with the information, but whoever they are, they knew that they had to get John Harkins out of the equation. They knew the U.S. could not afford a showdown between Harkins and us in light of the information we have now."

"How did Robert Stark take finding out it was John Harkins and not William Bucks involved in the bombing investigation cover-up?" Elizabeth asked.

"Not well at first," Jessica replied. "Stark liked John Harkins, so he never allowed himself to believe that it was Harkins who had the unidentified thumb removed from the forensics lab. Stark's focus on William Bucks wouldn't allow him to see what was right in front of him. As soon as Michael told me about the thumb I knew it was likely that Phillip Norton Taylor was on site the day of the bombing, and I knew it was the accomplice's thumb that had been found and then suddenly lost."

"So how did you get the connection to Steve Eddleton?" Elizabeth asked.

"Basically on a hunch," Jessica replied. "The whole mystery of Steve Eddleton was really puzzling me. Here was a man who Jason Johnson and the CMA took some risks to keep out of jail, and then for some reason they seemed to lose interest in him. Then I got the note from Emily Harkins that pointed to a deal between John Harkins and the CMA, somehow involving the Supreme Court. I was turning it all over in my mind, trying to figure out where it could lead, but I wasn't getting anywhere with it until Michael told me about the thumb. Now we had a missing man and a missing body part, and John Harkins's influence all over the bombing investigation. Suddenly Steve Eddleton's disappearance made sense, and I knew there had to be a connection."

"But it wasn't until later that you realized that Steve Eddleton had switched identity with Phillip Norton Taylor," Meagan said.

"Exactly," Jessica said. "We knew we were definitely onto something because we knew Eddleton had an arrest record from about fifteen years ago, but our initial search of public records came up empty. It took a fairly extensive search of media files to find a photograph of Eddleton. Then one of our agents noticed the resemblance between Eddleton and Taylor, and it was just a matter of getting the evidence we needed to prove our theory."

"I don't know if the Territory will ever be able to repay Katherine Hopkins for what she did to get that evidence," Meagan said.

Elizabeth looked over at Meagan, but said nothing.

Jessica nodded and said, "And Emily Harkins as well. After the dust settles from all of this, I'd really like to see her again."

Elizabeth looked over at Jessica. "I can understand that, but do you think it's a good idea? She has no idea what happened after you met her last month. She may ask questions. And I'm not sure how the CIA would read a visit from you, innocent though it may be." Elizabeth caught a quick flash of anger in Jessica's eyes, and she was in no mood for arguing with her. "Just give it some thought."

"What about Jason Johnson?" Meagan asked. "He shouldn't get away with his part in this, and his connections to the bombing ran deeper than John Harkins's."

"That's true," Jessica agreed. "But without Harkins, Johnson poses no real threat to the Territory. Who knows what will happen over the long run, but right now he will be sweating it out for a while. His whole charade down here has fallen apart and his main political ally is gone. I'll see some justice in watching him swing from his own rope."

"It will be interesting to watch Jason Johnson try to live with the sins of his past," Elizabeth said.

Jessica leaned toward Elizabeth's desk and deliberately laid out the bracelet she had been braiding before the news story broke. She ran her fingers down the unbraided leather strips to avoid Elizabeth's eyes as she asked, "What about you? What are you going to do with your past?"

Elizabeth looked at Jessica warily. "You mean Katherine."

"I mean Katherine," Jessica answered, now looking up at Elizabeth with certainty. "You have to see her sooner or later. If nothing else you should at least extend the official gratitude of the Territory."

Elizabeth stood and walked to the window to look out over the first traces of twilight falling across the gulf. Katherine—the ache that would never go away, the ache that had nearly torn Elizabeth apart during the four days of Belize. Meagan told Elizabeth everything when they returned—the risks Katherine had taken, the night she endured to prove Phillip Norton Taylor was still alive, the hollow, blank stare in Katherine's eyes the morning she came back from the boat. And now Katherine was back in the Territory, asking for nothing but the right to stay and do her work.

Just two days after returning from Belize Katherine settled back into the grueling routine of Mozingo's MIC team, working as if her three weeks of absence had never happened, again forming the backbone of the pathology team. Katherine had even convinced a reluctant Thomas to agree to share custody, pending their final divorce papers. Soon Thomas would be arriving in Tallahassee to begin house hunting and interviewing with three firms Jessica had set up, even though all three were well known as staunchly conservative. After all, Thomas would only go so far. The lawyers were still arguing as to whether Katherine would share custody in the Territory or if she would be forced to see her children only outside Territory boundaries. But at least Jacob was alive, and though his father still did not know it, he was cured.

"I have to be sure what I'm going to say to Katherine when I see her," Elizabeth said, still looking out the window. "We all know it will be more than just a simple thank-you."

"Yes, it will," Jessica replied as she stood up. "But time waits for no one, my friend," she said as she walked across the office. "I'll see you both in the morning," she said at the door. "A future like we've never known begins tomorrow. John Harkins is gone." Jessica nodded once to Meagan, and then left them.

"She's right, you know," Meagan said as she stood from her rocking chair and walked toward Elizabeth. "John Harkins has been an unfortunate part of our lives for a very long time. The future will be a different place for us now." Meagan looked up at Elizabeth and reached for her hand. "In fact, there is something I need to speak to you about."

Meagan led Elizabeth to the office couch and sat down beside her. She took both of Elizabeth's hands with a deep breath and looked at her earnestly. "Elizabeth, I don't know how to tell you this, so I'll just say it. I want to leave the Territory for a while. I'd like to take a leave of absence and go out to Arizona to be with Jill. I still love her, Elizabeth. I realized that when I was with her last month."

Elizabeth nodded and returned an understanding smile. It wasn't obvious, but Elizabeth had seen the same things in Jill she had seen in Chris: a passion for her work, a refusal to back down, commitment to people she believed in. And, as with Chris, there was the need for a nurturing soul to tend the hidden vulnerabilities. Elizabeth knew Meagan thrived on being that nurturing soul, and she knew that Meagan had finally let go of her grief for Chris.

Meagan kept her eyes down on their interlaced fingers as she spoke, "Elizabeth," she said, "there is another reason I want to go to Arizona. It has to do with the decision I talked you into twelve years ago when we decided to work with President Bucks. I told you then that I believed Chris was growing tired of fighting for gay rights, that she might be willing to take the fight down a path that would be easier for us. When I was driving over this afternoon it occurred to me that in that belief I was still trying to protect Chris. I wanted to let her rest in peace. *I* was the one who wanted to take Chris Landry, even her name and her memory, away from the fight. I knew that as long as you and I stayed in the States her name and what happened to her would be used to galvanize the gay rights movement, and I was too shattered to be a part of that. But now, with everything that has happened, I believe that Chris is with me in a whole new way. That hollow ache for her is finally gone, and I'm beginning to feel her strength again. Chris doesn't want to rest in peace. She wants me to keep fighting, so I'm going to start a political action organization called the Chris Landry Foundation. I believe it's important for me to carry on the work that Chris believed in—to continue the fight for our civil rights. Of course, I want this Territory to continue to thrive, but I believe it should be a place where people move by choice, not because they can't have their rights in their own home states."

Meagan gave Elizabeth's hand a gentle squeeze and looked up with her eyes focused intently. "Katherine gave us that gift of choice, Elizabeth. Because of what she did we'll never have to worry about the politics of the States again. No one can touch us now, so you won't need me as much in the Territory. I want to continue Chris's fight, and I can never do that here in the Territory."

Elizabeth nodded. "You're right. We do need to continue Chris's fight. Maybe I should consider joining your effort when my term is over."

"No," Meagan replied. "You're so much a part of this Territory; you have to stay here. You may not always be governor, but you will always be a vital part of the Territory's future. Your energy and dedication is needed by the people who count on you to make this crazy place work. Besides, you deserve a chance to sit back and enjoy everything you've worked so hard for."

Elizabeth smiled with the thought. "Sit back and enjoy, huh?" she said with a soft laugh. "Do you think I can really do that?"

"With the right partner, yes, I think you can," Meagan replied. "Katherine is waiting to hear from you, you know."

Elizabeth stood up and walked to her desk. She sat against it and said, "I don't know, Meagan. I love her and want her as much as I ever did, maybe even more. I can't tell you how crazy I was when both of you were in Belize. The thought of losing either one of you was killing me. I must have run sixty miles or more in the four days you were gone. But now you're both back safely and I just don't know. I can't start up with her again if it's not going to last. And I don't know if the trust is there for that."

Meagan came over to Elizabeth and lightly leaned against her. She spoke softly as she said, "Trust is difficult, Elizabeth. You and I trust each other in ways lovers never can. We tell each other things, we cry on each other's shoulders, we rely on each other, but even though I know things about you that no one else ever will I would never have done what Katherine did for you. She took the risk that night on the boat because she loves you, and she knew when she did it that she may never get you back."

"What about Jacob?" Elizabeth asked. "Wasn't he part of her decision?"

"No, not really," Meagan answered. "We agreed he would get the meds when Katherine agreed to go to Belize. She did what she did because of you." Meagan moved her hand up and down Elizabeth's arm as she studied her thoughtful eyes. "I think you should go to the beach," Meagan said after a moment. "Let the spirits help you with this one."

"Who said I'm ready to make a decision?"

"You are ready," Meagan replied. "Trust me on this. You are."

Meagan wrapped her arms around Elizabeth and held her close for a long moment, and then she looked into her eyes. "You are," Meagan said. Without another word she turned and walked out of the office.

As the door closed Elizabeth sat still in the silence of her office with Jessica's words and the case that resided in the deep recesses of her mind marching through her head. *A future like we've never known . . . Roe versus Idaho.* The words marched bolder and bolder, as if gathering for a great battle in her consciousness. Elizabeth leaned back and rubbed her hands across her eyes, sighing with the realization that she stood at yet another crossroad in her life. She knew Meagan was right. She had to go to the beach.

Elizabeth grabbed her keys and darted out the door.

ELIZABETH DROVE FORTY minutes to find a secluded stretch of beach. She made the drive in silence: no music, no talk radio, nothing but the hum of the BMW and the whip of the September wind. A slight chill blew in from the Gulf, and Elizabeth knew the end of the tourist season was near. She parked in a deserted parking lot and walked the boardwalk to the white sand below. This wasn't her usual place. She hadn't been back there since the night she shared it with Katherine. She hoped somewhere along this new stretch of beach she would find the same resolve. She walked about a mile before she found the right place, a deep gap etched between two dunes. Elizabeth settled into the sand and looked out to the Gulf. Slowly, thought by thought, she cleared her mind and sat quietly, waiting.

She wasn't aware of the passing time, but after a while a sandpiper flew in and landed beside her. She looked over, and the tiny bird looked back. He stood still, watching her. He seemed to be waiting. In a moment, he scuttled a few feet and turned around, watching her again. Elizabeth stood up and looked into his patient, round eyes. She took a step, and the bird scurried four more feet, stopped and again waited. Without question she followed him to the shoreline.

There, as if by design, he scurried along the upper edge of the surging film of tide. Elizabeth followed him until once again he stopped and looked at her. Then the waves went out, and in a mad dash, he rushed toward the Gulf. She watched his footprints form into the sand, and just as quickly as he had made them the next wave tumbled in. With that, the sandpiper flew away. Elizabeth looked down to his footprints as a sliver of Gulf water swept over the last of them. The footprints were gone, washed away by the forgiving sea. "Got ya," Elizabeth said in the direction the sandpiper's flight. "Thank you."

She turned and ran the mile back to the car. Katherine's condo was twenty-five miles from here.

KATHERINE'S CAR WAS NOT in the parking lot. Elizabeth called the condo, but there was no answer. She backed into a space in a dark corner near the entrance and settled into the leather seat of her BMW, turning her face up to the stars. She would wait here all night if she had to. Two cars drove by, passing Elizabeth without notice. The third was the Volvo. It passed just in front of the BMW, then stopped abruptly and backed up. Katherine turned it into the space next to Elizabeth.

"Will you go for a ride with me?" Elizabeth asked as Katherine rolled down her window.

Katherine looked at her strangely. Go for a ride, just as if it were any other night? These were the first words Elizabeth was going to say to her since the night before she left for Belize? Day after day since Katherine had returned she waited to hear something from Elizabeth—a phone call, or a visit to the lab, an e-mail, anything, but there had been nothing—no word, no note, nothing. Reluctantly Katherine had begun to build her defenses, knowing she may never see Elizabeth again. Now, in the past two days, living through the national drama of watching John Harkins fall dead, Katherine had finally convinced herself she didn't want to see Elizabeth. But here Elizabeth was, asking for a chance to be alone with her, and even it was just for another hour Katherine knew she didn't have the will to say no.

Without a word Katherine got out of the Volvo. Elizabeth mindlessly gripped the steering wheel and watched Katherine's quick steps and squared, tight shoulders moving in the way she knew to be Katherine's annoyed gait. She looked over as Katherine sat down in the passenger seat, noting the reservation in her eyes and the tense, drawn lines around her mouth. Katherine pulled the door closed, gave Elizabeth a quick, hesitant smile and turned her eyes ahead.

The windy roar of the open convertible quelled most opportunity for conversation as they drove. At traffic lights and stop signs Elizabeth filled the time with questions she already knew the answer to: how was Jacob, when would Katherine see her children again, and how was the research going?

Katherine answered mechanically, as if she were talking to a stranger. But she wanted to say so much more. She wanted to shout at

Elizabeth. She wanted to demand to know why Elizabeth hadn't called. She wanted to insist that she never intended to hurt her. She wanted to know what in hell else would she have to do to make it up to her, and why couldn't Elizabeth understand that she was only trying to save her child? She had never intended to fall in love with Elizabeth in the first place. And, in spite of her best efforts, she still was.

Katherine looked over at Elizabeth, watching her as she drove. Elizabeth seemed content in a solitary world of her own thoughts. Maybe it had been a mistake to come with her. Maybe she would just ask Elizabeth to drop her off. She could get a cab back to the condo.

"Elizabeth," Katherine began. She didn't get out the next words before Elizabeth flipped up the turn signal and slowed down. Katherine knew this right turn would lead to Elizabeth's house, and she knew that Elizabeth would not take her there simply to tell her they were through.

After the right turn Elizabeth looked over at Katherine with a familiar trace of a smile. Katherine had seen that smile a hundred times, and she knew it was only for her. The six inches between them suddenly seemed too far. Katherine wanted to touch Elizabeth everywhere, at least to wrap her fingers in Elizabeth's as they drove. Contentedly Katherine turned her face to the wind. The world was alive again, and for the first time in weeks, she wanted to be in it.

Elizabeth stopped in front of her house and turned off the engine. "Will you stay for a while?" she asked. "I'd like for us to talk."

"Yes, of course," Katherine replied. She looked out across the moonlit yard toward the clear spring just down the hill and listened to the distant hum of the crickets and the baritone song of the bullfrogs. A whip-poor-will added his reply to the chorus. Katherine laid her head back against the headrest, feeling the gentle breeze from the pines brushing across her face, bringing with it the fresh aroma of the early fall. She loved this place. She could stay here forever.

Elizabeth looked over at Katherine and smiled again, and then got out of the car and walked to the front steps of the porch to sit down. Katherine watched Elizabeth for a moment, and then followed her.

"Katherine," Elizabeth began with a deep breath of reservation, "I know I should have come by to see you sooner, but I was just so mixed up about things I didn't know what I would say to you. So," she said, shrugging her shoulders, "I just decided to concentrate on what was happening with John Harkins." Elizabeth looked up to the sky, her face filled with the uncertainty of apology. "But now, after what has happened in the past two days, I know we'll never have to worry about the politics in the States again," she said. She turned back to Katherine and reached for her hand. She held it protectively as she talked. "I know the Territory owes much of that to you. Because of what has happened in the past few weeks, no politician or lobbyist or even the CMA will ever be able to touch us. We would never have that freedom if it weren't for you. And, the odd thing is, no one will ever know the sacrifice you made except me and a few other people. The people of the Territory will never be able to thank you, but *I* want to thank you for what you did."

Katherine turned away and stared down at the ground, pushing back the sordid memory of that night in the Caribbean. She couldn't look at Elizabeth right now, imagining what Elizabeth must be thinking of her and the lover that she had allowed. Katherine did not regret the sacrifice she had made that night on the boat, but she knew she would never completely forget it either.

Elizabeth saw the struggle in Katherine's eyes and gripped her hand tighter as she spoke again. "But now it comes to you and me and what everything that has happened has meant for us—for our life together. I knew that while you were in Belize I felt I loved you like never before, but when you got back home I just didn't know what to do with it. We've hurt each other so deeply. I knew what it felt like to lose you, and I never wanted to feel like that again. I was so lost about us, Katherine, but after some persuasion from Meagan I went to the beach to clear my head. While I was there I met this sandpiper."

Elizabeth told the whole story, how the sandpiper had coaxed her, the footprints in the sand, the washing away in the waves. Katherine listened quietly, knowing how Elizabeth trusted the lessons of the beach.

When Elizabeth finished the story she looked at Katherine and said, "Tonight the beach told me that a mighty force can wash away the mistakes we make along the way, and that the future is not always bound by the past. After those waves washed away the sandpiper's footprints, I knew I had to see you." Elizabeth reached over to take both of Katherine's hands. She held them gently and said, "I know it's early, but I know I want you to be my in future, Katherine, and I'd like to ask if you will consider the same. Maybe you and I could live together someday, right here in this house."

Katherine looked up at Elizabeth and turned a slow smile as she looked around the shadowed yard. "Do you suppose we could put in a swing set, maybe right over there?" Katherine asked, pointing to a flat spot in the back of the yard.

"Absolutely," Elizabeth replied. "We'll have Henri build the best, sturdiest swing set in the Territory. It will still be here for your grand-children to play on."

Katherine leaned into Elizabeth's shoulder and rested her head on her chest. "Or maybe our grandchildren," she said with a contented smile.

Elizabeth's face brightened, for the first time considering a future she had never allowed herself to contemplate. Jessica's words ran across her mind again. *A future like we've never known.*

With two fingers Elizabeth lifted Katherine's face up to meet her own eyes. "Our grandchildren, huh?" Elizabeth said. "I like the sound of that." She took Katherine's hands and softly kissed the inside of both wrists. "Would you like to go inside?" Elizabeth asked as she stood and pulled Katherine to her.

"Absolutely," Katherine replied.

ABOUT THE AUTHOR

Perry Wynn was born and raised in Alabama and now lives in North Carolina with her partner and their two dogs, two cats, and a bird. She has spent more than twenty years working in the field of natural resources and is currently working on her second novel.

ALICE STREET EDITIONS™
Southern Tier Editions
Judith P. Stelboum
Editor in Chief

Zach at Risk by Pamela Shepherd

An Inexpressible State of Grace by Cameron Abbott

Minus One: A Twelve-Step Journey by Bridget Bufford

Girls with Hammers by Cynn Chadwick

Rosemary and Juliet by Judy MacLean

An Emergence of Green by Katherine V. Forrest

Descanso: A Soul Journey by Cynthia Tyler

Blood Sisters: A Novel of an Epic Friendship by Mary Jacobsen

Women of Mystery: An Anthology edited by Katherine V. Forrest

Glamour Girls: Femme/Femme Erotica by Rachel Kramer Bussel

The Meadowlark Sings by Helen R. Schwartz

Blown Away by Perry Wynn

Shadow Work by Cynthia Tyler

Dykes on Bikes: An Erotic Anthology edited by Sacchi Green
and Rakelle Valencia

Order a copy of this book with this form or online at:
http://www.haworthpress.com/store/product.asp?sku=5706

BLOWN AWAY

_____in softbound at $19.95 (ISBN-13: 978-1-56023-607-8; ISBN-10: 1-56023-607-8)

310 pages

Or order online and use special offer code HEC25 in the shopping cart.

COST OF BOOKS_____

☐ **BILL ME LATER:** (Bill-me option is good on US/Canada/Mexico orders only; not good to jobbers, wholesalers, or subscription agencies.)

POSTAGE & HANDLING_____
(US: $4.00 for first book & $1.50 for each additional book)
(Outside US: $5.00 for first book & $2.00 for each additional book)

☐ Check here if billing address is different from shipping address and attach purchase order and billing address information.

Signature_____

SUBTOTAL_____

☐ **PAYMENT ENCLOSED: $**_____

IN CANADA: ADD 6% GST_____

☐ **PLEASE CHARGE TO MY CREDIT CARD.**

STATE TAX_____
(NJ, NY, OH, MN, CA, IL, IN, PA, & SD residents, add appropriate local sales tax)

☐ Visa ☐ MasterCard ☐ AmEx ☐ Discover
☐ Diner's Club ☐ Eurocard ☐ JCB

Account # _____

FINAL TOTAL_____
(If paying in Canadian funds, convert using the current exchange rate, UNESCO coupons welcome)

Exp. Date_____

Signature_____

Prices in US dollars and subject to change without notice.

NAME_____

INSTITUTION_____

ADDRESS_____

CITY_____

STATE/ZIP_____

COUNTRY_____ COUNTY (NY residents only)_____

TEL_____ FAX_____

E-MAIL_____

May we use your e-mail address for confirmations and other types of information? ☐ Yes ☐ No
We appreciate receiving your e-mail address and fax number. Haworth would like to e-mail or fax special discount offers to you, as a preferred customer. **We will never share, rent, or exchange your e-mail address or fax number.** We regard such actions as an invasion of your privacy.

Order From Your Local Bookstore or Directly From
The Haworth Press, Inc.
10 Alice Street, Binghamton, New York 13904-1580 • USA
TELEPHONE: 1-800-HAWORTH (1-800-429-6784) / Outside US/Canada: (607) 722-5857
FAX: 1-800-895-0582 / Outside US/Canada: (607) 771-0012
E-mail to: orders@haworthpress.com

For orders outside US and Canada, you may wish to order through your local
sales representative, distributor, or bookseller.
For information, see http://haworthpress.com/distributors

(Discounts are available for individual orders in US and Canada only, not booksellers/distributors.)
PLEASE PHOTOCOPY THIS FORM FOR YOUR PERSONAL USE.
http://www.HaworthPress.com   BOF06